Susanna Gregory was a police officer in Leeds before taking up an academic career. She has served as an environmental consultant, doing fieldwork with whales, seals and walruses during seventeen field seasons in the polar regions, and has taught comparative anatomy and biological anthropology.

She is the creator of the Thomas Chaloner series of mysteries set in Restoration London as well as the Matthew Bartholomew books, and now lives in Wales with her husband, who is also a writer.

DEATH OF A SCHOLAR

Susanna Gregory

sphere

SPHERE

First published in Great Britain in 2014 by Sphere

A CIP catalogue record for this book
is available from the British Library.

ISBN 978-0-7515-4975-1

Typeset in New Baskerville by Palimpsest Book Production Limited,
Falkirk, Stirlingshire
Printed and bound in Great Britain by Clays Ltd, St Ives plc

Papers used by Sphere are from well-managed forests
and other responsible sources.

MIX
Paper from
responsible sources
FSC® C104740

Sphere
An imprint of
Little, Brown Book Group
100 Victoria Embankment
London EC4Y 0DY

An Hachette UK Company
www.hachette.co.uk

www.littlebrown.co.uk

For my mother

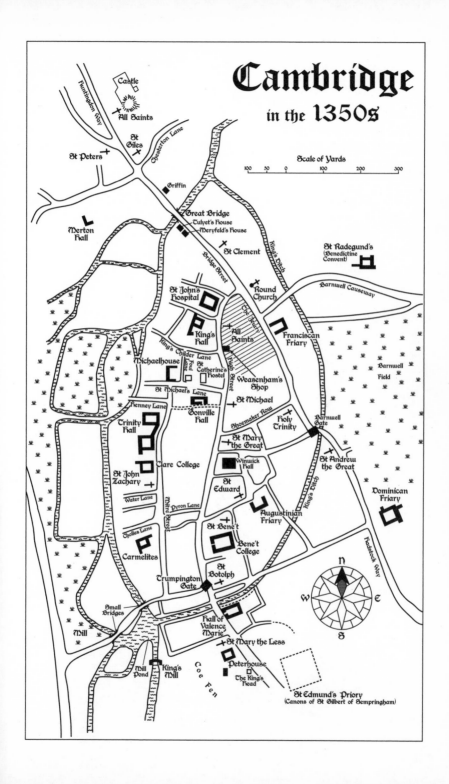

PROLOGUE

Cambridge, Lammas Day (1 August) 1358

Oswald Stanmore knew he was dying. He also knew it was time to push earthly concerns from his mind and concentrate on his immortal soul, but he could not bring himself to do it. At least, not yet. His beloved wife Edith sat at his bedside, and her good opinion was important to him – he did not want her to learn that not everything he had done during his long and very successful career as a clothier had been legal or ethical.

He had managed to destroy all evidence of his more serious transgressions – the reek of burnt parchment still hung about him – but what about the rest? It had not been easy to be a merchant in such turbulent times. The interminable war with France, famine, plague, years of unpredictable weather – all had taken their toll on trade, and only the strongest had survived. Stanmore had done what was necessary to protect his family from the wretchedness of poverty.

He closed his eyes, aware that he was deluding himself, which was hardly wise at such a time. The truth was that he loved the darker side of commerce – outwitting competitors, avoiding the King's taxes, driving a ruthless bargain. His willingness to bend the rules had given him an edge his rivals had lacked, and had made him one of the wealthiest businessmen in the shire. Edith knew nothing of it, of course, and the thought that she might find out when he was dead sent a pang of distress spearing through him. He groaned aloud.

'Doctor Rougham will be here soon,' said Edith, misunderstanding the cause of his anguish. Her bright smile reminded him that she had no idea of the gravity of his condition. 'You have chosen a bad time for a fever, dearest. Matt is away.'

She referred to her brother, Matthew Bartholomew, considered by the family to be the town's best physician. Rougham, on the other hand, was an indifferent practitioner, more interested in making money than in his patients' welfare. Stanmore grimaced. He could hardly blame Rougham for that – a fondness for money was a failing he owned himself.

The door clanked, and Rougham entered the room. As befitting a man of his academic and social standing, he had spent a small fortune on his clothes. The material had come from the Stanmore warehouses, naturally, but there was a flaw in the weave that prevented the tabard from hanging as well as it might, and Stanmore was gripped by a sense of shame. He remembered that particular bolt, and should not have charged Rougham full price for it.

'Marsh fever,' announced Rougham, after the briefest of examinations. 'It always strikes at this time of year. Indeed, I have only just recovered from a bout of it myself.'

Stanmore knew otherwise, but made no effort to say so. Why bother, when it would make no difference? Rougham and Edith began to discuss remedies and tonics, so he let his mind wander to what he had done that day.

He had spent most of it in his solar, frantically destroying records in the hope of sparing Edith some worrisome discoveries – a difficult task when the deceitful was so intricately interwoven with the honest. A summons had come in the early evening, inviting him to a secret meeting. He had gone at once, hoping it might win him a little more time. It had not, for which he was heartily sorry – another day would have seen evidence of *all* his misdeeds eliminated, and he could have died safe in the knowledge that Edith would never learn what he had kept from her for so many years.

If he had known then that he would not see another dawn, he would have hurried home and spent his last few hours finishing the task he had started. Instead, he had attended a gathering of the Guild of Saints. The Guild was a charitable organisation that he himself had founded as a sop to his nagging conscience. He had encouraged other rich citizens to join, too, and was proud of the good work they had done. He had gone that night to reassure himself that it was strong enough to continue after his death. After all, it might count in his favour when his soul was weighed.

He had started to feel unwell during a discussion about the widows' fund, but he had paid the signs no heed. However, when he had stood up at the end of the meeting, he had known that something was badly amiss. He had hurried home, and succeeded in burning a few more documents before pain and weakness drove him to his bed, at which point Edith had sent for Rougham.

Stanmore glanced at the *medicus*, who was haughtily informing Edith that the only remedy for marsh fever was snail juice and cloves. How the man could have made such a wildly inaccurate diagnosis was beyond Stanmore – Matt would certainly have seen the truth. But there was no point saying anything; it was not important. In fact, perhaps it was even better this way.

'I have changed my will, Edith.' Stanmore felt as though he was speaking underwater, every word an effort. 'You will inherit this house, the manor in Trumpington and the business. Richard will have everything else. He will be pleased – he has never been interested in cloth, and this leaves him rich without the bother of overseeing warehouses.'

Edith blinked. 'You are not going to die! You will feel better in the morning.'

He did not try to argue. 'Richard is not the son I hoped he would be. He is selfish and decadent, and I dislike his dissipated friends. Do not turn to him for help when I am gone. Zachary Steward knows the business, and can be trusted absolutely. Matt will support you with everything else. He is a good man.'

A good man who would be guilt-stricken for being away when he was needed, thought Stanmore sadly. It was a pity. He would have spared him that if he could.

'Stop, Oswald!' cried Edith, distressed. 'This is gloomy talk.'

He managed to grab her hand, but darkness was clawing at the edges of his vision, and he sensed he did not have many moments left. He gazed lovingly at her, then slowly closed his eyes. He did not open them again.

Mid-September 1358

Few foundations had ever been as unpopular as Winwick Hall. The University at Cambridge, a body of ponderous, exacting men, liked to take its time over important decisions, and was dismayed by the speed with which the new College had sprung into existence. One moment it had been a casual suggestion by a wealthy courtier, and the next it was a reality, with buildings flying up and Fellows appointed. Now, it was to receive its charter – the document in which the King formally acknowledged its existence – which would be presented at a grand ceremony in St Mary the Great.

John Winwick, Keeper of the Privy Seal, smiled his satisfaction as the University's senior scholars began to gather outside the church, ready to process inside and begin the rite. Winwick Hall was *his* College, named after him. *He* had bought land on the High Street, *he* had hired masons to raise a magnificent purpose-built hall, and *he* had chosen its first members. He had even worked out the curriculum that would be taught.

It had all been an unholy rush, of course. Indeed, the mortar was still damp in places, and haste had rendered the roof somewhat lopsided, but Winwick was an impatient man who had baulked at the notion of waiting years while the University deliberated about whether to let him proceed. He wanted students to start their studies that term, not in a decade's time.

Unfortunately, his aggressive tactics had earned enemies for the fledgling foundation. The other Colleges felt threatened by it, jealous of its prestigious position on the High Street and its connections to Court, while the hostels envied its luxurious accommodation and elegant library. The townsfolk were a potential source of trouble, too – they hated the University anyway, and were appalled by the notion of yet more scholars enrolling to swell its ranks. Bearing all this in mind, John Winwick had taken measures to safeguard his creation.

First, he had arranged for sturdy walls and stalwart gates to be raised, like the ones that protected the other Colleges, and had employed the most pugnacious porter he could find to oversee its security. Second, he had chosen as Fellows men who knew their way around the dark corridors of power, who would be adept at fighting back should rivals like Bene't, King's Hall or Michaelhouse conspire to do it harm. And third, he had secured an alliance with the Guild of Saints, a masterstroke of which he was inordinately proud.

The Guild of Saints was unusual in that it boasted both townsfolk and scholars as members, although only those who were very wealthy were invited to join. Oswald Stanmore had created it to help the poor, but its objectives had been changed since his death, so it now supported a much wider range of worthy causes. Winwick had persuaded it that his College was one, and had cajoled it into making a substantial donation. This was a clever move on two counts: it eased the pressure on his own purse – a relief, given that the venture had cost twice what he had anticipated – and it gave the guildsmen a vested interest in the place. They would defend it, should he not be on hand to oblige.

Now all he had to do was sit back and enjoy the fruits of his labour, although he would have to do it from afar. He would be with the King, making himself indispensable in the hope of winning yet more honours and wealth. And in time, clerks from his College – law was the only subject that would be taught at Winwick Hall – would help him in his designs, men who would be grateful for the chance they had been given, and who would repay him with loyal service and favours.

He smiled. Life was good, and he looked forward to it being even better. Smugly, he turned to his scholars, and told them the order in which he wanted them to process into the church. Unfortunately, both the Guild and the academics themselves had other ideas, and an unseemly spat began to blossom. A short distance away, three men watched as tempers grew heated. They were the University's Chancellor and his two proctors.

'I still cannot believe this happened so quickly,' said the Senior Proctor, a plump Benedictine named Brother Michael. 'I go to Peterborough for a few weeks, leaving you two to maintain the status quo, and I return to find Winwick Hall half built and its doors open to students.'

'Its founder has a very devious way with words,' said Chancellor Tynkell defensively. He was a timid, ineffectual man, and it was common knowledge that it was Michael, not he, who ran the University. 'I found myself agreeing to things without realising the consequences.'

'I did suggest you let me deal with him,' said John Felbrigge, a stout, forceful individual who liked being Junior Proctor because it gave him the opportunity to tell other people what to do. 'I would not have been bullied.'

'No,' agreed Michael, not entirely approvingly. Felbrigge

had not been in post for long, but had already managed to alienate an enormous number of people. Moreover, he had designs on the Senior Proctorship, and Michael disliked an ambitious underling snapping at his heels. 'Having a ninth College does make our University stronger, yet I am uneasy about the whole venture.'

'You worry needlessly,' said Tynkell, comfortable in the knowledge that he would retire soon, so any trouble would not be for him to sort out. 'Besides, would you rather John Winwick took his money to Oxford?'

'Of course not!' Michael hated the Other Place with every fibre of his being. 'But I do not like the kind of men who have flocked here, hoping to study in Winwick Hall.'

'True,' agreed Felbrigge. 'There have already been several nasty brawls with the townsfolk.'

'Things will ease once term starts,' said Tynkell, although with more hope than conviction. 'These young men will either become absorbed in their studies, or Winwick Hall will decline to take them and they will leave.'

'You are half right.' Michael eyed him balefully. 'Many *will* leave when their applications are rejected. However, some will win places, and as Winwick Hall is taking only the richest candidates, regardless of their intellectual ability, we shall have a lot of arrogant dimwits strutting around.'

All three looked towards Winwick's Fellows. So far, there were five and a Provost, although provision had been made to add more during the year. They were resplendent in their new livery – blue gowns with pink hoods – a uniform far more striking than the sober colours favoured by the other foundations.

'*Provost* Illesy,' said Michael sourly. 'Why not Master or Warden, like everywhere else? "Provost" implies that he has control of a collegiate church, and as Winwick Hall is in the parish of St Mary the Great, he might try to take the place over. And *we* work in that church.'

'It *is* a concern,' agreed Felbrigge. He lowered his voice to a gossipy whisper. 'John Winwick said that he chose Illesy as Provost because he is the most talented lawyer in Cambridge. Yet I cannot forget that Illesy has represented some very unsavoury clients in the past – criminals, no less. However, I have taken steps to keep him and his College in their place.'

Michael was indignant at the presumption. 'What steps?'

'I am a member of the Guild of Saints, as you know,' replied Felbrigge. He smirked superiorly: Michael and Tynkell would never be asked to join, as neither was sufficiently affluent. 'And we have a say in what happens at Winwick Hall, because it could not have been built without our money. So I have used my influence to install one or two safeguards.'

'Such as?' demanded Michael.

'I am afraid I cannot say, Brother. Blabbing about them will undermine their efficacy. But do not worry. Everything is under control.'

'I am sure it is,' said Michael tightly. 'But if it affects my University, I want to know what—'

'*Your* University?' interrupted Felbrigge insolently. 'I thought it belonged to all of us.'

Michael was so unused to anyone challenging his authority that he was startled into silence. Then Winwick's procession began to move, and his belated rejoinder was drowned out by shouts from onlookers – a few cheers, but mostly catcalls and jeers. He heard a hiss and a thump over the clamour, but thought nothing of it until Chancellor Tynkell issued a shrill shriek of horror.

He turned to see Felbrigge on his knees, an arrow protruding from his middle. He glanced around quickly, but the road was so full of buildings and alleys that the archer might have been anywhere. Pandemonium erupted. Scholars and spectators scrambled for cover, while Felbrigge slumped face-down on the ground. A physician hurried to help him.

'Dead?' asked the monk unsteadily, when the *medicus* sat back on his heels, defeated.

'I am afraid so, Brother.'

Chesterton, the Feast of St Michael and All Angels
(29 September) 1358

John Potmoor was a terrible man. He had lied, cheated, bullied and killed to make himself rich, and was hated and feared across an entire region. No crime was beneath him, and as he became increasingly powerful, he recruited more and more like-minded henchmen to aid him in his evil deeds. Yet it was a point of pride to him that he was just as skilled a thief now as he had been in his youth, and to prove it, he regularly went out burgling.

Although by far the richest pickings were in Cambridge, Potmoor did not operate there – he was no fool, and knew better than to take on the combined strength of Sheriff and Senior Proctor. Then an opportunity arose. Sheriff Tulyet was summoned to London to account for an anomaly in the shire's taxes, and Brother Michael went to Peterborough. Potmoor was delighted: their deputies were members of the Guild of Saints, as was Potmoor himself, and guildsmen always looked after each other. He moved quickly to establish himself in fresh pastures, and they turned a blind eye to his activities, just as he expected.

Not every guildsman was happy with his expansion, though: Oswald Stanmore had objected vociferously to Potmoor's men loitering around the quays where his barges unloaded. Then Stanmore died suddenly, and those who supported him were quick to fall silent. By the time Brother Michael returned, Potmoor's hold on the town was too strong to break, and the felon was assailed with a sense of savage invincibility. But he had woken that morning feeling distinctly unwell.

At first, he thought nothing of it – it was an ague caused by the changing seasons and he would soon shake it off. But he grew worse as the day progressed, and by evening he was forced to concede that he needed a physician. He sent for John Meryfeld, and was alarmed by the grave expression on the man's normally jovial face. A murmured 'oh, dear' was not something anyone liked to hear from his *medicus* either.

At Meryfeld's insistence, Surgeon Holm was called to bleed the patient, but the sawbones' expression was bleak by the time the procedure was finished. Unnerved, Potmoor summoned the town's other medical practitioners – Rougham of Gonville, Lawrence of Winwick Hall and Eyer the apothecary. The physicians asked a number of embarrassingly personal questions, then retreated to consult their astrological tables. When their calculations were complete, more grim looks were exchanged, and the apothecary began to mix ingredients in a bowl, although with such a want of zeal that it was clear he thought he was wasting his time.

A desperate fear gripped Potmoor at that point, and he ordered his son Hugo to fetch Matthew Bartholomew. Although the most talented of the town's *medici*, Potmoor had resisted asking him sooner because he was Stanmore's brother-in-law. Potmoor did not know the physician well enough to say whether he had taken his kinsman's side in the quarrel over the wharves, but he had been unwilling to take the chance. Now, thoroughly frightened, he would have accepted help from the Devil himself had it been offered.

Hugo rode to Cambridge as fast as his stallion would carry him, but heavy rain rendered the roads slick with mud on the way back, and Bartholomew was an abysmal horseman. Hugo was forced to curtail his speed – the physician would be of no use to anyone if he fell off and brained himself – so the return journey took far longer than it should have done.

They arrived at Chesterton eventually, and the pair hurried into the sickroom. It was eerily quiet. The other *medici* stood in a silent semicircle by the window, while Potmoor's henchmen clustered together in mute consternation.

'You are too late,' said Surgeon Holm spitefully. He did not like Bartholomew, and was maliciously gratified that his colleague had braved the storm for nothing. 'We did all we could.'

Hugo's jaw dropped. 'My father is dead? No!'

'It is God's will,' said Meryfeld gently. 'We shall help you to lay him out.'

'Or better yet, recommend a suitable woman,' said Rougham. It was very late, and he wanted to go home.

'But he was perfectly well yesterday,' wailed Hugo. 'How can he have died so quickly?'

'People do,' said Lawrence, an elderly gentleman with white hair and a kindly smile. 'It happens all the time.'

'How do you *know* he is dead?' demanded Hugo. 'He might just be asleep.'

'He is not breathing,' explained Meryfeld patiently. 'His eyes are glazed, he is cold and he is stiff. All these are sure signs that the life has left him.'

'Declare him dead so we can go,' whispered Rougham to Bartholomew. 'I know it is wrong to speak ill of the departed, but Potmoor was a vicious brute who terrorised an entire county. There are few who will mourn his passing – other than his equally vile helpmeets and Hugo.'

Bartholomew stepped towards the bed, but immediately sensed something odd about the body. He examined it briefly, then groped for his smelling salts in the bag he always wore looped over his shoulder.

'*Sal ammoniac*?' asked Eyer in surprise, when he saw the little pot of minerals and herbs that he himself had prepared. 'That will not work, Matt. Not on a corpse.'

Bartholomew ignored him and waved it under Potmoor's nose. For a moment, nothing happened. Then Potmoor sneezed, his eyes flew open and he sat bolt upright.

'I have just been in Heaven!' the felon exclaimed. 'I saw it quite clearly – angels with harps, bright light, and the face of God himself! Why did you drag me back from such a paradise?'

'That is a good question, Bartholomew,' muttered Rougham sourly. 'Why could you not have left him dead?'

CHAPTER 1

Cambridge, early October 1358

It was an inauspicious start for a new College. Geoffrey de Elvesmere of Winwick Hall lay dead in the latrine, sprawled inelegantly with his clothes in disarray around him. Matthew Bartholomew was sorry. Elvesmere had been a fastidious, private man, who would have hated the indignity of the spectacle he was providing – three of his colleagues had come to gawp while his body was being inspected. Establishing why he had died was a task that fell to Bartholomew, who was not only a physician and a Doctor of Medicine at Michaelhouse, but also the University's Corpse Examiner – the man responsible for providing official cause of death for any scholar who shed the mortal coil.

'Our first fatality,' sighed Provost William Illesy. He was tall, suave, sly-eyed and wore more rings than was practical for a mere eight fingers and two thumbs. 'I knew we would lose members eventually, but I was not expecting it to be quite so soon.'

'It will look bad in our records,' agreed a small, sharp-faced Fellow named Ratclyf. His expression turned thoughtful. 'So perhaps we should pretend he never enrolled. Officially, we are not part of the University until term starts next week, so there is no reason why—'

'You do not mean that,' interrupted the last of the trio sharply. Master Lawrence was unusual in that he was not only a *medicus*, but a lawyer as well. His long white hair and matching beard made him distinctive, and although he had not been in Cambridge long, he was already noted for his compassion and sweetness of manner. 'It is shock speaking. Elvesmere was a lovely man, and we should be proud to count him as a colleague.'

Bartholomew kept his eyes on the corpse, lest Lawrence should read the disbelief in his face. He had only met Elvesmere twice, but had considered him rude, officious and haughty. A long way from being 'lovely' in any respect.

'I suppose he suffered a seizure,' mused Illesy. 'He was very excited about the beginning of term ceremony, and I said only last night that he should calm himself.'

Bartholomew blinked. 'What ceremony? There is nothing to mark the occasion except a long queue to sign the register and a short service in St Mary the Great.'

'This year will be different, because of us,' explained Ratclyf smugly. 'We are to be formally incorporated into the University, so there will be a grand procession.'

But Bartholomew's attention had returned to the body, and he was no longer listening. Elvesmere was in an odd position, one he was sure the man could not have managed by himself. 'Has he been moved?'

'No,' replied Illesy, pursing his lips in disapproval. 'Although he should have been. It is disrespectful for an outsider like you to see him in such an embarrassing situation.'

'But Lawrence would not let us,' added Ratclyf, treating his colleague to a cool glance. 'Even though we are not quite members of the University, he said its Corpse Examiner would still need to inspect Elvesmere *in situ*.'

There was a distinct sneer in Ratclyf's voice as he spoke Bartholomew's title, but the physician chose to ignore it. The post had been created by the Senior Proctor as a way to secure help with the many suspicious deaths that occurred in the town – when Brother Michael had first started calling on his expertise, Bartholomew had vehemently objected, feeling his duty lay with the living. Now he earned three pennies for every case, he was happy to oblige, as he needed the money to supply medicine for his enormous practice of paupers.

There was another reason why his objections had diminished, too: familiarity with cadavers had taught him that there was much to be learned from them. He felt this knowledge made him a better physician, and he was sorry the study of anatomy was frowned upon in England. He had watched several dissections at the University in Salerno, and it was obvious to him that they should form part of every *medicus*'s training.

'Lawrence doubtless hopes that you will do for Elvesmere what you did for Potmoor,' Ratclyf went on. 'Namely raise him from the dead.'

'Potmoor was not dead,' said Bartholomew shortly. Reviving such an infamous criminal had earned him almost universal condemnation, and he was tired of people berating him for it. 'He would have woken on his own eventually.'

'So you say,' harrumphed Ratclyf. 'But you should have let him—'

'Enough, Ratclyf,' interrupted Provost Illesy irritably. 'Potmoor has been very generous to our new College, and it is ungracious to cast aspersions on the way he earns his living.'

'I am not casting aspersions on him, I am casting them on Bartholomew. If he had not used magic potions, Potmoor would have stayed dead. It was witchcraft that brought him back.'

'Actually, it was smelling salts,' corrected Lawrence with one of his genial smiles. 'We call them *sal ammoniac*. Like me, Matthew buys them from Eyer the apothecary, whose shop is next door.' He gestured down the High Street with an amiable wave.

'Well, he should have left them in his bag,' grumbled Ratclyf. 'Potmoor might give us princely donations, but that does not make him respectable. It was God's will that he should perish that night, and Bartholomew had no right to interfere.'

'Certain ailments produce corpse-like symptoms,' began Bartholomew. He knew he was wasting his time by trying to explain, just as he had with the many others who had demanded to know what he thought he had been doing. 'One is catalepsia, which is rare but fairly well documented. Potmoor was suffering from that.'

'I came across a case once,' said Lawrence conversationally. 'In a page of Queen Isabella's. They were lowering him into his grave, when he started banging on the lid of his coffin.'

'Yes, but *he* was not a vicious criminal,' sniffed Ratclyf. 'Bartholomew should have found a way to keep Potmoor dead.'

Bartholomew disliked people thinking that physicians had the right to decide their patients' fates. 'I swore an oath to—'

'You saved one of the greatest scoundrels who ever lived,' interrupted Ratclyf. 'And if that is not bad enough, Potmoor believes that his glimpse of Heaven means he is favoured by God. Now his wickedness will know no bounds.'

'How can you call him wicked when he gave us money to build a buttress when our hall developed that worrying crack last week?' asked Illesy reproachfully. 'There is much good in him.'

'You *would* think so,' sneered Ratclyf. 'You were his favourite lawyer, and it was your skill that kept him out of prison for so many years.'

'How dare you!' flashed Illesy, irritated at last by his Fellow's bile. 'You had better watch your tongue if you want to continue being a Fellow here.'

Bartholomew was embarrassed. Most halls kept their spats private, and he did not like witnessing rifts in Winwick. Lawrence saw it, and hastened to change the subject.

'I was probably the last person to see Elvesmere alive,' he

told his fellow physician. 'It was late last night. He said he felt unwell, so I made him a tonic. He was not in his room when I visited at dawn, so I assumed he was better and had gone to church, but I found him here a little later.'

'He is cold and stiff,' remarked Bartholomew. 'Which means he probably died hours ago. Why was he not discovered sooner? Latrines are seldom empty for long, even at night.'

'Because no one uses this one except him and me,' explained Lawrence. 'The seats are not fixed yet, you see, and have a nasty habit of tipping sideways when you least expect it.'

'The rest of us prefer the safety of a bucket behind the kitchen,' elaborated Ratclyf. He addressed his Provost archly. 'Do you think Potmoor will pay to remedy *that* problem, or is it beneath his dignity as a member of the Guild of Saints and an upright citizen?'

'Is something wrong, Bartholomew?' asked Lawrence quickly, thus preventing the Provost from making a tart reply. 'You seem puzzled.'

'I am. You say Elvesmere has not been moved, yet I doubt he died in this position.'

'He must have done,' said Illesy. 'You heard Lawrence: he and Elvesmere are the only ones who ever come here. And Lawrence is the one who insisted that nothing be touched until you came, so you can be sure that *he* has not rearranged anything.'

'His position looks natural to me,' said Lawrence, frowning. 'The fatal seizure caused him to snatch at his clothes in his final agony, which is why they are awry.'

'His final agony was not the result of a seizure,' said Bartholomew. He eased the body forward to reveal a dark patch of red. 'It was because he was stabbed.'

Provost Illesy turned so pale after Bartholomew's announcement that the physician was afraid he might faint, so he asked Lawrence to take him somewhere to sit down. Then, with Ratclyf watching his every move with discomfiting intensity, he finished his examination. Afterwards, they wrapped the body and carried it to St Mary the Great, where it would lie until it was buried.

'Come to our *parlura* and tell us what you have deduced,' instructed Ratclyf, once they were outside. A *parlura*, or place to talk, was Winwick Hall's name for the Fellows' common room; other Colleges used the rather less pretentious term 'conclave'. 'It is only right that we should hear your conclusions before you report them to the Senior Proctor.'

Bartholomew was frantically busy. He had more patients than he could properly manage, and if he did not prepare lectures, reading lists and exercises for his students before the beginning of term, he would sink beneath the demands of a ridiculously heavy teaching load. Moreover, his sister was still in mourning, so any free moments he did have were spent with her. Thus he did not have time to linger in Winwick Hall. Yet he knew *he* would want details, if one of his colleagues had been murdered, so he nodded assent and followed Ratclyf across the yard.

He looked around him as he went, studying for the first time the place that would soon become the University's latest addition. Like all Cambridge Colleges, it was protected by high walls and a stalwart gatehouse. Set in the exact centre of the enclosure was the hall. This was a magnificent building on three floors, perfectly symmetrical, with a large arched doorway in the middle. The ground floor comprised the *parlura* to the left, and a library to the right. The first floor was a huge room for teaching and dining, with imposing oriel windows and a hearth at either end, while the top floor was a spacious dormitory for students.

In addition to the hall, Winwick boasted living quarters for the Provost and his Fellows, a kitchen block with accommodation for servants, several stables, and sheds for storage. Most were new, and workmen still swarmed over the parts that were not quite completed. Some of the labourers were Bartholomew's patients, and nearly all had called on him to tend cuts, bruises and even broken bones as a result of the speed with which the founder had compelled them to work.

'I hear Brother Michael is no further forward with solving the murder of his Junior Proctor,' said Ratclyf as they walked. 'Why should we trust him to keep us safe, when he cannot catch his own deputy's killer? Personally, I think he should resign.'

'It only happened two weeks ago,' objected Bartholomew. 'Give him time.'

'Yet I cannot say I was surprised when Felbrigge was shot,' Ratclyf went on. 'He antagonised not only half the University with his hubris, but most of the town, too.'

'You exaggerate,' said Bartholomew curtly. He had not particularly liked Felbrigge, but he detested gossip, especially from someone like Ratclyf, who was hardly a paragon of virtue himself.

'I do not! And had he lived, there would have been trouble. He had a heavy hand with students, and they would have rebelled. Michael is well rid of him.'

'How many pupils have enrolled at Winwick Hall?' asked Bartholomew, pointedly changing the subject to something less contentious.

'Twelve. But we shall have ten times that number by the beginning of term. Men flock to apply for places, and I anticipate that we shall be bursting at the seams in no time at all.'

Bartholomew was sure of it, as the town was currently full of men who had come in the hope of being offered a place. It was always a dangerous time of year, because the applicants did not officially become students until they had matriculated – registered with a College or a

19

hostel – and so were outside the University's jurisdiction. *Ergo*, there was nothing the Senior Proctor or his beadles could do about their boisterous high spirits, and the town resented them. Affrays were frequent and sometimes serious.

The discussion ended as Ratclyf led the way into the *parlura*, a pleasant chamber that smelled of wet plaster and new wood. Its walls were plain, still to be covered with tapestries or murals, and its floorboards had not yet been stained or waxed. When it was finished, it would be a delightful place to sit of an evening.

Illesy was by the hearth, with his Fellows clustered around him, so Ratclyf began to make introductions. First he indicated Master Lawrence.

'As you know, our lawyer-*medicus* was the late Queen Isabella's personal physician. But most of us are distinguished in our fields, so his appointment is in keeping with the high standards we at Winwick Hall aim to promote.' Ratclyf turned to his Provost, and suddenly his voice was far less friendly. 'And you have met Illesy, of course. Legal adviser to the villainous Potmoor.'

'And plenty of other clients,' added Lawrence quickly, when Illesy began to scowl. 'No one knows more about criminal law than he, and we are lucky to have him. When they graduate, most of our students will be bound for Court, so such knowledge will be very useful.'

He beamed affably, although Bartholomew was disconcerted to learn that the men who ran his country might need to call upon someone who possessed the same kind of sly skills that had kept Potmoor from the noose.

'I am not the only member of Winwick with links to Potmoor,' said Illesy tightly. 'Lawrence is his physician, a post he took when the last *medicus* was dismissed for failing to save him. I understand the honour was offered to you, Bartholomew, but you declined it.'

Bartholomew had, because he had no wish to be at the

beck and call of wealthy criminals, although the excuse he had given was that he had too many patients already.

'I *like* Potmoor,' said Lawrence. 'And I have seen nothing but generosity and kindness in him.'

'And here are our last two Fellows,' Ratclyf went on, treating the claim with the contempt he felt it deserved by ignoring it. 'Albizzo di Nerli is from Florence, and is an expert in civil law. He has a string of degrees from the University at Salerno, and will certainly attract the best students.'

Nerli was a darkly handsome man with long black hair, an olive complexion and hooded eyes. He did not smile when Bartholomew bowed, and there was something cold and predatory about his manner. He stood apart from the others, as if he did not consider them sufficiently worthy company.

'I have been a scholar all my life,' he said. The others had been speaking French, but Nerli used Latin, which he pronounced with a strong Florentine accent. 'But only in the country of my birth. Thus I am delighted with the opportunity to ply my skills farther afield.'

'And finally, William Bon will teach our students how to be notaries public,' finished Ratclyf.

Bon had a sharp, narrow face and wispy fair hair. The pupils of both eyes were white, and a student had been detailed to stay with him to ensure he did not fall. He moved confidently across the *parlura* to greet Bartholomew, though, and the physician suspected he would fare better still once the College was not strewn with workmen's tools and building materials.

'So now we all know each other,' said Illesy snappishly. He turned to Bartholomew. 'What have you learned from examining our unfortunate colleague?'

'Very little,' replied Bartholomew. 'Except that I suspect he was stabbed elsewhere and was brought to the latrine after he died, perhaps to delay his discovery.'

21

'So he was definitely murdered?' asked Lawrence in a small voice.

'Yes. However, the wound would not have been instantly fatal, so I fail to understand why he did not call for help.'

'Perhaps he did,' suggested Ratclyf. 'But starting a new College is exhausting work, and we all sleep very soundly.'

'The killer will be a member of another foundation,' said Bon unpleasantly. He had a shrill, nasal voice, and its tone was acidic. 'King's Hall, Gonville, Valence Marie, Michaelhouse – they all resent us, and would love us tainted by scandal.'

Before Bartholomew could object to the claim, the door opened and the porter entered. His name was Jekelyn, a surly, belligerent man who was not above greeting visitors with torrents of unprovoked abuse. He jerked his thumb over his shoulder.

'Visitor,' he announced sourly. 'John Knyt, Secretary of the Guild of Saints, who is probably here to make sure the donations it has given us are not being squandered. Although it is none of his business if they are.'

Bartholomew had always liked Knyt, a principled, compassionate man who was generous to the poor. He had been the obvious choice to lead an organisation that was committed to doing good works, a task he had inherited in August after the sudden death of Oswald Stanmore.

'Knyt!' cried Illesy gushingly, indicating with a sweep of his arm that the visitor was to enter. 'You have caught us at a bad moment, I am afraid. Poor Elvesmere has been murdered.'

'Murdered?' echoed Knyt, shocked. 'I heard he was dead – servants gossip, and one of yours told one of mine – but no one said anything about murder. What happened?'

'He was stabbed,' replied Ratclyf. 'I imagine it was Potmoor's doing.'

'It was not,' snapped Illesy. 'Why would he do such a thing?'

'I am inclined to agree,' said Lawrence, as Ratclyf drew breath to argue. 'There is a tendency to blame everything on him these days, and he cannot be guilty of *every* crime.'

'No,' said Ratclyf flatly. 'Of course not.'

There was no more Bartholomew could tell the Provost and his Fellows, so he took his leave. Knyt went with him, murmuring that the College should be left to grieve in peace. He and the physician walked across the yard, where the great gates that led to the High Street were detached from their posts and stood propped against a wall – the carpenter had ordered the wrong hinges, so they were waiting for a set that would fit.

'How is Edith?' asked Knyt. 'I see her at Guild meetings, and she is always so very sad.'

Bartholomew knew this all too well. Although his sister's marriage had been arranged, she had loved her husband dearly, and his death had left her grief-stricken and lonely. Bartholomew hated seeing her so low, but was acutely aware that there was nothing he could do to help.

'She buries herself in work,' he replied. 'Running Oswald's business.'

'He was wise to have left it to her,' said Knyt. 'Not only because it gives her life purpose while she mourns, but because I doubt your nephew would make a good clothier. Two dozen people rely on that venture for their livelihoods, and it is safer with Edith than with Richard.'

Bartholomew nodded, although he feared that Edith's increasing familiarity with the work might teach her things about it that she would rather not know. Like most successful merchants, Stanmore had not always been gentle or honest, a fact he had carefully concealed from his wife and son. Bartholomew might have remained in ignorance, too, were it not for patients who had complained to him. Thus every time Edith spoke with a customer or opened a ledger, he braced himself for her dismay at discovering something upsetting. Ten weeks had passed without incident, but this only meant that the shock would be all the greater when she did find something amiss.

'I am surprised Richard is still here,' Knyt went on. 'His father's death left him a very rich man. I thought he would have dashed straight back to London to make the most of it.'

Bartholomew was also bemused by Richard's disinclination to leave, as his lawyer-nephew had always professed to find Cambridge dull after the heady delights of the city. Unfortunately, rather than being a comfort to his mother, Richard was a strain. She could pretend he was sober and hard-working when he was away, but it was difficult to maintain the illusion when he was living under her roof.

'Poor Stanmore,' sighed Knyt. 'His death was a great shock to us all. It was so sudden.'

It had certainly been a nasty blow for Bartholomew. Stanmore and Edith had raised him after the early loss of his parents, so his brother-in-law had been part of his life for as long as he could remember. He might have deplored Stanmore's shabby antics in commerce on occasion, but he had loved him as a kinsman, and his death left a hole that would never be filled.

'The University's students are returning, I see,' remarked Knyt, as they stepped on to a High Street that teemed with people. 'Is it my imagination, or are there more of them than usual?'

'There *are* more,' replied Bartholomew. 'Most have come to apply to Winwick Hall. I did not realise that law was such a popular subject.'

Knyt laughed. 'Stanmore always said you were unworldly, and that remark proves it. Everyone knows that law is the most lucrative of professions.'

'Is it?' Bartholomew had never cared about money. He

could have made a princely living if he had confined himself to calculating horoscopes for affluent townsmen, but he was more interested in genuine diseases, which meant that most of his clients were poor and unable to pay.

'Oh, yes. We have several lawyers in the Guild, and they are by far our richest members. And look at the clerk who founded Winwick Hall – one of the wealthiest men in the country.'

'So I have heard.'

'Yet I would not trade places with him for the world. He might have power and pots of money, but *I* live in a town I love, surrounded by friends and family. And as Secretary of the Guild, I spend a lot of time helping people in need. What could be more rewarding than that?'

They stepped aside to let a gaggle of young men strut past. Bartholomew supposed a senior member of the University and the Secretary of the Guild of Saints should have stood their ground, but he disliked pointless confrontation, and was glad Knyt did, too. Unfortunately, they were seen by several apprentices, who scoffed at their pusillanimity. He grimaced, suspecting there would be serious trouble between the newcomers and the town before long.

'Have you heard about the recent increase in burglaries?' asked Knyt, as they resumed their journey. 'They coincide with Potmoor's resurrection.'

Bartholomew groaned. 'Potmoor was *not* dead – he had catalepsia. And it is not my fault that he has decided to indulge in a crime spree either.'

'I quite agree,' said Knyt soothingly. 'Personally, I do not believe that Potmoor is the culprit, and I spoke not to rebuke you, but to warn you – there *are* folk who think you are to blame, so be on your guard. We cannot afford to lose the only physician who helps the poor.'

'Lawrence helps the poor.'

'Yes,' conceded Knyt. 'But not to the same extent. Still, he is better than the other *medici*, who do nothing at all. Especially Surgeon Holm, who refuses point blank when I ask him to tend deserving cases. Incidentally, he seems to have taken a rather violent dislike to you.'

Bartholomew blushed. Holm's antipathy stemmed from the fact that Bartholomew was in love with his wife. The surgeon was naturally indignant, but his homosexuality meant he was not in a strong position to win her back. The couple had reached an understanding about the friendships each wished to pursue, but that did not mean that Holm was happy about being cuckolded.

'Will you be at the Cambridge Debate tomorrow?' asked Knyt when there was no reply to his observation. 'The Guild has agreed to sponsor the refreshments afterwards.'

'I will not,' said Bartholomew vehemently. 'The topic is apostolic poverty, with monks arguing that friars should denounce all property and privileges, and friars arguing that they should be allowed to keep them. I am neither a friar nor a monk, and do not want to be drawn into it.'

'The monks have a point: friars are meant to live like Christ, simply and modestly. They are not supposed to lounge in luxurious convents, eating and drinking like princes. Monks, however, live contemplative lives, which you cannot do effectively with a growling stomach.'

Bartholomew laughed, amused by the simplification of a row that was threatening to tear the Church apart. 'I would not repeat that to a friar if I were you. You would never hear the end of it.'

Michaelhouse was the third College to be founded at Cambridge, and had recently celebrated its thirty-fourth birthday, although opinions were divided as to whether it would see its thirty-fifth. Its founder had endowed it with a pleasant hall, land in the centre of town, several houses and a church, not to mention the tithes of four parishes. Unfortunately, mismanagement and a series of unwise investments meant it was currently on the brink of ruin.

Bartholomew opened the gate and paused for a moment to survey the place that had been his home for more years than he could remember, and that he would miss horribly should the pessimists be right about the seriousness of its financial problems.

The courtyard had once been grassed, but was now an expanse of mud. On the far side was the hall, a large but shabby building with kitchens below and two large chambers above. The bigger room was the refectory, which boasted a pretty but glassless oriel window and a sizeable hearth; trestle tables were set out for meals, then stacked away when it was time for lessons. The other room was the conclave, exclusive domain of the Master and his Fellows.

At right angles to the hall were the two accommodation blocks. Bartholomew lived in the older, more dilapidated wing, where he had been allocated two rooms. He shared one with his students, while the second, no more than a cupboard, was used for storing medicines. He sometimes slept there, as the other was a tight fit at night when all the students unrolled their mattresses.

He arrived to find his pupils involved in an angry-voiced discussion that stopped the moment he opened the door. His current senior student, a red-haired, merry-faced lad named Aungel, quickly began to read aloud from the copy of Theophilus's *De urinis* that lay on his knees, although his guilty expression suggested the quarrel had been about something else entirely – probably the results of their illicit gambling ring, or the proscribed delights of the town's prostitutes.

'I do not see why we should study before term begins,' said John Goodwyn, a haughty newcomer who was older than the rest. Bartholomew had not chosen to teach him – indeed, he would have rejected the lad had he interviewed him himself – but the Master had been bribed with the offer of double fees. Bartholomew was not pleased: Goodwyn was a disruptive influence, leading the others to grumble when they normally would have been compliant.

'Sitting in a tavern would be much more fun,' agreed Aungel wistfully.

'Taverns are forbidden to scholars.' Bartholomew raised his hand to quell the immediate objection that Goodwyn started to make. 'And do not say you will not be a scholar until next week, because you became one when you signed our register.'

Goodwyn fell silent, although he shot his teacher a resentful glare. Bartholomew ignored it, and set the class an exercise that would keep them busy for the rest of the day. He knew he drove them hard, but the country was still desperately short of qualified physicians after the plague, and he was determined that the ones he trained would be worthy to replace those who had died.

When he was sure they had understood his instructions, he left Aungel to supervise, and retreated to the storeroom. He closed the door to block out the sound of Goodwyn's whine, and slumped on a stool. He was exhausted. Lawrence had taken on some of his patients, but he still had far too many, and he was not sure how he would cope when teaching began the following week.

He glanced at the treatise on fevers he had been writing for the past few years, originally intended to be a brief guide for students, but now extending to several volumes. He could not remember when he had last added to it. Admittedly, some of his spare time had gone on trying to invent a decent lamp for night-time consultations – experiments from which he was now banned after they had gone disastrously wrong – but how much longer would he have to struggle against increasingly impossible workloads?

Sighing wearily, he pulled Galen's *Prognostica* towards him and started to write the commentary he would need to provide as his students slogged their way through it. He had only been working a few moments when the door opened and Brother Michael stepped in. The monk was his closest friend, but Bartholomew still felt a surge of annoyance at the interruption.

'Where is your wine?' Michael demanded. 'I need a drink.'

He snatched the flask from the shelf before Bartholomew could reply, and poured himself a generous measure. It was the cheapest claret available, used in medicines where its taste was irrelevant, and he winced as it went down. The sour flavour did not prevent him from taking a second swig, though. Then he plumped himself down on a bench, where an ominous creak made both scholars tense in alarm – Bartholomew afraid for furniture he could not afford to replace, and Michael worried for his dignity. But the joints held, and the two of them relaxed.

Besides being a Benedictine theologian of some renown, Michael was also Senior Proctor, and his years in post – he stubbornly refused to allow an election that might allow someone else a turn – had made him the most powerful man in the University. The Chancellor, who should have been in charge, was a mere figurehead, there to take the blame when things went wrong.

'Well?' Michael asked.

Bartholomew regarded him blankly. 'Well, what?'

'Well, what can you tell me about Elvesmere? It was I who sent you to Winwick Hall, if you recall, and who will pay you threepence for it.'

'Oh, yes. He was stabbed at some unknown location,

29

then dragged to the College latrine. Poor Elvesmere. He would have been mortified to know what had been done to him.'

Michael stared at him in horror. '*Stabbed?* You mean murdered? And it did not occur to you to tell me immediately?' He waved away Bartholomew's sheepish apology. 'Stabbed by whom?'

'The killer left nothing to incriminate himself, Brother. All I can say is that the wound would not have been instantly fatal.'

'Could you have saved him, had you been called at once?'

Bartholomew shook his head. 'The blade punctured a lung. At least, I assume it did. It is impossible to be sure without looking inside him.'

'Then we shall accept your educated guess,' said Michael briskly, well aware of his friend's controversial views on the art of anatomy. 'Could you deduce anything else? Such as whether Elvesmere knew his assailant?'

'Of course not! However, there were no signs of a struggle, which means that either his killer attacked without warning, or Elvesmere did not consider him a threat.'

'Poor Winwick Hall! A murder on the eve of its entry into the University will do its reputation no good whatsoever. Did you meet the other Fellows while you were there? And perhaps observe their reactions when you told them that one of their number had been unlawfully slain?'

'Illesy was shocked, but I think it was more fear of the harm it might do his College than dismay for the victim. Lawrence had to take him to sit down. Ratclyf seemed more indignant than distressed, and the other two – Nerli and Bon – had heard the news before I went to their *parlura*, so I have no idea how they responded. Why? Do you suspect one of them of the crime?'

'Well, they are the ones with access to the place where the victim died,' Michael pointed out.

'Not so, Brother. The gates are off their hinges, which means that anyone can wander in and out. Jekelyn has been hired as a porter, but he is not very conscientious.'

'True.' Michael's green eyes were wide in his chubby face. 'How am I supposed to find a culprit when there is so little in the way of clues? Moreover, I am still busy with the murder of my Junior Proctor, not to mention struggling to keep the peace between the townsmen and the new *matriculands* who are flocking to enrol in the University.'

'Felbrigge,' mused Bartholomew. 'How is that enquiry progressing?'

'Slowly. But I will catch his killer if it is the last thing I do. I must, or the culprit may set murderous eyes on another University official.'

When the bell rang to announce the midday meal, Bartholomew and Michael started to walk towards the hall, joining the streams of scholars emerging from the accommodation wings and gardens. Meals in College were obligatory, and no one could absent himself without the Master's permission. Fortunately for Bartholomew and Michael, the Master was a pragmatic soul who appreciated that physicians and senior proctors sometimes needed to obey more urgent summons, and rarely took them to task if they were missing.

His name was Ralph de Langelee, a tall, barrel-chested individual who had been a henchman of the Archbishop of York before deciding that the University was a better place to ply his range of dubious skills. He knew little of the philosophy he was supposed to teach, but he was an able administrator, and his Fellows were mostly satisfied with his rule. He spotted Michael and Bartholomew as he came out of his quarters, and changed direction to intercept them.

'You know the College statutes, Brother,' he said shortly. 'Is there anything in them that I can use to stop Father William and Thelnetham from sniping at each other? Their feud has lasted for months now, and I am heartily sick of it. It is even worse now that Hemmysby is back.'

'Is it?' asked Bartholomew, startled. Simon Hemmysby was a diffident theologian, who spent half his time teaching in Cambridge, and the other half as a canon in Waltham Abbey. Bartholomew could not imagine him aggravating spats.

'William preached a sermon saying that Waltham is home to the Devil,' explained Langelee. 'So now Hemmysby joins with Thelnetham in deploring William's excesses, and clamours at me to dismiss him on the grounds of bigotry. Can I, Brother? I would do anything for peace.'

Michael considered; he loved the minutiae of College rules. 'Unfortunately, William has been a Fellow too long for us to object to his character now. If we dismiss him for extremism, he will appeal the decision and will probably be reinstated – after which he will be more insufferable than ever. However, there is a statute that says all disputes are to be adjudicated by the Master—'

'I know,' said Langelee acidly. 'You were rash enough to mention it in front of them once, and I have been plagued by demands to arbitrate ever since. I have better things to do than sort out their quarrels. They come to me two or three times a day, and I am at the end of my tether.'

'What do they argue about?' asked Bartholomew.

Langelee regarded him askance. 'That is a question only a man with his head in a corpse would pose! They squabble about everything – who should have which part of the hall for teaching, who should stand where in church, who should have first loan of a book from the library—'

'How many students should be admitted next term.' Michael took up the list, having also been dragged into their rows. 'Whether we should use white tablecloths on

Sundays. Whether we should apologise to Ovyng Hostel for the racket made by our porter's pet peacock. Whether Hemmysby should be a member of the Guild of Saints—'

'Why should he not?' interrupted Bartholomew. 'It is a body of people committed to worthy causes. It is good for us to be associated with it, and all the Fellows of Winwick have joined.'

'William claims it is only open to very wealthy folk, and he disapproves of elitism,' explained Langelee. 'Hemmysby is rich, what with his stipend here and what he earns at Waltham. I suppose Winwick's Fellows must be similarly affluent.'

'Actually, they were admitted because their founder wants as close a connection between the Guild and his new College as possible,' said Michael. 'They are members by default, although I doubt they mind – its functions are very lavish. But the real reason why William objects to Hemmysby's involvement is because *he* was not invited to join – he is jealous.'

'He is not a man to rejoice in the good fortune of others,' sighed Langelee. 'However, what worries me more are his mad views on apostolic poverty, which is a deeply contentious subject.'

Michael agreed. 'Have you heard what is happening in Oxford because of it? The debate has inspired so many fanatical theologians to air their opinions that some bishops refuse to let men from their dioceses study there. The King has been forced to issue an edict forbidding anyone from discussing it, but too late – the whole *studium generale* is already seen as a hotbed of heresy.'

'Yet apostolic poverty has been chosen as the subject for tomorrow's Cambridge Debate,' remarked Bartholomew.

'It is a calculated gamble on my part,' explained Michael. 'We get the matter out in the open, but in strictly controlled conditions and before most of our students arrive back. Then it will become a banned topic until further notice.'

'Do you think Oxford's current reputation for dissent is why John Winwick chose to found his new College here?' asked Langelee.

'I am sure of it,' replied Michael. 'Especially after what happened to Linton Hall.'

'And what was that?' asked Bartholomew, when Michael pursed his lips in disapproval.

'You have not heard? Its members defied the King's edict and wrote a tract challenging the most recent papal bull on apostolic poverty. In response, His Majesty dissolved their hostel, and His Holiness excommunicated all its scholars.'

Bartholomew blinked. 'That seems harsh!'

'Pope and King have decreed that other foundations will suffer the same fate if they follow Linton's example. I do not want *my* University sullied by that sort of thing, so the subject will be off limits once term starts, and anyone who does not like it can go and study somewhere else.'

'You had better tell William, then,' said Langelee. 'Because his beliefs will be just as radical as those of Linton Hall. Personally, I fail to understand why a subject so tedious can excite such fervour. I am sick of hearing about it.'

'You will not be at St Mary the Great to hear us discuss it, then?' asked Michael wryly. 'I shall speak myself, of course. I cannot wait to put those uppity friars in their place.'

'If you do, William will never forgive you,' warned Bartholomew. 'While Thelnetham will be intolerable if he thinks he has your support.'

'He is right, Brother. Please watch what you say.' Langelee sighed wearily. 'Incidentally, the trustees of the Stanton Hutch – namely me, William and Thelnetham – are due to meet after dinner.'

Hutches were chests containing money that could be borrowed by College members. In return for coins, they could leave something of equal or greater value, such as a book or jewellery, and if the loan was not repaid by a specified date, the hutch kept whatever had been deposited. Michaelhouse had several, although the Stanton was by far the richest.

'They will quarrel,' the Master went on. 'And I need some excuse to keep them apart, or I shall be hard-pressed not to run them through. Can you think of anything?'

'How about attending the meeting unarmed?' joked Bartholomew.

'Perhaps I had better,' sighed Langelee without the flicker of a smile, causing Bartholomew and Michael to regard him in alarm. Weapons were forbidden to scholars, and although Langelee had always ignored this particular stricture, he was at least usually discreet about it. 'I do not want to be arrested for murder, although they would try the patience of a saint.'

'Is the Stanton Hutch doing well?' asked Michael, after a short silence during which he decided that he was not equal to disarming the head of his College that day. 'Matt and I manage the Illeigh Chest, but that is virtually dead. We have dozens of useless baubles, but no coins at all.'

'The Stanton is loaded with money,' said Langelee gloomily. 'Because if William supports an application, Thelnetham vetoes it, and vice versa. We have not made a loan in months. They will not even let me have one, and a few marks would help enormously with the expenses we always incur at the beginning of the academic year.'

'The statutes forbid its use for that sort of thing,' preached Michael. 'And rightly so. If we did not have the facility to lend our students money, some would never pay their tuition fees.'

Langelee waved the remark away and turned to Bartholomew. 'I understand you make remedies for Thelnetham's biliousness. How well do you know your toxins?'

'I sincerely hope you are jesting,' said Bartholomew,

although looking at Langelee's disagreeable expression, he suspected not.

Langelee scowled when he saw he was not going to be rid of the problem so easily. 'I do not want William *or* Thelnetham in my College. Now I know how Henry the Second felt when *he* had to manage turbulent clerics.'

'So Langelee views himself as a beleaguered monarch,' mused Michael when the Master had gone. 'No wonder he walks around armed to the teeth and wants you to poison his enemies.'

Bartholomew had always liked Michaelhouse's hall, although it was more pleasant in summer than in winter. The windows had once contained glass, but that had been broken over the years, and the scholars were now faced with the choice of a warm but dark environment with the shutters closed, or a bright but chilly one with them ajar. As the weather was mild that morning, they were thrown wide open, and sunlight streamed in, bright and cheering.

He stood behind his seat at the high table, and watched his colleagues take their places. The Master was in the centre, with Father William on one side and Michael on the other. Bartholomew was next to Michael, with the College's Dominican, John Clippesby, next to him. Clippesby was generally deemed to be insane, because he talked to animals and claimed they answered back. Yet he was gentle, honest and patient with his students. Hemmysby was at the end, quiet, priestly and in desperate need of a haircut – his normally neat curls had been allowed to blossom into a thick thatch that was faintly ridiculous.

Unfortunately, the rules of seniority put Thelnetham next to William, something that might have been avoided if Suttone the Carmelite had been willing to move. Suttone refused, on the grounds that he had no wish to have one adversary on either side of him, predicting – probably justifiably – that they would just continue to argue across him.

With eight days still to go before the start of term, the hall was only half full, as many students had yet to return. Bartholomew was the only Fellow who insisted that his pupils begin studying the moment they arrived, although Michael's sombre theologians were hard at work of their own volition, as were a number of youthful first-years, eager to make a good impression.

When everyone was standing behind his seat and the clatter of conversation had died away, Langelee intoned one of his peculiar graces, which comprised half-remembered clips from other prayers, all jumbled together without reference to content or meaning. He spoke with a booming confidence that impressed anyone who had no Latin but bemused those who did, after which everyone sat, and waited for the servants to bring the food.

Meals were supposed to be taken in silence at Michaelhouse, the only voice that of the Bible Scholar reading the scriptures. In reality, Fellows were a talkative horde, and rarely paid heed to this particular rule. The students followed their example, so it was not long before the hall was full of animated banter. At the high table, Michael began to list all the Colleges, hostels and houses that had been burgled of late – cleverly executed crimes that neither he nor the Deputy Sheriff had been able to solve. Thelnetham cut across him.

'I really must complain, Master. William has stolen the ale I bought for the paupers in the choir. It is a disgusting act of selfishness.'

Thelnetham – refined, fastidious and with a penchant for enlivening the plain habit of his Order with outrageously colourful accessories; there were yellow bows on his shoes that day – was one of the most able scholars in the University, and it was inevitable that he and the grubby, dim-witted William should fall out.

'I thought it was there for everyone, and I was thirsty,' objected William, using the loud, hectoring tones he reserved for spats with Thelnetham. He had originally been with the Inquisition, but had been ousted because his cronies had deemed him too zealous. Bartholomew and Michael were used to his idiosyncrasies, but the newer Fellows found him difficult to take. He was physically repellent, too: his Franciscan habit rarely saw the laundry, and he had thick, greasy hair that sprouted untidily around a lopsided tonsure.

'We shall observe silence today,' declared Langelee promptly. 'It is the Feast Day of Saint Gratinule, and we should all reflect on his martyrdom.'

'Saint who?' Thelnetham narrowed his eyes. 'I hope you have not invented him, because you decline to address my complaint.'

'How did he die?' asked William ghoulishly.

'He choked on a walnut,' replied Langelee, seeing a bowl of them on the table in front of him.

'That is hardly martyrdom, Master,' said William, doubtfully. 'And—'

'He perished while giving the Host to the King of Rome,' elaborated Langelee. 'He was very devout, and we must all contemplate his great holiness.'

'Why was he eating walnuts while celebrating Mass?' asked William suspiciously. 'And I was not aware that Rome went in for kings.'

'It was a long time ago,' stated Langelee, the curt tone of his voice indicating that the discussion was over. 'When things were different. Now let us pray.'

He bowed his head and clasped his hands in an entirely uncharacteristic pose of piety, forcing those who were in holy orders to do likewise. As this was all the Fellows except Bartholomew, there was blessed peace, broken only by the rattle of spoons on pewter bowls.

The fare was dismal as usual, comprising a watery stew

laced with gristle and undercooked onion – fuel was expensive, and one economy was not lighting the kitchen fire until later in the day, which meant that food was often served semi-raw. There was nothing else except a few late nuts from the orchard, so it had to be eaten, but Fellows and students alike grimaced their distaste. Langelee was about to say a final grace when Cynric, Bartholomew's book-bearer, appeared. Bartholomew started to stand, assuming he had come with a summons from a patient, but Cynric went to the Master instead.

'I cannot find the Stanton Hutch,' he said, perturbed. 'You asked me to collect it from the cellar and put it in the conclave, ready for your meeting. But it is not there.'

Langelee turned to William and Thelnetham. 'Have either of you taken it?'

Both Fellows shook their heads. 'However, I can tell you that it contains fifty marks and five pence,' said William.

'Fifty marks and *nine* pence,' corrected Thelnetham crisply.

'More,' gulped Langelee, speaking in a low voice so that the students would not hear. 'A *lot* more. A couple of weeks ago, I discovered that rats had attacked the box where we keep the College's valuables. I put them in the Stanton Hutch instead, as it is thicker and I thought they would be safer. If the chest has gone, then it means the College is penniless. Literally!'

CHAPTER 2

It did not take Michaelhouse's agitated Master and Fellows long to determine that the heavy box containing the money, books and jewels of the Stanton Hutch, along with virtually every other item of value the College owned, was not on the premises. After a brief and very panicky search they met in the cellar beneath the kitchen, where the hutches were stored.

'But it cannot have gone!' breathed Langelee, white-faced with horror. 'Everything is in it, including all the fees I have collected for the coming term.'

'I hope you did not put the deeds for our various properties in it,' said Michael worriedly. 'Without them, we cannot prove ownership.'

'Of course I did! Documents are far more vulnerable to rats than coins, and I aimed to protect them. I repeat: *everything* is in there, even the Stanton Cup.'

There was renewed consternation. The Stanton Cup had been bequeathed by their founder, and was by far their most cherished possession. Silver gilt and studded with precious stones, it was priceless, but although the College was constantly struggling for funds, it would never be sold.

'Someone will give it back,' said Hemmysby soothingly. 'Do not worry.'

'Give it back?' spluttered Langelee. 'What kind of thief returns his spoils? We shall never see it again, and this disaster means we face the biggest crisis in our existence.'

'It is certainly the biggest crisis in mine,' gulped Thelnetham. 'I left a pledge in the Stanton Hutch – a bestiary with a gold-leaf cover. My Prior General lent it to me, and

I was going to redeem it this week, because he wants it back. What shall I say to him? He will skin me alive!'

'You borrowed the money to buy yourself a pair of red shoes,' said William with gleeful spite. 'So it serves you right.'

'What shall we do?' asked Suttone, his shocked voice cutting through Thelnetham's waspish retort. 'How will we buy food, fuel and teaching supplies? Or pay the servants?'

'Easily,' replied Hemmysby. 'We shall forfeit our stipends.'

Bartholomew was appalled. He had no other income, given that most of his patients could not afford to pay him, and while he was not concerned for himself, it would mean an end to free medicine for a sizeable proportion of the town's poor. He had thought his troubles on this front were over when he had been left some money by his brother-in-law, but it had been needed to repair the wall roof after a violent storm, leaving him as impecunious as over.

'That is very kind,' said Langelee wretchedly. 'But our stipends have gone, too. We have five marks due in tithes from our church in Cheadle, along with fees from those students who have not yet arrived. And that is all. We shall have nothing more until Christmas. Nothing!'

There was a dismayed silence.

'Then I had better see about catching the thief,' said Michael eventually.

'How?' asked Langelee in despair. 'Nearly every College and decent home in Cambridge has been burgled over the last two weeks, and you have told me countless times that the thief leaves no clues. This is just one in a long chain of crimes.'

'Potmoor,' said Thelnetham, shooting Bartholomew a disagreeable glance. 'We all know he is the culprit. You must arrest him at once, Michael.'

'I *have* arrested him,' said the monk crossly. 'But with

no actual proof that he is guilty, I was forced to let him go again.'

'But Potmoor is a wealthy man,' said Bartholomew doubtfully. 'I do not see him demeaning himself by clambering through windows in the dead of night.'

'Well, he does,' retorted Michael. 'He is always braying that he likes to hone the expertise he acquired as a novice felon. It is a point of honour to him that he can still burgle a house with all the skill of Lucifer. And if you do not believe me, ask him. He will not deny it.'

'It is true, Matt,' said Hemmysby. 'He claims he would never ask his henchmen to do anything he cannot manage himself, and he is reputed to be one of the most able housebreakers the shire has ever seen.'

'And his henchmen are nearly as talented,' added Langelee glumly. 'Even if he is innocent, the chances are that one of them is responsible – with or without his blessing.'

Michael took a deep breath. 'So let us see what we know about the crime he committed against us. Who was down here last?'

'Me,' replied Langelee. 'I collected the fees from Bartholomew's new medics after supper last night, and I came to put them in what I thought was a safe place. The hutch was here, whole and intact. And before you ask, yes I *was* careful to lock up again afterwards.'

'He was,' interjected Cynric. 'I came down here with him, to hold the lamp.'

'Did anyone see or hear anything unusual after that time?' asked Michael.

Everyone shook their heads, and Langelee closed his eyes in despair. 'So it is no different from all the other burglaries – executed with a ruthlessly brilliant efficiency that shows the perpetrator to be a felon of some distinction.'

'Potmoor,' put in Thelnetham a second time. 'And we all know it.'

'We shall have to keep this quiet,' said Suttone worriedly. 'If our students think we cannot supply what they have paid for, they will demand a refund so they can go elsewhere. When we fail to oblige, we will lose our charter. This *must* stay between us.'

'How?' asked Bartholomew. 'One of them might have seen something that will help us identify the culprit, but to find out, we shall have to ask questions. We cannot do that without revealing what has happened.'

'True,' agreed Michael. 'So I suggest a compromise: we admit that the hutch has gone, but the loss of all the College's money and deeds will remain our secret.'

'How long can we last without funds?' asked Hemmysby. 'I know we have enough fuel for a few weeks, because I bought some in August, but what about food? If we have any more nuts, we should sell them. They will fetch a good price at the market, and they are a silly extravagance anyway – I cannot abide the things.'

'We had the last of them today,' replied William, who was a regular visitor to the kitchen and its stores. 'But we have peas and beans for a month. The hens will stop laying soon, so I suggest we eat them and—'

'*No!*' said Clippesby fiercely. He had one of the birds in his arms, and he hugged her protectively. 'There is nothing wrong with living on vegetables and grain for a while.'

'I am not giving up meat,' stated Michael. 'I would rather go naked.'

'Let us hope it does not come to that,' said Thelnetham, shuddering at the prospect. 'However, *I* can dine in the Gilbertine Priory, so I am not concerned about food. What does worry me is the loss of the deeds that prove we own our churches and manors.'

'I shall forge replacements,' determined Michael, ignoring the blatant selfishness of Thelnetham's remark. 'And we will just have to brazen it out if anyone challenges them.'

'Fair enough,' said William. 'No one will question our probity.'

'Someone might question yours,' muttered Thelnetham, eyeing the grimy Franciscan in distaste. 'Then we shall all be exposed as liars.'

'You have not seen the high quality of Michael's forgeries,' said Hemmysby with a smile, speaking before William could respond. 'They will convince even the most distrustful of sceptics.'

'I blame Winwick Hall, personally,' said William. 'The town hates the idea of another College, while our fellow scholars are suspicious of a place that has been founded with such unseemly haste. Someone has burgled us in revenge.'

'That makes no sense,' said Thelnetham impatiently. 'Why pick on us?'

'Because the Senior Proctor lives here,' explained William. 'And he runs the University. They think *he* brought Winwick into being, even though we know he is innocent.'

'It is possible,' sighed Hemmysby soberly. 'Winwick Hall has caused a lot of resentment. Perhaps someone *has* decided to punish us for Michael's role in bringing it into being.'

Thoroughly rattled, Langelee organised a more systematic search of the College and its grounds to ensure that a student had not hidden the chest as a prank, leaving Michael to question the other two hutch managers. The monk spoke to Thelnetham and William in the cellar, while Bartholomew prowled with a lamp, looking for clues and listening with half an ear to the discussion.

'When did you last see the Stanton Hutch?' Michael asked them.

'In July,' replied William promptly. 'We have had no requests for loans since then, so there has been no need to look at it.'

'I saw it last week.' Thelnetham regarded William coolly. '*I* take my responsibilities seriously, even if you do not. I check regularly to ensure it is safe.'

'I did not think it was necessary,' countered William. 'We never had trouble with thieves before *you* arrived. Yet you must get the money from somewhere to pay for your fripperies . . .'

'I inspected the chest six days ago – Tuesday,' said Thelnetham to Michael, not gracing the accusation with a response. 'I did not open it, but it was in its usual spot. However, it occurred to me then that it was vulnerable – Langelee keeps the key to the cellar in his quarters, which he often leaves unattended. It would not be difficult for someone to walk in and take it.'

'We have a good porter,' objected William. 'He repels anyone he does not know.'

'That assumes the thief came from outside,' Thelnetham pointed out. 'But if that were true, how did he know where to find the key? And the door *was* opened with a key, because there would be scratch marks on the lock if it had been forced or picked, and there are none.'

Bartholomew stopped prowling to stare at him. 'I hope you are not suggesting that a member of College is responsible.'

'It is an unpleasant notion, I know,' replied the Gilbertine. 'But the reality is that the culprit knew exactly how to get in.'

'No,' said Bartholomew firmly. 'No one here would do such a thing.'

Michael asked a few more questions, then nodded to say that William and Thelnetham could go. They bickered as they went, their haranguing voices echoing as they climbed the stairs.

'Actually, Thelnetham makes a good point,' said Michael when it was quiet again. 'No stranger would be aware of the fact that Langelee keeps the cellar key in his room.'

'Thieves can be cunning and determined,' argued Bartholomew. 'One might have been planning this invasion for weeks, gathering information and watching what we do. Moreover, our porter is effective when he is at the gate, but what happens when he does his rounds?'

'True,' acknowledged Michael. 'And I am much happier with the notion of the culprit being a stranger than a viper from within. However, we must remember that a lot of new students have enrolled this term, and we do not know them yet.'

'Their seniors will keep them in order,' said Bartholomew firmly.

Michael nodded, but did not look convinced. 'I know you are busy, but I shall need your help with this. No, do not argue! How will you physick your paupers if you have no stipend to spend on medicine? Your best hope is to help me catch the culprit before he squanders it all. Then you might still be paid.'

Bartholomew gave his reluctant assent, wondering whether Lawrence would agree to treat more of the town's needy until the situation was resolved. And the lectures he had to prepare for the coming term and his daily visits to Edith? He supposed he would just have to forgo more sleep.

'Thank you,' said Michael. 'We shall start by speaking to our colleagues, to see if they have remembered anything new now that they have had time to reflect.'

Clippesby, Suttone and Hemmysby were in the conclave. The Dominican still held the hen, a feisty bird who chased any cat or dog that dared trespass in her domain, and who ruled the other fowl with a beak of iron. She was gentle with Clippesby, though, and her eyes were closed as she dozed on his lap.

'I noticed nothing odd.' Hemmysby ran a hand through his bushy hair. 'I forgot we owned the thing, to tell you the truth. I do not manage a hutch, so I never think about them.'

'I saw Thelnetham go down to the cellar last Tuesday,' supplied Suttone. His plump face was troubled. 'I hope *he* did not take it, aiming to have William blamed. I would not put it past him. I wish they would end this silly feud. Such rancour is hardly seemly for men in holy orders.'

'Are you *sure* none of you saw anything unusual?' pressed Michael desperately. 'Clippesby? What about your animal friends?'

The Dominican had a habit of sitting quietly to commune with nature, which meant he often saw things not intended for his eyes. His observations had helped with enquiries in the past, although the intelligence he provided invariably required careful decoding.

'No,' he replied, uncharacteristically terse. 'Or I would have said the first time you asked.'

Although Michael and Bartholomew spent the rest of the day asking questions of Fellows, students and servants, they learned nothing useful. Everyone was shocked by the news, especially when they heard that the Stanton Cup had gone, too, and Bartholomew did not relish the prospect of eventually confessing that the College's entire fortune had disappeared into the bargain.

At sunset, he went to visit Edith. She lived in a pleasant manor in the nearby village of Trumpington, but since her bereavement, she had preferred to stay at the handsome, stone-built house on Milne Street, from which the family cloth business was run. Bartholomew was glad, feeling its lively bustle was better for her than the quiet serenity of the countryside.

Edith was in the solar, a comfortable room with thick rugs on the floor, and a warm, homely aroma of herbs and fresh bread. Lamps were lit, which imparted a cosy golden glow. She and Bartholomew were unmistakably siblings: both had dark eyes and black hair, although her locks now had a significant sprinkling of silver. He experienced a surge of mixed emotions when he saw Richard was with her – pleasure, because he was fond of his nephew; irritation, because he could see that Edith was upset.

'She has found a box of Father's personal documents, and aims to paw through them,' Richard explained sulkily, when Bartholomew commented on the icy atmosphere. 'It is not right.'

Bartholomew studied his nephew meditatively, trying to see in the man who lounged by the hearth the fresh-faced, carefree boy he had known. Soft living had furnished Richard with an unflattering chubbiness, while his eyes had an unhealthy yellow tinge. He wore his hair long, but the style did not suit him, and made him look seedy. Despite his arrogant confidence, Richard was not a good lawyer, and although he had secured a series of lucrative posts, he had kept none of them for long. The most recent had been with the Earl of Suffolk, where there had been a scandal involving a pregnant daughter. A considerable sum of money had been required to appease the outraged baron.

'Of course it is right,' said Edith irritably. 'Some might be unpaid bills, or other matters that require my attention.'

'They won't – Zachary says so,' Richard shot back.

'Zachary is not in charge,' countered Edith coolly. 'I am. And besides, you neglected to mention that I found this box in the garden, atop a small fire – which the culprit had neglected to mind, so its contents were undamaged. Zachary denies putting it there, so perhaps Oswald . . .'

'If it had been Oswald, surely you would have found it before now,' said Bartholomew. 'While Zachary is not the sort of man to burn someone else's documents.'

'Well, he seems to have had a go at these,' said Richard sullenly. He turned back to his mother. 'But it is not for you

48

to paw through them. They might be nothing to do with the business, and pertain to *my* part of the inheritance.'

'In which case I shall pass them on to you,' said Edith, exasperated. 'Now, did you mention that you were going out this evening?'

Richard saw the defiant jut of her chin, and evidently realised that this was a confrontation he would not win, because he grabbed his cloak and stalked out. Bartholomew watched him go, sorry the easy friendship they had once enjoyed was lost. Richard considered him dull company compared to his London cronies, and the rare evenings they spent together were strained affairs with each struggling to find common ground for conversation.

'He looks well,' he remarked, after the door had been slammed closed.

Edith pulled a disagreeable face. 'He looks like what he is – someone with too much money and too many dissolute companions eager to help him spend it. To be honest, I have no desire to trawl through that chest, but the fact that he tried to stop me . . . Indeed, I cannot help but wonder whether *he* was the one who tried to destroy them.'

'Do you want me to do it?' The prospect did not fill Bartholomew with enthusiasm, and would be yet another demand on his precious time, but there was little he would not do for Edith.

She shook her head. 'I wish Oswald were here, though. He would know how to handle Richard. I wake up each morning thinking it has all been a bad dream, and that he is still alive.'

'Me, too,' admitted Bartholomew.

'His death . . . I know we have discussed it ad nauseam, Matt, but I am sure there was something amiss. *Why* did he die of marsh fever? His previous attacks were never very serious.'

'I do not know,' replied Bartholomew, as he had done many times before. 'I was not there.'

'No,' said Edith bitterly. 'You were off running errands with Michael in Peterborough when he needed you. If you had been in Cambridge, Oswald would still be alive.'

While Bartholomew knew that Edith's words were born of grief, they still hurt, and he returned to Michaelhouse with a heavy heart. He doubted his presence at Oswald's deathbed would have made any difference, given Rougham's account of what had happened, but he still wished he had been there. While his colleagues slept, he sat in the conclave working on his lectures, aiming to distract himself from the guilt of failing Edith during the darkest hours of her life.

Michael arrived after a fruitless evening investigating Elvesmere's murder, and immediately began forging deeds. He gave up when the words began to blur before his eyes, leaving Bartholomew slumped across the table, fast asleep. It was an uncomfortable position, and the physician woke with a stiff neck and backache when the bell rang for Mass the following dawn.

It was a subdued College that attended church. The only person who seemed unaffected by Michaelhouse's desperate predicament was Goodwyn, the new medical student, who sang lustily and wore a smug grin through the entire rite. Michael homed in on him when the service was over.

'I am dissatisfied with your explanation regarding your whereabouts for the time of the theft,' he said briskly. 'Tell me again.'

'You cannot remember that far back?' quipped the student with breezy insolence. 'Shall I mix you a remedy for senile forgetfulness, then?'

'That remark has cost you sixpence, payable by the end of the day.' Michael held up an authoritative hand when a startled Goodwyn started to object. 'It is expensive to annoy the Senior Proctor, so I recommend you curb your tongue. Now, to business. The hutch was stolen between nine o'clock on Sunday evening, when Langelee visited the cellar, and yesterday at noon, when Cynric discovered it missing. Where were you during all that time?'

'Doctor Bartholomew set us a lot of reading on Sunday, sir,' said Aungel, before Goodwyn could land himself in deeper trouble by arguing. 'And it took us until supper to finish. Afterwards, we were restless after being cooped up all day so we went for a walk. We returned to Michaelhouse just as the bells rang for compline.'

'Then we played dice . . . I mean we read our bibles until Doctor Bartholomew came back from seeing a patient,' continued Goodwyn. Gambling was forbidden in College, on the grounds that it led to fights. 'He will testify that we were all there – and that we stayed until morning. After that, we went to church, had breakfast, and read in the hall with the other Fellows.'

Bartholomew nodded, but the truth was that he was an unusually heavy sleeper, and the entire class could have thundered out during the night without waking him, so he was the last person who should be used as an alibi. Michael knew it.

'Goodwyn is the culprit,' he growled, as he and the physician walked back to Michaelhouse. 'You were sleeping too deeply to notice he had gone, and his classmates are wary of exposing him as a liar, because he is older and bigger.'

'And did what with the stolen hutch?' asked Bartholomew. 'It is not in my room, I assure you.'

'Hid it somewhere else.'

'Where? Cynric searched the College from top to bottom, and Goodwyn is new to the town – he will not know any safe places outside.'

'Perhaps he has accomplices.' Michael turned to glare; Goodwyn glowered back, unfazed by the monk's hostility. 'And even if it transpires that he is innocent, you should watch him. Langelee should never have taken him on.'

'He did it for the double fees.'

'Fees that have now disappeared,' remarked Michael caustically. 'But let us review again what we know about the hutch. The cellar was opened with the key from Langelee's room, which was then replaced. You were out on Sunday evening. Did you notice anything odd when you came back?'

'No, but the porter was away on his rounds, so I let myself in.' A stricken expression crossed Bartholomew's face. 'Perhaps someone saw how easy it was, and simply copied me.'

'Unlikely – Thelnetham was right to point out that if it were a random crime, the thief would not have known where to find the key.' Michael's expression hardened. 'The culprit made a mistake when he targeted our home. You offered to help me catch him yesterday—'

'I did not offer. You coerced me.'

'—but I need help with the murders of Felbrigge and Elvesmere, too. No one has offered to take Felbrigge's place, and it is difficult to manage so much without a Junior Proctor.'

'I cannot, Brother,' said Bartholomew tiredly. 'Unless you can arrange for more hours in the day. I am struggling to cope as it is.'

'Felbrigge and Elvesmere were fellow scholars. You should want justice for them.'

'I do, but—'

'Good, it is settled then,' said Michael, with such relief that Bartholomew glanced sharply at him. There were dark bags under his friend's eyes, and he realised that he had been so wrapped up with his own problems that he had failed to notice the toll Michael's responsibilities were taking on him – murders to solve, a huge influx of matriculands to control, all the difficulties surrounding the birth of a new College, and now the stolen hutch.

'I can give you until the start of term, Brother. A week. After that I shall be swamped with teaching. We both will.

So we had better make a start. What have you learned about Felbrigge?'

'Nothing,' replied Michael bitterly. 'He was standing next to me when he was shot, but neither I nor anyone else saw a thing to help. My beadles found the bow, and we were able to deduce that it probably belonged to a professional archer, but that is all. In short, we still have no idea who did it or why.'

'Perhaps Felbrigge was not the intended victim,' suggested Bartholomew. 'Maybe this professional archer was aiming at the Chancellor or you – the University's most powerful scholar.'

'I have already assessed that possibility and dismissed it. Such men do not miss their targets, and nor could they have mistaken Felbrigge for me or Tynkell. I wear my habit, Tynkell is thin and grey, and Felbrigge was short, fat and clad in a ceremonial robe of scarlet. The three of us look nothing alike.'

'When I was at Winwick yesterday, Ratclyf said that Felbrigge was unpopular.' Bartholomew spoke hesitantly, never happy with gossip. 'That he was disliked by scholars *and* townsmen.'

'It is true. Felbrigge managed to antagonise an extraordinary number of people while you and I were away in Peterborough. Clearly, I should never have left him in charge.'

'Did you know he was arrogant and abrasive when you appointed him?'

'Yes, but he was the only one who applied for the job, and I was desperate for help.'

It was no surprise that scholars were not queuing up to be Michael's helpmeet. He was dictatorial, impatient with mistakes, and hated being challenged. Moreover, the post was poorly paid, sometimes dangerous and involved everything Michael did not fancy doing himself.

'Did you like him?' Bartholomew asked.

'Not really. On his first day in office he told me that he intended to step into my shoes by the end of the year. The audacity of the man! Anyway, he obviously angered someone less tolerant than me, and he paid for it with his life. Of course, he was a member of the Guild of Saints . . .'

Bartholomew regarded him uneasily. 'Are you saying that one of them killed him? Lord, that would be awkward! They comprise the town's most influential people – folk who will not appreciate being accused of murder. Who is on your list of suspects?'

'I do not have a list, Matt. I have no evidence, remember? However, I keep coming back to the fact that Potmoor is in the Guild of Saints, and he is no stranger to murder . . .'

Bartholomew sincerely hoped he was wrong. It was bad enough being held responsible for all the burglaries Potmoor was supposed to be committing, but if the felon had murdered a senior member of the University . . . He changed the subject uncomfortably. 'What did you learn about Elvesmere yesterday?'

'Very little. You say the knife wound was not instantly fatal, but no one heard him cry for help. And you say he was moved after he died, but my beadles found no bloody puddles anywhere in Winwick Hall – and they explored it very thoroughly.'

'Is that all?'

'Yes, other than the fact his colleagues disliked him. Their porter – Jekelyn – let slip that Elvesmere was always arguing with them.'

'Do they have alibis?'

'No. They claim to have been in bed all night – alone. Jekelyn says no one came a-calling and that he never left his post. It is a lie, of course – all porters slip away to nap from time to time. So all we know for certain is that Elvesmere was alive when the scholars of Winwick Hall went to sleep, and dead when they awoke.'

* * *

Because William had conducted the morning Mass, and he was noted for the speed with which he could gabble through the sacred words, the Michaelhouse men arrived home before breakfast was ready. Agatha, the formidable lady who oversaw the domestic side of the College, emerged from the kitchen to inform them that the food would not be ready until she said so. Women did not normally hold such sway in University foundations, but she had been Michaelhouse's laundress for so long that not even Langelee was brave enough to challenge her authority.

It was a pleasant day to loiter in the yard, though, and no one minded. The Fellows stood in a huddle near the door, while the students retreated to the far end of the yard, where they could chat about things they did not want their teachers to hear – ways to smuggle women into their bedrooms, secret stashes of wine, and the illicit gambling league established by Goodwyn.

The weather was mild, and the sun shone in a pale blue sky. The trees were just starting to change colour, so summer green was mixed with autumn gold and orange. A blackbird sang from one, answered every so often, somewhat more shrilly, by the porter's peacock. The chickens scratched happily in the dirt, and Clippesby went to talk to them when William raised the subject of the hutch, muttering that he could not bear to hear more speculation about the thief.

'Perhaps *he* took it,' said Thelnetham. A bloodstained rag around one finger marred his otherwise pristine appearance. 'I know for a fact that he admired the bestiary I left in the chest, and he *is* mad. He told me last night that a goat plans to take part in today's debate.'

'It will be an improvement on some of the coxcombs who intend to speak there,' remarked William, casting a pointed glance at the Gilbertine's bright puce shoes.

'What happened to your hand, Thelnetham?' asked Bartholomew, before they could argue.

'I cut it on the church door,' explained the Gilbertine. 'The latch has always been awkward, but recently it has been much worse.'

'It never sticks for me,' said William immediately, watching Bartholomew unwind the bandage to inspect the wound. 'Obviously, God does not want you in there.'

'It *does* stick for you,' countered Hemmysby. 'I saw you wrestling with it only yesterday.'

William scowled. 'You are confusing me with someone else.'

'I doubt that is possible,' said Thelnetham unpleasantly, then jerked his hand away with a screech. 'That hurt, Matthew! Have a care!'

'We should replace that latch,' said the portly Suttone. 'It has been a nuisance for years.'

'How?' asked Langelee. 'We cannot justify hiring a craftsman when we have no money for victuals. Indeed, it would not surprise me if breakfast this morning comprised nothing but sawdust and dung.'

'I said ten free masses for the locksmith's wife last year,' mused Hemmysby. 'I am sure he would give us a new mechanism if I asked nicely.'

'So ask,' ordered Langelee promptly. 'Go now.'

'Tomorrow,' said Hemmysby with a smile. 'I am one of the main speakers at today's debate, and I should spend the morning preparing. Will you be going, Master?'

'No, I have camp-ball practice,' replied Langelee, referring to the vicious sport at which he excelled. 'However, I am sure College honour will be satisfied without me. Michael is also participating, I believe.'

The monk nodded. 'It is time the friars listened to what I have to say. The concept of apostolic poverty is—'

'We friars will win,' interrupted William rudely. 'Because you monastics do not know what you are talking about. Our right to property and influence is a free gift from God, and you have no right to question His will.'

'The loss of rightful dominion through sin is in conflict with sacerdotal power to consecrate the Eucharist independently of a state of grace,' stated Thelnetham with considerable authority, launching into a part of the debate that his less intelligent rival was unlikely to understand. 'That is the nub of the matter. What do you think, William?'

'Our camp-ball team is looking good this year,' began Langelee, aiming to nip the discussion in the bud. William was not the only one who struggled with the complexities of the dispute, and Langelee had no wish to listen to his clerics airing arguments that might have been in Ancient Sumerian for all the sense they made to him. 'We have two new—'

'The debate will see the friars victorious.' William interrupted again, although not to answer Thelnetham's question, as he had no idea whether it was the nub of the matter or not. 'How could it not, when sensible priests like me and Hemmysby have important things to say?'

'*You* are speaking?' asked Suttone in alarm, an expression mirrored in the faces of the others. Michaelhouse did not enjoy an especially distinguished academic reputation, but what little it did have would be lost if William was allowed to hold forth.

'Chancellor Tynkell invited William, who then very kindly agreed to let me take his place,' said Hemmysby, much to everyone's profound relief. 'I have never spoken at the Cambridge Debate before, and I am touched by his generosity of spirit.'

'Just wait until I see Tynkell,' growled Michael. 'He approached William for spite, just because I told him to stop trying to make a name for himself before he retires next year. First there was that new library, and now we have Winwick Hall. The man is a menace.'

'Naturally, *I* shall be speaking,' said Thelnetham, wincing as Bartholomew smeared his finger with a healing paste. 'I shall not take long to demolish the friars, after which we shall all enjoy the refreshments provided by the Guild of Saints.'

'Eat as much as you can,' instructed Langelee, cutting across William's immediate objections to the Gilbertine's predictions. 'I shall dine there, too, after camp-ball. Then we can cancel supper and conserve our supplies.'

'Matt and I will not have time for such pleasures,' said Michael, with the air of a martyr. 'We shall be hunting thieves and killers. I will have to leave the church once I have said my piece, although I doubt any mere friar will be able to refute my conclusions.'

'*Gently*, Matthew!' cried Thelnetham, jerking his hand away a second time. 'I am not a corpse, needing rough treatment to haul me back to the world of the living. I am already here.'

'More is the pity,' muttered William.

'Speaking of corpses, I overheard Potmoor telling a henchman about Heaven yesterday,' said Suttone. 'He claimed he was quite happy there, and resented being dragged back to Chesterton.'

'He was never in Heaven,' declared William. 'He was in Hell. He only thought it was Paradise because Matthew rescued him before he could get a good look at it.'

'I still think he stole our hutch,' said Thelnetham. 'To prove to his nasty henchmen that he has not lost his touch.'

'I doubt it,' said Hemmysby. 'If I had to pick a suspect, it would be someone from Winwick Hall. Their College was built too fast, and they need money to shore it up before it falls down around their ears.'

'Do you have any particular reason for mentioning them?' asked Michael keenly. 'You know its people better than the rest of us – from being a fellow member of the Guild of Saints.'

Hemmysby shrugged. 'I am afraid not, Brother. I was just saying what I felt.'

'You had better not indulge in unfounded statements this afternoon,' warned Thelnetham. 'Or you will make Michaelhouse a laughing stock. Still, better that than what Matthew and William are doing, one with his love of anatomy, and the other with his crass stupidity.'

'I have no love of anatomy,' objected William, startled. 'It is a very nasty—'

'It is a pity anatomy is frowned upon,' said Hemmysby. 'Lawrence from Winwick tells me it is greatly beneficial to our understanding of the human form. Personally, I applaud the practice.'

'If that is the kind of thing you discuss at Guild meetings,' said Thelnetham in distaste, 'then I am glad I have not been invited to join.'

When the breakfast bell rang, the Fellows abandoned their discussion to hurry up the spiral staircase to the hall, Michael and William vying for first place. Bartholomew let the students go in front of him, because he disliked being shoved and jostled, especially when the victuals were unlikely to be worth the scramble.

'John,' he called to Clippesby, who was still talking to the hens. 'You will be late, and I do not want my new students following your example.'

'No,' agreed the Dominican, reluctantly abandoning avian company for human. 'You have an exceptionally unruly horde this year. Aungel is a decent lad, but Goodwyn will lead him astray. And where Aungel goes, the others follow. Ethel told me.'

'Who is Ethel?' asked Bartholomew.

'The College's top hen,' replied Clippesby. 'She is an observant bird when she is not eating, and she has been watching your lads carefully. Incidentally, five more applied to join them last night. I told Langelee that you would not appreciate such a large group, but he said we needed the money, and refused to listen.'

'*Five?*' Bartholomew was horrified. 'But that will give me even more than I had last year – and I struggled then! How does he expect me to teach them properly?'

'He does not care about that – he just wants their fees. You should see the size of William's class. *He* does not mind, though, as he equates higher numbers with personal popularity. However, it will not take these young men long to realise that they are wasting their money by being with him, and then there will be trouble.'

'Lord!' muttered Bartholomew. 'I had better speak to Langelee.'

'Please do. Ethel says Langelee is wrong to overload our classes, as she believes we will not be in dire financial straits for long.'

'Then let us hope she is right,' said Bartholomew fervently.

'Here come your new pupils now,' said Clippesby, nodding to where a gaggle of young men were being conducted towards the hall by Goodwyn. 'You must excuse me, Matt. I saw them tease a dog last night, and I have no wish to exchange pleasantries with cruel people.'

Bartholomew regarded the newcomers warily, thinking they did not look like aspiring *medici* to him. They were beautifully dressed, and their elegant manners suggested that they would be more at home at Court than dealing with the sick. He could only suppose that Langelee had accepted them without explaining what being a physician entailed.

'Doctor Bartholomew,' said Goodwyn unctuously. 'Here are your latest recruits. I am sure we shall all become very fine physicians under your expert tutelage. Did I tell you that we are acquainted with your nephew, by the way? Richard said you tried to make *him* a physician, too, but he saw the light, and became a lawyer instead. There is money in law.'

'So I understand,' said Bartholomew, coolly, disliking

the lad's disingenuous tone. 'Perhaps you should consider studying it.'

Goodwyn laughed. 'Perhaps I shall, but not until I have seen what you have to offer.'

'How do you know Richard?' asked Bartholomew, wondering whether Goodwyn would transfer to another tutor if he overwhelmed him with work. He decided it was worth a try.

'From a tavern we all frequent in London. We are delighted that he has decided to stay in Cambridge for a spell, as life would not be nearly as much fun if *he* returned to the city.'

'Life will revolve around lectures and reading,' warned Bartholomew. 'So unless he plans to join you in the library, your paths will seldom cross.'

He walked away, smothering a smile at the newcomers' immediate consternation.

The meal did not last long, as there was very little to eat, and Langelee's prediction of inedibility was more accurate than was pleasant. There was no dung – at least, not that was readily identifiable – but the bits floating in the pottage were almost certainly wood shavings. When it was over, Bartholomew snagged Langelee before he could disappear to punch, bite, kick, scratch and maul his team-mates in the name of sport.

'Your new students came with testimonials from their parish priests *and* licences to matriculate,' said the Master, immediately guessing the reason for the physician's irritation. 'But more importantly, they can pay a term's fees up front, and one donated a book to our library.'

'What book?' asked Bartholomew. 'A medical one?'

'Law. Do not ask me the title – it was something in Latin.' Langelee began to walk away. 'And you cannot grumble about the extra work either. We must all put our shoulder to the wheel if we are to survive.'

'Unfortunately, he is right,' said Michael, who had been listening. 'You are not the only one who has been burdened with unsuitable pupils. He gave *me* three Cistercians!'

'Gracious,' said Bartholomew, although he failed to understand why Cistercians should be deemed so undesirable. 'But we had better make a start with your enquiries, or we shall still be investigating when we are supposed to be teaching. Our new recruits will not be impressed by tutors who fail to arrive for class.'

They left the College and walked up St Michael's Lane. When they reached the High Street, Bartholomew was again astonished by the huge number of would-be students who had descended on the town – at least twice as many as usual.

'They are certainly keeping my beadles busy,' said Michael, when the physician remarked on it. 'Unfortunately, we have no jurisdiction over them – they are not yet members of the University, as they are always quick to remind us.'

'Some will be,' said Bartholomew. 'The ones who have been offered places.'

'If only that were true! But don't forget that they're not bound by University rules until they have signed our register and that's not until next week. It is not usually a problem, as most new lads are eager to make a good impression.'

'So why are this year's applicants different?'

'I wish I knew. The current intake is abnormally objectionable, the worst of them all being your loathsome Goodwyn. He is still my prime suspect for stealing the Stanton Hutch, you know.'

'But he has just paid a huge sum of money to study here. Do you really think he would promptly turn around and steal from us?'

'You are too willing to see the good in people, Matt,

and it is not a virtue. Goodwyn is a worm, and you would be wise to recognise it.'

'The townsfolk do not like these undisciplined louts either,' said Bartholomew, watching one particularly arrogant throng strut past. 'Cynric told me that they are making it easy for the burglar to operate – there is so much brawling that any suspicious sounds are masked.'

Michael sniffed. 'Potmoor – if he *is* the culprit – is such an experienced criminal that he will not need help from noisy matriculands. Incidentally, I have lost count of the number of times that I have been told you should have kept your necromantic skills to yourself and left Potmoor dead.'

Bartholomew groaned. 'I used smelling salts, not witchery. And if Meryfeld, Rougham, Lawrence, Eyer the apothecary and Surgeon Holm had been halfway competent, they would have done the same.'

'Perhaps they thought it was time that his reign of terror was ended. You, on the other hand, gave him the opportunity to continue.'

'He would have woken anyway – patients with catalepsia usually do. Where are we going?'

'To Winwick Hall. Hemmysby said they might have stolen our hutch.'

'He also said he had no particular reason for thinking so.' Bartholomew was alarmed that they were about to visit the new College on so frail a pretext.

'I know. But I also have my reservations about the place – reservations that make me want to keep an eye on it. On the one hand, I am delighted that Winwick Hall is here, not in Oxford, because another endowed foundation will make our University stronger and more attractive to benefactors and students.'

'But on the other?'

'On the other, it arrived too quickly, and we were not

ready for it. We are an old, staid organisation, and we require time to adjust to new situations.'

'Oxford never needs time to adjust. They are far more forward thinking than us.'

Michael scowled. 'No, they are not, and you would do well to remember that if you value your position here. Anyway, I wish we had been given more time to consider. Better arrangements could have been made, especially regarding its location.'

'What could be more suitable than a site next to St Mary the Great?'

'Precisely! It is the best position in the entire town, and shades even King's Hall. Moreover, it will use St Mary the Great as a chapel, and the fact that its head is called a Provost implies a degree of ownership over the place. It is the *University* Church – it belongs to all of us, not just one College.'

'If you had been Chancellor, none of this would have happened. Winwick's charter would have needed your signature before it was sent to the King, and you could have procrastinated. Perhaps you should consider standing for election when Tynkell resigns.'

'But I do not want to be Chancellor! I like things the way they are, with me making all the important decisions, and him taking the blame if things go wrong.'

'When he retires, he may be replaced by a less malleable man,' warned Bartholomew.

'True – which would be a nuisance. Perhaps I should arrange to have myself elected, then. It will look good for when I am promoted to a bishopric or an abbacy.'

It was not the first time Michael had voiced the expectation that he would achieve high rank, and Bartholomew had always been amused that he expected to rise in a single bound, without the tedious steps in between. It had also not escaped his notice that Michael clearly intended to rig the vote, rather than risk the democratic process.

Meanwhile, Michael was eyeing a gaggle of youths on the other side of the road, some of whom bore obvious signs of brawling – torn clothes, bruised fists and bloody faces.

'Yet another spat with the town, I warrant,' he grumbled. 'And no Dick Tulyet to help me keep these louts in order.' He referred to the Sheriff who, besides being very good at his job, was also a friend. 'It is unfortunate that his deputy is next to worthless. But here we are at Winwick Hall. Let us see what its Fellows have to say for themselves.'

The new College's gates still leaned against the wall waiting for their hinges, and Jekelyn the porter stood in the gap ready to repel any visitors he did not like the look of. He regarded Bartholomew and Michael suspiciously when they asked to see the Provost, but stood aside for them to enter. As they walked across the yard, Bartholomew saw that scaffolding had been erected around part of the hall since his visit the previous day.

'Subsidence,' explained Illesy, as he came to greet them. 'Our land is boggy, so it is to be expected. Have you seen our lovely library, by the way? Do come and look. The workmen finished laying the floor last night.'

He opened a door to reveal a room that was as handsome as any in Cambridge. Its walls were covered in bright white plaster to improve the light for reading, and its shelves had been fashioned from pale wood. They were poorly planed in places, though, and Illesy yelped as he ran a heavily beringed hand along one, only to be rewarded with a splinter. The windows were glazed, an almost unimaginable luxury, but not all the panes had been properly fitted, and several had dropped out – yet another indication of the speed with which the building had been thrown up.

Bartholomew began to browse the books, but was quickly disappointed. Winwick had been founded for clerks, so there was not a medical tome in sight. He scanned the titles. Most were standard texts that all lawyers would need to learn, and none were very good copies. In short, he thought the fine room was wasted on them.

'The Guild of Saints has promised to buy us some carrels,' Illesy was telling Michael with proprietary pride. 'We aim to have them installed by the beginning of term.'

'I hear you have a problem with your endowment,' said Michael. 'That the deeds to the churches and manors that will provide you with your steady income have not yet been delivered.'

Illesy waved a dismissive hand. 'A minor delay, no more. They will be here soon.'

Just then, the door opened and the Fellows trooped in. Bartholomew studied them carefully, wondering whether there was any justification in Hemmysby's belief that one might have stolen the Stanton Hutch. It took no more than a moment for him to decide there was not. All five were obviously wealthy, and their liveried tabards were made from the best cloth money could buy. Nerli's and Bon's were edged with fur, while Lawrence and Ratclyf had elegantly embroidered hems. Illesy was even more extravagantly attired, with a silk undershirt poking from one sleeve, and a beautiful lambswool cape around his shoulders.

None seemed particularly pleased to see the visitors, except Lawrence who smiled with his customary sunny charm. Ratclyf was irritable, clearly resenting the intrusion, while Nerli the Florentine had a sombre, brooding face that was not made for cheery greetings anyway. Meanwhile, Bon's attention was on negotiating the still-unfamiliar terrain, and he clung hard to the arm of the student at his side.

'We came to warn you about the recent spate of burglaries,' lied Michael. 'Michaelhouse was targeted last night, and we lost a valuable loan chest.'

'How terrible,' said Nerli in his oddly accented Latin, and Bartholomew was struck again by the man's darkly sinister appearance. It was even more apparent when he stood next to the white-bearded Lawrence, who radiated jollity and charm. 'Still, I imagine you have plenty more. We have been told several times that you older Colleges have pots of money, and are thus more likely to survive than us youthful upstarts.'

'No one phrased his remarks quite like that,' objected Lawrence. 'They—'

'The deed for the manor of Uyten – our founder's home village – will be here within a week,' interrupted Bon. 'I oversaw the arrangements myself. Well, perhaps *oversaw* is the wrong word, given my affliction, but I certainly ensured that all was in order.' He smiled, obviously proud to have been of service. 'It is the first of many, because our founder wants us to have the biggest endowment in the country.'

The reference to his ailment caused Bartholomew to study him with professional detachment, and note that he suffered from hypochyma – a clouding of the lens behind the eye. He also observed that Bon's student guide had the same thickened ears that Langelee was acquiring from camp-ball, where they were so frequently battered that they changed shape.

'That is why the other Colleges are jealous of us,' bragged Ratclyf. 'Along with our fine buildings, good location and connections with Court. In time, we shall outshine them all.'

'In time, we shall become friends,' corrected Lawrence, a little sternly.

'Perhaps,' shrugged Bon. 'After all, there are more worthy enemies than our colleagues from King's Hall, Michaelhouse, Bene't and Gonville.'

'Yes, like the town,' agreed Nerli unpleasantly. 'They hate us, too.'

'They do,' agreed Michael baldly. 'Which means you might be vulnerable to thieves.'

'I hope you have not been swayed by the common prejudice that Potmoor is responsible for all these crimes,' said Illesy. 'There is no evidence to suggest he is guilty. My appointment as Provost means I can no longer be his lawyer, but I will not see him unjustly maligned even so.'

Michael raised his eyebrows. 'I malign no one. I merely warn you to be on your guard.'

Bon smiled in the monk's approximate direction. 'We should be safe. Our walls are thick, and we have Jekelyn as a porter.'

'Whatever possessed you to hire such a surly rogue?' asked Michael disapprovingly. 'I could have suggested some far more suitable candidates.'

'Our founder picked him,' explained Ratclyf. 'Hopefully, his reputation as a brawler will make this vile burglar think twice about paying us a visit.' He glanced archly at Illesy, making it clear that *he* did not share the conviction that Potmoor was innocent.

'He might make scholars think twice before paying you a visit, too,' retorted Michael tartly. 'No one likes being subjected to impertinent remarks when he comes to see colleagues.'

'We shall not have time for entertaining once term starts,' said Bon. 'We will not become the biggest, most prestigious College in the University by fooling around with guests.'

'We shall entertain!' cried Lawrence, dismayed by the bleak prospect that Bon was painting. 'It will be a poor existence if we do nothing but work.'

The others' doubtful looks suggested he might be alone in that belief.

'Your students will certainly want to relax with friends,' said Michael. 'And speaking of students, let me give you some advice. They will do anything to avoid paying their fees, so you might want to establish some hutches. Once there is a facility for borrowing, no one will have an excuse not to give you what is owed.'

'Have you found Elvesmere's killer?' asked Illesy, his curt tone making it clear he did not appreciate being told how to run his College. 'Is that why you came? To tell us his name?'

'I am afraid not,' replied Michael. 'Although progress has been made.'

'Has it?' Lawrence smiled warmly, eyes crinkling at the corners. 'I am so glad. I am not vengeful, but I dislike the notion of a murderer at large.'

'So do I,' agreed Bon. 'It might deter students from applying here, and that would be a pity – for them as much as us.'

'You would not fear that if you could see,' said Ratclyf smugly. 'Our yard was thronged with hopefuls all day yesterday, and we accepted another twenty lads last night. It will not be long before we have so many pupils that we shall be by far the richest College in Cambridge.'

Bartholomew and Michael exchanged a wry glance. Increasing the size of *their* classes had done nothing for Michaelhouse's coffers. Indeed, the reverse was often true, as the lads then had to be housed and fed, which – due to fluctuating market prices – sometimes cost more than the fees they had paid.

'Did Elvesmere want Winwick Hall to be the biggest College in Cambridge?' asked Michael.

'Actually, he was of the opinion that we should curb our enthusiasm for growth,' replied Illesy. 'It was something about which we disagreed.'

'His caution was misplaced,' asserted Bon. '*We* have no reason to limit ourselves. *We* are Winwick Hall, and our founder is a favourite of the King.'

'He also thought we should teach only canon law,' added Illesy. 'However, *civil* law is where the money lies – wills, medico-legal issues, property disputes. That is what the bulk of our students will want to study. Thus he disapproved of everyone except Ratclyf, who is our other canonist.'

'He was particularly opposed to criminal law,' said Nerli slyly. 'And he made some very harsh remarks to our Provost about the skills he honed while representing Potmoor.'

'He made some very harsh remarks to you, too, Nerli,' retorted Illesy spitefully. 'He denigrated your degrees from Salerno, just because it is a foreign school.'

Nerli scowled so angrily that Bartholomew and Michael exchanged another glance. The Florentine was powerfully built, and the knife he carried in his belt was too big for sharpening quills and paring fruit. Bartholomew could easily imagine him stabbing a colleague in the dark.

'He did not *denigrate* Nerli's qualifications,' said Lawrence, ever the peacemaker. 'He merely said that he did not know there was such a thing as a Master of Civil Law—'

'Well, there is,' snapped Nerli. 'Salerno does not follow the same style as other universities.'

This was news to Bartholomew, although in fairness, he had spent time in its medical school, not its Law Faculty, so was not in a position to contradict the Florentine.

'And he thought your post was a sinecure, Lawrence,' Ratclyf went on. 'That medico-legal studies are not a serious subject, and that you are being paid for nothing.'

'Then let us not forget the words *you* exchanged with him,' flashed Bon. 'He despised you for the sly way you deal with tradesmen.'

'I am the College bursar – if I do not deal slyly with tradesmen, they will cheat us,' snapped Ratclyf. He jabbed an angry finger at his accuser. 'You were his closest friend, but it did not grant you immunity from his bile.' He turned to the visitors. 'Bon is illegitimate, which Elvesmere feared might damage our reputation. He was always harping on it.'

'Enough,' cried Illesy. 'Do you want the Senior Proctor to include *us* on his list of murder suspects? He was unimpressed yesterday to learn that none of us can prove our whereabouts at the time of Elvesmere's killing, and now you make our harmless tiffs sound like reasons for wanting him dead. I suggest you say no more until you are in control of your tongues.'

'They *are* on the Senior Proctor's list of murder suspects,' said Michael, once he and Bartholomew were out on the street again. 'Lord only knows what else might have been added had Illesy not silenced them.'

'On the contrary, he let them continue on purpose,' said Bartholomew. 'Had he stopped them at the beginning of the spat, we would have gone away thinking *he* was the only one Elvesmere had offended. Now we know that Elvesmere alienated them all.'

'Illesy is certainly a prime suspect. Not only will he have learned a lot about dispatching opponents from his association with Potmoor, but no Head of House wants a malcontent in his midst. Look at Langelee, who is always after us for ways to get rid of William and Thelnetham.'

'Yes, but not by killing them.' Then Bartholomew remembered that the Master had asked about poisons, and hurried on. 'The others' motives are just as strong. For example, Ratclyf clearly hates criticism, and Elvesmere condemned the way he performs as bursar.'

'Meanwhile, there is something decidedly sinister about that gently smiling Lawrence. And he is a *medicus* – trained at Oxford, no less. I am sure *they* taught him how to ply a knife.'

'Nonsense, Brother,' said Bartholomew impatiently. 'Lawrence is a good man. Besides, whoever wielded the dagger was *not* an expert – Elvesmere took some time to die.'

'If you say so.' Michael's tone of voice made it clear he disagreed. 'Nerli is a strong candidate, too. He is sensitive about his foreign qualifications, and he has a black and dangerous look about him. In fact, Langelee thinks he is a soldier, not a scholar at all.'

'What about Bon?' asked Bartholomew. 'I cannot imagine he was pleased to be reminded of his illegitimacy, especially if he and Elvesmere were supposed to be friends.'

'His bastardy has been nullified by papal dispensation – I have seen the documents myself. I doubt Elvesmere's remarks meant anything to him. Besides, I imagine a blind man would be at a severe disadvantage in a killing.'

'Hypochyma,' mused Bartholomew. 'Rougham and Lawrence will tell you that it is caused by corrupt humours collecting in the *locus vacuus* between the pupil and the eye, but my Arab master said it was because pigments accumulate on the lens, thus preventing light from—'

'This may not be the best time to air controversial opinions, Matt,' interrupted Michael. 'Not with royal and papal ears alert for any hint of heresy – we do not want Michaelhouse to suffer the same fate as Linton Hall. And your unorthodox views are immaterial to our discussion anyway, which is that Bon cannot see, so committing murder would be something of a challenge. Especially one that involved lugging bodies around, given that you say Elvesmere was killed elsewhere.'

'And I *am* sure that is what happened, which may be enough to exonerate *all* the Winwick men. If the body was moved, why not take it away from the College altogether?'

'Perhaps the killer panicked, or did not want to risk going out with a corpse. My beadles have been assiduous in their patrols of late, because of all the new students who flock to join us.'

'Then perhaps that is where we should be looking for a culprit – at the matriculands.'

'It is possible . . . Oh, Lord! Here comes Cynric, and I can tell from the expression on his face that he has unpleasant news. I hope it has nothing to do with Michaelhouse.'

'You have been summoned, I am afraid,' said Cynric

to Bartholomew. 'By Dickon Tulyet, who has been bitten by a horse.'

Michael backed away. 'We are friends, Matt, but there are limits to what I will do for you, and helping with Dickon is well past them. I am afraid you must confront the little beast alone.'

'Sheriff Tulyet should have taken Dickon with him when he went to London,' said Cynric as the monk departed with impressive speed for a man his size. 'His son is Satan's spawn, and should not have been left for his mother to manage on her own.'

There was a time when Bartholomew would have defended Dickon, but he had suffered far too much at the child's vengeful hands to bother. Dickon was the Sheriff's only son, a strapping lad who looked older than his nine or ten years. His father doted on him, although his mother had begun to recognise his faults. Dickon terrorised other children and the household servants, and even the grizzled veterans at the castle were wary of him. For a juvenile, he was a formidable figure.

'Perhaps *he* stole the Stanton Hutch,' suggested Bartholomew, aware that he was dragging his feet. He had good reason: treating Dickon was dangerous, as the boy was prone to kick, bite, punch and scratch. Worse yet, his misguided father had recently given him a sword.

'And killed Felbrigge and Elvesmere,' nodded Cynric. He was outspoken for a servant, confident in the knowledge that he was indispensable, and a friend into the bargain. 'I would not put it past the brute. Would you like a charm to ward him off?'

Bartholomew declined, suspecting his priestly colleagues would have something to say if he was seen sporting pagan talismans. Cynric was the most superstitious man in Cambridge, and crucifixes and pilgrim badges jostled for space on his person with 'magic' ingredients tied in little leather bags around his neck. Bartholomew noticed that there were more of them than usual.

'Because of the evil that I sense will soon befall us,' the book-bearer explained matter-of-factly. 'It is an inevitability with all these strangers wandering around our town.'

'They want to be students,' objected Bartholomew. 'There is nothing sinister about them.'

'I beg to differ. Then there is Potmoor, who is more wicked than ever now he thinks he is destined for Heaven. There are rumours that *he* killed Felbrigge, you know.'

'Yes, I have heard them, but Michael tells me that he has an alibi for the shooting – he was with his son and several henchmen. Besides, that was before he rose from the— before he was ill.'

'He would not have bloodied his own hands,' said Cynric scornfully. 'He would have ordered one of his minions to oblige him. God knows, he has enough of them.'

CHAPTER 3

It was a market day, and as Bartholomew headed towards his ordeal with Dickon, he could hear the familiar clamour of commerce echoing through the streets: the cry of vendors hawking their wares, the clatter of iron-shod cartwheels on cobbles, and the heavier trundle of wagons carrying bulk goods to and from the wharves by the river. The taverns were busy, too, and beadles were out in force, ousting those drinkers who were students. Trouble arose when the matriculands challenged the beadles' authority to give them orders, and more than one inn rang with acrimonious voices.

As Bartholomew passed the jumble of houses known as The Jewry, he glanced, as always, at the cottage that had once belonged to Matilde, the love of his life. He had been tardy in asking her to marry him, which had led to her leaving Cambridge one fine spring morning. He had spent months searching for her, travelling to every place she had ever mentioned. He had failed to find her, but had recently discovered that she had not gone as far away as he had believed. Their paths had crossed, and she had made a vague promise of a future together.

As always when he thought of her, he experienced a sharp stab of loss, although the feeling was now tempered by confusion. He had believed he would never love another woman, but that was before he had met Julitta, wife of the town's only surgeon.

He was perplexed by the emotions that assailed him. Neither woman was available, as one had disappeared again and the other was married, but that did not stop him pondering which one he should choose. Until that summer, he would have picked Matilde, but their recent encounter – if it could be called that; he had been asleep at the time, and he was still hurt that she had opted to communicate by letter rather than wait for him to wake – had opened his eyes to flaws in her character he had not known she possessed. She and Julitta were on a much more even footing in his mind now, so it was perhaps fortunate that neither was clamouring for an immediate answer.

He was obliged to watch his step when he reached Bridge Street, to navigate the chaos of ruts outside St Clement's Church. When he looked up again, his spirits soared: Julitta was walking towards him. He smiled – until he saw she was with her husband. All thoughts of an enjoyable tête-à-tête fled, and he glanced around for a suitable hiding place. Then he reminded himself that he was a senior scholar, and should not be scuttling down alleys to avoid uncomfortable meetings.

The Holms were a handsome couple, and as Julitta had inherited a fortune from her father, which allowed them to buy whatever clothes took their fancy, they were beautifully attired. Her money also meant that Holm did not have to work, and he had been quick to pare down his practice in order to concentrate on what he considered to be his true vocation – inventing patent medicines. So far, he had marketed a powder to cure baldness and a method for dislodging kidney stones, both of which had been spectacular failures. Even so, there was arrogance in his stride – his disappointments in the world of healing had done nothing to temper his high opinion of himself.

Julitta wore a blue kirtle that matched her remarkable eyes. Her long, silky hair was in a plait, an unusual style for a married woman, but one that suited her. She had adored her pretty husband when they had first been wed, but it had not taken many nights before the cold truth had dawned. Her happy innocence was replaced by some-thing graver and wiser, but she declined to let Holm's preferences dismay her. She had simply turned to Bartholomew for comfort, although she retained a touching devotion towards the surgeon that Bartholomew felt Holm did not deserve.

'Have you heard what people are saying about you, physician?' Holm asked with a smirk. 'That you used witchcraft to snatch Potmoor from Hell.'

'Will is right, Matt,' said Julitta worriedly. 'You made no friends when you saved him.'

'I had no idea that smelling salts could be so potent,' Holm went on. 'I bought a bottle from Eyer the apothecary afterwards, but he says the one he sold you must have been different from his usual brews, as *sal ammoniac* does not usually restore life to corpses.'

'Potmoor was not dead,' said Bartholomew irritably. 'As you know perfectly well – you were there. And when we discussed catalepsia later, you said you had witnessed several cases of it.'

'That was before accusations of necromancy started to fly about, so I have reappraised my memory in the interests of personal safety. However, I would not mind owning the *sal ammoniac* you used on Potmoor. Will you sell it to me? It might come in useful.'

'Useful for what, Will?' asked Julitta uneasily. 'You are not thinking of restoring life to corpses yourself, are you?'

'Not I,' averred Holm. 'But I still conduct surgery on one or two favoured patients, and a more pungent mixture might help to rouse them when things do not go quite according to plan.'

'I threw it away,' said Bartholomew shortly. Rank superstition had led him to toss the little pot in the College midden – a ridiculous fear that the smelling salts might indeed have held some diabolical power.

'That was wise,' said Julitta, although Holm looked disgusted. Then she smiled and changed the subject. 'We are summoned to yet another urgent gathering of the

Guild of Saints. There are a great many of them these days, most requiring speedy decisions about money.'

Like many social and religious fraternities in Cambridge, the Guild of Saints not only accepted women as members, but encouraged them to take an active role in its running. Willing and efficient ladies like Julitta – and Edith before she had been lumbered with her husband's business – were kept extremely busy with its various undertakings.

'It is tiresome,' said Holm sulkily. 'And making beggars happy is a waste of time, if you ask me, although I must say I enjoy the Guild's monthly feasts.'

'Perhaps this meeting is to discuss the role Winwick Hall will play in the University's beginning of term ceremony next week,' Julitta went on, ignoring him.

'Really?' Bartholomew was puzzled. 'Why would your friends be interested in that? It is a University matter, and none of the Guild's concern.'

'Our members have given Winwick Hall a lot of money,' explained Julitta. 'So we have a say in what it does and when.'

'The other scholars hate us having such influence over a foundation that will soon belong to their *studium generale*,' gloated Holm. 'And next week's ceremony is just the start. Winwick will soon be the largest College in Cambridge, and by controlling it, we shall control the University.'

'Take no notice,' murmured Julitta, squeezing Bartholomew's hand as her husband strutted away. 'He is in a bad mood because he had a row with Hugo Potmoor. It was over the Michaelhouse Choir if you can believe it.'

The choir in question was Michael's concern, a body of spectacularly untalented individuals who attended practices solely for the free bread and ale afterwards. They had a reputation for performances so loud that they could be heard miles away, and Bartholomew had never understood why Michael, an accomplished musician, steadfastly refused to accept that they were a lost cause.

'Michael wants to use them in the ceremony,' Julitta elaborated. 'Hugo thinks it is an excellent idea, but Will has heard them sing. Will does not *want* to argue with the son of a man who is . . . well, suffice to say, *I* should not like to cross a Potmoor.'

Bartholomew continued his journey, wishing with all his heart that Julitta's father had not betrothed her to Holm. Then he would have wed her, and Matilde would not have re-entered his life to create such a turmoil of conflicting feelings. Of course, it would have meant giving up the teaching he loved, as scholars were not permitted to marry. Then a vision of Goodwyn came to mind, along with all the lectures he needed to prepare, and a change of career suddenly seemed rather appealing.

He arrived to find the Tulyet house in uproar, which was not uncommon when Dickon had hurt himself – he was the kind of lad who wanted everyone else to suffer, too. The servants had retreated to the back of the house for safety, and Dickon himself was in the kitchen, bawling at the top of his very considerable voice.

'Dickon, please!' his mother was begging. 'What will your father think when he hears about the fuss you have made?'

'He will have forgotten by the time he comes home,' yelled Dickon. He had thick, heavy features, and bore no resemblance to either of his slim, graceful parents; it was widely believed that his mother had entertained the Devil the night he had been conceived. 'Which might be weeks yet. He said so in the last letter he wrote to you – the one you keep in your little purple box.'

'You poked about in my personal things?' cried Mistress Tulyet, shocked. 'Dickon!'

'Go away!' howled the boy when he saw Bartholomew. 'Or I shall stab you with my sword.'

The weapon was on the table, and the physician's lunge towards it was marginally quicker than Dickon's. The boy's eyes widened in fury when he saw the blade in the hands of his opponent.

'Give it to me,' he ordered between gritted teeth.

'Behave yourself, Dickon,' commanded his mother. Her voice was so unsteady with shock and distress that it carried scant conviction. 'Or I shall tell Deputy de Stannell.'

The boy sneered. 'He is not a *real* soldier. He pretends to be like Father, but he cannot even ride. I watched him all last night in the castle – he is taking secret lessons from Sergeant Helbye, so he will not make an ass of himself when he sits on a horse in town processions.'

'You should have been in bed,' said Mistress Tulyet weakly. 'And what have I told you about spying on people?'

Needless to say, Dickon was unmoved by the reprimand. 'It was fun. The lesson started at midnight, and finished at dawn. Poor Helbye was exhausted by the end of it, although de Stannell still cannot ride. But what can you expect from a man who looks like a monkey?'

'He is very good at administration,' said Mistress Tulyet, somewhat feebly. 'And that is more important than horsemanship while your father is away.'

Tiring of the discussion, Dickon made a grab for the sword, obliging Bartholomew to raise it above his head where it could not be reached. He felt ridiculous, like a statue of Neptune wrestling a sea-serpent he had once seen in Rome, and he laughed out loud. Dickon regarded him with small, malevolent eyes, then sat down suddenly and presented his damaged hand. Bartholomew examined it cautiously, keeping a firm grip on the weapon, knowing the boy intended to retrieve it at the first opportunity. If Dickon succeeded, blood would be spilled – and it would not be his own.

As usual, the injury was superficial, and would have been disregarded by most children. Still on his guard, Bartholomew smeared it with a soothing paste.

'What happened?' he asked.

'The horse bit me,' pouted Dickon, submitting more readily to Bartholomew's ministrations once he realised it was not going to hurt. 'And I am going to shoot it in revenge.'

'No, you are not,' said Mistress Tulyet sharply. 'You bit it first.'

'He bit a horse?' blurted Bartholomew.

'It was looking at me,' said Dickon. 'Can I have my sword back now?'

'No,' said Bartholomew, and because Mistress Tulyet looked pale and tired, he mixed a mild soporific that would send Dickon to sleep and give her a few hours' respite. He was not in the habit of drugging children, but Mistress Tulyet was also his patient, and her health was just as important as her hellion son's. 'Drink this and go to bed.'

'I shall not,' said Dickon, folding his arms sulkily. 'I am not thirsty.'

Bartholomew was good with children, and rarely had trouble persuading them to take what he prescribed. Dickon was the exception, and the physician was ashamed of the dislike the boy always engendered in him. He was just trying to decide whether to let Dickon go without a battle, or stick to his guns and pour the medicine down the brat's throat, when Edith walked in.

'I heard there had been a mishap,' she said. 'So I came to help.'

'You are not wanted here,' snarled Dickon rudely. 'Go away.'

Bartholomew gripped the sword rather tightly. While he did not care what Dickon said to him, his beloved sister was another matter altogther, and he was about to say so when she stepped forward.

'Is this Dickon's medicine?' she asked, picking up the cup from the table.

'To make him better,' replied Mistress Tulyet, and Bartholomew was not sure whether he heard or imagined the murmured 'if only that were possible' that followed.

'Then drink it,' said Edith, holding it out. When Dickon hesitated, her expression became forbidding, and Bartholomew had a sudden flash of memory back to his own childhood, when some youthful prank had displeased her. 'Or there will be trouble.'

Intimidated by the steel in her voice, Dickon accepted the cup and sipped the mixture. He pulled a face and opened his mouth to complain, but Edith raised an authoritative forefinger, which was enough to see the potion swallowed and the cup set meekly back on the table.

'Now go to bed,' she ordered. 'And not a sound until morning, or you will answer to me.'

Dickon went without a word, and Mistress Tulyet followed, her face full of startled wonder. Edith grinned wanly once she and Bartholomew were alone.

'I learned how to deal with naughty children when I raised you.'

'I hardly think I was anything like Dickon,' objected Bartholomew.

'No, but you were worse than Richard by a considerable margin. He was an angel, and it is difficult to understand what has happened to him.'

'There is still time for him to settle down,' said Bartholomew, although he did not believe it, and neither did she. Richard was well into his twenties, so youthful exuberance could no longer be blamed for the deficiencies in his character.

'I owe you an apology, Matt,' Edith began. 'Last night, I said it was your fault that Oswald died, because you were away when he was ill. It was unkind – I know he would have passed away regardless. Yet I cannot escape the sense that something was amiss . . .'

'Many bereaved people do,' said Bartholomew kindly. 'It is perfectly natural.'

She shot him a baleful look. 'This is different. And I hate to admit it, but perhaps Richard was right about me sorting through that chest. There was a document this morning . . .'

'What did it say?'

Edith glanced around quickly before lowering her voice. 'It is all rather unclear, but I think Oswald charged too much for a consignment of cloth that went to King's Hall. The figures do not tally, and his notes on the transaction seem to imply that he knew it.'

Bartholomew could hardly say that he was not surprised. 'Perhaps you should let Richard sort through these records. He did offer.'

Edith grimaced. 'I am not sure he is capable, to be frank. And nor would he appreciate being obliged to work when he could be out drinking with his cronies. Thank God Oswald left the business to me. Richard would have sold it by now – or run it into the ground with ineptitude – which would have been a disaster for the people we employ.'

Bartholomew agreed, but felt it would be disloyal to say so. 'Is he going to the meeting of the Guild of Saints? I heard that one has been called.'

'Of course,' said Edith bitterly. 'Wine will be served afterwards.'

'Oh,' said Bartholomew, trying to think of words that might comfort her. None came to mind.

Edith sighed unhappily. 'He told me this morning that several friends have applied to Winwick Hall, so he has decided to stay on here, to enjoy their lively company. I never thought I would say it, Matt, but I wish he would leave Cambridge and go back to London. Just because I

83

am a widow does not mean that I want a grown son under my feet – especially one who has an annoying aversion to anything that might be considered work.'

'He will not be here much longer,' predicted Bartholomew. 'Carousing will be forbidden to his scholar friends once term starts, so he will find himself drinking alone. He will soon tire of it.'

Edith gave him a hopeful smile and changed the subject. 'There are a lot of nasty rumours circulating at the moment, including one about Michael . . .'

'That he intends to inflict the Michaelhouse Choir on the beginning of term ceremony? It will not make our College very popular.'

'Oh, Lord, does he?' gulped Edith. 'I had no idea. Perhaps that is why the Guild has called an emergency meeting – to discuss ways to prevent it. But I was talking about the gossip that says he arranged for Felbrigge to be shot for daring to set covetous eyes on the senior proctorship.'

'Then the gossipmongers do not know Michael. He is perfectly capable of defeating rivals through non-fatal means.'

'I am just reporting what is being said. However, the only way to put a stop to these nasty tales is by finding the real killer.'

'Yes,' sighed Bartholomew. 'The only problem being a marked absence of clues.'

It was not long before Mistress Tulyet reported with a relieved sigh that Dickon was asleep. The servants began to creep back, speaking in whispers lest they woke the brat, while the horse that had sparked the incident was whisked away to safety. Bartholomew walked Edith to the Guild of Saints' headquarters, a timber-framed hall near St Clement's Church. She was still a member, although a less active one since inheriting her husband's large and complex business.

She faltered at the door, assailed by memories of happier times, so Bartholomew took her by the hand and led her inside. He would not be permitted to stay long, but no one would mind him escorting her to Richard. He entered the main chamber, and was astonished to find it packed with people – the Guild had not been half as big in Stanmore's day. Most members stood, while the officers and more important individuals sat on a long bench at the front.

'I thought this was an exclusive organisation,' he whispered. 'Open only to wealthy folk who are willing to be generous to the poor.'

'It is. But people clamour to join because it is prestigious – a symbol of high status. Anyone who can pay an entrance fee is enrolled these days. Unlike when Oswald was in charge.'

Bartholomew said nothing, but knew for a fact that Stanmore had not been as particular as she believed. For a start, he had admitted Potmoor, a man who was openly proud of his criminal achievements. Bartholomew glanced around, suddenly uneasy. He had not seen Potmoor since tending him on his 'deathbed' and had no wish to renew the acquaintance.

'Is John Knyt here?' asked Edith, struggling to see over the heads of the people in front. 'He is our Secretary, but I can only hear his assistant de Stannell speaking.' She lowered her voice. 'I cannot abide de Stannell – he has sly fingers in every pie.'

'Deputy Sheriff de Stannell? He is Assistant Secretary of the Guild as well?'

'He seems to like being second in command,' said Edith with uncharacteristic acerbity. 'Or perhaps he intends to oust both his betters, and run shire and Guild at the same time.'

Aware that he would soon be asked to leave, Bartholomew looked around for Richard, but his eye lit on Julitta instead. She would look after Edith. He steered his sister towards her, glad that Holm had abandoned his wife for Hugo, with whom he was muttering and giggling.

'I thought you told me that they had quarrelled,' he said, watching the pair in distaste. It was inappropriate behaviour for two grown men in a public place.

'They made up,' Julitta replied, and Bartholomew experienced a surge of anger against Holm when he saw the misery in her eyes. She made an obvious effort to suppress it, and smiled as she brought Edith up to date with the meeting's progress. 'We are discussing the Michaelhouse Choir. Potmoor says they should be allowed to sing at the ceremony next week. Everyone else disagrees.'

'Then let us hope the majority prevails,' said Edith fervently, 'or the occasion will be ruined. Oswald always said that he could not hear himself think once they started caterwauling.'

Heads together, she and Julitta began to exchange tales of their experiences with the singers, and seeing Edith was in kindly hands, Bartholomew aimed for the door. A number of Stanmore's old friends nodded amiable greetings as he passed, and the patriarch of the powerful Frevill clan came to offer belated condolences.

'I miss him,' he sighed. 'And I am sorry to say it, Bartholomew, but your nephew is not his equal. Not by a long way.'

It was true, but Bartholomew was unwilling to admit it to a man he barely knew. He mumbled a noncommittal reply, and was almost at the door when he was intercepted by another guildsman – Potmoor. He experienced a stab of alarm when the felon smiled, as there was something not entirely nice about the expression.

Potmoor looked like a criminal. He had small, shifty eyes, a flamboyant moustache of the kind favoured by pirates, and thinning hair kept in place by the application of copious amounts of goose-grease. He was not very big, yet he exuded an aura of evil menace, and Bartholomew was perfectly prepared to believe the many tales about his barbarity, greed and ruthlessness.

'I never thanked you,' Potmoor said. 'For bringing me back from the dead.'

'You were not dead,' replied Bartholomew, although he knew he was wasting his time: Potmoor was enjoying the prestige that accrued from his so-called resurrection. 'Catalepsia is—'

'I was dead, and I saw the bright glory of Heaven,' countered Potmoor, a little dangerously.

'It was an illusion. There were a lot of candles burning in your bedchamber that night.'

'I know what I saw. Or are you telling me that I mistook you and your medical colleagues for God and His angels?' Potmoor gave a low, creaking laugh.

Bartholomew frowned, taking in the man's pale face and unsteady hands. 'Yet you are still not recovered. What ails you? Headaches? Fevers?'

'Headaches, which I attribute to setting eyes on the face of Our Lord. Meryfeld's remedies were worthless, so I dismissed him, and hired Master Lawrence instead. Provost Illesy recommended him, as he was once *medicus* to Queen Isabella, although he has not cured me either. Would you like the job? I am a very rich man.'

'I have too many patients already,' said Bartholomew, trotting out the excuse he had used the last time Potmoor had asked. 'I am sure Lawrence will find a medicine that helps you soon.'

It was a lie, as he was not sure at all. Such symptoms should have eased by now, and their persistence did not bode well. Potmoor launched into another subject.

'Has your sister recovered from her tragic loss?'

'No,' replied Bartholomew shortly, recalling that Oswald had vigorously opposed Potmoor's expansion into

Cambridge and his untimely death had certainly been to Potmoor's advantage. Naturally, there had been rumours, although they had fizzled out eventually, due to a lack of evidence. However, Bartholomew did not like the smirk on the felon's face.

'Pity.' Potmoor changed tack yet again. 'Hugo informs me that we never paid you for bringing me back to life. I would rather have remained in Heaven, of course, but I am not a man who reneges on his debts. Here is your fee.'

'There is no need.' Bartholomew refused to take the proffered purse. He was being watched, and it would do his reputation no good whatsoever to be seen accepting money from such a man.

'I hope you are not suggesting that my life is not worth it,' said Potmoor coldly.

'No, of course not, but—'

'Good.' Potmoor grabbed Bartholomew's hand and slapped the pouch into it. 'From what I hear, your College could do with a windfall.'

'What do you mean?' Was this an admission that Potmoor *had* raided Michaelhouse?

Potmoor smiled, and Bartholomew struggled to prevent himself from shuddering at its reptilian nature. 'Just that I am sure you can put my donation to good use.'

Bartholomew left the guildhall confused and unsettled. He shoved the purse into his medical bag, disliking the greasy touch of it on his fingers. The encounter had made him feel grubby, and he hated to think how the exchange would be interpreted by the people who had witnessed it. He swore under his breath, wishing he had had the sense to cut the conversation short.

His reverie was interrupted when someone collided with him so heavily that he was almost knocked off his feet. The culprit did not stop, but continued down Bridge Street, head bowed and hands tucked inside his green cloak. One of Bartholomew's patients saw the incident.

'Some folk got no manners,' he muttered. His name was Noll Verius, a slovenly, loutish ditcher who was not known for courteous behaviour himself. 'It is because you are a scholar, see. The University is unpopular with normal folk at the moment.'

He went on his way before Bartholomew could respond, moving so fast that the physician wondered if he aimed to catch up with the fellow and berate him for his clumsiness. Bartholomew started to call out to stop him, but suddenly became aware of the acrid stench of burning. It was coming from St Clement's Church, along with the sound of drunken singing. Bemused, he recognised the voice of its vicar, William Heyford, a man noted for preaching vicious sermons against the University. But Heyford claimed to be an abstemious soul who rarely touched wine, so Bartholomew went to investigate. Smoke billowed out as he opened the door, and he could hear flames devouring dry wood within.

'Fire!' he yelled at the top of his voice.

No passer-by needed to be reminded of the dangers of a blaze in a town where houses were timber-built and thatch-roofed. There was an instant flurry of activity. Buckets, bowls and even boots were frantically filled with water from the well, but the effort was disorganised and far too much of the precious liquid was spilled as it was slopped towards the burning building.

With his sleeve over his nose and mouth, Bartholomew groped his way inside, aiming for the spot where he could still hear Heyford. The priest was lying on the chancel floor, crooning and chuckling to himself, while the high altar was a bright rectangle of flames. He heard a sound behind him and turned quickly.

'Is he drunk?'

Eyer the apothecary had followed him in. He was a

89

comparative newcomer to the town, a pink-faced man with a round head. He always wore a clean white apron, and his air of venerable geniality made people more willing to trust his remedies. His clean, pleasantly fragrant shop on the High Street had become a refuge for the town's physicians, and Bartholomew in particular sought sanctuary there when pressure of work threatened to overwhelm him. Eyer had recently been elected to the Guild of Saints, and Edith said he had already donated large sums to worthy causes.

Yet despite his generosity, there was something about the apothecary that Bartholomew did not quite trust, and he knew the other *medici* felt the same. None could put his finger on what made them draw back from the proffered hand of friendship, but the inconsistencies in the stories Eyer told about his past did not help: small contradictions, it was true, but enough to raise eyebrows.

Together, physician and apothecary pulled Heyford to his feet, and half dragged, half carried him into the street, where they deposited him, still chortling, next to a horse trough. Two of his deacons came to hover anxiously over him. Heyford reeked of wine, and his eyes had the dull glaze of a man who was barely conscious. Bartholomew suspected it would be some time before he was sober enough to answer questions.

'I had not taken him for a drinking man,' remarked Eyer wonderingly. 'And certainly not one who would imbibe so much that he would set his own church alight.'

'He did nothing of the kind,' said one of the deacons indignantly. 'He is ill, not drunk.'

'We shall take him home,' said the other. 'The poor man needs to rest.'

They hauled him upright and hustled him away, taking a circuitous route so that as few people as possible would witness his condition. Bartholomew turned his attention back to the fire.

There were many willing hands, but no one had organised them, so the result was a chaotic mêlée, with folk bumping into each other and water slopped needlessly. The Guild of Saints had abandoned its meeting. A few members were toting buckets, but most were too grand to soil their hands, so confined themselves to offering impractical advice. The Deputy Sheriff, who should have taken charge, was more interested in cornering Potmoor. Watching, Bartholomew saw that Dickon was right to say he looked like a monkey – de Stannell had a long, protruding nose, close-set eyes and bushy facial hair.

'Perhaps he is trying to charm another benefaction for our Guild's continuing good work,' shrugged Eyer, seeing where Bartholomew was looking and reading his thoughts. 'Potmoor has been generous since . . . recently.'

'I would have thought that saving the town is rather more pressing at the moment.'

Eyer clapped him on the shoulder. 'Spoken like a man with no head for finance! But look – your sister and Mistress Holm have taken charge. De Stannell's authority is not needed anyway.'

Briskly competent, Edith and Julitta shepherded people into a line so that water could be poured into the church more effectively. Bartholomew and Eyer joined it, the physician glancing around quickly to see who had done likewise.

Provost Illesy and his Fellows had pitched into the affray, Illesy speaking in a loud, important bray to ensure that everyone knew Winwick Hall was doing its bit. Lawrence worked quietly at his side, his white beard full of cinders, while Nerli toiled with soldierly efficiency. Bon dropped more buckets than he passed, but at least he was trying – unlike Ratclyf, who kept his distance.

'The Cambridge Debate will start soon,' said Eyer, when Bartholomew remarked on it. 'Ratclyf is scheduled to speak, and will not want to arrive looking like a drowned rat.'

'That does not seem to worry anyone else.'

Eyer shoved a bucket at Bartholomew with such urgency that most of its contents sluiced down the physician's front. 'Perhaps he is just more fastidious than the rest of the University.'

Another man who considered himself a cut above hefting pails was Potmoor, his mustachioed face wearing a sly look that made Bartholomew wonder whether he was responsible for the blaze. Nearby, his hulking son Hugo stood with Holm, both watching Julitta. Bartholomew could not tell if the surgeon was proud or resentful of his wife's organisational skills. With a stab of disappointment, he saw Richard was not helping either – he was with Goodwyn and the other new medical students, laughing in a way that suggested he did not care that the town was in danger.

'You will have trouble with them,' came a voice at his side. It was Hemmysby. The gentle Michaelhouse theologian was also trying to keep his finery clean for the debate, but that did not stop him from working as hard as anyone. 'It is a pity Langelee accepted them.'

'Perhaps they will leave once they realise that reading medicine is hard work,' said Bartholomew hopefully.

'It is with you!' Hemmysby's smile took the sting from his words. 'You drive your lads harder than any other master in the University, although it has its rewards. Five of the seven who graduated last year secured excellent posts in noble households.'

This was a sore point. Bartholomew had hoped they would dedicate themselves to doing something more useful than calculating horoscopes for the wealthy, and their appointments made him feel as though he had wasted his time. He called over to their replacements, and ordered them to join the line. They obeyed with ill grace, Richard trailing at their heels.

'I do not see why I should labour like a peasant,' grumbled Goodwyn. 'There are more than enough low types here for that, and I . . .'

He faltered when he saw the dark expression on his teacher's face, and promptly turned his attention to his duties. Richard laughed uproariously at the exchange, although there was a brittle quality to his guffaws that made them sound more mocking than amused.

At last the town's frenzied labours paid off, and someone called out the welcome news that the fire was out. People flexed aching arms and shoulders, congratulating each other on their efforts. But all asked the same question: how had it started?

'I expect it was that drunken vicar,' said Eyer. 'He must have knocked over a candle.'

'Or Potmoor,' suggested Goodwyn. 'Look at him – you can see from here that he is disappointed the church is saved. He is a killer and a thief, and arson is nothing to him.'

'Potmoor *is* a thief,' whispered Hemmysby to Bartholomew. 'But I doubt he stole our hutch, so I hope Michael does not accuse him of it. It will be someone else. Winwick Hall, perhaps.'

'You said that earlier,' recalled Bartholomew. 'But you had no evidence.'

'And I have none now. Yet I sense that all will turn out well in the end.' Hemmysby laughed suddenly. 'Lord! I sound as credulous as Cynric!'

'Who is that fellow lurking at the back of the church?' asked Goodwyn, pointing with a bony finger. 'One of Potmoor's henchmen? He looks very suspicious.'

'That is Nicholas Fulbut,' supplied Richard. 'He is a mercenary, and he does sell his services to Potmoor on occasion. De Stannell told me that he is wanted for all manner of crimes.'

'Then have you told de Stannell that he is here?' asked

93

Hemmysby archly. 'Or, as I am sure you are a model citizen with a sense of duty and justice, why have you not arrested him yourself?'

'Oh, he has disappeared now,' said Richard. 'What a pity.'

'A pity indeed,' murmured Hemmysby coolly.

Rudely, Richard turned his back on the priest and addressed his cronies. 'I wonder why Knyt did not attend the Guild meeting today. *He* would not have let the Michaelhouse Choir sing next week. De Stannell was like clay in Potmoor's hands over the matter.'

'Colic confines him to bed,' explained Eyer. 'His wife told me when she came to collect bryony root to make him a soothing tonic.'

'I think *I* shall join Michael's choir,' said Goodwyn, grinning impishly at his classmates. 'I understand a lack of musical talent is no barrier, and there is free ale afterwards.'

'Then I shall inform him of your interest,' said Hemmysby sweetly. 'He is always looking for volunteers to help serve the food and drink, and I am sure you will not mind waiting on paupers.'

When the bell in St Mary the Great chimed to announce that the Cambridge Debate was about to begin, most scholars hurried away. A number of matriculands lingered, though, eyeing a group of apprentices and clearly ready for a brawl. Michael dealt with the would-be students, but de Stannell was no better at exerting authority on unruly youths than he was at fighting fires, and the town lads continued to loiter. Unwilling to go far until they had dispersed, Michael went to inspect the church, picking his way up the aisle carefully, lest water or ashes should soil his best habit.

'Have you spoken to Heyford?' asked Bartholomew, following him inside and flapping at the smoke that

94

still swirled. 'To determine whether this is arson or accident?'

Michael gave a disgusted snort. 'He is in a drunken stupor, and is likely to remain that way for hours. His deacons told me that someone sent him a gift of exceptionally strong wine, which, as a usually abstemious person, he should not have touched. It seems he then knocked over a candle as he staggered around. Foolish man!'

'The altar *was* blazing when I found him.' Bartholomew coughed as he looked around. 'Fortunately, the damage does not seem to be too severe.'

'A bit of scrubbing and a new table, and all will be right again. I was unimpressed with de Stannell's reaction to the crisis today. He did nothing to take command of the situation, preferring instead to curry favour with Potmoor.'

Bartholomew started to describe his encounter with the felon in the guildhall, but Michael was not very interested, and cut across him with a lengthy account of his own efforts to identify the burglar who had visited so many of the University's hostels and Colleges.

'I know most people think Potmoor is the guilty party,' he said. 'And they may well be right. However, I feel obliged to investigate other suspects, too. I ordered my beadles to round up a few likely offenders, and I have passed the time since we last met with some very unsavoury villains.'

'Did any confess to stealing our hutch?'

'No. They all have alibis of one kind or another. My beadles will check them, but I imagine we shall be forced to let them go. I would have been spared the ordeal if Dick Tulyet were here – it is the Sheriff's responsibility to interview these people, not mine. I asked de Stannell to oblige, but he said he is too busy. That man is a disgrace! Dick should never have left him in charge.'

When they returned to the street the apprentices had gone, so they aimed for the town centre, Michael walking unusually briskly, so as not to miss more of the debate. They joined three other scholars who were also heading in that direction – Bon, clinging to Lawrence's arm, and Doctor Rougham, the haughtiest and least likeable of the town's four physicians.

Rougham was Acting Master of Gonville Hall, and an inflexible traditionalist, which meant he and Bartholomew were diametrically opposed in their approach to medicine. Time had rendered their association a little less volatile, but relations were currently strained because Bartholomew had failed all Rougham's students in their summer disputations. Rougham had still not forgiven him, although it should have been obvious even to his indignant eyes that his lads were well below par.

'I am astonished to learn that Heyford was drunk,' Rougham said. 'Especially after his sermon on Sunday advocating abstinence.'

'There is much to be said for abstinence,' said Lawrence, eagerly seizing the opportunity for a medical discussion. 'The great Maimonides says—'

'It is for fools,' interrupted Rougham uncompromisingly. 'And I shall never practise it myself, or recommend it to my patients.'

As neither Bartholomew nor Lawrence were inclined to tackle such a rigidly held conviction, the debate ended there and then.

'How are your enquiries into Elvesmere's death, Brother?' asked Bon, stumbling over a rut and scowling at Lawrence for failing to warn him. 'The murder has not affected the number of lads who want to study with us, thank God, but I still do not like it hanging over our heads.'

'Then help me,' said Michael. 'Have you remembered anything that might point to his killer, no matter how silly or insignificant it may seem?'

'There is one thing,' replied Bon. 'We had a visitor late on the night that Elvesmere died. Potmoor, whom I distinctly heard leaving the Provost's Suite.'

'Provost's Suite,' sneered Rougham under his breath. 'Why not Master's quarters, like everyone else? I cannot abide these pretensions of grandeur.'

'Potmoor might be a fellow guildsman and generous with donations,' Bon went on. 'But he is a criminal, and I do not want him inside my College. Moreover, I am not sure Illesy is fit to be Provost if he keeps that sort of company.'

'There is nothing wrong with Potmoor,' said Lawrence, more sharply than was his wont. 'He is always perfectly gentlemanly when he summons me to remedy his headaches. However, this is a matter we should discuss later, Bon.'

His pointed glance was wasted, for obvious reasons, but Bon caught the physician's meaning from the warning tone in his voice and fell silent, albeit reluctantly.

'We had better have a word with Potmoor,' murmured Michael to Bartholomew. 'It would be a tidy solution if *he* murdered Elvesmere.'

The physician nodded without enthusiasm, then turned to help Lawrence guide Bon across a particularly uneven section of the High Street. Lawrence thanked him, but Bon did not bother, and went on the offensive instead.

'How are your enquiries into Felbrigge's murder, Brother? *I* do not believe you ordered him shot, of course.' The tone of his voice suggested otherwise. 'But the rumours that you did are damaging the University – and what damages the University also harms Winwick. I do not want my College sullied by association. Perhaps you should consider tendering your resignation.'

'Bow to the dictates of petty gossip?' demanded Michael indignantly. 'I most certainly shall not, especially as the only people who believe such ludicrous tales are fools and scoundrels.'

Bon's mouth tightened at the insult. 'If your continued presence harms my College, I shall write to the King and demand your removal.'

Michael regarded him thoughtfully. 'It usually takes years for new foundations to inspire such deep loyalty among its members, yet Winwick Hall has—'

'Yes, I *do* love Winwick,' interrupted Bon fiercely. 'And do you know why? Because I have much to offer academia, but no one else would hire me. Our founder alone saw past my blindness and recognised my abilities, so the least I can do is give his College my complete devotion.'

'Yet your ailment must be a disadvantage,' mused Michael. 'How do you study the texts you are obliged to teach?'

'I learned them by rote before my eyes grew dim. And if I need to refresh my memory, I pay students to read to me. There is nothing wrong with my mind, Brother. It is just as sharp as yours.'

'Is that so?' Michael tended to the opinion that few colleagues were his intellectual equal.

Bon bridled, and his voice turned even more acidic. 'So what *are* you doing about Felbrigge's killer? Or are you just grateful to the culprit for ridding you of an ambitious junior?'

'Bon,' murmured Lawrence warningly. 'You shame us with these intemperate remarks.'

'Yes, you do,' agreed Michael coolly. 'However, since you ask, Felbrigge's murder is solved. The culprit will be in my cells by the end of the day.'

'Will he?' blurted Lawrence. He sounded alarmed, and Bartholomew wondered why. 'Oh, look! We are at Eyer's shop. I think I had better buy a remedy for queasiness, as I feel most unwell.'

'He must be nervous about the debate,' said Rougham,

watching him dart inside. 'He is unused to public speaking.'

'Will you be taking part, Rougham?' asked Bon.

'Of course not,' replied Rougham scathingly. 'Do I look like a friar or a monk to you?'

Bon's expression was cool. 'You do not *look* like anything to me. I am blind, if you recall.'

'Oh,' said Rougham uncomfortably. 'I suppose you are.'

Leaving the Gonville man to make obsequious apologies, all of which were received with icy disdain, Bartholomew and Michael continued alone.

'Do you really know who killed Felbrigge, Brother?' asked Bartholomew.

'Yes and no. I have the identity of the archer – Cynric heard him bragging in the King's Head last night. However, word is that he was hired by someone else, who is the *real* culprit in my opinion. The archer will talk once he is in my cells. I have never met a mercenary yet who was prepared to sacrifice himself for his paymaster.'

'A mercenary?' asked Bartholomew, thinking of how Richard had described the man they had seen lurking behind St Clement's. 'What is his name?'

'Nick Fulbut. My beadles are hunting him as we speak.'

Bartholomew stopped walking. 'He was watching the fire just now.' He repeated what Richard had told him, omitting the uncomfortable truth that his nephew had made no attempt to report the matter to the authorities, regardless of the fact that he knew Fulbut was a wanted man.

Michael hurried back as fast as his legs would carry him, Bartholomew at his heels, but neither scholar was surprised to discover that their quarry was no longer there. The monk instructed two beadles to monitor the church lest the archer reappeared, then he and Bartholomew turned towards St Mary the Great again.

'The news that Fulbut works for Potmoor is disturbing,'

said Michael. 'Why would Potmoor want my Junior Proctor dead? And if Fulbut was lurking near the burning church, do you think *he* gave Heyford the strong wine and lit the fire? On Potmoor's orders?'

'I thought you said it was an accident. Besides, what can Potmoor have against Heyford?'

'A lot of vicious sermons that accuse him of all manner of crimes. I have warned Heyford to curb his tongue, but he is not a man to listen to sound counsel.'

Despite his intention to stay away, Bartholomew did attend some of the debate. He heard Michael speak with his usual incisive eloquence, which had even friars nodding their appreciation. After Michael came Ratclyf, whose language was so flowery that it was difficult to distil any meaning from it, and Bon, who was uninspired and unoriginal. Hemmysby was next, and demolished the Winwick men with an intellectual agility that earned him a standing ovation.

'Michaelhouse is doing well,' murmured Lawrence, standing at Bartholomew's side. 'But I fear Winwick's entry into public disputation has been less than distinguished, and I doubt my contribution will redeem us. I am too nervous to shine.'

'Address your remarks to your friends, and do not look at anyone else,' advised Bartholomew. 'Speak slowly, clearly and loudly, and ignore any jeers.'

Lawrence smiled wanly. 'Thank you. Oh, Lord! The Chancellor is waving to me – it is my turn to speak. Into the valley of the shadow of Death . . .'

He was far too diffident for the boisterous arena of the Cambridge Debate, and had barely finished his opening remarks before the hecklers weighed in. Tynkell should have silenced them, but he was a meek man himself, and his timid exhortations were ignored. When he saw the discussion had reached the point where no one was going to be allowed to finish a sentence, Bartholomew returned to Michaelhouse to work on his lectures.

He made reasonable progress, and by evening he knew he could manage the first week with something approaching competence. Of course, that still left the rest of term, and he wondered whether he would be reduced to using last year's material. Other masters did it, but he considered it a lazy habit and wanted to avoid it if possible.

After a miserable supper of stale bread smeared with some sort of brown paste, washed down with a liquid Agatha claimed was broth but that might equally well have been something in which she had washed the pots, he went to visit Edith. She was in angry tears following another spat with Richard over the documents she had been examining, but her seamstresses were providing fierce female solidarity, and Bartholomew sensed that his presence was an unwanted intrusion. He returned to Michaelhouse, and went to the conclave, where there was a lamp that was significantly better for reading than the flickering tallow candle in his own room.

'I understand Potmoor paid you a princely sum today,' said Langelee, watching him set scrolls, ink and pen on the table. He held out his hand. 'It may stave off disaster for a few days.'

'Who told you?' asked Bartholomew resentfully. He had intended to replenish his medical supplies with the money – a matter of urgency now that there was no stipend to come. 'Michael?'

'Surgeon Holm.' Langelee snatched the purse eagerly. 'He was aiming to make trouble for you, so I lied and told him I already knew. That took the wind out of the bastard's sails. I do not blame you for making a cuckold of the fellow. Julitta deserves a proper man.'

'Let him keep a few coins for medicine, Master,' said Hemmysby, watching Langelee pocket the lot. 'I should not like to think of the poor suffering as a result of our temporary penury.'

'It is not temporary,' growled Langelee. 'It is permanent. Even if Michael does manage to lay hold of the culprit, the money will have been spent by now.'

'I disagree,' said Hemmysby. 'It is an enormous amount, far too large to dispose of without attracting attention. I am sure we shall have most of it back, if not all.'

No one else shared his optimism, but they did not argue about it for long, preferring instead to discuss how best to use Potmoor's money. While they debated, Bartholomew struggled to work. The lamp had been turned low to save fuel, and the cheap oil smoked badly. It made his head ache, but he persisted anyway, and was still reading when Cynric arrived with a summons.

'You are needed at John Knyt's house, boy,' the book-bearer announced. 'You know – the Secretary of the Guild of Saints.'

'I am?' asked Bartholomew in surprise. 'Why? He is Rougham's patient.'

'Rougham is unavailable, apparently. But Knyt lives on the Chesterton road, which is in Potmoor's domain, so I had better go with you.'

Bartholomew was glad to escape from the reeking lantern. He hurried across the yard to collect his cloak, but as he approached his storeroom he detected a terrible smell emanating from within. He opened the door to see all his students crammed inside, amid a chaos of dirty flasks, broken pots and careless spillages. The far wall was barely visible through a thick fug of fumes, which was impressive, given the chamber's modest size.

'We are experimenting,' explained Aungel brightly. 'It was Goodwyn's idea. We are testing what happens when you add different things to boiling urine. We aim to find one that explodes.'

'Why?' asked Bartholomew, perplexed. 'What use would such knowledge be?'

'All knowledge is useful,' declared Goodwyn loftily. 'Aristotle said so.'

Bartholomew was sure the philosopher had said no such thing. 'I sincerely hope you did not use any of my supplies to test this ridiculous theory. I need them for patients.'

'It is not ridiculous,' objected Goodwyn indignantly. 'And I am sure you cannot object to us expanding our minds. If you do, you should have locked your door.'

Bartholomew had locked it, but now it stood open. He looked up at the top shelf, where he kept his most expensive and dangerous compounds, and was horrified to see that the jars had been thoroughly raided. He also noticed that several lads were green about the gills, so he ordered them all outside into the fresh air.

'I thought I had made it clear that no one was to enter the storeroom without me,' he said, once the coughing and wheezing had eased. His voice was soft, but even the densest student could hear the anger in it. 'Some of those mixtures are poisonous, and you are not yet qualified to handle them. And especially not to conduct silly experiments unsupervised. If it happens again, you can all find another College.'

'You cannot dismiss us,' said Goodwyn challengingly. 'We paid good money to—'

He stopped speaking when Bartholomew glowered furiously at him, and stared at his feet instead, flushing a deep, resentful red. The other students exchanged uncomfortable glances, and there was a tense silence until Cynric broke it.

'Knyt, boy,' he said softly. 'We should go.'

'I will sort out the mess later,' said Bartholomew in the same tightly controlled voice. He would have liked to tell the students to do it, but there was a danger that two substances might come together and harm them, and tempting though it was to wish the likes of Goodwyn in the cemetery, he had no wish to put the others in danger.

He stalked away. Goodwyn and the other newcomers immediately began muttering, and he was half inclined to sneak back to see if they were plotting revenge, but he was a senior scholar and such antics were beneath him. He kept walking, Cynric trotting at his side and Knyt's servant scurrying behind. Eventually, he shot the book-bearer a rueful grin.

'Now we have even more reason to find the Stanton Hutch. I want it back so we can return Goodwyn's fees, because I am *not* teaching him next term. He is a bad influence on the others.'

'Good,' said Cynric fervently. 'Because I do not like him either. Did I tell you that I caught him stealing wine from the kitchen today? He was fortunate it was me, not Agatha.'

'Yes,' said Bartholomew drily. 'So if he does it again, stand aside and let him walk into the dragon's mouth. That would solve all our problems.'

'Damn!' Cynric was disgusted with himself. 'Why did I not think of that?'

It was a long way to Knyt's house, a pretty mansion on the Chesterton road. The weather had changed since Bartholomew had been in the conclave. Clouds had scudded in, brought by a gusty wind that made the trees sway and roar. It was unusually dark, too, and although Cynric had brought a torch, it was not easy to see the ruts and potholes in its guttering light. The air smelled of the fens, a dank, rich aroma of stagnant water and rotting vegetation, but there was also the sharper, cleaner tang of fresh-fallen autumn leaves.

After a while, they saw another torch bobbing on the road. It was a servant sent to meet them. The man grabbed

Bartholomew's arm and urged him into a trot, sobbing that Knyt was the best master in the country, genuinely loved by everyone who worked in his household.

When they arrived, Bartholomew's cloak was whisked off, and he and his bag were bundled with polite but urgent speed along a corridor and up a flight of stairs; Cynric was escorted with equal briskness into the kitchen for refreshments. The house spoke of quietly understated wealth, Knyt's affluence visible not in showy tapestries and gaudy ornaments, but in the quality of the furniture and the discreet luxury of the rugs on the floor.

In a large chamber on the upper storey, a fire crackled comfortably and lamps emitted a gentle, golden glow. It was dominated by a bed piled with furs. A number of servants stood around it, nearly all of them weeping. A woman stood at its foot, and Bartholomew recognised her as Olivia, Knyt's wife of twenty years or more.

'You are here at last,' she said with a wan smile. 'Good. My husband died an hour ago, but you raised Potmoor from the dead, so now you can do the same for John.'

Bartholomew took several steps away, cursing himself for a fool. Knyt had never been his client, and he should have been suspicious of a summons out of the blue. Then he saw Rougham in the shadows by the window, while Surgeon Holm, physicians Lawrence and Meryfeld, and Eyer the apothecary stood near the hearth. Bartholomew's arrival meant that all Cambridge's medical professionals were now present, just as they had been when Potmoor had 'died'.

'Mistress Olivia would like a miracle,' explained Rougham icily, clearly outraged by the fact that she had called the others. 'She will not believe me when I say her husband is gone.'

'He had a seizure,' added Eyer helpfully. 'A major one, of the kind that is always fatal. I have seen many such cases before, so it was not difficult for me to diagnose it in Knyt.'

Bartholomew regarded him askance. Eyer was an apothecary, not a physician, so had no authority to draw such conclusions. He glanced at the others, and saw they were similarly bemused.

'I conducted my own examination, naturally,' said Rougham, his cool glance telling Eyer that he had overstepped his mark. 'It was a colic-induced seizure, brought on by a surfeit of oysters. Lawrence and Meryfeld agree.'

Eyer pulled an unpleasant face at the snub by omission, but it was nothing compared to the scowl Holm gave at the bald reminder that physicians were at the top of the medical profession, and everyone else was well below them.

'Then there is nothing I can do, Mistress,' said Bartholomew. He took a step towards the door, eager to leave, but two servants blocked his way. He tried to move past them, but they shoved him back, not roughly, but enough to tell him that he was not going anywhere.

'It will not take a moment,' said one quietly. 'Just wave your *salt almanac* at him.'

'*Sal ammoniac*,' corrected Bartholomew. 'And it worked with Potmoor because he was not dead, no matter what he claims now. He was suffering from a condition that—'

'Just cure him,' interrupted the servant. 'John Knyt is a decent, honest soul, and he should not die while Potmoor lives. It would not be right. Just apply your *salt almanac*, and the whole town will praise you as an angel of God.'

Bartholomew refrained from remarking that it was more likely to seal his reputation as a necromancer, and turned towards the sickbed, knowing he would not be allowed to leave until he had at least examined the patient.

It did not take him long to see that Knyt was far beyond his skills, and had been for some time.

'I am sorry,' he said gently to Olivia. 'My colleagues are right. Your husband is dead.'

'There,' said Rougham in satisfaction. 'May we go now? We cannot do any more to help, and it is very late.'

Olivia ignored him. 'Put your *salt almanac* to his nose, Doctor Bartholomew, like you did to John Potmoor.'

'It will make no difference.' It was not the first time someone had refused to believe that a loved one had gone, and Bartholomew knew the only way to convince Olivia was by patient kindness. He sat on a bench and gestured that she should perch next to him, so he could explain.

'Do you have your *salt almanac* with you?' she asked, not moving.

'Yes, but—'

'Then use it,' she ordered. 'Now, please.'

'Just do it, Bartholomew,' said Rougham irritably. 'It will do no harm, and none of us will be permitted to leave until it is done.'

Very reluctantly and feeling like a ghoul, Bartholomew rummaged in his bag for the new salts he had bought after he had superstitiously discarded the ones he had used on Potmoor. Rougham snatched them from his hand and waved them under Knyt's nose, evidently intending to claim the credit if it worked. It did not, so he handed them back without a word. Bartholomew turned apologetically to Olivia, but her face was grim as she indicated that he was to do it himself.

He did what she ordered, but her husband remained as dead as ever.

CHAPTER 4

The wind picked up through the night, rattling the tiles on Michaelhouse's roof and making mysterious clunking sounds that might have been nothing, but that equally well might have been something about to break. Bartholomew slept poorly, starting awake at every thump, and once, after an especially loud clatter, getting up to ensure that the roof was still attached.

'You normally sleep through storms, sir,' said Aungel the following morning. 'Are you ill?'

'No,' replied Bartholomew shortly, unwilling to reveal that his restlessness had been caused by the episode in Knyt's house. He hated losing patients, even ones who were dead before he was called. Then he realised that Aungel was trying to make amends for his bad behaviour the previous day, and the curt answer had been churlish. He forced a smile. 'It was just very noisy.'

'It was,' agreed Aungel. 'The roof always knocks when the wind is from the east. It terrified me when I first came three years ago, but I have learned since that it is nothing to worry about.'

Bartholomew was far from sure about that. He took the lad to the storeroom, leaving the others to roll away mattresses, fold blankets and take dirty clothes to the laundry. He surveyed the mess wearily, then began to scrub the spilt substances off the workbenches while Aungel swept the floor. Anger gripped him again when he saw how free the experimenters had made with his supplies. His poppy juice was almost gone, and he wondered if Eyer would let him have more on credit until he earned some money. Or perhaps Edith would lend him a few pennies.

'God's teeth,' he exclaimed, holding up a flask containing a fluid that was bright blue. When he swirled it, it adhered to the sides, and he was quite sure that if any spilled, it would stain whatever it touched permanently. 'What is this?'

Aungel grimaced. 'It was not that colour last night! Goodwyn will be disappointed – he wanted red, so he could daub rude messages about the townsfolk on the guildhall's door.'

'If he does, I shall expel him.' Bartholomew looked at the mixture. 'What is in it?'

'I cannot remember. We filched wine from the kitchens, and added pinches of this and glugs of that. Goodwyn had some powders of his own, which he *said* he bought, but . . .'

'But what?' Bartholomew sensed he was about to be told something he would not like.

'But he does not have much money now his fees are paid,' confided Aungel unhappily. 'And Brother Michael keeps fining him. I think he may have stolen them. I know he was in Apothecary Eyer's shop with your nephew. He might have palmed a few things then, for mischief.'

'Richard was his accomplice?' Bartholomew was horrified.

'Oh, no, sir! He was there to purchase a hangover remedy. I imagine Goodwyn pinched the stuff while Eyer was serving him.'

Bartholomew sniffed the blue mixture cautiously, and recoiled at its toxic stench. He wondered what to do with it. He could not pour it down the drain, lest it did something terrible to the river. Irritably, he shoved it on the top shelf behind the pennyroyal, thinking it would have to wait until he had time to dispose of it in the midden.

'It was not my idea to conduct those tests,' said Aungel sheepishly. 'I said we should ask you first, and so did most of the others, but Goodwyn told us . . .'

'If he suggests anything else, refuse. You are the senior student, not him.'

'Yes, but he is older than me,' said Aungel miserably. 'He and the other new men did the trivium and most of the quadrivium at Oxford, which is why Master Langelee took them. He can charge advanced scholars higher fees, you see.'

'If they are trouble, I shall send them down, along with anyone else who follows them into mischief,' said Bartholomew warningly. 'So do not let them lead you astray.'

Aungel nodded, but it was clear the task might be beyond him. 'They are an evil influence. They met up with Mistress Stanmore's apprentices last night and caused trouble in the Cardinal's Cap. They escaped before the beadles arrived, but I heard them sniggering about it afterwards.'

'Then tell Langelee. We do not want them bringing disgrace on the College.'

'Very well. But if Goodwyn finds out that I am a sneak, and I am forced to flee in fear of my life, I shall want a refund on my fees.'

The wind was still strong when Michaelhouse's scholars processed to church, but the gusts were moderating. It had blown leaves into rusty piles in the corners, while small twigs and bits of branch littered the streets. The students burst out laughing when Langelee, wrestling with the temperamental latch on the porch door, released a string of obscenities that would have made the most foul-mouthed of guttersnipes blush.

'Thank God you are going to see the locksmith today,' he muttered to Hemmysby, inspecting a torn fingernail. 'We shall be pinched, sliced and maimed no more.'

'I am afraid it will have to be tomorrow,' said Hemmysby apologetically. 'There was not enough time for everyone

110

to speak at the debate yesterday, so the Chancellor suggested that we resume again this morning. I am called to clarify certain points from Ockham's *Opus nonaginta dierum* – ancient tenets raised by the silly Bon from Winwick Hall.'

'Tynkell really is inept,' said Michael in disgust. 'He failed to restrict the discussion to new arguments, so inexperienced debaters like the men from Winwick Hall dredged up lot of old material. And for the first time ever, the Cambridge Debate will span two days.'

'It is partly your fault, too, Brother,' said William. 'You plan to ban apostolic poverty after Tuesday, so everyone is keen to have his say before the injunction comes into force. It is a poor decree. There is nothing wrong with a bit of theology.'

'It is not a bit of theology,' said Michael crossly. 'It is heresy, and I have no wish to share Linton Hall's fate. But I wish Tynkell had kept the debate on track. I do not have time to monitor it myself, what with catching killers and making arrangements for the ceremony next week.'

'And looking for our hutch,' added Langelee pointedly.

'Moreover, my choir needs to rehearse the *Conductus*,' Michael went on, 'or they will disgrace themselves with their indifferent grasp of polyphony.'

'They will disgrace themselves by opening their mouths,' muttered Thelnetham. He spoke a little louder. 'Do you have any of that remedy for biliousness, Bartholomew? The thought of those heathens performing has made me feel quite sick.'

'It is all the poison inside you,' declared William. 'If you were a nicer man, you would not need a tonic. Biliousness is a sign of a disagreeable character.'

'We did well at the debate yesterday,' said Clippesby, speaking quickly to avert a spat. He had Ethel in his arms, and clearly intended to take her to the service. The hen's leery expression suggested she was not entirely comfortable with the idea, but she made no attempt to flap away.

'*I* did well,' gloated Thelnetham. 'Michael and Hemmysby were adequate.'

'Hurry up with the door, Master,' ordered William. 'I want to return to the tract I am composing. I have some concluding remarks to make, and then it will be ready for your enjoyment and edification. You will learn a great deal from it, I promise.'

'I am sure he will,' said Thelnetham snidely. 'Such as the fact that you have wasted a lot of perfectly good ink and parchment on your foolish ramblings.'

A row blossomed, but Bartholomew stopped listening when Goodwyn gave Aungel a shove that was vigorous enough to make the younger lad stagger. Both returned to their places when they saw they were being watched, but he suspected Goodwyn would not behave for long. Langelee had noticed, too, but was unsympathetic when Bartholomew put his case for expelling troublemakers.

'Impossible! How will we refund their fees? And think yourself lucky. Yours at least *look* respectable – the ones enrolled with me have the appearance of escaped convicts.'

Goodwyn and his cronies, along with the ruffians from Langelee's class, shuffled and snickered all through Mass, although they settled down at breakfast. Bartholomew poked dispiritedly at the pottage in his bowl. It comprised a watery broth flavoured with fish heads, accompanied by the kind of oat mash that was more usually fed to horses.

Afterwards, Cynric was waiting with a long list of patients, while the other Fellows – and Ethel – went to attend the rest of the debate. Before he left, Michael murmured that he would need Bartholomew's help that afternoon, as they had to follow up on what Bon had told them the previous day – that Illesy had entertained Potmoor at Winwick Hall on the night that Elvesmere had been murdered.

'And a gold candlestick has been stolen from Gonville,' the monk added. 'Rougham assures me that the culprit is Potmoor, so we had better interview him, too.'

'Does Rougham have evidence for this accusation?'

'If only! He bases it on the brag that Potmoor once made to his henchmen – that he commits burglary as a way of ensuring that he does not lose his felonious touch.'

'Did Potmoor really say that, or has it been quoted out of context?'

'Oh, he said it, and not in jest either. However, as I keep telling everyone, he is not the only burglar in the shire, and I shall continue to hound other suspects. Seven hostels, three Colleges and the Dominican Priory have been targeted now, while de Stannell says he has lost count of the number of thefts in the town. It is imperative that the culprit is caught before he beggars us all.'

'What about Fulbut? You said you would arrest him yesterday, and persuade him to tell you who ordered the murder of your Junior Proctor. Did he identify the culprit?'

'Unfortunately, he has disappeared and my beadles cannot find him.' Michael sighed. 'It is one step forward and two back with these cases. But do not be too long with your patients. We must make some headway today, or term will be on us and we shall expire from the pressure.'

Bartholomew began his rounds by visiting those patients who lived south of the College, walking carefully along a High Street that was littered with debris from the storm. There were a lot of smashed tiles on the ground outside Winwick Hall, but builders were already scrambling across the roof to replace them. Lawrence and Bon were watching, Lawrence describing what he could see to his colleague. Bartholomew went to exchange pleasantries with them.

'No, we did *not* enjoy yesterday's debate,' snapped Bon, turning his milky eyes to the grand church next door, from which already came the sound of haranguing voices. 'Michaelhouse savaged us cruelly, which was unkind, given that it was our first appearance.'

'Your colleagues could have been gentler, Matthew,' agreed Lawrence. 'But Illesy and Nerli will salvage our reputation today, and the refreshments we shall provide afterwards will put us in everyone's good graces. Ah, here comes Eyer with the poultice for your eyes, Bon.'

'About time,' muttered Bon savagely. 'He is late again.'

'I do not like to speak ill of a colleague,' muttered Lawrence, as Bon stamped away on the apothecary's arm, 'but Bon really is a surly devil. He cannot open his mouth without saying something unpleasant, and living with him will be a sore trial, I fear.'

Bartholomew suspected he was right.

The physician arrived at the home of his first patient – a carpenter with a broken hand. Technically, this was Holm's domain, but Bartholomew did not trust him, and regularly performed procedures that were traditionally the prerogative of surgeons. It was unorthodox, but he felt his patients deserved the best treatment available – which would not be forthcoming from an incompetent like Holm. He set the bones carefully, half listening as he was regaled with complaints about the number of matriculands who had arrived that year. The next two visits saw him bombarded with vitriol about the Guild of Saints, which had decreased the amount of charity it dispensed after Stanmore had died, and was expected to cut back even further now that Knyt was no longer in charge.

'Father Heyford told us so in a sermon,' confided a resentful rat-catcher. 'The Guild used to support beggars and needy widows, but now it gives all its money to Winwick Hall.'

Bartholomew broke away from paupers to make a visit to King's Hall, where a scholar named Geoffrey Dodenho, whose academic abilities were not as great as he thought they were, was suffering from a swollen knee. Dodenho had no complaints about the Guild of Saints or the number of matriculands, but he had a great deal to say about the unseemly speed with which Winwick Hall had come into being.

'King's Hall does not approve. It took *us* twenty years to go from a writ to a fully fledged College, but that place did it in a few days. It is not right, and there will be trouble.'

'Probably,' said Bartholomew. 'Flex your knee now. Does that hurt?'

'No. And all the while, the hostels laugh at us, because they think we are jealous. We are not: we are concerned. Did you know that John Winwick has not even sorted out its endowment yet, owing to some legal hiccup? Without it, his foundation is not really a College at all.'

'I suppose not. What about this? Is that sore?'

'No. Winwick Hall is beneath us in other ways, too. It does not have *royal* connections, like we do. Or the support of powerful churchmen, like Michaelhouse. It cannot even claim to have been founded by the town, like Bene't. It is a cuckoo, and one established by a lawyer into the bargain.'

'Stand up. Is there any pain when I push here?'

'No. John Winwick might be Keeper of the Privy Seal, but he hails from *common* stock and his hall will attract *common* members. It is not to be borne.' Dodenho jerked away suddenly. 'God's blood, Bartholomew! That hurt!'

One call took the physician to the sparsely populated area north of the river, once a thriving community but wiped out in a few days by the plague that had swept across the country a decade before. Again, there was talk about the increasing miserliness of the Guild of Saints. On his way back, he passed St Clement's, where Heyford was sweeping his porch.

'No, I am *not* well,' the vicar snapped in reply to Bartholomew's polite enquiry. 'I have a headache. Someone sent me a jug of very powerful wine yesterday, and it made me sick.'

'You made yourself sick,' countered Bartholomew. 'No one forced you to drink it.'

'I was thirsty,' said Heyford tetchily. 'As the villain doubtless knew I would be after I had given that long sermon about the wickedness of the Cambridge Debate.'

'Why do you consider it wicked? Because the subject is apostolic poverty?'

'Do not be ridiculous! Apostolic poverty is an excellent topic for discussion. No, my objections stem from the fact that *I* was not invited.'

Bartholomew was nonplussed. 'Why would you be? You are not a member of the University.'

'Of course not – I would never deign to join such a vile institution. But I still have a right to speak, and I have views about the greedy excesses of monks. And speaking of greedy monks, what is Brother Michael doing to catch the arsonist who tried to incinerate me?'

'I thought it was an accident. A candle falling over while you were dr— while you slept.'

'That is what everyone was meant to think, but the villain set light to my altar deliberately. He sent me that strong wine, too, to ensure that I would die in the resulting inferno. And why? Because I am honest and say what I think. Someone probably took offence at something I preached – a scholar from that diabolical Winwick Hall, perhaps. Or Potmoor.'

Bartholomew did not grace the claim with a response, but it did not matter, because the vicar's attention had already turned to something else that was not to his liking: a party of young men. All were older than the lads who usually applied to study at the University, and Bartholomew did not like the fact that they were armed with swords.

'They are here for Winwick Hall,' Heyford said darkly. 'But if they are rejected – and not even that bloated abomination can accept them all – they will find themselves a master and establish a hostel. We shall be knee-deep in lawyers, and our poor town will be like a foretaste of Hell!'

Bartholomew's next port of call was a woman who lived next to St Clement's. Ylaria Verius had been his patient for years, and was currently suffering from a persistent cough. Her husband – whom Bartholomew had met just before the fire the previous day – was a ditcher, but as he was too lazy to work he often supplemented his income with petty theft. Their meagre shack was gloomy, damp and cold, and Bartholomew was not surprised that Ylaria's health improved slowly.

'Your sister's apprentices caused a terrible rumpus in the Cardinal's Cap last night,' said Ylaria, when the examination was over and they were waiting for water to boil for a soothing syrup. Normally, Bartholomew would have sent Verius with a note asking Eyer to prepare what was needed, but such luxury was impossible now he had no stipend.

'I heard,' said Bartholomew, not liking to admit what Aungel had claimed: that the new medical students had joined them there. 'I will speak to her.'

'Do not bother her with it,' said Ylaria. 'Corner your nephew instead. Tell him, Noll.'

'Yes, tackle Richard,' nodded Verius. 'He was the one who led them inside.'

Bartholomew was annoyed. Townsfolk never visited that particular establishment, as it was the acknowledged domain of scholars – although taverns were off limits to academics, the Cap was a discreet exception, as it was frequented by sober clerics who never caused trouble. Richard should have known better than to take apprentices there.

'Some friars asked them to leave,' Verius went on, 'but Richard refused. Insults were traded and there was a brawl, although your nephew did not join in.' The ditcher was clearly disdainful of such unmanly behaviour.

'Was anyone hurt?' asked Bartholomew anxiously.

'No, although Richard did his best to goad it into something worse. I know, because I was watching from the Angel Inn opposite. That Richard is an odious ba—'

'Easy, Noll,' interrupted Ylaria hastily. 'Doctor Bartholomew may like him.'

'I doubt it,' averred Verius. 'No one could be fond of a sly dog like him. He—'

'There is a lot bad feeling towards the University at the moment, Doctor,' said Ylaria quickly, cutting her husband off a second time. 'Mostly because we dislike all these new students invading our town. There are far more of them than usual.'

'Winwick Hall,' spat Verius. 'The showy place on the High Street – *that* is what is attracting all these pompous louts. I wish the Guild of Saints would not give it so much money.'

'Money that should go to the poor,' agreed Ylaria. 'The Guild is not what it was when your brother-in-law was in charge, Doctor. There still are some nice people in it, but most are villains – such as the Fellows of Winwick, Deputy de Stannell and Potmoor.'

'Potmoor is all right,' objected Verius. 'Nicer than the scholars.'

'Rubbish – he is a rogue!' Ylaria turned back to Bartholomew. 'I am none too fond of that Julitta Holm either. I am sorry to say it, as I know you and her are close, but she used to be such a kind lady. Now she never gives money to the poor and—'

'There is a rehearsal for the Michaelhouse Choir tonight,' interrupted Verius, bored with the tirade. 'I am a member, as you know, and Brother Michael has promised to execute a conductor for us. I am not sure who he plans to kill, but it will be interesting to see.'

'It means he has written some music for you to sing,' explained Bartholomew. 'A processional piece, called a *Conductus*.'

'Oh,' said Verius, disappointed. 'Well, no matter. I shall probably enjoy myself anyway. Ylaria says I have the voice of an angel, and Brother Michael has pledged me a solo part.'

Bartholomew did not like to imagine what manner of sound the gruff Verius would produce. He took his leave and walked towards the Jewry, but had not gone far before he met Edith and Richard. They were walking stiffly side by side, and he was sorry they no longer linked arms as they would once have done. Edith looked worn and haggard.

'Matt,' she said with a strained smile. 'I have been looking for you.'

Bartholomew glanced at his nephew. 'Because of the Cardinal's Cap?'

'No,' said Richard quickly, and promptly went on a spiteful offensive of his own, to ensure events in that particular tavern were not discussed in front of his mother. 'Have you seen Julitta Holm this morning? She has unveiled a plan to withdraw free bread for paupers, and some of the prostitutes have asked me to speak to her about it. She is your lover, so I thought you . . .'

He pretended to trail off guiltily, but his ploy to expose Bartholomew's peccadillos failed. Edith knew all about her brother's affection for Julitta, and considered it none of her business. Instead, her eyes narrowed, and she homed in on what Richard had said.

'I sincerely hope you have not used prostitutes while living under my roof.'

'Of course not,' said Richard, although he had the grace to blush. He changed the subject in a transparent attempt to avoid a lecture. 'Did I tell you that I plan to apply for a Fellowship at Winwick Hall? Provost Illesy said he would put in a word for me with the College's founder.'

'You want to be a scholar?' asked Bartholomew, startled.

Richard shrugged. 'Such a life has much to commend it – long holidays, not much to do during the day, sumptuous feasts in the evenings.'

Bartholomew laughed.

'I was sorry to hear about Knyt,' said Edith. She stood a little taller and looked her brother straight in the eye. 'He was a decent man, and I shall miss him.'

Bartholomew regarded her warily. He knew that particular posture. It meant she was leading up to something – a something that would almost certainly horrify or disconcert him.

'His wife is not decent, though,' gossiped Richard meanly. 'I was just telling Mother – I happened to be walking past their house yesterday morning, and I saw Potmoor sneaking out through the back door. He should not have been visiting Olivia when Knyt was out.'

'How do you know Knyt was out?' asked Bartholomew.

It was Edith who replied. 'Because Knyt was with *me* when Richard was on the Chesterton road. We were discussing the number of blankets we shall need for the poor this winter.'

'Was his house burgled yesterday?' Bartholomew felt a surge of hope. Perhaps this would allow Michael to arrest Potmoor and charge him with the thefts. A search of his home might even reveal the Stanton Hutch, and Michaelhouse's problems would be over.

'Not as far as I know,' said Edith briskly. 'But its owner died a few hours later. *That* is what I wanted to discuss with you.' She glanced at Richard. 'With both of you.'

Richard frowned uneasily. 'I am not sure I follow. Are

you suggesting that Potmoor had something to do with Knyt's death?'

'Yes,' replied Edith with total conviction. 'And it is not the first time he has killed either.'

'No,' agreed Richard wryly. 'The taverns are full of tales about his many victims – some slaughtered by his own hand, and others by that army of henchmen he has recruited. Of course, not everyone believes he is such an outright villain. Provost Illesy says—'

'Everyone thinks that Oswald died of marsh fever,' interrupted Edith. 'But I have never been happy with that explanation, as you know. I have thought of little else these last few weeks, and Knyt's sudden and unexpected death has given me the answers I have been looking for. He was poisoned. And so was Oswald.'

Bartholomew blinked. This was a wild conclusion, even for a woman desperate to understand why a much-loved spouse had been snatched away with so little warning. 'I hardly think—'

'By Potmoor,' finished Edith. 'He is a wicked slayer of innocent men, and I mean to bring him to justice. And I want your help.'

CHAPTER 5

Bartholomew scrubbed hard at his face with his hands. His sister was not easily dissuaded from a course of action once she had decided on it, and preventing her from tackling one of the most dangerous criminals the town had ever known was going to be a challenge. He glanced at Richard, hoping that a combined assault by both would convince her that her deductions were questionable, and that accusing Potmoor was certainly not something Oswald would have wanted.

But Richard's expression was troubled, and Bartholomew's unease intensified. Was Edith's allegation a possibility that Richard had already considered? Or was his nephew merely afraid that such an accusation might damage his chances of being accepted at Winwick Hall – a place that benefited from Potmoor's largesse?

'Oswald was not murdered,' said Bartholomew, quietly but firmly in the hope that calm reason might nip the situation in the bud before it blossomed into something dangerous. 'Whatever gave you such an outlandish idea?'

'There is evidence,' replied Edith, and Bartholomew's heart sank. She had spent too much time brooding, and he realised he should have done more to prevent it. 'Oswald challenged Potmoor when he first began to ply his nasty trade in Cambridge, and Potmoor did not like it. Oswald was also a powerful voice in the Guild of Saints, and took his responsibility to the poor seriously. So did Felbrigge, Elvesmere and Knyt, and now all four are dead. Tell me that is not suspicious.'

'It is not suspicious,' said Bartholomew promptly. 'Oswald and Knyt died of natural causes, and you cannot compare their deaths to what happened to Felbrigge and Elvesmere. If you wander down that path, you will drive yourself mad.'

'I am right,' insisted Edith. 'I guessed the truth ages ago. Now Knyt is dead, I am sure of it.'

'She may have a point,' said Richard. Bartholomew shot him an exasperated glance: encouraging her was hardly helpful. 'But we shall need solid evidence to convict Potmoor in a court of law.'

'I have it,' said Edith with savage triumph, pulling a piece of parchment from her sleeve. 'I found it today when I was sorting through Oswald's documents.'

Richard frowned. 'The ones in the box? I told you to leave those alone.'

Edith shot him a look that expressed exactly what she thought of his gall in daring to give her orders, then turned to Bartholomew. 'It is a letter inviting Oswald to a meeting, to discuss "certain delicate business". Well, Potmoor's dealings with him were certainly "delicate". Oswald refused to listen to anything that vile rogue had to say.'

With Richard peering over his shoulder, Bartholomew read the message quickly. It was in French, nicely penned and perfectly grammatical – and nothing like the kind of communication the boorish Potmoor was likely to send.

'It is unsigned,' noted Richard. 'How do you know it is from him?'

'Because it is on expensive parchment,' Edith replied, 'which he is wealthy enough to afford.'

'So are many others,' Bartholomew pointed out. 'Especially Oswald's merchant friends.'

'Yes, but *they* would have sent a servant with a verbal invitation,' she argued. 'Potmoor is the only man obliged to converse by letter. He cannot ask his horrible henchmen to recite messages on doorsteps, because no one would be foolish enough to answer their knocks.'

Bartholomew regarded her sceptically. He could name

dozens of people who penned communiqués to friends, kinsmen and acquaintances. Moreover, when Potmoor had been ill, he had used Hugo to fetch medical help, thus proving that he *did* issue verbal invitations.

'I doubt Potmoor speaks French,' he said. 'And even if he does, or he hired a clerk, he is not so stupid as to leave written evidence of a murder he planned to commit.'

'Perhaps he did not intend to kill Oswald when he sent it. Maybe he just wanted to persuade him to turn a blind eye to the illicit activities on the wharves. And when Oswald refused . . . Look at the date on this letter: Lammas Day.'

Bartholomew was bemused. 'What is the significance of that?'

'You were not here, so I suppose there is no reason for you to remember,' said Edith bitterly. 'Oswald died on Lammas Day.'

'Are you sure he actually went to this meeting?' asked Richard, while Bartholomew flailed around for a way to tell her that it was probably just coincidence.

'Of course.' She shot him a disdainful glance, one that then turned to her brother. 'I remember everything about that day, as I have told you on countless occasions before. It was a lovely warm evening, and there was to be a Guild function later. Oswald and I were in the hall with Agatha, who happened to be visiting, when this letter arrived.'

'How do you know it was that letter?' pounced Bartholomew.

'Purple ink,' replied Edith, showing it to him. 'It is unusual and distinctive. And there is the date, of course. Anyway, Oswald read it, then told us that he needed to go out before the Guild gathering, to take care of a small piece of business.'

'But he did not specify that the "business" was with Potmoor,' said Bartholomew. They were covering old ground – he had lost count of the number of times they had combed through every last detail of his brother-in-law's final few hours.

'No, but this missive proves it was,' said Edith stubbornly.

Bartholomew did not want to be unkind, but he had to make her see sense before there was a serious problem. 'Not all Oswald's affairs were wholesome, Edith,' he said as gently as he could. 'Perhaps that invitation is from another dubious contact who—'

'Matt!' cried Edith, while Richard's face darkened with anger. 'He might have sailed a little close to the wind on occasion, but he was always honest.'

Not for the first time, Bartholomew marvelled at the extent to which Stanmore had managed to pull the wool over his family's eyes regarding his creative business practices. He tried again to reason with her. 'Yet you told me only yesterday that you had uncovered evidence of unscrupulous dealings with King's Hall.'

'There was another with Mistress Tulyet, too,' said Edith unhappily. 'I discovered it this morning. But these were isolated incidents, and I am sure there was a good reason for them.'

'Of course there was,' snapped Richard, clenching his fists at his side. 'And if you had left his personal affairs alone, as I suggested, we would not be having this shameful discussion.'

'Shall I tell you again what happened when he returned home that night?' asked Edith, and before either could tell her there was no need, she began. 'He was sombre, which was odd, as he usually enjoyed Guild meetings.' She favoured Bartholomew with a frosty glare. 'And it was *not* because he had had too much to drink.'

At one point, Bartholomew, familiar with maudlin drunks from College feasts – back when Michaelhouse had been able to afford them – had asked how much Oswald had imbibed. Edith had still not forgiven the impertinence of the question.

'He said he felt unwell and wanted to retire,' she

continued. 'I stayed chatting to Agatha for a while, then went to see if he needed a tonic. He was clearly ill, so I asked her to fetch a physician. You were in Peterborough, so she called Doctor Rougham.'

Bartholomew did not look at her, afraid he would see accusation in her eyes again for being away. 'Why do you find it so difficult to believe that he had marsh fever? He had bouts of it in the past, and August is a bad month for such ailments. Moreover, Rougham said—'

'Rougham!' spat Edith. 'You have never trusted his diagnoses before. Why start now?'

'Because he suffers from marsh fever himself. He knows the symptoms.'

'But, as I keep telling you, Oswald's last illness was not like his other attacks. I have spoken to his friends at the Guild, and they all say the same – he was not himself that evening. And I now know why: because Potmoor enticed him to a meeting first, and gave him poison.'

Bartholomew turned to Richard for support but his nephew was nodding slowly, an expression on his chubby features that was dark and rather dangerous.

'I have often wondered why he succumbed so quickly to this so-called fever,' Richard said. 'Perhaps Potmoor *is* responsible. Or a so-called friend, jealous of Father's success and integrity.'

'So now you know the truth,' said Edith, hands on hips as she regarded them both challengingly. 'What are we going to do about it?'

'Nothing,' replied Bartholomew firmly. 'I doubt Potmoor is a poisoner. It is too subtle a method of execution for a man like him.'

'Not with a victim like Oswald,' argued Edith. 'An official investigation would have exposed him as the one with the obvious motive for murder. But he will not get away with it, not as long as I have breath in my body.'

Bartholomew could tell that she had resolved to do

what she thought was right, and the anger in Richard's eyes suggested that he might help her. If he wanted to keep them safe, he had no choice but to explore the matter himself, or at least go through the motions.

'I will look into it,' he promised. 'But on two conditions. First, that you say nothing to anyone else about your suspicions, and second, that neither of you will try to investigate.'

'But we will be more efficient together,' objected Edith, dismayed.

'No, he is right,' said Richard. 'We may damage his chances of success if we butt in with questions of our own. We should let him work alone.'

Bartholomew regarded him sharply, not sure what to make of the remark. Was it a blind, and Richard actually intended to initiate an inquest of his own? Was he genuinely acknowledging that two enquiries might be counterproductive? Or was he a coward, unwilling to tackle killers himself?

Edith considered the proposal for a long time before finally inclining her head. 'Very well. But I *am* right about this. I have never been more sure of anything in my life.'

Bartholomew entered the Jewry in an unsettled frame of mind, wondering how he was going to prove to his family's satisfaction that Oswald had died of natural causes. It would be yet another demand on his time, and he was not sure how he would manage. He grew more flustered still when he remembered that his next patient lived in the house that Matilde had once owned.

It was not easy to enter a place that held so many poignant memories. Matilde's parlour had been bright, clean and welcoming, full of the scent of herbs and honey. He associated it with laughter, love and warmth. The current occupant, however, had transformed it so completely that he would not have known it, which was simultaneously a relief and a disappointment. It was crammed with dark, heavy furniture and horsehair pillows, and there was a powerful stench of burning fat.

The patient was Marjory Starre, a woman of indeterminate age, sometimes said to be a witch. She hated scholars with a passion that was barely rational, although she graciously allowed Bartholomew to tend her for a recurring tetter, a rash that was interesting enough to compensate for her insistence on outlining all the evils of his University each time they met. That day, however, she was more concerned with the storm that had battered the town the previous night.

'It blew for John Knyt. Everyone knows that a strong wind means a great man is dead.'

Bartholomew had known no such thing, but most of his attention was on her hands, which exhibited an unusual and intriguing degree of inflammation.

'Potmoor murdered him, of course,' she went on. 'Because back in the spring, Knyt voted against his election to the Guild of Saints. Potmoor was not the kind of man Knyt wanted in that venerable body, see.'

'Knyt was not murdered,' said Bartholomew. 'He died of—'

'Potmoor murdered Felbrigge and Elvesmere for the same reason.' Marjory cut across him, as was her wont with anyone who tried to argue. 'It would not surprise me to learn that he disposed of your brother-in-law, too. Of course, while Stanmore always claimed to dislike Potmoor, I happen to know they got on very well together.'

Bartholomew regarded her sharply, wondering if she somehow knew about the discussion he had just had with Edith and Richard. Or perhaps she had put the notion of murder into Edith's head in the first place. Regardless, there was a sly cant in her eyes that he did not like at all.

'I hope you are not suggesting that Oswald was a criminal,' he said coolly.

128

'He was too clever to treat with Potmoor publicly, although arrangements were certainly in place behind the scenes,' she replied artfully. 'He sold cloth, which he imported via the river that flows through Chesterton – Potmoor's domain. If you dig deep enough, you will find connections. No wind blew for him, of course, which means he was *not* a great man.'

'He was to his family,' said Bartholomew with quiet dignity. 'And that is what counts.'

'Is it indeed?' asked Marjory archly. She continued her rant. 'The wind did not blow for Felbrigge and Elvesmere either. But it blew for Knyt, and it will blow again soon.'

'Who for?' asked Bartholomew, although his mind was back on her tetter, with which he felt a good deal more comfortable.

'Many folk,' she said, with such sober conviction that he looked at her in surprise. 'Death is in the air. I can feel it and smell it. You must take extra care, Doctor.'

Bartholomew left her house even more unnerved than when he had arrived, although he knew her words were rank superstition and he should pay them no heed. He turned the corner, and then did not know whether to feel pleased or more disquieted still when he bumped into Julitta. She saw where he had been, and smiled sympathetically – he had told her about Matilde, although not the possibility that he might receive an offer of marriage in the future, one that he might well accept. Or would he? When he was with Julitta, he tended to long for a life with her instead.

'I am going to another Guild meeting,' she said, after they had exchanged pleasantries. 'It has been called to announce the death of John Knyt, although the news is already common knowledge.'

'Who will take his place?'

'Assistant Secretary de Stannell will serve out the rest

of Knyt's term, and we shall hold an election next Easter. Will plans to stand, and I hope he wins.'

'You do?' said Bartholomew. Her eyebrows rose in surprise, and he hastened to explain. 'The Guild is committed to helping the poor, but Holm has never been very interested in . . .'

He faltered, aware that defaming her husband was not the best way to keep her good graces. She might have suffered a cruel shock when she discovered Holm's true nature, but that did not mean she appreciated disloyal remarks about him. It was an attitude Bartholomew failed to understand, but he supposed it could be attributed to her rigidly traditional upbringing. He was just glad her nuptial devotion did not prevent her from pursuing a relationship with him.

'He knows the Guild's work is important,' she said, a little defensively. 'I have been spending a lot of time on it of late.'

'Is that why people have said that you are less involved with other charitable concerns?'

She nodded. 'There is not enough time for it all, so I have decided to concentrate on the Guild for now. We are very busy with arrangements for the beginning of term ceremony.' Her expression turned rueful. 'Several scholars have voiced their displeasure at our "meddling", but it will mark Winwick Hall's entry into the University – which could not have happened without *our* money.'

Holm appeared before Bartholomew could respond, annoyed by the sight of his wife and the physician chatting so amiably together in public. 'It is a pity you let Knyt die, Bartholomew,' he said coolly. 'He was a fine man, and will be sorely missed.'

'You were there first – why did *you* not save him?' Bartholomew shot back, then wished he had kept a dignified silence. Why demean himself by sparring?

'I am sure you both did your best,' said Julitta

soothingly, but Holm was not in the mood to be appeased, and attacked on another front.

'I met Hugo Potmoor today. He says his father often dreams of Heaven. You have given that scoundrel serious delusions about himself, ones that even his son cannot dispel.'

'I hardly think that is Matt's fault,' objected Julitta. 'He—'

'Yes it is. He bears responsibility for *all* the crimes Potmoor has committed since he was snatched from the grave. And his victims now include us. *We* were burgled last night.'

'Are you all right?' Bartholomew addressed his question to Julitta, far more concerned about her than her dreadful spouse.

She nodded. 'The thief only got as far as the workshop before we heard him and drove him off. All he got was a few herbs and potions.'

'Herbs and potions that cost money,' sniffed Holm. 'And that I would not have to replace, if Bartholomew had not raised Potmoor. I intend to consult a lawyer today, and see about suing him.'

'No, you will not,' said Julitta firmly. She shot the physician a wan smile. 'It is shock speaking. Will has never been burgled before.'

'No, and I am more angry than I can say,' snarled Holm. 'The next time you revive a felon, please reflect on the impact it will have on decent, hard-working folk.'

Irritated and disconcerted by the encounter with the Holms, Bartholomew went on his way, but had not gone far when he saw Rougham, Meryfeld and Lawrence. He went to join them, hoping a medical conversation might restore his equanimity. They were talking about the previous night, when they had been summoned to tend Knyt.

'You should have refused to go,' Rougham was saying

131

waspishly. 'He was my patient, and I do not approve of poaching. Especially the lucrative cases.'

'My apologies,' said Lawrence, trying to prevent his long white beard from flapping in the wind. 'The servant who fetched me claimed that Knyt wanted a fellow guildsman. I was stunned to learn it was a lie. Knyt had been insensible for hours, so could have made no such request.'

'The same tale was told to me,' said Meryfeld, rubbing his grubby hands together. 'I demurred, because I dislike going out in gales, at which point the fellow threatened to carry me there by force. It was all most distressing.'

'And I was told you were unavailable,' finished Bartholomew. 'I am sorry, Rougham.'

'Very well,' conceded the Gonville man, mollified. 'I shall overlook it just this once. It is not the first time a desperate wife has summoned every *medicus* she knows in order to save a spouse. However, we should all be on our guard. There are rumours that Knyt was murdered, and we do not want to be associated with that sort of thing.'

'Murdered by whom?' asked Meryfeld, shocked.

'By Potmoor, of course,' replied Rougham. 'Who else?'

'Oh, yes,' said Lawrence drily. 'The person deemed responsible for every foul deed and mishap in the town. Well, all I can say is that he must spend very little time eating and sleeping, or there would not be enough hours in the day to get around to them all.'

Rougham glared at him. 'He definitely burgled Gonville Hall – a fine foundation like ours will certainly attract his greedy eyes. However, I am willing to concede that he might be innocent of making off with the town's maypole last night. It does not seem like his kind of crime.'

'That was probably your sister's apprentices, Matthew,' said Lawrence. 'I saw them inspecting it yesterday, and I thought then that mischief was in the offing.'

'It was dumped in the river, where it poses a

considerable nuisance to shipping,' added Meryfeld. 'But we digress. *Was* Knyt murdered? I thought he had a seizure.'

'He did have a seizure,' said Rougham irritably. 'We are not often unanimous in our diagnoses, especially when Bartholomew is involved, but we all agreed on that one. The rumour about Potmoor killing him is a silly lie put about by fools who aim to make trouble. Of course, I cannot blame them. Potmoor flaunts his misdeeds like banners, which is galling for us victims.'

'You should not have saved him, Matthew,' admonished Meryfeld. 'Not only did it make the rest of us look incompetent, but the whole town despises you for it.'

'Catalepsia,' mused Rougham, before Bartholomew could defend himself. 'I confess that possibility had not occurred to me. I wish it had, because I would have recommended that he be buried as soon as possible. Then he would have woken up inside his coffin, and no one would have been any the wiser. Except him, of course.'

Bartholomew was shocked. 'You would never condemn anyone to such a terrible fate!'

'I agree,' said Lawrence reproachfully. 'It is hardly commensurate with our calling.'

'Our calling is to prevent suffering,' countered Meryfeld loftily. 'And eliminating such a wicked rogue would have done just that. I side with Rougham. Potmoor grows stronger every day, and I abhor him *and* his evil deeds. I am glad he is no longer my patient.'

He shot Lawrence a sour glance that belied his words and made it clear that he bitterly resented losing such a profitable source of income.

'Yet Bartholomew should not bear sole responsibility,' said Rougham. 'I sniffed the *sal ammoniac* that woke Potmoor, and it almost melted my eyeballs. I have since learned that Eyer made a mistake with his ingredients.'

'Who told you that?' demanded Bartholomew. Eyer was a painstaking practitioner, and while errors were always a possibility, he seriously doubted that the apothecary had made one with the potent ingredients that were involved in producing smelling salts.

'Eyer himself.' Rougham shrugged sheepishly. 'In so many words.'

'Does anyone know what gave rise to the tale about Knyt being unlawfully slain?' asked Meryfeld before Bartholomew could press the matter further. 'Was it because Potmoor was Olivia's lover, and liked to slip into her house while Knyt was out?'

Bartholomew stared at him, recalling what Richard claimed to have seen. Could the rumour be true? He shook himself impatiently. Why would Olivia dally with the unsavoury Potmoor? If the man had visited Knyt's house when its master was away, then it would have had nothing to do with her. So what *had* Potmoor been doing there? A small, nagging voice began to scratch at the back of his mind, telling him that perhaps he was wrong to dismiss Edith's claim so precipitously.

'*Are* we sure Knyt had a seizure?' he asked, thinking how easy it would be to enter an empty kitchen and slip something toxic into a dish of food. 'You said we were unanimous in our diagnosis, but that is untrue. I did not venture an opinion, because I only saw him after he was dead.'

'Quite sure,' replied Rougham curtly. 'Please do not fuel these silly tales by disagreeing with the rest of us. A surfeit of oysters gave him colic, which brought on a fatal attack. And I am more sorry than I can say.'

'Yes,' agreed Lawrence sadly. 'The town will be poorer without his goodness and charity.'

'*I* shall be poorer without *him*,' said Rougham sourly. 'He was my richest client.'

CHAPTER 6

A little while later, Bartholomew entered St Mary the Great to find Michael at the back of the church. The nave rang with splenetic voices, ones far too agitated to pay heed to Chancellor Tynkell, who was struggling to impose order.

'Normally, I would rescue him,' said the monk. 'But it was his idea to continue the debate for a second day, so he can manage by himself. That will teach him to make decisions without me.'

'I thought it would be over by now,' said Bartholomew.

'It should be, but it will drag on into the evening, given that Tynkell is incapable of preventing our more wordy colleagues from repeating everything six times. I shall leave him to it. Heavens! Here is Langelee. It is rare to see him at this sort of occasion.'

'Have you seen William's tract?' demanded the Master without preamble. 'The one he has been working on these past two weeks?'

'Not yet,' replied Michael. 'Although he aims to annoy Thelnetham with it, so I imagine it will be rich in reckless bigotry. Why?'

'Because not only does it attack the Dominicans, the Gilbertines, Waltham Abbey and John Winwick in ways that will have the King and half the priests in England clamouring for our blood, but he has written about apostolic poverty.'

Michael sighed. 'Then burn it before any of his victims see the thing. I am not worried about his ravings on religion – he is not clever enough to devise a thesis that will attract followers, and his ponderings will likely be laughed into oblivion.'

'If only that were true, Brother. Unfortunately, he managed to acquire a copy of the text that caused Linton Hall to be dissolved and its members excommunicated. He has copied it out, and aims to pass it off as his own. I am no theologian, but even I can tell it is heresy.'

Michael regarded him in alarm. 'Then why is it not on the fire already?'

'Because he has hidden it and refuses to tell me where. You will have to use your authority as Senior Proctor to wrest it from him. And while you are at it, tell him that if he tries my patience again, I shall not be responsible for the consequences.'

'Very well,' sighed Michael wearily. 'I shall come at once.'

'He is here, listening to the debate, and will make a fuss that will attract unwanted attention if you haul him out in front of everyone. Nab him this evening, Brother, but for God's sake do not forget or we shall be finished.'

'William really is a nuisance,' muttered Michael, as the Master turned on his heel and stalked away. 'Why did he have to choose now to be controversial? But never mind him. We need to visit Potmoor before any more of the day is lost.'

'Must we?' asked Bartholomew without enthusiasm. 'Is there no other way forward?'

'None that I can see. Other than asking Illesy what he has to say about entertaining the villain on the night Elvesmere died – which we shall do as soon as we have Potmoor's side of the story.'

As it transpired, they were spared a trek to Chesterton because they met Potmoor on the High Street. The felon was with his hulking son Hugo, and at his heels were men who wore the greasy half-armour of the professional lout.

He was exchanging greetings with Olivia Knyt, who was pale and subdued. When the two scholars approached, she took the opportunity to hurry away from him.

Michael began his interrogation with some innocuous remarks about the recent spate of burglaries, but Potmoor only acknowledged them with grunts, his attention fixed on Olivia's retreating form. His expression was hungry, making Bartholomew suspect he *did* harbour a hankering for her, although that was not to say that it had ever been reciprocated.

At that moment Illesy joined them. He was breathless, giving the impression that he had seen his former client waylaid, and had raced to give him the benefit of his legal skills. Bartholomew studied him carefully, but could read nothing in the bland, oily face. He could certainly read Michael's, though: the monk quickly lost patience when Illesy began to reply to questions that were directed at Potmoor.

'What do you think of Winwick Hall?' asked Michael, finally devising one that Illesy could not possibly answer on Potmoor's behalf.

'I cannot say – I have never been inside.' Potmoor smiled, revealing long yellow teeth beneath his dangling moustache, although the eyes remained cold and beady. 'But that will change next week, as I have been promised a tour after the beginning of term ceremony. Certain members of the Guild of Saints have been invited to dine there, see.'

'How odd,' mused Michael. 'I suppose those witnesses were mistaken when they said they saw you there the night that Elvesmere was murdered.'

Hugo stepped forward and shoved Michael hard enough to make him stagger, a considerable feat given that the monk's bulk was not easily shifted.

'If you are accusing my father of killing Elvesmere—'

'Hugo, Hugo,' interrupted Potmoor mildly. 'I am sure

the good Brother meant nothing of the kind. He knows that those of us who have seen the face of God would never commit base crimes.'

'No?' asked Michael archly. 'Then what about your boast that you still enjoy breaking into people's homes, despite the fact that you have an army of henchmen to do it for you?'

Potmoor continued to bare his amber teeth. 'I did once enjoy plying the skills God gave me. However, I have not used them since my glimpse of Paradise. And you cannot prove otherwise.'

'I can prove that you are lying about your visit to Winwick Hall. I have witnesses, as I said.'

'He is not lying,' intervened Illesy smoothly. He turned to the felon with an obsequious smile. 'You did come to see us. It must have slipped your mind, since it was only for a moment. You came to donate ten marks. Do you remember now that I have jogged your memory?'

'Oh, yes,' said Potmoor flatly. 'Forgive me, Brother. I did not intend to mislead you.'

'Good,' said Michael. 'Then perhaps you will tell us where you were at dusk last night. Gonville lost a valuable candlestick, and someone answering your description was seen in the vicinity. Obviously, we are keen to eliminate you from our enquiries.'

'I was out on business,' replied Potmoor shortly. 'Alone – as I usually am whenever someone important is burgled. I cannot help it if the villain always chooses to strike when I am not in a position to provide you with alibis.'

'But you *do* have alibis,' countered Illesy with another greasy smile. 'You were accompanied by servants. Would you like me to bring them to you, Brother? Tomorrow, perhaps?'

Bartholomew stared at him, wondering how the Provost could demean himself by manipulating the law to let a criminal remain at large. And Illesy clearly believed that

Potmoor was guilty, or he would not be fabricating a defence for him.

'Do not trouble yourself,' said Michael, aware that Potmoor's henchmen would be only too pleased to perjure themselves for their master. 'It would be a waste of time for us all.'

'Quite,' said Potmoor. 'And now, if you will excuse me, it is time I went home. I have another headache. Those of us blessed with holy visions do, you know.'

'Really?' asked Michael. 'I wonder why no saint has ever complained of them. But I have one last question before you go: where is Nick Fulbut? I know he is in your pay.'

'Not any more. He is a mercenary, and I have no need of such men now that I have made my peace with God.'

Eyebrows raised, Michael glanced pointedly at the louts who had ranged themselves behind him, but Potmoor only stared back insolently, a half-smile on his sallow face.

'No one in Potmoor's employ knows where Fulbut might be found,' said Illesy. 'Although you are right to hunt the man, Brother. There is a rumour that he shot your Junior Proctor.'

'Fulbut is a slippery devil,' added Potmoor, 'and will work for anyone who can pay him. Perhaps you should liaise with the Deputy Sheriff, as I doubt your beadles will catch him on their own.'

'Olivia Knyt suggested the same,' said Bartholomew.

It was untrue, but Potmoor's gloating confidence had irked him and he wanted to disconcert the man. He was wholly unprepared for the result. Potmoor's smirk vanished, to be replaced by a look of such dark, brutal fury that Bartholomew took an involuntary step backwards. He was not the only one to be unnerved: Hugo and the henchmen promptly edged away.

'Your father is tired, Hugo,' said the Provost quickly.

'Not yet recovered from his brush with death. You should take him home.'

Hugo reached for Potmoor's arm, although with obvious trepidation. There was a moment when it seemed Potmoor would resist, but he glanced at Illesy, and something in the lawyer's face caused him to nod and allow himself to be led away. The henchmen followed, but at a safe distance.

'Have you found Elvesmere's killer yet, Brother?' asked Illesy, when they had gone. 'If not, I suggest you refrain from harassing innocent citizens, and concentrate on hunting him instead.'

'That is exactly what I have been doing,' retorted Michael.

Illesy regarded him coldly. 'Then have you visited King's Hall, Gonville or Bene't, to ask what they know about the vicious murder of one of our scholars? That is where the culprit will be – in another College. You know they hate us, and revel in anything that does us harm. *They* murdered Elvesmere, not Potmoor.'

He turned on his heel and stalked away.

'That was a waste of time,' grumbled Michael when he and Bartholomew were alone again. 'I did not expect Potmoor to confess to robbing half the town and arranging the deaths of Felbrigge and Elvesmere, but I had hoped for something in the way of clues.'

'I did not, and we were rash to have challenged him, especially once Illesy was on hand to ensure that nothing incriminating was said. However, we did learn something.'

'Potmoor's obvious fancy for Olivia Knyt?'

Bartholomew nodded. 'Richard saw him leaving her house the morning before Knyt died, and Meryfeld thinks they are lovers. Yet I doubt Olivia would entertain a lout like him . . .'

'My beadles inform me that she *does*. He is a powerful man, and women find that attractive. I speak from personal experience, of course – there is nothing more desirable to a lady than strength and charisma. But speaking of strength and charisma, it is time we visited a man who has neither.'

'Deputy de Stannell?'

'Yes. Potmoor was right – we *should* combine forces to catch Fulbut.'

They began to walk towards the castle. Bartholomew was silent for a while, reflecting on Potmoor's unnerving flare of rage. 'My sister thinks he murdered Oswald,' he confided.

Michael sighed. 'I wondered how long it would be before she decided that Oswald's death was suspicious. I can see why – he was hale and hearty one moment, but dead the next.'

'It happens, Brother. And there is no reason to doubt Rougham's diagnosis.'

Michael raised his hands in a shrug. 'Well, you had better make a show of investigating, or she will do it herself. And she bakes the best Lombard slices in the shire. I should hate to be deprived, just because she accuses Potmoor and he takes umbrage.'

Bartholomew winced at the thought. 'Unfortunately, she will know if I try to deceive her. She always does. And then there will be trouble.'

'I will think of something,' promised Michael. 'Do not worry.'

They climbed Cambridge's only hill, where a motte had been raised by the Normans shortly after the Conquest. The castle had expanded since, and was now a formidable structure – a tall curtain wall bristling with towers and fighting platforms, which enclosed a huge bailey containing barracks for soldiers, a gaol, courtrooms, kitchens, stables, pantries, workplaces for clerks and repositories for records. It had never seen a serious attack, and its resources were mostly channelled into more peaceful purposes, such as collecting taxes.

The centre of operations was the Great Tower, a stalwart, cylindrical structure that formed the most secure part of the complex. Its first floor comprised the spacious chamber that Sheriff Tulyet used as an office, and de Stannell was sitting by its hearth with Ratclyf from Winwick Hall when Bartholomew and Michael arrived. The deputy's face was flushed with wine, which made him appear more like an angry baboon than ever. Ratclyf, however, looked decidedly furtive.

'I must be going,' he said, standing abruptly and turning towards the door. 'Thank you for your understanding, de Stannell. It is always good to do business with another guildsman.'

'He came to ask for more help from the Guild of Saints,' explained de Stannell, once the clatter of Ratclyf's footsteps on the stairs had faded. He preened himself. 'Now Knyt is dead, it falls to me to make the important decisions.'

'Can you do that as well as your duty to the shire?' asked Michael.

'Of course. I am no Tulyet, who can only manage one post at a time. Today is a case in point. I gave Ratclyf a loan to repair the roof that was damaged in last night's storm, and in return he will pay a higher tariff on Winwick's fuel. I did Guild and county business in a single stroke.'

Ratclyf's hasty departure and reputation for guile made Bartholomew suspect that de Stannell had just been cajoled into an agreement that would allow Winwick to prosper at the shire's expense. He hoped it would not lead to more trouble between the town and the University.

'We came to discuss Fulbut,' said Michael. 'And the possibility of you and I working together to lay hold of him.'

'No, thank you,' replied de Stannell briskly. 'I would rather rely on my own men. He set St Clement's alight, so I want him in *my* cells, not yours.'

'Of course,' said Michael stiffly. 'However, he also shot my Junior Proctor, so I would like the opportunity to question him if you catch him first. I want to ask who hired him to do it.'

'I am afraid your enquiry is secondary to mine. *I* am investigating crimes against townsfolk, but your victim was only a scholar. And if you do not like it, complain to Tulyet when he returns.'

'Oh, I shall,' vowed Michael tightly. 'But how do you know Fulbut burned St Clement's?'

'It is obvious,' replied de Stannell. 'Heyford was sent strong wine just before the fire started – by Fulbut, who aimed to ensure that his victim would be too drunk to douse the flames.'

'Then perhaps he was following Potmoor's orders. I learned today that Heyford was reckless enough to make Lazarus the subject of his Sunday sermon, to Potmoor's detriment.'

'I shall bear it in mind. Now if you will excuse me, Brother, there are *important* matters requiring my attention.'

Michael railed about de Stannell's manners all the way to St Mary the Great, where they were astounded to discover the debate still in full flow, and in serious danger of extending into a third day.

'How can Tynkell let this nonsense drag on?' he cried. 'Winwick Hall has offered to provide refreshments afterwards, but we shall be eating at midnight at this rate. Where are *you* going?'

'To visit Eyer,' replied Bartholomew. 'Rougham thinks he made a mistake with the *sal ammoniac* I used on Potmoor. I doubt it, but I had better make sure.'

Michael was more interested in his own troubles. 'If

Dick Tulyet does not come home soon, he will have no town left to rule – that ridiculous de Stannell will have destroyed it with his crass stupidity. Do you think *he* killed Knyt, in order to take command of the Guild of Saints?'

'According to my medical colleagues, Knyt had a seizure brought on by a surfeit of oysters.'

'And you believe them? When Olivia was betraying him with the greatest criminal the town has ever known, and the slippery de Stannell wasted no time in filling his shoes? Knyt's death is very convenient for them both, is it not?'

'It is, but that does not mean he was murdered.'

Michael sighed, and some of the anger went out of him. 'I had better brief my beadles for their evening patrols.' He glanced at the sky. 'Then I shall partake of Winwick's refreshments.'

'I thought those were for the men taking part in the debate. You have missed most of it.'

'So what? The fare will be more appetising than boiled kidneys and leeks, which is what is on offer at College tonight. I recommend you do the same. And I shall need something decent inside me, because first I must confront William over his poached views on apostolic poverty, and then I have choir practice. A lot of new members have enrolled, so I need to assess them all for talent.'

Or lack of it, Bartholomew thought, but dared not say.

'After choir, I shall visit Winwick Hall,' the monk went on. 'We have been told that Elvesmere and Bon were particular friends, so perhaps Bon will tell us a little more about our murder victim. He is likely to be feeling wretched, and may appreciate a kindly ear.'

'Why will he be feeling wretched?'

'Because Hemmysby savaged him in the debating chamber again today. He should have kept quiet, but he would insist on speaking, and Hemmysby led him into several cunning traps.'

The daylight was fading when Bartholomew reached Eyer's shop. He entered, breathing in deeply the pleasing aroma of aniseed, cloves and blackcurrant. There were no customers, and the apothecary was in the process of shutting up, bustling about with a lantern in his hand. He smiled when he saw Bartholomew, and led him to the private parlour at the back.

'Are you hungry?' he asked, and before Bartholomew could reply, had slapped some yellow-brown sludge into a bowl. 'Eat this. It will do you good, and you are too pale for my liking.'

'What is it?' asked Bartholomew, when a tentative chew yielded no recognisable flavour.

'Boiled caterpillars. It is very nutritious, and will set your humours right in no time at all.'

Manfully, Bartholomew resisted the urge to spit it out. He had forgotten that the apothecary had a penchant for peculiar food, and it was not the first time he had been fed unpalatable snacks. He set the bowl on the table and sat on a bench, glad of some peace after his hectic day. Eyer busied himself with a fire to ward off the evening chill, his face flushed with pleasure at having company.

'Do you need more *aqua imperialis*?' he asked. 'I made a new batch today.'

'I do, but I cannot pay.' Bartholomew was about to explain why when he remembered that Michaelhouse's predicament was meant to be a secret.

Eyer took a bottle from a shelf. 'Tell your patients that I gave it to you for free. I am still new here and it will do no harm for me to be seen as generous.'

'You are seen as generous already, for the money you give to the Guild of Saints for its charitable work. No one doubts your munificence.'

Eyer grimaced. 'Between you and me, these donations are beyond my means, but I must be *seen* to be wealthy, or customers might think I skimp on my ingredients. I do not, of course, but reputation is all in my business.'

'It is,' agreed Bartholomew. 'And Rougham told me today that you made a mistake with the *sal ammoniac* I used on Potmoor.'

'I did not! I merely said that I might have been a little liberal with the ammonium. However, I have no wish to share the blame for raising Potmoor, so I have been telling people that you prayed over it, to improve its efficacy.'

Bartholomew was dismayed. 'You accused me of witchery?'

'Praying is not witchery,' said Eyer sternly. 'And it would not be the first time that one of my potions was rendered more powerful by invoking God's name. It is entirely possible that He imbued my *sal ammoniac* with unusual potency.'

'But you just said you used too much ammonium.'

'*May* have used too much ammonium. I shall certainly deny it should anyone else ask, and Rougham had no right to reveal something I told him in confidence.' They sat in awkward silence until Eyer ranged off on another subject. 'Poor Knyt. I recognised the symptoms of a seizure as soon as I set eyes on him, of course, although it was easy to do when he was still alive. I cannot imagine how you arrived at a diagnosis from a corpse. You are a braver man than me!'

'I diagnosed nothing.' Bartholomew spoke shortly, as apothecaries did not usually question physicians, and he was not sure he liked it. 'I left that to Rougham, Meryfeld and Lawrence.'

'I wonder what anatomical changes occur in seizures,' mused Eyer, pouring wine into two goblets. Afraid it might be concocted from earwigs or some other undesirable ingredient, Bartholomew declined to take it. 'I have long felt there is much to be learned from dissection. We might even be able to tell what medicines actually *do*, which would be of great value to those in my profession. Have you ever witnessed one?'

Bartholomew did not want to lie, but nor was he willing to discuss a practice that was frowned upon by the Church. 'The universities in Salerno, Padua and Montpellier are very advanced compared to us,' he hedged.

'So I have heard.' Eyer lowered his voice. 'You will find no enemy of progress in me, Matt. Indeed, if it were in my remit, I would urge you to dissect Knyt. The resulting knowledge would be of great benefit to any medical man.'

'It would,' agreed Bartholomew. 'But I cannot see the Guild of Saints being very pleased. Or his wife, for that matter.'

Eyer sighed. 'Ignorance is ever the enemy of advancement.' At that moment, there was an ear-splitting wail that made him leap to his feet in alarm. 'Christ God! What is that?'

'The Michaelhouse Choir, warming up.'

'Lord!' breathed Eyer. 'I had better stay open late tonight, because I imagine remedies for shattered nerves will be much in demand later.'

Bartholomew winced as a crescendo blossomed. 'There is fever in the Dominican Priory, so I think I shall spend the evening there. The sound will not carry that far.'

'Do not be so sure,' said Eyer grimly.

Ever hospitable, the Dominicans invited Bartholomew to share their supper, so it was late by the time he returned to Michaelhouse. He walked towards the hall, intending to work for an hour before retiring to bed. As he climbed the spiral stairs, a rank stench told him that he had dined far better than his colleagues. He met Agatha the laundress by the door, carrying an empty pot.

'Have you found the Stanton Hutch yet?' she asked. 'You have been out all day, so you must have some news.'

'I am afraid not.' Bartholomew hesitated, but then

forged on, because Edith was very much on his mind. 'Will you tell me again about the night that Oswald died? I know we have been through it several times already, but my sister . . . well, she continues to fret.'

'You mean she suspects foul play?' asked Agatha baldly.

Bartholomew shrugged. 'She has her concerns, as do many who lose loved ones suddenly.'

Agatha's habitually fierce expression softened. 'Well, I am sorry he is gone. He was one of the best members of the Guild of Saints, and the poor miss him. They will miss John Knyt, too.'

'Edith will continue their good work. So will Richard.'

'Richard!' spat Agatha. '*He* does not care about beggars. He voted in favour of Potmoor's proposal to withdraw their free bread this winter.'

Bartholomew was stunned, both by the fact that Potmoor would suggest revoking such a basic service, and by Richard's betrayal of his father's legacy. Why would Richard support a man who made no secret of his criminal activities? Was it because he hoped to curry favour with Winwick Hall, of which Potmoor was a patron? And would he turn against the felon now that Edith had raised the possibility that Potmoor might have poisoned his father? If so, Bartholomew hoped he knew what he was doing, as men like Potmoor tended to react badly to what they saw as betrayal.

'You did not know,' surmised Agatha. 'I am not surprised – he is probably ashamed of himself now.' She sighed. 'The Guild did much good when Master Stanmore was alive, but it has since come under the control of less kindly members – Surgeon Holm, Potmoor and the Winwick men are more interested in what the Guild can do for them, than what they can do for the poor.'

'Julitta will put matters right. She told me only today that she plans to devote more time to it.'

Agatha sniffed. 'Unfortunately, she is married to a

148

greedy, selfish rogue who has other ideas. But you asked about Master Stanmore's death. Shall I tell the whole story again?'

'If you would not mind.'

'My cousin's boy Mark works for your sister, and I made him a cake. When I arrived, Master Stanmore was getting ready for a Guild function, and he and Edith were chatting in that teasing, affectionate way they had with each other. Do you know what I mean?'

'Yes,' replied Bartholomew, experiencing a sharp pang of sadness. 'I do.'

'She was sewing a button on his tunic when a message arrived.'

'The one asking Oswald out for a meeting,' recalled Bartholomew.

Agatha nodded. 'When he read it his manner changed – he went from happy, to strained and nervous. He told your sister that he had some business to attend, and left at once.'

'Did you see the letter?'

'It would not have mattered if I had, because *I* do not read.' Agatha never said she *could* not read, always that she *did* not read. There was a subtle, but significant difference.

'And were you still there when he returned a few hours later?'

'Yes, because young Mark ate too much cake, and made himself sick. Edith and I put him to bed, then sat talking. Master Stanmore came home eventually, but went straight upstairs, saying he felt unwell. Your sister and I chatted a while longer, then she went to offer him a tonic. She found him ailing, and sent me for help. You were away, so I fetched Doctor Rougham.'

'Did Rougham come at once?'

'Oh, yes.' Agatha's expression was wry. 'Master Stanmore was wealthy, and handsome fees were at stake. He diagnosed marsh fever, and Master Stanmore slipped away shortly thereafter.'

'Did Oswald say anything about his evening when he came home?'

'No. He just poked his head around the door to say he felt a little off-colour, and was going to bed. He did not retire immediately, though, because I could hear the floorboards creak as he walked around the solar.'

'Did he seem feverish to you?'

'Not at all. Indeed, it would not surprise me if your sister was right, and someone *did* do him harm. He knew some very nasty people, so I am glad she wants you to look into the matter.'

Bartholomew stared at her. Was Edith right after all, and Stanmore *had* been fed a toxic potion, either at the mysterious meeting or with his Guild friends afterwards? He decided to find out a little more about his kinsman's last evening, to set his own mind at ease, as much as hers. After all, a few innocent questions could do no harm. Could they?

To reach the conclave, Bartholomew had to cross the hall. It was full of students, most of them newcomers, so unfamiliar. Some were reading, some were chatting and some were dicing – although the illicit cubes were quickly palmed when he walked by. Goodwyn and the other new medical students had claimed a shadowy corner, and Bartholomew was glad Aungel and his class were not with them, sure they were plotting mischief.

He entered the conclave. A lamp had been lit, but it was turned so low to conserve fuel that all he could see of his colleagues were silhouettes. Most of them were there. Clippesby had Ethel on his lap; portly Suttone was positively slender next to Michael's impressive bulk; Father William was identifiable by his unkempt hair and smelly habit; and Thelnetham sat with his knees pressed together and a pomander to his nose. Langelee was by the hearth, holding a sack in his meaty fist.

'Good, we are all here at last,' the Master said, aiming for the table and indicating that his Fellows were to join him. 'I suggest we begin immediately.'

'Begin what?' asked Bartholomew, hoping it was nothing to do with William's heretical tract. Michael was clutching a sheaf of parchment covered in the Franciscan's distinctive scrawl, and tightly pursed lips told Bartholomew all he needed to know about what had been written there. 'And we are not all here, anyway. Hemmysby is missing.'

'He is still at the post-debate refreshments,' said Langelee with a grimace of disapproval. 'They finished ages ago, and I cannot imagine what is keeping him. However, he is the one I want to discuss, so it suits me that he is out.'

'Is it about his manoeuvres to stop William from taking part?' asked Thelnetham. 'If so, I think he did the right thing. We would have been a laughing stock if *he* had been allowed to hold forth. Or excommunicated as heretics. Have you finished reading his silly tract yet, Brother?'

'His *stolen* tract,' corrected Suttone disapprovingly. 'Really, William! If you must purloin other people's work, you could at least choose some that has not drawn the angry attention of the King *and* the Pope.'

William glared at them both. 'I explained why I did it,' he said tightly. 'To annoy this acid-tongued Gilbertine. I have no intention of letting anyone outside College see it. And I do not understand what all the fuss is about anyway. The piece seemed theologically sound to me, and Thelnetham is a fool for whining so.'

'No!' snapped Langelee, as Thelnetham drew breath to retaliate. 'You will *not* distract us with a quarrel. I have something nasty to report, and you will sit quietly and listen. Are you ready? Here we go then. Hemmysby stole the Stanton Hutch.'

There was a stunned silence, the only sounds a faint hissing from the lantern and a muted cheer from the students next door as someone won at dice.

'Have you been drinking, Master?' asked William, the first to recover his composure.

'I wish I had! It is not pleasant to learn that one of my Fellows is a thief.'

'Hemmysby is not a thief,' declared Clippesby, hugging the hen. 'He is a priest.'

'And priests do not steal?' asked Langelee archly. 'I could cite a dozen cases to prove otherwise, and so could you.'

'On what grounds do you make this accusation?' asked Michael worriedly.

'On the evidence I found in his room.' Langelee reached into the sack and withdrew an object they all recognised immediately. It was the Stanton Cup, its silver-gilt and precious stones glittering brightly, even in the dim light. 'This was sitting on his table. He did not even bother to hide it.'

'Perhaps one of his students put it there,' suggested Bartholomew. 'He shares with—'

'They are all staying at the Brazen George until term begins, to avoid our food,' interrupted Langelee. 'He sleeps alone. And I checked with the servants: none of them have been in there, because he locks the door. And now we know why – to conceal stolen goods.'

'How did *you* get in, then?' asked Thelnetham suspiciously.

'I went to borrow some ink. The stuff he buys is better than the muck the rest of you use.'

It was a bald admission that Langelee raided his Fellows' quarters in search of supplies he should have purchased himself, and that he picked locks in order to do so, but no one took issue with him over it. All were more concerned with Hemmysby.

'The fact that the cup was in plain sight suggests to me that someone else put it there,' said Michael. 'If he stole it himself, he would have kept it hidden.'

'Hemmysby is *not* a thief,' repeated Clippesby, more loudly. His eyes were wild, and Bartholomew suspected they were in for one of his turns; such matters always touched him more deeply than the others. 'The money will turn up sooner or later. Ethel here is sure of it.'

Michael ignored him. 'Obviously, the real culprit realised that the cup is not something that can be sold, as it is too readily recognisable. So he decided to return it.'

'That is not possible,' said William in a low voice. 'Since we lost the hutch, I have been watching the gate. No one has come in who should not have done. However, I did see Hemmysby acting oddly before today's debate . . .'

'Explain,' ordered Thelnetham.

'He was scurrying,' replied William uncomfortably. 'Walking oddly hunched, like Judas in the mystery plays. Yet I cannot believe—'

'Hah!' exclaimed Thelnetham. 'That is evidence enough for me.'

'Well, it is not for me,' said Bartholomew firmly. 'I suggest we refrain from drawing conclusions until we have spoken to Hemmysby and heard what he has to say.'

'Quite right,' agreed Michael. 'There will be an innocent explanation for this.'

'Yes, there will,' said Clippesby softly. 'It is—'

'There will not,' declared Thelnetham. 'Look at the facts. Hemmysby is guilty, so accept it.'

'Nonsense,' argued William, although whether he believed it or just could not bring himself to side with the Gilbertine was difficult to say. 'You do not know what you are talking about.'

'I am not sure what to think,' said Suttone miserably. 'The evidence suggests . . . yet . . .'

'So Bartholomew, Michael, Clippesby and William

deem Hemmysby innocent, Thelnetham and I judge him guilty, and Suttone wavers,' summarised Langelee. 'What shall we do? Go to St Mary the Great and demand some answers?'

'Lord, no! That would set tongues wagging.' Thelnetham stood. 'We shall await his return, and while we do, I suggest we visit his lair, and see what else he has secreted there.'

Hemmysby's quarters were in the south wing, where the rooms were larger, newer and in better repair than the ones where Bartholomew lived. Its ceiling did not leak, and there were thick rugs on the floor and books on a shelf above the hearth. The bed was loaded with blankets, and the students' mattresses were stacked neatly beneath it. It smelled pleasantly of the spices that hung above the door to ward off agues, and of the lavender that was heaped in a silver bowl on the windowsill.

Bartholomew watched Langelee and Thelnetham rummage in the iron-bound box that held Hemmysby's personal belongings. Spare habit, underclothes and shoes were tossed out with callous indifference, along with a lovingly embroidered blanket from the priest's mother. Bartholomew picked it up and folded it carefully, deeply uncomfortable with what they were doing.

'Someone else left the Stanton Cup here,' he continued to insist. 'William cannot have kept watch all day, so the real thief waited until he was not looking.'

'Yes,' nodded Clippesby. 'Of course that is what happened.'

Thelnetham regarded them both in distaste. 'Clippesby is mad, so can be excused asinine remarks, but you should know better, Matthew.'

'Here are the deeds that prove we own our churches and manors!' exclaimed Suttone, seizing a pile of documents that lay openly on the bed. 'How did you miss them when you were here earlier, Master?'

'I did not linger – I just grabbed the cup and hurried

to the conclave to talk to you,' replied Langelee. 'Are they all there?'

Michael rifled through them quickly. 'Yes, thank God! What about the money? Is there any sign of that?'

'And my bestiary,' added Thelnetham.

A more detailed search revealed no more. It was now very late and Bartholomew was worried, fearing that Hemmysby might have learned what was happening and be afraid to return lest his explanations were rejected. Cynric was sent to find him, but returned alone.

'St Mary the Great is empty,' he reported. 'And I do not know where else to look.'

It was decided that he might be in the College church, so Bartholomew and Michael went to see. As they walked there, the physician reiterated his certainty of Hemmysby's innocence.

'I agree,' said Michael. 'He has plenty of money, and his needs are modest. He has no reason to steal. Besides, the placement of the cup and the deeds in his room had a contrived feel about them. I seriously doubt he put them there himself.'

They entered St Michael's graveyard and approached the porch, where Michael began the laborious business of jiggling the awkward latch – more difficult in the dark than in daylight.

'Hemmysby will never mend this if he learns that Thelnetham and Langelee have declared him a felon,' he said. 'And it would serve them right. Lord! The wretched thing is stickier than ever tonight. It must be the damp. You try.' He stepped back to give the physician room, then released a yelp of surprise as he toppled backwards.

'Are you hurt, Brother?' asked Bartholomew, struggling to keep the amusement from his voice. It was not often that Michael lost his dignity.

The monk replied with some pithy obscenities that made Bartholomew laugh aloud.

'I tripped over a . . . Oh, Christ!' While Michael was not averse to swearing, he rarely blasphemed, and the exclamation put an abrupt end to Bartholomew's mirth. 'Help me, Matt! Quickly! I am sitting on someone. A *dead* someone!'

Bartholomew groped about in the blackness, locating a chest and then a face. There was no breath, and the skin was cold. Michael was right: it was a corpse. He felt something else, too – a familiar pectoral cross and a head of wildly bushy hair.

It was Hemmysby.

CHAPTER 7

It was a dismal night for Bartholomew. He carried Hemmysby into the church, while Michael fetched the other Fellows. All watched in shocked silence while he inspected the body just carefully enough to say that the priest had not been shot, stabbed or battered. He would conduct a more thorough examination the following morning, when he could see what he was doing.

As a mark of respect, they decided to keep vigil for the rest of the night. Bartholomew took the first shift, standing over his dead colleague until Langelee relieved him at midnight. He returned to Michaelhouse and fell into an exhausted drowse, but woke two hours later and could not go back to sleep, so when a summons came to tend a case of fever, he was relieved to turn out. Medical matters kept him busy until six o'clock, after which he went to visit Edith, because he saw a light burning in her solar.

Sleep had eluded her, too, and he spent an hour listening to her repeat her conviction that Potmoor had murdered Oswald. Prudently, he did not add fuel to the fire by saying that Marjory Starre and Agatha thought she might be right. She had also discovered two more documents proving that Oswald had overcharged trusting customers, although Richard had declared they did no such thing, and they had quarrelled about it.

'Where is he?' Bartholomew asked, coming angrily to his feet. 'Upstairs in bed?'

Edith rolled her eyes. 'Of course not. He is out with his friends, as usual.'

Richard was still out when Bartholomew left. The physician walked slowly through the lightening streets, and arrived at the church just in time for morning prayers. Although Hemmysby was invisible to view – Langelee had moved him to the Stanton Chapel, the small chamber next to the high altar – everyone was acutely aware of his presence. The students cast frequent glances at the chapel door, and some of the younger ones had clearly been crying.

'Langelee found the Stanton Cup in Hemmysby's room yesterday,' Bartholomew heard Goodwyn whisper to Aungel. 'He was a thief, so do not mourn him. And he is not the only Fellow with an unsavoury reputation: our own tutor raises criminals from the dead and consults with the Devil on his more difficult cases, while Brother Michael arranged for his deputy to be shot.'

'Then you should watch I do not "arrange" for the same thing to happen to you,' said Michael, making Goodwyn jump in alarm by speaking in his ear. 'But this time I shall settle for threepence, which is the price of brawling in the Griffin last night.'

'It was not my fault!' Goodwyn pointed accusingly at Bartholomew. 'It was his nephew who took us there. And poor Uyten from Winwick Hall lost three teeth in that skirmish.'

'Then my fine will remind you not to be so foolishly gullible again,' said Michael sweetly. 'And later, you can help Agatha wash the jugs we used at choir practice last night.'

'Clean up after peasants?' But Goodwyn reached for his purse when a steely expression suffused the monk's face. However, it did not stop him from muttering, 'It was choir practice that sent us in search of strong drink in the first place. That rendition of Wycombe's *Alleluia* . . .'

'I assume you were going to furnish us with a compliment,' said the monk tightly. 'If not, you will pay two shillings for gross impudence.'

'You cannot . . .' began Goodwyn, then forced a smile. 'Your choir is unique, Brother, and I can honestly say that I have never heard anything like it. I cannot wait for the next rehearsal.'

'I must browse the statutes for a way to eject him,' said Michael through gritted teeth as Goodwyn slunk away. 'I do not want him in Michaelhouse.'

Nor did Bartholomew. He joined the procession to return to the College for breakfast, but Langelee had other ideas.

'Inspect Hemmysby properly, then come back and tell me what you find,' he instructed. 'I imagine he took his own life. He must have felt guilty about stealing the hutch, so he left the deeds and the cup where he knew they would be found, and took the easy way out.'

Bartholomew disagreed. 'Why would he commit suicide outside a church? Moreover, he was at the debate all day yesterday. People do not attend those sorts of events and then kill themselves.'

'I might, if *I* had been obliged to listen to that claptrap for so many hours,' said Langelee. 'But his death is a bitter blow on two counts. First, because now we cannot ask him to give us back our money. And second, because he was a good teacher, who will be difficult to replace.'

Bartholomew waited for everyone except Michael to leave, and locked the door behind them. He did not do anything overtly gruesome when inspecting corpses, but Goodwyn's remark made him wary of exacerbating the tales of his association with the Devil.

'Ignore him,' said Michael, guessing the reason for his caution. 'He has a poisonous tongue, as evidenced by his gossip about me.'

'Edith heard that particular rumour, too.'

Michael waved dismissively. 'I can think of far more creative ways of dealing with upstart minions than hiring archers to shoot them, and anyone who matters knows it. Still, it is galling to think that I am the subject of tittle-tattle by the likes of Goodwyn.'

'Have your beadles found Fulbut yet?'

'No, and I am beginning to suspect that whoever

159

employed him has taken steps to ensure that he will never spill his secrets.'

'You mean he might be murdered himself?'

Michael nodded. 'There must be some reason why he has disappeared so completely.'

'Do you think de Stannell is right to accuse him of setting light to St Clement's? After all, I saw him skulking near the back of it shortly afterwards, and its vicar freely admits to giving a damning sermon with thinly disguised references to Potmoor's "resurrection".'

'It is possible – Heyford is his own worst enemy with his nasty orations. But you had better make a start. We cannot stay locked in here too long, or people will wonder what you are doing.'

Bartholomew made no move to oblige. 'These rumours about the Devil and necromancy would not be so galling if I had not tried so hard to conform – keeping my opinions to myself, never discussing the teachings of my Arab master, bowing to traditionalism at every turn . . .'

'Then just imagine what folk would be saying if you had not taken steps to toe the line. Be thankful for small mercies. Now are you going to begin or not?'

Bartholomew was thorough, but there was no sign of violence, self-inflicted or otherwise, and everything indicated that Hemmysby had just fallen over dead in the churchyard.

'He must have been taken ill after the debate,' he said eventually. 'And came here as the nearest refuge, but the sticky latch defeated him and he died outside.'

'Died of what?'

Bartholomew shrugged. 'Some failure of the vital organs, I suppose. Heart, brain or liver.'

'Natural causes?' asked Michael sceptically. 'That is very convenient, given what we found in his room. Are you sure he has not been poisoned?'

'No. Some toxic substances leave obvious marks

– discoloration, rashes, swelling and so forth – but many are untraceable.' Bartholomew leaned against the wall. 'I witnessed a dissection at Salerno once, where poisoning was suspected. There were no external signs, but the anatomist discovered plenty internally. His diligence allowed a killer to be brought to justice.'

'How did he do it? By slitting the victim open from chin to toes?'

'Hardly! He made an incision in the neck, and the lesions were immediately apparent. He could have stopped there, but he removed the stomach, liver and intestines as well, to show us that damage had occurred in those, too.'

Michael was silent for a long time, staring down at their dead colleague. 'I do not believe Hemmysby died naturally,' he said at last. 'And I do not believe he stole the Stanton Hutch either. I think someone is trying to lead us astray.'

'What are you saying? That he *was* poisoned? Murdered?'

Michael nodded slowly. 'Yes, because we also have two other untimely "natural" deaths – Knyt and Oswald Stanmore. Like Hemmysby, both were guildsmen.'

'Rougham said Oswald died of marsh fever . . .'

'But Rougham is not a good *medicus*, and you do not trust his opinion,' finished Michael.

'I will quiz him about it today. Again.'

'Do. Meanwhile, I dislike the notion that someone might be using Hemmysby to mislead us, and I will not let him be buried amid rumours of dishonesty and suicide. I want his name cleared.'

'So do I, but how will you go about it?'

Michael looked up at him very slowly, and the physician was disconcerted by the haunted expression in his eyes. 'By asking you to look inside him.'

Bartholomew's jaw dropped. 'You want me to *dissect* Hemmysby?'

'Not dissect,' corrected Michael, distaste clear in his face.

161

'Just make a small incision to look for these telltale lesions. I do not expect you to . . . pull anything out.'

Bartholomew regarded him in alarm. 'But you have always said you would never permit such a procedure, yet here you are encouraging me to do it on a friend. In a church!'

Michael winced. 'If there was another way, I would take it, believe me. But I can think of none, and I will not see Hemmysby in a suicide's grave – which is where he will go unless we prove his innocence. Thelnetham will see to that.'

'He will. But I cannot do what you ask, Brother. Hemmysby would not have liked it.'

'I disagree. He said not two days ago that he approved of anatomical studies, and I am sure he would rather suffer a little judicial slicing than lie in unconsecrated ground for eternity.'

'Looking inside him might – *might* – disclose whether he swallowed poison, but not whether he did it himself or was given it by someone else. Thus a dissection will not provide you with the answers you want, and nor will it save Hemmysby from an anonymous hole outside the town gates.'

'Perhaps,' conceded Michael. 'But it would give us a place to start.'

Bartholomew was surprised by the depth of his disinclination to do what Michael asked, especially as he had always championed dissection as an enlightened way to learn more about the mysteries of the human body. He shook his head. 'I will not do it, Brother. Not on Hemmysby.'

Michael made an irritated sound at the back of his throat. 'Why not? You have been itching to try it for years, but the moment I give you my blessing, you baulk. Where lies the problem?'

Bartholomew did not want to admit the truth, which was that he was sometimes assailed with the uncomfortable sense that God did not approve of what he did to the dead in the name of justice, and that weighing in with knives and forceps was likely to make the feeling a lot worse. He hedged.

'I have no training in the art. Watching once or twice is not the same as being taught how to do it properly. I am not qualified.'

'It cannot be that different from all the illicit surgery you conduct. Indeed, I imagine it will be a sight easier, as Hemmysby is unlikely to move.'

'But he was a friend, Brother,' said Bartholomew wretchedly. 'It would not be right.'

'What is not right is failing to do all in our power to clear his name and ensure he lies in the grave he deserves. I am not happy with desecration either, but I am prepared to set aside my aversion for the sake of justice. And if you care anything for Hemmysby, you will agree.'

Bartholomew was acutely unhappy. 'There must be a better way . . .'

'If there is, then I am all ears. If not, please make a start. I shall stand guard outside – we cannot have anyone walking in on you, and it will relieve me of the obligation to watch.'

When Michael had gone, Bartholomew stood motionless, looking at the body that lay before him as he tried to make sense of the whirlwind of conflicting emotions that raged within him. He had thought for years that dissection was the only way to establish accurate causes of death, but now he had permission to put his beliefs into practice, he was nervous, hesitant and afraid.

Yet at the same time, Michael was right: Hemmysby deserved to be exonerated, and an internal examination would provide a place to start. Heart thumping, he took a scalpel and made an incision. It was easier than he had anticipated, and once it was done, the intellectual part of his mind took over. He was able to disregard the fact that he was looking inside a friend, and concentrate on what he had learned at Salerno. It did not take him long to do what was necessary or to stitch up the holes he had made.

When all was done, and Hemmysby was lying decently in a clean robe, Bartholomew washed his hands in a jug of water and went outside. He found Michael looking pale and furtive.

'I do not want to hear anything other than what you found,' said the monk in a low voice. 'I have been praying, to ask if what we are doing is right, but the only reply has been a resounding silence. I almost ran back inside to stop you, but the thought of Hemmysby's eternal repose kept me rooted here among these graves.'

Bartholomew slumped down next to him, oddly exhausted now the deed was done. 'He *was* poisoned. The signs are identical to those I saw in Salerno. The toxin then was a substance called *dormirella*, from the Latin for sleep, and I suspect the same one was used here. It contains many potent ingredients, including realgar, dwale and hemlock, which are deadly, as you know.'

Michael regarded him askance. 'I know no such thing! And what are dwale and realgar? I have never heard of them.'

'Dwale is belladonna, and realgar is a reddish mineral used for dyeing cloth, tanning leather—'

'Enough! I do not need an alchemy lesson.' Michael swallowed hard. 'I do not know whether to be smug that I was right or appalled that something so terrible has happened. Did he suffer?'

'I imagine he just felt increasingly sluggish until he was overwhelmed with the need to sleep – hence the name *dormirella.* He may have been a little dizzy or feverish, and there may have been a slight burning in the throat, but this is a toxin that kills its victims quietly and without a fuss.'

'Thank God for small mercies.' Michael crossed himself. 'How long does it take to work?'

'It depends on the dose, which I have no way of determining.'

'And there is nothing to say whether he swallowed it accidentally or otherwise?'

'The contents of his stomach suggest it was probably in some cake. Thus it was unlikely to have been suicide – he would have swallowed it straight from the bottle if it had been self-murder.'

'Cake?' cried Michael, shocked all over again. 'What kind of cake?'

'One with dried fruit in it, although I cannot be more specific, I am afraid. I suppose I could take a sample to—'

'No!' Michael raised a hand to stop him. 'I am sure we can manage without molesting him further. However, we can certainly dismiss accidental poisoning. Such a substance is unlikely to fall into food by mistake, which means it was put there deliberately.'

'Yes, probably. So he was murdered, which means he can go in the churchyard. At least we have done that much for him.'

Michael closed his eyes, trying to push his continuing disquiet to the back of his mind. 'So who wants Hemmysby blamed for stealing the Stanton Hutch, and dead so he cannot deny it? Someone from Michaelhouse? His students liked him, but he earned the displeasure of others for backing Thelnetham in his feud with William. And our College is currently full of strangers . . .'

'I hope you are wrong.' Bartholomew hated the notion of a killer in their home.

'We need to locate the generous soul who gave him cake. There was none in his room – I would have noticed – so he must have eaten it at the post-debate refreshments.' He regarded the physician in sudden alarm. 'Lord! I hope there are no more victims among our theologians.'

'If so, you would have heard about them by now.'

'True. Now what about Knyt? I doubt Rougham, Meryfeld

and Lawrence are capable of telling the difference between a natural attack and the insidious effects of this sly toxin.'

That had already occurred to Bartholomew, along with the fact that Potmoor had been in the Knyt house shortly before its owner had died – and Potmoor was the man whom Edith suspected of poisoning her husband. He shrugged at Michael's question.

'It is impossible to know without looking inside him.'

Michael grimaced. 'It is one thing anatomising Hemmysby, safe in the knowledge that no one will ever find out, but another altogether to do it to a wealthy merchant. It would be discovered, and you would be denounced as a warlock.'

'Then how will we learn the truth?'

Michael spread his hands. 'Simple – you listed the symptoms that Hemmysby would have suffered as the potion worked. If our other victims were similarly affected, then we can infer that they were fed *dormirella*, too. It should not be difficult. Knyt had a wife, servants and *medici* who watched him in his final hours, while Oswald had Edith, Agatha and Rougham.'

'Perhaps we should include Elvesmere in our enquiries, too. The wound in his back was not instantly fatal, as I said, and his death has puzzled me from the start. He was also a guildsman, like Oswald, Knyt and Hemmysby.'

'You mean he was knifed, but when that did not kill him, he was made to drink poison?'

'Or he drank poison, but it took too long to work, so his killer stabbed him. So how shall we go about unravelling this muddle? By asking Rougham to describe Oswald's death?'

Michael patted his arm. 'I understand his fate is the most important to you. However, I suggest we start with Hemmysby, by finding witnesses who saw him at the debate. Next we shall see what we can learn about Knyt's last hours. And if we run into Rougham, we shall see what he can tell us about Oswald.'

Bartholomew smiled ruefully. 'This is the point where I usually tell you that I am too busy with patients and teaching. But Oswald and Hemmysby deserve the truth.'

'So do Knyt and Elvesmere,' said Michael soberly.

Before they began their enquiries, they were obliged to report their findings to Langelee. The Master was no stranger to violent death, and Bartholomew knew for a fact that he had been responsible for more than a few himself while in the employ of the Archbishop of York, but he still paled when he heard what they had discovered.

'How do you know it was *dormirella*?' The way the name tripped off his tongue suggested he was more familiar with it than was appropriate for the head of a Cambridge College. 'I thought that was undetectable.'

'Not to a physician,' replied Michael smoothly.

'Nonsense. It leaves no visible marks . . . Oh, God! Bartholomew looked inside him! I *knew* it was only a matter of time before his ghoulish curiosity would get the better of him.'

'We needed the truth,' said Michael defensively.

'But how will you reply when people ask how you have managed to detect the undetectable?' Langelee sounded appalled and angry in equal measure. 'I absolutely forbid you to tell the truth. You will have to lie. Say it was narcissus poisoning, which leaves a rash.'

Bartholomew regarded him askance. 'How do you know?'

Langelee ignored the question. 'If word gets out that you anatomised a corpse, we shall all be decried as sorcerers. Damn it, Bartholomew! Why could you not restrain yourself?'

'It was under my orders,' said Michael curtly. 'And we had no choice. If we had done nothing, Hemmysby would be buried under a cloud of suspicion, and the killer would be laughing at us. Do you want that?'

'No, of course not.' Langelee fought down his

exasperation and became practical. 'You must find the villain as soon as possible. It will be catastrophic if our students decide they do not feel safe here and demand their fees back. You are both excused College duties until the matter is resolved. However, I can only grant you this freedom until the beginning of term.'

'Next Tuesday,' mused Michael. 'Five days. Let us hope that is enough.'

The first place Michael and Bartholomew went after leaving College was St Mary the Great, to ask Chancellor Tynkell whether he had noticed Hemmysby at the debate. It took longer than usual to reach the church because they kept meeting people they knew – Eyer and Meryfeld, Warden Shropham of King's Hall, and Weasenham, the University Stationer. Bartholomew, uncomfortable, after Langelee's reaction, with what he had done to Hemmysby, could not meet their eyes, and mumbled shifty responses to their friendly hails.

'Would you like a banner saying you have done something untoward?' asked Michael. 'Even that would be more discreet than this abjectly guilty behaviour.'

'I should not have done it,' said Bartholomew wretchedly. 'Perhaps there are good reasons why the Church frowns on the practice. It felt wrong – like sacrilege.'

'Rank superstition! God gave you your skills for a reason, and He would be disappointed if you were prepared to let a killer go free, just for the want of a few judicious slits.'

Bartholomew might have been comforted had he thought the monk believed what he said, but he could tell the words were empty – Michael was also wrestling with his conscience over the matter. However, all thoughts of dissection flew from his head when he saw Edith, who was looking pale, tired and older than her years.

'Is it Richard again?' he asked, concerned.

She rolled her eyes. 'He took the chest containing

Oswald's personal documents, the one I found half-burned in the garden, although no one seems to know how it came to be there – and hid it, so I had to order him to give it back. He refused, and we both said things we shall probably regret. In the end, he all but hurled it at me before storming out.'

'Why does he want to keep it from you?' asked Michael, while Bartholomew clenched his fists at his sides, a wave of anger washing through him at his nephew's boorish behaviour.

'Because he thinks we should respect Oswald's privacy. But I have uncovered several unpaid bills, and another instance where a customer was overcharged. It is incumbent on me, as Oswald's heir, to make good on these . . . oversights.'

Bartholomew glanced at her ashen face, and knew she was beginning to understand more than was comfortable about the way her husband had run his business. Richard, of course, would prefer to remain in blissful ignorance, taking the lawyerly view that he could not amend what he did not know was wrong. Both scholars set about trying to raise her spirits, but although she was slightly more cheerful when they parted ways, Bartholomew suspected it would not be long before she was cast down again, if not by reading Oswald's documents, then by Richard's shabby antics.

He and Michael were just passing St Michael's Church when they met Julitta. Surgeon Holm was not with her for once, and she looked especially pretty in a green kirtle with gold embroidery. Bartholomew's heart swelled with affection for her, which went some way to easing the ache caused by Edith's unhappiness, his concern for his wayward nephew, and his continuing unease over Hemmysby.

'You are a member of the Guild of Saints,' said Michael, after they had exchanged warm greetings – very warm on Bartholomew's part. 'What can you tell us about Felbrigge?'

'Your Junior Proctor?' asked Julitta, startled by the

question out of the blue. 'I barely knew him, Brother. He tended to spurn anyone he thought would not be useful to him.'

'He did not think your friendship was worth cultivating?' asked Michael, surprised. 'But you are wealthy, and therefore have a voice in Guild politics.'

'Not as loud a voice as people like Mayor Heslarton, Mistress Mortimer, John and Hugo Potmoor, the Frevill clan, and the Fellows of Winwick,' replied Julitta. 'And Knyt, Hemmysby and Oswald Stanmore when they were still alive.'

'When they were still alive,' echoed Michael. 'But they are dead, along with Elvesmere and Felbrigge himself. That makes *five* guildsmen gone within a few weeks of each other. Have there been any rumours about that? Any hint that something odd is unfolding?'

Julitta regarded him in astonishment. 'Surely you do not think there is a connection? How could there be, when three died of natural causes, one was shot, and the other was stabbed?'

'We know Felbrigge was unpopular,' said Bartholomew, unwilling to burden her with their suspicions. 'But what about the others?'

'Knyt was loved by everyone, while Stanmore was a hero among the poor for his unstinting munificence. Elvesmere was also quietly generous, as was poor Hemmysby.'

'I was sorry to learn you were burgled,' said Michael, launching into another subject. 'Your husband complained bitterly to me about it yesterday.'

Julitta sighed. 'Poor Will. He has never been the victim of a crime before, and it unsettled him badly. The culprit made a terrible mess in his workshop.'

'Workshop?' asked Michael uncertainly. 'Why would a surgeon have one of those?'

'He performs very little cautery these days, and spends most of his time making medicines.' Julitta smiled

170

indulgently. 'His pill for gout is almost ready, although his paste for whitening teeth suffered a serious setback when the thief stole some of his key ingredients.'

Bartholomew regarded her uneasily. 'Not a substance called *dormirella?* It cannot be used for whitening teeth – at least, not sensibly – but Holm might have had it for another purpose.'

'He does use *dormirella* in his tooth-paste,' said Julitta, a little coolly. 'It is perfectly safe if you know what you are doing, and Will has a rare talent with such matters.'

'Right,' said Bartholomew flatly. 'So did the thief steal some from him?'

'I believe so.' She started to add more, stopped, then spoke in a gabble. 'Signor Nerli. I was walking past Winwick Hall the other day, and I saw him practising his swordplay with Potmoor in the yard. He was far more competent than is respectable for a scholar, and he may well have other sinister talents – like a familiarity with compounds that have Italian-sounding names.'

'He might,' agreed Michael. 'And I had better find out just how friendly he is with Potmoor.'

The expression on Julitta's face remained troubled. 'Nerli is not the only Winwick scholar who worries me. I like Master Lawrence very much, but Will tells me that he killed Queen Isabella with incompetence – that he did not retire to dedicate the rest of his life to teaching, but because he was ousted from his post by the King.'

'Typical Oxford man,' muttered Michael. 'I am not surprised that Lawrence—'

'Spiteful gossip,' interrupted Bartholomew shortly. 'You should not believe it.'

Julitta nodded, although doubt remained in her eyes. 'Speaking of Will, you had better not come for our usual evening tomorrow, Matt. He cannot visit Knyt, as he usually does on Fridays, so he has offered to sing to me instead. I have not yet heard his voice, given that he has suffered so many sore throats since our wedding day, but I am sure it will be beautiful.'

The surgeon was marginally less easy on the ears than a braying donkey, and it was testament to his skills as a liar that he had managed to conceal it from his wife for so many months. Bartholomew had no doubt whatsoever that an excuse would be invented for the following evening, thus allowing Holm to escape with his musical reputation intact. The man was nothing if not resourceful, and Bartholomew thought Julitta a fool for swallowing so many of his falsehoods.

'Perhaps he should audition for the Michaelhouse Choir,' he said, uncharacteristically acidic because he resented losing what was the highlight of his week.

'I do not need more members, thank you,' said Michael in alarm. 'It is already bigger than ever before, and I shall struggle to conduct it if it grows any further.'

'Gracious,' said Julitta, wide-eyed. 'I must remember to stand well back when they perform at the beginning of term ceremony. So as to appreciate the quality of their performance,' she added quickly when Michael's eyes narrowed.

They made their farewells, and the scholars resumed their walk to St Mary the Great. Bartholomew was thoughtful, mulling over the possibility that Holm's *dormirella* had killed Hemmysby, along with the fact that so many members of the Guild of Saints were dead. He also pondered Nerli, a man with odd skills for a scholar, whose qualifications Elvesmere had questioned. Had he fabricated them, or did the University at Salerno really award Masters of Civil Law?

'You play with fire, Matt,' said Michael. 'Enjoying brazen assignations with another man's wife. You are fortunate the Senior Proctor is your friend, or you might have found yourself fined for inappropriate relationships. Women *are* forbidden to scholars, you know.'

172

'We meet to practise her reading.'

'You can call it what you like,' said Michael. 'But I have seen the way you look at each other. However, you should watch yourself, given that her husband has access to poisons. If he sends you a cake, try it out on Goodwyn before eating any yourself.'

'I was thinking much the same. Not about experimenting on Goodwyn, but that Holm might be responsible for killing Hemmysby. They were both guildsmen, and now we learn that he has a supply of *dormirella*.'

'You want him to be guilty because you love Julitta.'

'Nonsense,' said Bartholomew stiffly. 'He was probably never burgled at all, and invented the tale to explain why some of his supply is missing. Doubtless, he is afraid that you will ask everyone to account for any *dormirella* they have bought in the past.'

'You had better hope not,' said Michael drily. 'Because if so, it means he predicted that we would learn Hemmysby was poisoned, and as *dormirella* is supposed to be undetect-able, he will know what we did for answers.'

Bartholomew gaped at him in horror. 'He will accuse me of defiling Hemmysby, and one look at the corpse will prove him right! No one will care that he stands accused of murder, because what I did will be considered worse.'

'Then I suggest we visit Eyer, and find out who has bought *dormirella* recently. If Holm is the only one, we shall arrest him before he can blare any nasty allegations. However, while I understand him wanting *you* dead, I do not see why he should have taken against our other victims. What would his motive be?'

'To win a louder voice in the Guild of Saints? They deal with enormous sums of money, and he probably hankers after the power such influence will give him.'

Michael regarded him askance. 'Holm does not care about the kind of "power" that accrues from giving money to worthy causes. Love is playing havoc with your reason, my friend! What will Matilde say when she returns to find that your heart belongs to another man's wife?'

'She may never come,' said Bartholomew shortly, disliking the reminder of his confused feelings. 'And even if she does, I am not sure we could be happy together.'

The Chancellor had an office in St Mary the Great, although it was smaller and less well appointed than his Senior Proctor's. He was busy when they arrived, almost buried under a mound of parchment. Students in holy orders needed dispensations from their priories, abbeys or convents before they could enrol at the University, while others needed licences from bishops. All had to be checked and acknowledged, and it was tedious work. Michael had long since delegated the task to Tynkell on the grounds that he himself had more interesting matters to attend.

Tynkell was sitting back massaging his neck when the monk walked in. He had an unfortunate aversion to personal hygiene, which meant his company was often disagreeable. There was something peculiar about his physiognomy, too, and Michaelhouse's students had once started a rumour that he was pregnant. Bartholomew knew what made the Chancellor different, but steadfastly refused to tell.

'Poor Hemmysby,' Tynkell sighed, when asked what he remembered about the debate. 'He argued with great eloquence that the property and jurisdiction of friars are free gifts from God, and was so persuasive that even the monastics applauded his thesis. It is a great pity that he died before he could bask in his success.'

'Did his opinions offend anyone?' asked Bartholomew.

'Not his opinions, but he was ruthless with those whose minds are less incisive than his own. A number of inexperienced, inept or careless speakers fell prey to his impeccable logic. And no one likes being made to look a fool in front of his peers.'

'So a number of people might have meant him harm?'

'Harm in a future debate, perhaps – to maul him, as he did them – but I cannot imagine anyone wishing him physical hurt. We are scholars, not politicians.'

'Did you see anyone give him a piece of cake?' asked Michael.

Tynkell regarded him balefully. 'You may not have left me much in the way of authority, but I have enough to prevent scholars from eating in church. However, there were refreshments in the vestry afterwards, provided by Winwick Hall. You must remember, Brother – you were there.'

'Only long enough to grab the merest morsel. I had to go to choir practice.'

Prudently, Tynkell passed no remark on either statement. 'It was kind of Winwick to provide the food yesterday. The Guild of Saints obliged on the first day, but refused to do it a second time, lest we debated until Christmas, and they were compelled to feed us every night.'

'From what I saw, that was not an unreasonable concern,' muttered Michael.

'But Winwick was caught out by the number of scholars who appeared for the victuals, especially as many had not bothered with the debate, and only wanted the food.' Tynkell did not look at Michael. 'So several guildsmen came to their rescue. De Stannell sent wine, Meryfeld marchpane, Eyer nuts and Edith Stanmore some magnificent fruitcake.'

'My sister?' Bartholomew was alarmed. 'And Hemmysby ate some?'

'We all did,' replied Tynkell. 'There must have been two hundred of us, and we all enjoyed her baking. Hemmysby stood in my little group in the vestry. I am fairly sure he took some cake. He had no wine, nuts or marchpane, though. There was not enough of the first, and he did not like the second and third.'

'Who else was in this group?' asked Michael, while

Bartholomew remembered that Hemmysby often mentioned his aversion to nuts and anything containing them.

'William and Thelnetham, who spent the time bickering over some tract one of them had penned; Rougham, who did not attend the debate and only came for the food; and Illesy and his Fellows, along with that loutish student who acts as a guide for Bon – Uyten. He hails from John Winwick's home village, you know, and he has taken the name to—'

'When did these refreshments finish?' interrupted Michael curtly, not interested in irrelevancies.

'About halfway through your choir practice, which we could hear quite clearly from here. I was vexed because everyone left me to do the clearing up alone, even the Winwick men, who used the excuse that they were expecting a visit from you. I pointed out that you would not come as long as the choir was singing, but to no avail.'

'I did visit,' said Michael. 'They were settled in their *parlura* by then.'

'A few scholars chatted outside the door while I laboured,' Tynkell went on. 'I sent them packing when I finished. It was dark, so I cannot tell you who they were. However, one was definitely Hemmysby, because he stumbled over something and we exchanged words about it.'

'What did he say?'

'That he felt unwell, but it was a passing remark, and I did not know he was suffering the beginnings of a fatal fever – obviously, or I would have tried to help him. I last saw him walking up the High Street alone. I assumed he was going home.'

Michael looked at Bartholomew. 'You were right in what you suggested last night: he must have felt too ill to reach Michaelhouse, so he headed for our church instead. But he could not open the door and he died in the graveyard.'

Tynkell crossed himself. 'At least he breathed his last on holy ground.'

'That is some consolation, I suppose,' said Michael bleakly.

'What now, Brother?' asked Bartholomew, as they stood outside St Mary the Great. 'And please do not say we should visit Edith and demand to know why she poisoned her cake. If she were the culprit, there would be two hundred casualties, not just one – you included.'

'I did not have any fruitcake,' said Michael soberly. 'Warden Shropham cornered me to gripe about Winwick Hall, and it had all gone by the time I managed to escape. I had to make do with a few scraps of marchpane and a handful of nuts. And wine, of course. So the poison was not in those. Or at least, it was not in the few morsels that I managed to snag.'

'There was no wine inside Hemmysby,' said Bartholomew. 'I would have smelled it. And Tynkell was right: Hemmysby disliked nuts, so would not have taken them or the march-pane. However, this does not mean that Edith killed him. Perhaps he had cake twice yesterday – the poisoned one *and* what he took in the vestry.'

'How? He was at the debate all day, and Tynkell would not have let him devour pastries in the church.' Michael was thoughtful. 'How long does *dormirella* take to work?'

'It is immediate. However, what you really want to know is: when would he have noticed? And the answer is that it depends how much he was given, which is beyond my skills to determine.'

'Well, we know *when* he had it. The debate finished at dusk, and Tynkell has just told us that the following refresh-ments were over halfway through choir practice. That means Hemmysby ate the poison between seven o'clock and half-past eight.'

'He lingered afterwards, chatting. He told Tynkell he was unwell, but he could not have been too ill or he would have asked for help. I imagine the accolades of admiring colleagues kept him lively, but once he was alone, he began to feel lethargic. He probably decided to rest at St Michael's on the way home, but when the latch stuck, he collapsed and slipped into unconsciousness.'

'So our first duty is to speak to the others who were with him in the vestry – William, Thelnetham, the men from Winwick Hall and Rougham. And we are in luck, because here comes Rougham now.'

The Gonville physician had treated himself to a new gown for the beginning of term; it fitted snugly around his ample paunch. He pointed across the road as he approached, to where Holm and Hugo were just entering Eyer's shop.

'Those two are always together,' he remarked. 'Almost as much as you and Julitta.'

Bartholomew felt himself blush. 'I do not—'

'Yes, you do,' countered Rougham. 'And it is reckless to cavort with the wife of the town's only surgeon. He might take deadly revenge if you are ever in need of his services.'

'Have you heard that Hemmysby is dead?' asked Michael, tactfully changing the subject. When Rougham nodded, he continued. 'Tynkell tells me that you were in the group which enjoyed refreshments with him after the debate. Did he seem ill to you then?'

'He said he had a headache, but that is not surprising, considering he was shut inside a stuffy church all day, listening to clamouring voices. What killed him? A seizure?'

'Yes,' lied Michael. 'But its suddenness has perplexed us, so we are trying to learn more about his last hours.'

Rougham thought carefully. 'I did not attend the debate, but in the vestry afterwards, it was clear that he was delighted with his performance – positively glowing. Perhaps he died because he was so pleased with himself.'

It was a ridiculous assertion and to avoid saying so, Bartholomew moved abruptly to Stanmore. 'I have been thinking about my brother-in-law's death—'

'What, *again?*' groaned Rougham. 'How many more times must I repeat myself? He was dying by the time I arrived. I wish I could have saved him, but some cases are beyond even my superior skills, and there was nothing I could do. I am sorry for Edith, but these things happen.'

'You said it was marsh fever. Are you sure?'

'Yes, because I suffer from it myself.'

'Did he say anything when you came to his bedside?'

'Not to me, but he talked to Edith about his will. However, as I have told you several times already, I met him on Bridge Street shortly before his Guild meeting and we exchanged greetings. He was not his usual cheerful self, but we all have days when we wish we had stayed in bed, and I thought nothing of it. With hindsight, it is obvious that he was ailing then.'

'What else do you remember about that discussion?'

'For God's sake, Bartholomew! It was ten weeks ago, and we only spoke for a moment. I just recall that he seemed tired and dispirited. That is all.' Rougham regarded him sharply. 'I hope you do not think there was anything unto-ward about his demise.'

'Oswald went to another meeting before going to the guildhall,' said Bartholomew, disinclined to answer. 'I do not suppose he mentioned that to you, did he?'

'No. However, I recommend you stay out of his affairs. He was not always scrupulous, and you may put yourself in danger. I know this is not something you want to hear, but it is true.'

'You think he was doing something unethical at this prior meeting?'

'Now you are putting words in my mouth. I spoke only to warn you that if you dig, you might not like what you uncover. Leave well alone, and let your family continue to honour his memory.'

'How do you know he was unscrupulous?' pressed Bartholomew. 'Did someone tell you?'

'It is common knowledge, man,' said Rougham, exasperated. 'Moreover, I saw him with Potmoor several times, heads together as they negotiated. And Potmoor is a criminal.'

'Edith believes that Oswald met Potmoor the night he died.'

'Perhaps he did. It would certainly explain his lack of cheer – I would not be easy after enduring the company of such an evil creature either. I am glad Lawrence is Potmoor's physician, not me.'

'Yet you attended Potmoor when he thought he was dying.'

'So did you,' flashed Rougham. 'I did it for money. Hugo enticed me there with the promise of a very princely sum, and I have a half-built College chapel. However, to return to Stanmore, Potmoor was not the only scoundrel with whom he associated.'

'Who else?'

'Guildsmen – Mayor Heslarton, de Stannell, Weasenham, the Frevill clan. All are wealthy, and did not become so by being gentle. None are men with whom you should trifle, especially if you intend to prove he was murdered. No, do not deny it – that is why you are asking me these questions. Edith has never been happy with my diagnosis, and she has persuaded you to her way of thinking.'

'But you are certain that marsh fever was the cause?'

'Quite sure. And I shall call for your resignation if you apply for permission to dig him up and prove me wrong. I know you have been itching to expand your skill with corpses, but anatomy is unethical, distasteful, and those who indulge in it are cursed by God.'

There was little that could be said after such a remark, and Bartholomew was glad when Cynric arrived with a summons from a patient, allowing him to escape. Michael chatted to the Gonville physician a little while longer, then continued his enquiries alone, questioning witness after witness about Hemmysby's behaviour at the debate, then interviewing the residents of St Michael's Lane about the theft of the Stanton Hutch. Despite his best efforts, he learned nothing useful. Tired and glum, he revived his flagging energies by inveigling an invitation to dine at the Dominican Priory. As he emerged, he met Master Lawrence, who had been for a stroll along the Hadstock Way.

'Why did you leave your lucrative post at Court?' he demanded without preamble. He disliked the Oxford-trained physician, and failed to understand why Bartholomew seemed to enjoy his sickly-sweet company.

Lawrence smiled seraphically. 'To give younger men a stab at the job, and to repay God for His goodness by dedicating the rest of my life to teaching.'

'Very noble,' murmured Michael. 'You were one of the last people to see Hemmysby alive. What can you tell me about the refreshments in the vestry at St Mary the Great?'

'I saw him eat some fruitcake, but he refused nuts and marchpane, and there was not enough wine. Have you solved Elvesmere's murder yet, Brother? Nerli tells me that Potmoor is your prime suspect, but I doubt he is responsible. He saw the face of God when Bartholomew raised him from the dead, and such men tend to be wary of sinning.'

'Is that so?' said Michael flatly.

CHAPTER 8

It was late afternoon before Bartholomew was free again. Irritated by the encounter with Lawrence, Michael took him straight to Winwick Hall, where they began the tortuous business of persuading the porter that they had legitimate business inside. Jekelyn was encouraged in his insolence by Uyten, the thick-eared student who acted as Bon's guide. The lad was newly missing his front teeth, and Bartholomew recalled that Goodwyn had mentioned them being punched out during a skirmish in the Griffin.

'I hail from our founder's birthplace,' he lisped, although neither Bartholomew nor Michael had asked. 'He invited me to study with Master Bon, as he believes I shall be a great asset to him at Court one day. He has promised to make me a College prefect next year.'

'The nepotism begins,' murmured Michael. 'Cambridge will soon be full of men whom John Winwick wants groomed to support him.'

Bartholomew stopped in surprise as he entered the courtyard. It heaved with students, and he could tell by the amount of baggage they had brought that most were wealthy. They were moving into the dormitory on the top floor of the hall, and there was a gale of laughter when a stair collapsed under the press of feet, sending one lad tumbling into the arms of his cronies.

'We have forty students already,' gloated Uyten. 'And Illesy plans to take even more.'

'Where will they all sleep?' asked Bartholomew, stunned.

Uyten shot him a superior look. 'In the hall and the Fellows' rooms. We have lots of space, and will soon be bigger than all the other Colleges combined. Moreover, our founder has pledged extra money for accommodation next year.'

'Heavens!' exclaimed Michael, watching Uyten go over to issue bullying orders to a handful of arrogant young men who clearly resented the impertinence. 'King's Hall told me today that they fear losing their status as largest and wealthiest College. I told them they had nothing to worry about. Perhaps I was wrong.'

'Or perhaps you weren't,' said Bartholomew wryly. 'I am sure the hall roof was straighter when I was last here, and you just saw that stair give way. Maybe the place will tumble about their ears before its members' ambitions are realised.'

'The building is just settling. The ground is soft, and all structures shift when they are raised in this part of the town. You should see the angle on Gonville's chapel.'

'There is Eyer,' said Bartholomew, seeing the pink-faced apothecary emerge from the hall and weave his way through the students. 'We can ask how much *dormirella* Holm bought.'

'Here,' said Eyer, dropping a flask of poppy juice into Bartholomew's bag as he passed. 'Young Aungel told me that Goodwyn used all yours in an experiment, and no physician should be without such a basic weapon in his armoury.'

'But I cannot pay—' began Bartholomew.

'Consider it a gift for the poor.' Eyer held up his hand when Bartholomew began to ask his question. 'Later, Matt. Bon was in urgent need of a poultice for his eyes, and I had to abandon my shop to bring it. Come to see me when you have finished here. Perhaps we can dine together.'

'Thank you,' said Michael, although the flash of surprise in Eyer's eyes said the monk had not been included in the invitation. 'We shall be there shortly.'

*   *   *

Provost Illesy and three of his Fellows – Ratclyf was missing – were in the *parlura*, enjoying warmed wine and Lombard slices. As these were Michael's favourites, he helped himself. Illesy's eyebrows shot up in surprise at the liberty, Nerli scowled, and Lawrence smiled affably. Bon sensed something was happening, and turned his head this way and that as he attempted to determine what.

'It is unmannerly to foist yourself on another College and start scoffing its comestibles,' said Nerli in his oddly accented Latin. 'Or is such behaviour encouraged in Michaelhouse?'

'He is welcome to share.' Lawrence smiled sweetly, showing red lips through his white beard. 'So is Matthew. Come, both of you, and sit by the fire. There is a nasty nip in the air today.'

'Have you caught Elvesmere's killer?' asked Illesy, leaning back in his chair and drumming beringed fingers on the table. 'I hope so. It has now been three days since we had the terrible shock of finding his body in the latrine.'

'I know,' said Michael, equally curt. 'And considerable progress has been made.'

'Good,' said Nerli, although Bartholomew thought the response lacked enthusiasm.

'You asked us to tell you if we remembered anything else that might help,' said Lawrence. 'So I have been thinking about Elvesmere's last evening. He complained of a headache. Perhaps *that* is why he left the College and ended up stabbed – he went out in search of fresh air.'

'How do you know he was killed outside the College?' pounced Michael. Lawrence frowned, but had no answer, so Michael asked his next question. 'Where is Ratclyf?'

'Ill,' explained Nerli. 'He drank too much wine last night, and is suffering the consequences.'

'He indulged himself with claret because he mourns

Elvesmere,' said Lawrence, shooting the Florentine an admonishing glance.

'Actually, he was more distressed about the fact that Hemmysby mauled him at the debate,' countered Nerli. 'He did not comport himself very skilfully, and was ashamed of his performance.'

'As well he should be,' muttered Illesy sourly. 'He should not have opened his mouth if he had nothing intelligent to say.'

'Elvesmere,' prompted Nerli. '*What* progress have you made exactly, Brother?'

'Quite a bit,' hedged the monk. 'But we shall resolve the matter much more quickly if you answer a few questions. Shall we begin with the Guild of Saints? I understand you are all members.'

'It is a perk of being Fellows here,' explained Illesy, although with obvious irritation that he was to be interrogated yet again. 'It has some lovely people, but also some dreadful villains.'

'Your old employer, Potmoor, being the greatest of them,' put in Nerli acidly. 'And Stanmore being another.'

'You knew Oswald?' asked Bartholomew, cutting across Illesy's indignant objection to the remark. 'I thought he died before you arrived.'

'We came a month before he passed away,' explained Lawrence. 'Winwick Hall did not exist then, of course, but our founder wanted us here anyway, to learn the lie of the land.'

'Did you see him the night he died?' asked Bartholomew. 'It happened not long after a Guild function.'

Nerli yawned. 'I do not recall. It was weeks ago now.'

'I remember,' said Bon sullenly. 'He accused me of taking a second goblet of wine before others had had their first. How was I supposed to know who had drunk what when I cannot see? Then he blathered on about the high tax on foreign wool. It was boring.'

'He was explaining why he could not give the widows' fund more money,' said Lawrence, gently reproachful. 'The King increased excise on imports, so he had less available cash.'

'That was Knyt's fault,' said Nerli. 'Stanmore usually smuggled his supplies through the Fens, but Knyt found out and told the Sheriff. A reception committee was waiting when Stanmore's barge docked, so he was forced to pay his dues.'

'Oswald was not a smuggler,' said Bartholomew, although he spoke more from loyalty than conviction. Prudently, Michael changed the subject.

'After yesterday's debate, you chatted to the Chancellor, Rougham and—'

'What does this have to do with catching Elvesmere's killer?' demanded Nerli.

'I am not at liberty to say,' replied Michael loftily. 'It may adversely affect the outcome of my enquiries. However, I want to know whether Hemmysby ate cake from the same plate as you.'

'What an extraordinary question!' exclaimed Illesy. 'Why should we answer that?'

'The good Brother has told us why,' said Lawrence quietly. 'It is pertinent to his enquiries about Elvesmere. However, *I* cannot help. I never eat between meals, as it is bad for the digestion, so I did not notice who had what last night.'

'I cannot help either,' said Bon, turning his milky eyes towards the monk. 'I had lots of fruitcake, marchpane and nuts, but I could not see the platters, let alone tell you who ate from them. However, I objected to Hemmysby joining us. He attacked me viciously in front of the entire University, then had the audacity to say it was nothing personal.'

'It was not,' said Nerli. 'You just happen to have easily crushed views on apostolic poverty.'

'It was Bon's first time in the debating chamber,' said

Lawrence reprovingly. 'And Ratclyf's. Hemmysby should have been kinder to them both, and I told him so.'

'You argued with him?' asked Michael keenly.

'It was not an argument,' hedged Lawrence. 'More an exchange of opinions. However, as he then died of a seizure, perhaps ill health led him to take such pleasure in humiliating others.'

'I recall what Hemmysby ate,' said Illesy acidly. 'Three slices of cake, which was greedy. He said it was to make up for the fact that he refused the nuts and marchpane.'

'Your sister made those pastries, Matthew,' said Lawrence. 'They were very nice, and we are grateful for her support. When we offered to provide refreshments, we assumed it would just be for those in the church, but every scholar who was hungry promptly announced an intention to descend on us.'

'The debate ended very abruptly,' mused Illesy. 'We were taking it in turns to mind the food – we did not want to leave it unattended lest thieves struck. I had only been in the vestry for a few moments, but I poked my head out to see how the forum was going only to discover that Tynkell had declared it over – no summing up, no declaration of a winner, no vote of thanks to the participants. I was stunned.'

'He was almost flattened in the ensuing race for victuals,' added Bon. 'With Michaelhouse being the quickest off the mark. Does your Master not feed you?'

'Have you heard of a substance named *dormirella*?' asked Michael, declining to dignify the question with a response.

'Of course,' replied Nerli. 'Some of its active ingredients are used in tanning.'

'Are you intimately acquainted with the process of leather-making, then?' asked Michael.

'It is general knowledge,' replied the Florentine, although he blushed angrily, and his eyes became harder and blacker. 'And I am widely read.'

'Do your studies extend to the theory of swordplay?' asked Bartholomew, aiming to make the surly Florentine admit to frolicking with Potmoor.

Temper flashed in Nerli's eyes, but was quickly masked. '*Are* there books on the subject? I would not know. I have no interest in the matter.'

'So you do not practise your martial skills with Potmoor?'

Nerli gazed at him. 'I do not. What a ridiculous notion!'

Bartholomew was about to press the matter further when it occurred to him that Nerli might guess that it was Julitta who had mentioned it, and an interrogation might put her in danger. He desisted abruptly enough to make Nerli regard him with suspicion, but fortunately Michael was ready with another question.

'Does anyone here own any *dormirella?*'

'No,' replied the Florentine, meeting his eyes steadily. 'Why would we?'

'I have never even heard of it,' put in Lawrence.

'Really?' Bartholomew was surprised. 'I thought you would have come across it at some point in your career.'

'I do not have much use for poisons, Matthew.' Lawrence smiled serenely.

'If you have never heard of *dormirella*, how do you know it is a poison?' pounced Michael.

'Because Nerli said it is used in tanning,' replied Lawrence genially. 'And you do not employ mild substances in that grim and filthy business.'

'*I* would not know,' said Bon in distaste. '*I* remain aloof from such coarse matters.'

'So do I,' said Illesy. He stood. 'And now if you will excuse us, there have been too many thumps and crashes from the dormitory upstairs. It is time we supervised our new charges.'

*   *   *

188

'None of the Winwick men succeeded in removing themselves from my list of suspects,' said Michael, once they were outside. 'Indeed, Nerli's answers won him a place at the top. Meanwhile, Bon and Ratclyf were offended by Hemmysby's treatment of them at the debate, while Illesy is a close friend of Potmoor.'

'Lawrence is a good man, though,' said Bartholomew. 'I could not have helped with your investigation if he had not taken on some of my paupers.'

'I cannot agree, Matt. There is something about him that I do not like at all – a jarringly false note in that mask of amiability. And you know what is said about him and Queen Isabella. I imagine the tale is true, because what sort of man abandons a lucrative post at Court in order to teach law to a lot of ingrates?'

Bartholomew thought he was wrong, but did not want to argue. 'Illesy said they all took turns to guard the food, which means they all had the opportunity to poison Hemmysby's cake. But how could the culprit know that Hemmysby would be the one to eat it? Or do you think someone else was the intended victim?'

'It was Winwick Hall's food – its Fellows decided which plate went where. And let us not forget that none of them have an alibi for Elvesmere's murder. They claim they were asleep, but no one can prove it. They all have a motive for wanting him dead, as he offended every one of them with his caustic tongue.'

'Lawrence said Elvesmere had a headache, which could have been from eating *dormirella*.'

Michael was thoughtful. 'Much as it galls me to admit it, I am beginning to appreciate that anatomy has its uses. I shall arrange for you to spend a few moments alone with Elvesmere tonight, and you can find out whether he ate cake, too. Like Hemmysby.'

'No, Brother,' said Bartholomew firmly. 'Besides, I am

not sure it will be possible after so many days. These things liquefy, you know.'

Michael shuddered. 'Just do your best. However, if I ever have the misfortune to die, I do not want you in *my* innards. My stomach contents are my own affair, thank you.'

'I shall bear it in mind,' said Bartholomew, amused by the fact that the monk seemed to regard death as optional. 'We should visit Eyer now. Perhaps he will tell us that one of our suspects bought *dormirella* recently, and thus solve the case without the need for another dissection.'

'You are here at last,' beamed Eyer, his pink face breaking into a beam of pleasure as Bartholomew and Michael entered his shop. 'Good! I am ravenous.'

'What are we having?' asked Michael keenly.

'Snake,' replied the apothecary. 'There are many who shun reptile, but I find it a most wholesome meat. We shall have it with grass soup, which will set us up splendidly.'

'I have just remembered that we are expected at Michaelhouse,' gulped the monk. 'What a pity. Incidentally, it was good of you to contribute victuals to the debate yesterday. Most generous.'

Eyer gestured towards a large sack of cobnuts. 'I told the Winwick men to help themselves, and they sent a student around with a bowl. It was all I had available at such short notice, although I appreciate that the shells are a nuisance in polite company.'

'Hemmysby would not have eaten those, Brother,' whispered Bartholomew, when the apothecary went to baste the snakes that were roasting over the fire. 'Remember, he did not like nuts. Besides, they could not have been poisoned while they were in their shells. At least, not easily.'

'Do you have any *dormirella* for sale, Eyer?' called Michael, determined to learn at least something useful from the visit.

Eyer turned to purse his lips. '*Dormirella* contains a mixture of potent ingredients that includes realgar, dwale and hemlock. It is very dangerous, and not something I sell to non-medical professionals. Why do you want it, Brother? Perhaps I can suggest a less toxic alternative.'

'But you sell realgar, dwale and hemlock on their own?' pressed the monk.

Eyer regarded him warily before addressing Bartholomew. 'You know I do – you buy hemlock and dwale from me regularly. What is this about?'

'Has Holm bought *dormirella* at all?' asked Bartholomew.

'Last week,' replied Eyer, looking from one to the other anxiously. 'For his experiments with whitening teeth. Why do you want to know?'

'Have you sold any other poisons recently?' asked Michael, ignoring the question.

Eyer spread his hands in a shrug. 'What is a poison? Virtually anything can be harmful if used incorrectly. Or conversely, a potent herb can be rendered worthless by ignorance. Take Olivia Knyt, for example. She bought bryony root for her husband's colic, but instead of boiling it in wine for him to drink, she made it into a poultice that she put on his feet. Useless!'

Bartholomew regarded him uneasily. 'What are you saying? That she deliberately misused the seeds so that his illness would kill him?'

'No,' said Eyer, but so quickly that Bartholomew saw he had his doubts. 'I am just pointing out that laymen have an unfortunate habit of misapplying what they buy.'

'What about *dormirella?*' probed Michael. 'Olivia did not buy any of that, did she? Or realgar, hemlock or dwale?'

'Not from me, although they can be obtained quite easily in the alleys behind St Mary the Great. But let me check my records.' Eyer produced a roll of parchment, and ran his finger down the entries. 'Holm bought *dormirella*, but he is the only one since Easter. However, Edith Stanmore bought a lot of realgar last week. See her name here?'

'My sister?' asked Bartholomew in alarm.

Eyer nodded. 'Realgar is expensive, so there are not many requests for it. Other than that, no one except *medici* have bought the ingredients you mentioned.' He handed Michael the scroll. 'You can look for yourself if you do not believe me.'

'Why would Edith want realgar?' asked Bartholomew. His mouth was dry and he felt sick.

'I am not sure, although she has been complaining about the number of rats in her warehouse recently. It is not a solution I would employ, of course, but one can never predict the foibles of laymen. But why all these questions? Is there a problem?'

Unhappily, Bartholomew trailed after the monk to Milne Street. A servant conducted them to Edith's solar, where she was working on a heap of documents. There was a plate of freshly baked Lombard slices at her elbow, and Michael reached for one automatically. Then he recalled what had happened to Hemmysby, and jerked his hand back as though it had been burned.

'Michael has agreed to help me look into what happened to Oswald,' said Bartholomew quickly, seeing her puzzled frown and not wanting to tell her why they were there. He ignored the monk's astonishment at the claim – the boot had been on the other foot often enough.

Edith smiled wanly. 'Thank you, Brother. I shall always be grateful.'

Michael nodded to the untidy pile of deeds in front of her. 'Does Richard not help with that sort of thing?'

'These are the ones he wants to destroy,' she replied. 'Most are simple receipts of sale, but some require action by Oswald's heirs – me, mostly.'

She looked down at the table, and Bartholomew knew she was lying: she had uncovered yet more evidence of Stanmore's deviation from the straight and narrow.

'Richard tells me that he means to apply for a place at Winwick Hall,' said Michael. 'I confess I am surprised. He has never expressed an interest in scholarship before, and now he has inherited most of Oswald's money, he has no need to do anything so taxing.'

'He had a sharp mind when he was a lad,' said Edith softly. 'Perhaps immersing himself in books again will remind him that he does not need to be drunk or surrounded by dissipated cronies to enjoy himself.'

Bartholomew hated to see the pain in her eyes, and felt a surge of anger against his nephew. How could Richard put her through such torment when she was still steeped in grief?

'Eyer mentioned that you have a problem with rats,' said Michael, changing the subject to one that was obviously a relief for Edith but that made Bartholomew's stomach churn – especially when he recalled the apothecary's remark about laymen misusing what they bought. He did not want to hear that she added a pinch to dough in the hope of making it rise, or some such nonsense.

Edith nodded. 'Yes, the wretched things are everywhere this year.'

'He sold you realgar?'

'He did, but not for rats. Why would I use an expensive and not terribly reliable poison on them? There are far better remedies available. I bought it for dyeing cloth.'

'Of course!' blurted Bartholomew, closing his eyes in relief. 'I should have remembered! It yields an orange-red pigment.'

'Do you have any to hand?' pressed Michael. 'In the kitchen, perhaps?'

'In the kitchen?' echoed Edith in disbelief. 'It is a poison, Brother! I do not allow those in a place where food is prepared. It is locked in one of the outside store-rooms. However, if you want some, you will have to give me a very good reason, because it can be dangerous if used incorrectly.'

'We appreciated the cake you made for the post-debate refreshments yesterday,' said Michael, and his sombre expression made Bartholomew's stomach lurch again: the monk was not yet convinced that she was innocent. 'It was kind of you.'

She smiled. 'It was a delight to see them so heartily devoured. I made four of them, and all that was left at the end were crumbs.'

'Were all four the same? Or did you use different recipes?'

Edith was obviously mystified by the interrogation, but answered anyway. 'I made them all with butter, because I thought you might be there, and I know you prefer it to lard.'

'And how did they get to the church? Did you take them there yourself?'

'Yes, with Zachary. We delivered them to the vestry while the debate was still raging in the church, and then we came home. But why—'

'Was anyone in the vestry to receive them?'

Edith regarded him askance. 'Signor Nerli helped us unpack, but then Bon was called on to speak, so he hurried off to the nave to listen to him. Why are you asking all this?'

'The security of cakes is an important matter,' replied Michael gravely. 'They might have been stolen when they were unguarded. Then where would we have been?'

Edith laughed, a genuine, bubbling guffaw that Bartholomew had not heard since he had returned from Peterborough to find her a widow. 'You are incorrigible,

Brother! I thought for a moment that there was something terribly wrong.'

'No,' said Michael. 'Not here, at least.'

When Michael professed a keen interest in keeping things safe, Edith showed him the shed where she stored the more deadly substances that were used in the preparation of cloth. The only key was on a chain around her neck, and the lock was substantial. Records were kept of what was used when, and it quickly became apparent that her supply of realgar had not been tapped to kill anyone. When he and Michael were outside in the street, Bartholomew heaved a sigh of relief.

'Thank you, Brother,' he said sincerely.

'I was skilful,' said the monk immodestly. 'She never once guessed that I was assessing whether she was a killer.'

'Actually, for making her laugh.'

Michael frowned. 'Yes, but I hope the willingness with which she did so does not mean she considers me a glutton. I eat very little – just a crust here, and a scrap there. I just have heavy bones, which give the *appearance* of corpulence, although I would be as light as a feather without them.'

Bartholomew grinned at him, but then became serious. 'Unfortunately, her testimony does not help us with Hemmysby's poisoner. The vestry is open to the street as well as the church – anyone could have slipped in and tampered with the food after she and Zachary left, and Nerli abandoned his post to listen to Bon pontificate. And that leads again to the question of whether Hemmysby was the intended victim.'

'True. Is that Uyten racing towards us? He should slow down – if he falls on his face, he will lose what few teeth he has left.'

'There you are, Doctor Bartholomew,' the student

195

gasped. 'Master Lawrence sent me to find you. You must come to Winwick immediately.'

'Must he indeed?' said Michael coolly. 'And why is that, pray?'

'Because shortly after you left, Master Lawrence went to visit Ratclyf and found him very ill. He does not know what to do, and begs urgent assistance.'

Bartholomew set off at a run. He was waved through Winwick's still-unattached gates by the porter, although Michael was challenged when he tried to follow. Bartholomew did not stop to intervene; the Senior Proctor needed no help from him in entering a College. Despite the exigency of the situation, Uyten was unable to resist a brag as they hurried towards the Fellows' rooms, which were located in a house opposite the hall.

'We will hire ten more teachers soon. Your nephew has applied to be one of them, which is good. He is exactly the kind of man we should appoint.'

If the remark was intended to impress, it did not succeed – Bartholomew would not want Richard in *his* College, setting a bad example with his indolence. He said nothing though, and entered Ratclyf's surprisingly sparse quarters. There was a single rug on the floor, the walls were bare, and the only personal items were a bronze statue that looked Italian and a pretty ceramic bowl.

The lawyer was pale and his breathing shallow. Bartholomew knelt by the bed, and felt a thready pulse and skin that was cold to the touch. Lawrence stood next to him, his amiable face a mask of distress, while Illesy, Nerli and Bon were by the door, keeping well back, as if they feared they might catch something.

'How long has he been like this?' Bartholomew asked.

'I am not sure.' Lawrence was almost as pale as his patient. 'He complained of a headache when he woke, and I assumed it was from the amount of wine he downed last night – so much that Nerli was obliged to put him to bed. I suggested healing sleep, and did not trouble him again until shortly after you left . . .'

'What about the rest of you?' asked Bartholomew. 'When did you last see him?'

Nerli had chosen to stand in a shadowy place, so his face was difficult to read. 'At dawn, when he was surly, but ambulatory. We heard no more from him until Lawrence raised the alarm.'

'*You* visited him, Provost,' said Bon, turning his milky eyes in Illesy's direction. 'You came mid-morning, to discuss taking on more Fellows.'

'Yes,' acknowledged Illesy, albeit reluctantly. 'But he was asleep, so I left again. How do you know? You obviously did not see me.'

Bon smiled without humour. 'I have learned to identify different treads, so I "see" more than you think. A blind man is not always—'

'Later, Bon,' interrupted Lawrence. His voice was anxious. 'Can you help Ratclyf, Matthew?'

Bartholomew examined the patient again, but Ratclyf was sinking fast and there was nothing he or anyone else could do. 'What has he eaten or drunk today?'

'A little pottage for breakfast,' replied Lawrence. He pointed. 'The bowl is on the table.'

Bartholomew examined it, to find it had been wiped clean. He sniffed it carefully and detected the faint odour of garlic. *Dormirella* released a garlicky aroma when heated.

'Did Ratclyf like his breakfast pottage highly flavoured?' he asked.

'The cook made a mistake with his flavourings today,' explained Nerli. 'We all ate the stuff, but I ordered the rest tipped away and the pot scoured out. You English have no idea how to cook with potent herbs.'

'It is remarks like that that made Elvesmere dislike you,' said Bon sharply. 'He was patriotic, and you offended him by insulting his country.' He turned his sour visage on the elderly physician. 'And you have not been entirely honest, Lawrence, because you failed to tell Bartholomew about the tonic you made. Surely you had not forgotten it?'

'I had, actually.' Lawrence smiled wanly. 'Mint and camomile. I prepared it myself, and he drank it all. Here is the empty cup.'

Bartholomew inspected that, too, but there was nothing to see or smell. He returned to Ratclyf, where he felt the life-beat growing steadily fainter under his fingers.

'Try your *sal ammoniac*,' whispered Lawrence. 'Mine did not work.'

There was nothing to lose, so Bartholomew pulled out the little phial, half wishing he had not thrown away the more powerful concoction he had used on Potmoor. It made no difference. Ratclyf was breathing too shallowly to inhale, and it was not long before he died.

There was a shocked silence when Bartholomew informed Winwick Hall that a second of their number was dead. Illesy sank on to a chair and put his head in his hands, Lawrence started to cry, and Bon comforted him by patting his shoulder, although he was so white that he looked as though he might faint himself. Nerli leaned against the wall with his arms folded, his face still and brooding. The only sounds were Lawrence's sobs, and Uyten shouting in the yard.

Then Michael arrived and took charge, briskly ushering the Fellows out of the bedchamber to go to the hall and wait in the *parlura*. He gestured that Bartholomew was to examine Ratclyf. The physician obliged, but, as he expected, found no suspicious marks or injuries.

'But was he poisoned?' whispered Michael. Although he had closed the door, both were acutely aware of the possibility of eavesdroppers.

'I cannot tell. His symptoms were certainly consistent

with a dose of *dormirella*, but they could equally well have been caused by a host of naturally occurring ailments. However, if he was poisoned, then it was not at the same time as Hemmysby, because their deaths are too far apart.'

'Then let us go and talk to Ratclyf's grieving colleagues, and see what they can tell us.'

Even though it was dark, there were workmen in the *parlura*, plastering over cracks in the walls. They put down their tools and left when Illesy said something in a low but authoritative voice. The three surviving Fellows were there, along with Uyten, who was guiding Bon through the treacherous muddle of equipment left by the labourers.

'I shall summarise what happened.' Illesy gestured for Bartholomew and Michael to sit on a bench, but he remained standing, giving himself the advantage of height. He was at his most oily, and had clearly used the intervening time to decide what the Senior Proctor and his Corpse Examiner were going to be told. 'To save unnecessary questions.'

'Very well,' said Michael cautiously. 'Proceed.'

'Ratclyf was distressed by the way Hemmysby belittled him at the debate, and drank heavily to expunge it from his mind. Nerli put him to bed but, not surprisingly, he woke this morning with a headache. He swallowed some pottage and Lawrence's tonic, and went back to sleep. He was dozing when I went to enquire after his health mid-morning—'

'I thought you visited him to discuss hiring new Fellows,' interrupted Michael.

'I intended to do both. But he was resting, so I left him in peace. Bon saw me come and go.'

'I did not *see* anything,' countered Bon pedantically. 'I *heard* you.'

'Just so,' said Illesy with a pained smile. He turned back to Michael. 'Shortly after you and Bartholomew left,

Lawrence went to see whether there was any improvement, and found Ratclyf unwell. He tells me that all the symptoms point to a failure of Ratclyf's heart, which was weak.'

Michael glanced at Bartholomew, who shrugged to say it was possible. As he had not been Ratclyf's physician, he did not know the man's medical history, and his brief time trying to help had not been enough for a reliable diagnosis. Michael returned to the fray.

'It is odd that you should lose a second Fellow so soon after the first.'

Illesy's eyes narrowed. 'I sincerely hope you do not suspect foul play with poor Ratclyf.'

'He means to accuse us of it,' said Bon sullenly. 'He is jealous that all the best students are coming here, and aims to wound us by soiling our reputation.'

'Stop!' cried Lawrence. 'There is no need for nasty words. Brother Michael knows the truth: Elvesmere might have been murdered, but Ratclyf died of natural causes.'

'Where is the wine that Ratclyf drank last night?' asked Michael, declining to comment.

'Inside him,' replied Bon promptly. 'He swallowed every last drop and did not offer to share.'

Bartholomew regarded him sharply. Was there a hint of gloating in the blind scholar's voice because he knew that Ratclyf had consumed the evidence, so the crime would never be proved?

'How was his health before this?' asked Michael.

'Poor,' replied Illesy, so quickly that it smacked of invention. 'He was often unwell, which is the lot of those with weak hearts. I speak from experience: my father was the same.'

'It is a pity you did not use your witchy skills to save him, Bartholomew,' said Nerli. 'He was a much more deserving candidate than Potmoor. I thought being guildsmen would spare us from being burgled by the villain, but we also became victims today.'

'We *were* raided,' said Illesy tightly. 'But not by Potmoor. The crime occurred this morning, when we were all in the hall telling the students . . .'

'Telling the students what?' demanded Michael when the Provost trailed off sheepishly.

'To be aware of our enemies,' supplied Bon spitefully. 'Namely King's Hall, Gonville, Michaelhouse and all the other Colleges who mean us harm.'

'You mean you were delivering speeches to encourage rivalry,' surmised Michael. 'You are right: we *do* dislike you, but it is your own fault. You gloat over your superior numbers and your fine hall, and you are arrogant and condescending. You could have won our affection, but instead you have nurtured an atmosphere of bitterness and confrontation.'

'We do not want your affection,' Bon flared up. 'We want you to acknowledge our rightful place as premier College. We—' He stopped abruptly when temper caused him to take several angry steps forward and he stumbled over a trowel. Uyten surged to catch him before he fell.

'What was stolen while you ranted in the hall?' asked Michael, treating Bon to a look of such contempt that it would have silenced anyone able to see it.

'We shall show you our mettle next Tuesday,' Bon snarled, pulling angrily away from his student guide. 'When we are inaugurated into the University. We may be ninth in the procession entering St Mary the Great, but we will certainly be first coming out.'

Michael blinked. 'Impossible! Peterhouse always leads, because it is the oldest, followed by King's Hall and Michaelhouse. You will never take precedence over us.'

'Oh, yes, we will,' declared Bon heatedly. 'And our founder will be here to see it. We received a letter from him this morning, saying that he will be here for the ceremony. Do not forget who he is – Keeper of the Privy Seal and one of the most powerful men in the country.'

201

'It makes no difference,' said Michael tightly. 'You will still be ninth in the procession. It is not for you, him or anyone else to change what has always been.'

'You will see,' sneered Bon. 'We have a plan to—'

'We lost nothing of value when we were invaded by the burglar,' interrupted Illesy quickly. 'I heard a suspicious sound and hurried to investigate, but the villain saw me coming and fled, snagging a dish as he went. A *cracked* dish, so at least he will not profit from his crime.'

'What plan?' demanded Michael, ignoring Illesy and addressing Bon.

Nerli clapped a hand on his colleague's shoulder, a gesture that warned him to say no more. 'We were just teasing, Brother. You need not fear a rumpus on Tuesday.'

'Good,' said Michael coldly. 'Because the Senior Proctor can make life very difficult for foundations that do not conform to the University's statutes and edicts. I should not like to think that Winwick Hall caused trouble for itself on its first day as a member.'

'The burglar,' gushed Lawrence in a transparent attempt to change the subject before Bon lost his temper again. He smiled, all amiable good humour. 'We were lucky, because he might have stolen Ratclyf's purse instead of a dish that no one will miss. They were on the table next to each other – poor Ratclyf was too drunk to take it with him last night – but the thief missed it.'

He held up a simple leather bag that looked too coarse to have belonged to the urbane bursar. Michael upended it on the table. There was a cloth for nose-wiping, two pennies, a glass for magnifying writing, and a small phial. Bartholomew picked up the bottle and removed its stopper.

'Ratclyf had a sore throat after speaking so long at the debate,' explained Nerli. 'He took some syrup of liquorice root to soothe it.'

Bartholomew blinked. 'But liquorice root should be avoided by patients with weak hearts.'

'Yes, it should,' agreed Lawrence, frowning in consternation. 'I wonder why he chose that remedy when there are others that would have suited him better.'

Bon stumbled towards the door and opened it, indicating with a curt sweep of his hand that it was time for the visitors to leave. 'Thank you for coming. It was kind of you to try to help Ratclyf, Bartholomew. But now you must excuse us, as we have much to do.'

CHAPTER 9

There was another storm that night, a gale that all but tore the window shutters from their fastenings, and that threatened to rip tiles from roofs. Bartholomew woke frequently, plagued by nightmares about Hemmysby's dissection. He kept thinking of Marjory Starre's claim, too – that strong winds marked the death of a good person. Did this one blow for Hemmysby, a generous and compassionate member of the Guild of Saints?

He drowsed again, only to start awake moments later from a dream in which he was to give a lecture, which he had not prepared, on apostolic poverty to a huge audience of clerics, all of whom were livid after reading William's inflammatory tract. Hemmysby was among them, hands to the incisions in his neck and middle, and a reproachful expression on his face.

Bartholomew half expected to be struck down when he attended Mass the following morning, and was again acutely aware of Hemmysby's corpse in the chapel. Guilt and remorse deprived him of his appetite at breakfast, and he refused the watery gruel that was on offer.

'We shall go to the Brazen George for something to eat,' determined Michael, when Langelee had intoned a final grace and the scholars were free to leave. 'You will need your strength if we are to solve these mysteries in the next four days. And solve them we must, because I cannot be distracted by murder while Winwick Hall stages some disagreeable coup in St Mary the Great during the beginning of term ceremony.'

Although taverns and inns were forbidden to scholars, Michael saw no reason why the rule should apply to the

Senior Proctor, and was such a regular visitor to the Brazen George that the landlord had set aside a room for his exclusive use. It was a pleasant chamber overlooking a pretty courtyard that boasted a well and a herb garden. Rubbing his hands in gluttonous anticipation, the monk began ordering enough food to victual an army.

'I am hungry,' he said defensively, although Bartholomew had passed no comment. 'And we must do some serious thinking, which I always manage better on a full stomach. Besides, it will set me up for later.'

'Why?' What is happening then?'

'Another choir practice. A lot of matriculands have joined, because they have no money and I provide free bread and ale. I suppose I should send them packing, but I do not have the heart to refuse hungry men. However, it does mean that I have three times as many singers as usual.'

'Three? God Almighty! They will be audible in Scotland!'

'Do not blaspheme,' admonished Michael sharply.

'Sorry. If these matriculands are so impecunious, how will they pay their tuition fees?'

'They all hoped to be taken at Winwick, which offers free schooling to a small number of paupers. Of course, most have been rejected. Some have managed to enrol in hostels – six were founded yesterday alone – while others roam aimlessly, hoping Winwick will change its mind.'

'How will you buy bread and ale for so many?'

Michael grinned. 'With the handsome fee that de Stannell paid for the documents he needs to calculate certain town taxes.'

'The ones you always give Dick Tulyet for free?'

'The very same.'

He was interrupted by the landlord, who brought platter after platter of meat and bread – no vegetables, of course, as Michael considered them a waste of valuable stomach space. He tied a napkin around his neck, flexed his fingers, and pitched in.

'We now have six deaths to explore,' began Bartholomew, watching him absently. 'Oswald, Felbrigge, Elvesmere, Knyt, Hemmysby and Ratclyf. Shall we start with Oswald?'

'Proceed,' said Michael, waving a hambone.

'I think he *was* poisoned. He was called to a secret meeting, and everyone says he was distracted and unhappy afterwards. Edith thinks Potmoor killed him, and it seems they did do business together. However, I learned yesterday that all Winwick's Fellows were here in Cambridge when he died.'

The bone was waved again; it had notably less meat. 'Why would they want him dead?'

'He founded the Guild of Saints to help the poor, but Winwick has been demanding ever bigger donations. I cannot see him approving – it was not what he intended.'

'Fair enough. The next death was Felbrigge, shot before the ceremony giving Winwick its charter. Moments earlier, he had been telling me how he had instigated measures to control the place. Fulbut was the archer, but he almost certainly acted on someone else's orders. We know Potmoor hires him, but Fulbut is a mercenary, and they will work for anyone. He is still missing, and I have a feeling he has been killed to prevent him from talking.'

'Oswald and Felbrigge – and Knyt – were leading members of the Guild of Saints. De Stannell is in charge now, a man who is far more malleable than they would have been.'

'Hemmysby felt strongly about looking after the poor, too,' said Michael, wiping grease from his chin. 'Now *he* was definitely poisoned, probably with cake eaten after the debate, although we do not know how. He died trying to reach our church. And if that is not bad enough, someone wants him accused of stealing the Stanton Hutch.'

'And the culprit knows Michaelhouse well enough to make off with the chest himself, then come back and leave the cup and deeds on display in Hemmysby's room.'

'I suspect Potmoor of killing Knyt,' said Michael. The hambone was stripped bare, so he turned his attention to the beef. 'He was in Knyt's house the day Knyt died, and he is enamoured of Olivia. But if Knyt was poisoned and Potmoor did it, then it means that Potmoor killed the others, too – I doubt we have two poisoners at large.'

Bartholomew agreed. 'I cannot prove Ratclyf was fed *dormirella*, but he certainly suffered symptoms consistent with it. I seriously doubt he died of a weak heart – it is too convenient. Moreover, he had liquorice root in his purse, something people with unsteady hearts should avoid.'

Michael stopped eating and regarded him sombrely. 'I hate to say it, Matt, but I fear you might have to make more of those judicious incisions. On Ratclyf, Elvesmere and—'

'No! Winwick would find out for certain.'

'But we need to know.' Michael's face was pale, and the food sat ignored on the platter in front of him, telling the physician that he was not the only one who uncomfortable with what was being suggested. 'And I thought you were keen to use this new tool against wicked killers, learning more about the human body in the process.'

'I am. Or rather, I *was*.' Bartholomew rubbed a hand through his hair. It was not easy to discuss, even with Michael. 'It felt very wrong, Brother. Perhaps because we did it in a church.'

'Next time, it will be in St Mary the Great.' Michael raised an oily hand when Bartholomew started to object again. 'We have no choice, Matt. We *must* have the truth, and I cannot think of another way to find it. Besides, surely the second time will less distressing than the first?'

'It will not,' said Bartholomew with finality. 'And I am not doing it.'

Michael regarded him balefully, then continued with their analysis, although his appetite had gone and he ate no more. 'But Potmoor is not our only suspect. Winwick is not a College at ease with itself – none of its Fellows like each other, with the exception of the cloying Lawrence, who simpers over everyone.'

Bartholomew ignored the last remark. 'All were alone with the ailing Ratclyf at some point, although none would have admitted it if not pushed by the others. Nerli put him to bed, Illesy visited mid-morning, and Bon must have been in the vicinity or he would not have heard Illesy.'

'And Lawrence took him a tonic,' added Michael pointedly.

Bartholomew ignored him a second time. 'They all behaved suspiciously: Illesy is eager for us to believe that Ratclyf had a weak heart; Bon wanted us to know that Ratclyf did not share the wine that made him drunk; Nerli ordered the garlicky pottage thrown away; and the cup used for the tonic looked to have been rinsed. It means we cannot test anything that Ratclyf swallowed.'

'Nerli worries me most – there is something deeply sinister about him. Also, *dormirella* is an Italian creation, and he hails from Florence. It would not surprise me to learn that he is a poisoner. Which would mean that Potmoor visiting Knyt's house on the morning of his death is irrelevant.'

'Nerli has a motive for dispatching the other victims, too,' mused Bartholomew. 'He clashed with Elvesmere over the validity of his foreign degrees, while Oswald, Felbrigge and Knyt may have objected to the Guild's support of his College. Meanwhile, it was to Nerli that Edith delivered the fruitcake for the debate . . .'

'Elvesmere,' said Michael. 'Let us consider him next. He was stabbed somewhere other than the latrine where he was found, and the wound in his back would not have been instantly fatal. You say he may have been poisoned, too.'

'It is possible.' Restlessly, Bartholomew crumbled a piece of bread in his fingers.

'Everyone at Winwick had the opportunity to kill him,'

the monk went on. 'He died in the middle of the night, when they claim to have been asleep, and all his colleagues disliked him: he denigrated Nerli's qualifications, despised Illesy for befriending Potmoor, scorned Lawrence for being a *medicus*, and even his friend Bon did not escape his bile.'

'He drew attention to Bon's illegitimacy,' recalled Bartholomew.

'But Bon is blind, which is a serious disadvantage for a killer. How could he be sure that no one was watching while he poisoned victuals, or indulged in a bit of stabbing? And what about his getaway? He stumbled in the *parlura*, a place he knows, so how could he manage outside? I suppose he could have hired someone to help him, but that would carry its own uncertainties.'

'Yet despite all this, I am not sure the Winwick men are ruthless enough for murder. Several members of the Guild of Saints are, though. You do not accrue riches and power by being gentle.'

'True,' agreed Michael. 'So our suspects are the wealthy guildsmen with Potmoor high on the list, the four Winwick men—'

'*Two* Winwick men,' interrupted Bartholomew. 'Lawrence is not a murderer and Bon has hypochyma. However, there is another guildsman you have not mentioned: Holm, who bought *dormirella*, and has a workshop in which he experiments.'

'I wondered how long it would be before you reminded me about him,' said Michael wryly.

As Bartholomew and Michael left the Brazen George, they met two scholars from Bene't College. John Samon was a short, ugly canonist with a cheery manner, while Master Heltisle was tall, aloof and unfriendly. Heltisle had never liked Bartholomew, but that day, he regarded the physician with more hostility than usual.

'We were burgled yesterday,' he said coldly. 'By Potmoor.'

'*Possibly* by Potmoor,' corrected Samon, shooting him a cautionary glance. 'Although I do not believe it, personally. I know he never has an alibi for these crimes, but I do not see a powerful villain like him demeaning himself with petty theft.'

'He does it to keep his skills honed,' explained Heltisle shortly. 'Our porters heard him say so.' He turned back to Bartholomew. 'And it is *your* fault for resurrecting him.'

'If you believe that *medici* can raise people from the dead, then you are a fool,' said Bartholomew, tiredness and his continuing unease over Hemmysby making him uncharacteristically curt. 'It is impossible, and anyone with a modicum of intelligence should know it. Potmoor was *not* dead, he was suffering from catalepsia.'

Heltisle took a step away, unused to the physician hitting back. 'Well, perhaps. However, there is another rumour you should hear, too. We had it from Weasenham.'

'What has he been saying now?' groaned Michael wearily. The stationer was an incurable gossip, who shamelessly invented stories when he was low on true ones.

'That Provost Illesy stole from the King when he was a clerk in Westminster. He was dismissed in disgrace, so he had no choice but to work for Potmoor until he was offered something better. It explains why he is so rich – he kept what he filched from His Majesty.'

Michael rolled his eyes. 'What utter nonsense! John Winwick would not have appointed a thief to run his College, and he would certainly know if Illesy had been caught with his fingers in the royal coffers. Weasenham is just trying to make trouble, as usual.'

'Do not be so sure,' said Heltisle. 'Winwick is full of rogues, and I hate them all. Upstarts!'

Samon hastened to explain. 'We have just been to the reading of Knyt's will. He always promised to remember

210

Bene't in it, but everything has gone to the Guild of Saints instead – which means that Winwick Hall is likely to get it all.'

'Winwick is an abomination,' spat Heltisle, 'and if it had not come into being so fast, I would have contacted my friends at Court and put an end to it. As it was, we were essentially presented with a fait accompli.'

'We were,' agreed Michael. 'But it is here now, and we must make the best of it.'

Heltisle drew himself up to his full, haughty height. 'I shall oppose it at every turn, and so will King's Hall, Gonville, Valence Marie, Bene't, Trinity Hall, Clare and Peterhouse. Its greed and selfishness are damaging our University, and we want it gone.'

He stalked away, leaving Michael staring after him unhappily, thinking about Winwick's intention to usurp precedence at St Mary the Great after the beginning of term ceremony. The other Heads of Houses would feel the same as Heltisle, and there would be trouble for certain.

'Tynkell let slip something yesterday,' he told Bartholomew, as they resumed their journey. 'That my Junior Proctor encouraged John Winwick to wait until I had gone to Peterborough before forging ahead with his new College. In other words, Felbrigge wanted to oversee the arrangements himself, so he could claim all the credit.'

Bartholomew was not surprised. 'You scoffed at the notion that Felbrigge was a threat, but he was ruthlessly ambitious. Yet his plan has misfired: no one thanks him for Winwick Hall.'

'He said he had put measures in place to control it. I wish I knew what they were, because the wretched place is beyond *my* sway. Are people still saying I killed him, by the way?'

'Not to me.'

'Here comes de Stannell,' said Michael, watching the

deputy trot towards them on a lively bay. It was too spirited for his meagre equestrian skills – the secret riding lessons at the castle clearly had some way to go – obliging him to cling hard to the edge of his saddle.

'There were more thefts in the town last night,' he panted, struggling to control the beast and talk at the same time. 'Including the Mayor, who lost a silver pot and five spoons.'

'Bene't was burgled, too, and Master Heltisle claims Potmoor is responsible.' Michael took the reins, and the animal immediately quietened; he had a way with horses. 'It is a serious allegation, and it is incumbent on you to investigate.'

De Stannell looked away. 'I cannot. Potmoor is a fellow guildsman.'

'If your post as Secretary interferes with your duties as Deputy Sheriff, you should resign one of them,' said Michael sharply.

'Do not tell me what to do,' bristled de Stannell. 'Besides, I did challenge him, and he told me he is innocent. He may have been lying, I suppose, but unless you have evidence to prove it, I suggest you let the matter drop. It is reckless to annoy vicious felons.'

'But you are Deputy Sheriff!' exclaimed Michael, stunned by the bald admission of cowardice. 'It is your duty to annoy vicious felons.'

'Rubbish! Besides, *he* thinks a scholar is the guilty party. I am inclined to believe he is right.'

'Unless you can support such claims with facts, you would be wise to keep them to yourself,' snapped Michael. 'Or you will learn to your cost that slandering the University is expensive.'

'Is that so? Well, for your information, the best lawyers are in Winwick, and they would never move against me. Who provided wine when they were struggling to supply refreshments after the debate? *I* did! They are in my debt.'

'Then it is a pity you made them look mean by being niggardly,' flashed Michael. 'There was not enough to go around, and you embarrassed them with your miserliness.'

Before de Stannell could take issue, Michael dealt the horse a sharp slap on the flank. It reared and shot off down the High Street with its rider hauling ineffectually on the reins. Even Bartholomew, no equestrian himself, was unimpressed.

'Heaven help us if we need *his* help to quell trouble next week.'

Michael and Bartholomew had interviewed Tynkell, Rougham and the Winwick men about the cake that Hemmysby had eaten at the debate, but they had not yet questioned the last two scholars who had formed the little group. They returned to Michaelhouse, where they found William and Thelnetham in the conclave. No one else was there, and the pair were bickering furiously.

'I can give you some of my duties if you have too much time on your hands,' said Michael acidly. 'Or Matt's. We are both worried about how we will manage next term, yet you two have leisure to lounge in here, sparring with each other.'

'We were discussing my tract,' said William, flushing guiltily. 'Everyone criticised me for copying Linton Hall's essay and passing it off as mine, so I have rewritten the whole thing in my own words. Although I left the fore-word because that was the bit I had written myself anyway – and I certainly needed no help from Linton to tell me what I think of Gilbertines, Dominicans or that shameless pluralist John Winwick.'

'And needless to say, the ideas in that poisonous rant are now more dangerous and asinine than ever,' interposed Thelnetham.

Michael glared at William. 'How did you rewrite it? We burnt your version *and* the original.'

'I had two copies of Linton's work and you only confiscated one.' William smirked triumphantly. 'You cannot complain, Brother. It is now an entirely original piece.'

Michael controlled his temper with difficulty. 'The issue was not the plagiarism, it was the content – views that saw a brother foundation closed and its members excommunicated. Destroy it at once, or I shall instruct the Bishop to eject you from the Church.'

William paled. 'You would never do such a thing.'

'To save Michaelhouse from dissolution? I most certainly would.' Michael felt he had made his point and moved on to another matter. 'I understand you stood with Hemmysby, Tynkell, the Winwick Fellows and Rougham for the refreshments after the debate. You may have been among the last people to see him alive.'

'I thought he looked wan,' said Thelnetham. 'But so were we all after listening to those ranting voices all day. And I would not have chosen the company of the rogues from Winwick Hall, but William called them over.'

'To say how much I enjoyed watching Hemmysby make asses of Ratclyf and Bon,' explained William, bouncing back quickly from Michael's reprimand, as was his wont. He grinned gleefully. 'They did not know how to respond!'

'Vile creatures, the lot of them,' spat Thelnetham. 'They belong to that nasty Guild of Saints, for a start. I told Hemmysby to refuse the invitation to join, but he would not listen.'

'He wanted to do good works,' said William. 'And with Stanmore at the helm, it was a benevolent force. Some awful scoundrels took the reins after he died, though. Potmoor, de Stannell, Mistress Mortimer, Mayor Heslarton, the Frevills . . .'

'They probably corrupted Hemmysby,' said Thelnetham. 'It is *their* fault he turned dishonest.'

'He was not dishonest,' objected Bartholomew. 'He—'

'You can ignore the evidence, but I shall not.'

Thelnetham turned to Michael. 'I was vexed when William hailed the Winwick men over, as they distracted me with their carping, and I only managed to snag one piece of Edith's fruitcake. Everyone else had two.'

'I got four,' put in William gloatingly. 'And they were all delicious.'

'From the same plate as Hemmysby?' asked Bartholomew.

Thelnetham nodded. 'Lawrence had a platter that he was intending to tote around the vestry, but our little group fell on it like vultures, and it was emptied in a trice. Why? Was something wrong with the pastries, and *they* were what caused Hemmysby to die?'

'Lord!' exclaimed William in alarm. 'Am I in danger then?'

Bartholomew was puzzled. The poison could not have been in Edith's cake if so many others had eaten it with no ill effects, yet there had been nothing else in Hemmysby's stomach. At least, nothing that he could identify. Of course, it was the first time that he had ever examined the sludge that remained in a man's innards after death. Had he missed something, and led the investigation astray with his inexperience?

'Hemmysby should have given those Winwick upstarts short shrift when Ratclyf demanded an apology,' said Thelnetham. 'If they cannot cope with having their theories demolished, there is no place for them in a university.'

'Is there any news on the hutch, Brother?' asked William, who did not like having *his* theories demolished either.

'There will never be any news,' predicted Thelnetham. 'Hemmysby hid it, and it is lost for ever. I am glad we retrieved the deeds and the cup, but I shall never forgive him for making off with my bestiary. I have no idea what I shall say when my Prior General asks for it back.'

'I know what he will say to you,' said William spitefully.

'That you should not have pawned property that does not belong to you in the first place.'

Michael stood to leave before Thelnetham could respond. 'Burn your new tract, Father,' he ordered, as he made for the door. 'No, do not lean back on that bench as if you intend to resume your quarrel with Thelnetham instead. I want it on the fire before I reach the gate.'

'I will do it,' offered Thelnetham eagerly. 'Suttone has it at the moment, but *I* shall ensure that no one else is corrupted by its heretical raving.'

'Thank you,' said Michael. 'Well? What are you waiting for?'

Determined to stop the rumours about Illesy and the money he was alleged to have stolen from the King before there was trouble, Michael set off to visit Weasenham. Bartholomew went with him, as Goodwyn was a sullen, distracting presence in his room, and working in the conclave would be impossible with Thelnetham gloating over William about the tract. The stationer's shop was on the High Street, near King's Hall, but they had not gone far before Bartholomew felt someone tug his sleeve. It was Ylaria Verius.

'My man has all but severed his thumb,' she said. Her voice was hoarse, but he was pleased to see that she had shaken off her cough at last. 'He is busily swallowing wine to dull the pain, but will you sew it back on when he is drunk enough?'

'I will come now,' said Bartholomew. 'These matters should not be left.'

She shook her head. 'He will still be sober, and you will never hold him down – the poor lamb is sensitive to pain. Come after noon. He should be ready then.'

She had drawn Bartholomew to one side, which put him in such a position that he had an unusual view of All Saints graveyard. He was surprised to see Potmoor there, leaning against a tomb with his thumbs hooked into his tunic. He appeared to be waiting for someone. Intrigued, Bartholomew ducked into the church porch to watch. Michael followed.

Within moments, Illesy sauntered along the High Street. He stopped by the lychgate and knelt, pretending to fiddle with his shoe while he looked around. Apparently confident that no one was watching, he made a curious sideways scuttle into the churchyard, where he hid behind a tree. After a few moments, he eased out and tiptoed towards Potmoor, whose eyebrows were raised in amusement. Michael gave Bartholomew a shove.

'We cannot hear what they say from here. Go and eavesdrop from behind that monument.'

'You do it,' objected Bartholomew. He would almost certainly be caught, which would be embarrassing – and potentially dangerous if Potmoor took umbrage.

'I cannot fit behind a tomb with my heavy bones. But those are two of our main suspects for killing Hemmysby, and they are obviously going to discuss something important, or Illesy would not be taking such elaborate precautions. It is your moral duty to listen.'

With a sigh, Bartholomew did as he was told, feeling a fool as he eased through the long grass on all fours. He sincerely hoped no one could see him from the road or there would be rumours galore – crawling through graveyards was hardly normal behaviour for a physician, even one with his dubious reputation. Eventually, he came close enough to hear.

'I do not agree,' Potmoor was growling. 'It should have been done by a professional. They are more careful about the spillage of blood.'

'Professionals are expensive,' snapped Illesy. 'We could not afford it.'

'Then perhaps you should have hired one, just to

maintain the illusion,' countered Potmoor. 'I have my reputation to consider, you know. Nerli is— What was that?'

Bartholomew had knelt on a twig, and it had cracked very softly. It had barely been audible to him, and he was amazed that Potmoor should have heard it. He tensed, ready to run, at the same time wondering whether having unusually acute hearing was a prerequisite for a successful thief.

'What?' asked Illesy, cocking his head. 'Do you mean that peculiar wailing? It is just the Michaelhouse Choir warming up for another rehearsal.'

'No, not that – I can tell the difference between good music and suspicious snapping sounds.'

Bartholomew peered around the tomb and studied the felon's face, searching for signs that he was jesting, but saw none. Had Potmoor's brush with catalepsia damaged his wits? The racket evidently reminded Illesy of what was to happen in four days' time.

'I am looking forward to leading the procession out of St Mary the Great on Tuesday, and the following feast will be exceptionally fine, thanks to your generosity. Our founder has promised to attend, and I am sure he will be impressed. He—'

'I heard it again!' hissed Potmoor, looking around wildly. 'Someone is listening to us! I told you we should have met in Winwick Hall.'

'We cannot,' replied Illesy tartly. 'You were seen the last time you came, and conclusions were drawn – conclusions that were bad for both of us.'

'Then next time you can visit me in Chesterton.' Potmoor began to stride towards Bartholomew's monument. He pulled a knife from his belt as he went, and the expression on his face was malevolent. 'I hate spies. If I find one here, I will—'

'Provost Illesy!' came Michael's voice from across the

cemetery. 'Is that you? I was just coming to pray over the grave of an old friend. Do you have loved ones here?'

Bartholomew had braced himself for discovery, but nothing happened. When he summoned the courage to peer around the monument, Illesy was talking to Michael, and Potmoor had gone.

'I buried an aunt here a year ago,' the Provost was saying. 'I often come to remember her before God, but I have finished now, so the churchyard is yours.'

When he was sure they were alone, Bartholomew stood up and glared at the monk.

'I rescued you, so do not glower at me,' said Michael defensively. 'No harm was done.'

'No harm?' demanded Bartholomew. 'I thought I was going to be skewered.'

Michael waved a dismissive hand. 'Tell me what you heard.'

With ill grace, Bartholomew obliged, repeating the discussion verbatim.

The monk was thoughtful. 'They must have been discussing the murder of Elvesmere, and were sorry that they had not chosen a more skilled man to do it.'

'It sounded as if they were referring to a more major spillage to me. Elvesmere's was not particularly profuse. Perhaps there is a victim we have not found yet. Fulbut, perhaps.'

'Lord,' breathed Michael. 'That is an unpleasant thought.'

The stationer's shop was always full, and scholars visited it not just to purchase pens, parchment, ink and exemplars – anthologies of the texts they were obliged to learn – but to enjoy its blazing fires, and to chat with friends. Bartholomew and Michael met a number of acquaintances inside, one of whom was Richard, who was with the dentally bereft Uyten from Winwick Hall.

'I came for sealing wax,' Richard said. 'To help Mother with her business.'

Bartholomew was not sure whether he was more irked by the lie or by the fact that Richard expected him to believe it. 'She has plenty already. You should not need more.'

But Richard's attention was elsewhere, and Bartholomew saw he was eyeing the stationer's wife with open lust. Ruth Weasenham did not seem to mind, and there were answering simpers aplenty. Bartholomew groaned, seeing more worry in the offing for Edith.

'I thought you would have learned your lesson with the Earl of Suffolk's daughter. You were lucky he did not kill you.'

Richard smirked. 'It was worth the inconvenience – she was a lovely lass. But so is Ruth, and I am sure that dry old stick of a husband cannot satisfy her.'

'Please do not antagonise Weasenham,' begged Bartholomew. 'He is a powerful man who—'

'I do not need advice about amours from you,' interrupted Richard crisply. 'I have far more experience in such matters.'

Bartholomew was sure he did, and was equally sure he was none the wiser for it. 'If you are caught, Weasenham will have his revenge by spreading tales that might hurt Edith. He has a vicious tongue. And she has been through enough grief already.'

'As have I. She is not the only one who misses Father, you know.' Richard changed the subject abruptly, perhaps to disguise the tears that pricked his eyes. 'Uyten here tells me that you think my mother's cakes killed Hemmysby and Ratclyf. Is it true?'

'No,' replied Bartholomew, wondering how Uyten had found out. He could only suppose that one of his discussions with Michael had not been as private as they had thought.

'Then let us hope no one tells her otherwise. She will be mortified. Shall we make an agreement? You say nothing about my dalliance with Ruth, and I say nothing about the fact that my mother is a murder suspect in one of your investigations.'

'She is nothing of the kind!' Bartholomew was stunned that Richard should resort to such tactics.

Richard's expression was unpleasantly calculating. 'If you say so.'

'We will be late,' said Uyten, tugging on his arm. 'The Guild meeting will start soon.'

'Not without me.' Richard's eyes were still locked on Bartholomew's. 'De Stannell hopes for a donation, and is afraid of offending me in any way. You should be proud that I hold such sway in so venerable a body, Uncle. But Uyten is right. I should put in an appearance at the guildhall. Then he and I are going to join the Michaelhouse Choir.'

'Really?' asked Bartholomew suspiciously. 'Why?'

'Because Goodwyn says it is fun. Of course, we might need a cure for broken ears later.'

He gave a mock salute and threaded his way through the busy shop to the door, leaving Bartholomew staring after him unhappily.

Weasenham was an unattractive individual in his sixties with long oily hair and a sly face, and Bartholomew was not surprised that his vivacious wife – Julitta's sister, in fact – had taken a shine to a man nearer her own age. It could not be easy to live with the stationer, and Bartholomew recalled that the man's previous spouse had sought comfort outside the wedding bed, too.

'The tale is quite true,' Weasenham was telling Michael, who had cornered him behind his counter. 'Illesy *did* steal from the King when he was a clerk in Westminster. I heard it from Heyford, who worked in the same place.'

'Heyford of St Clement's?' asked Michael. 'The vicar?'

'The very same. And it was *his* church that was set alight the other day . . .'

Michael frowned. 'What are you saying? That Illesy did it in revenge?'

'It stands to reason. Heyford thinks the same, which is why he gave a sermon about it today. It had everyone in a frenzy of outrage against Illesy. And against his former employer Potmoor, who doubtless helped him in his evil designs.'

'You should watch your tongue,' advised Michael. 'Or the pair of them might take offence.'

'Offence!' sneered Weasenham. 'What do I care? They have done their worst already.'

'Why? What has—'

'I was *burgled*, Brother! The culprit stole all my best ink and parchment, and several valuable books. And at the beginning of term, too, when demand is always highest.'

'I doubt Potmoor would be interested in those,' remarked Bartholomew.

'This is a University town,' said Weasenham acidly. 'There is a huge market for such items. Or do you think thieves only ever take what they want for themselves, not what can be sold?' He leaned forward suddenly and lowered his voice. 'But Potmoor has a weak point: Olivia Knyt. They are lovers, and he would do anything for her.'

'How do you know?' asked Michael.

'I have seen them together with my own eyes, kissing and pawing. There is no accounting for taste where passion is concerned.'

He stared so hard at Bartholomew that the physician wondered if he knew about Julitta. Then the stationer nodded a greeting at someone, and the two scholars turned to see Heyford standing behind them. The vicar was full of righteous indignation, and when Michael asked whether he had recovered from his near-incineration, he received a waspish reply.

'My altar table is destroyed and I burned a finger. And no, I do not want Bartholomew to tend it. He is alleged to commune with the Devil, and I am a priest.'

'He does nothing of the kind,' snapped Michael. 'And if I hear anyone else making that sort of remark, they will find themselves charged with slander. Do you hear me, Weasenham?'

'Tell him about Illesy, Heyford,' said Weasenham, unfazed by the threat.

'That scoundrel! Money went missing from the royal coffers when he and I were treasury clerks – this was several years before the plague – and Illesy was the only possible culprit. Rather than risk a scandal by exposing him, he was ordered to leave Westminster.'

'John Winwick would not have hired a thief as Provost of—' began Michael.

'John Winwick does not know,' interrupted Heyford. 'The affair was too thoroughly hushed up. I said nothing when Illesy first arrived in our town, and he doubtless thought I had forgotten, but I decided to speak out when his College began getting uppity. In revenge, he and Potmoor sent me strong wine, then set my church alight, intending me to burn inside it.'

'These are serious allegations,' warned Michael.

'Yes,' agreed Heyford haughtily. 'And arson and attempted murder are serious crimes.'

Bartholomew and Michael left the shop to find the High Street awash with noise – the Michaelhouse Choir was bawling a lewd tavern song. With a squawk of dismay, Michael raced away to stop them, while passers-by grinned or scowled, depending on how they felt about obscenities being howled in churches. Bartholomew went to the

Verius house, where the ditcher had imbibed sufficient alcohol to render himself insensible.

'I am afraid Surgeon Holm has come to help, though,' Ylaria whispered apologetically. 'I told him he was not needed – and that we could not pay – but he insisted on staying anyway.'

Bartholomew was mystified: Holm never did charity work. However, he stopped thinking about the surgeon when he saw that Julitta was there as well. She smiled in a way that made his stomach turn somersaults, and although he struggled to keep his face impassive, he obviously did not succeed, because Holm's voice was distinctly peevish when he spoke.

'Thumbs are notoriously difficult to treat, and only surgeons are qualified to approach them with needles and saws. One wrong move, and the humours will be seriously unbalanced, leaving the patient to die an agonising death.'

'Then you had better be careful,' said Bartholomew, surprised by the oblique reminder that he would be trespassing on Holm's domain if he operated. It had never happened before – being an indifferent practitioner, Holm was usually only too happy to let someone else try his hand.

'Will and Verius are friends,' said Julitta, smiling again. 'So we thought he should be here.'

'Are they?' Bartholomew would not have imagined the suave surgeon demeaning himself by associating with a common layabout like Verius.

'Not *friends*,' countered Holm, shooting her an irritable look. 'Passing acquaintances. Shall we begin the procedure before he wakes up?'

Bartholomew looked at the slumped, snoring figure on the floor, and thought it would be some time before that happened. He knelt and inspected the wound. There was a deep gash at the base of Verius's thumb, and it had bled profusely, but the bone was undamaged, and the laceration would heal with a few judiciously placed stitches, although he suspected the ditcher would never enjoy full feeling in it again.

'He cut it when he was working,' explained Ylaria, fondly stroking her husband's hair. 'People throw sharp things in streams, and do not care that others might be hurt by them.'

Such injuries were an occupational hazard for ditchers. However, Verius's was very clean, and Bartholomew suspected he had lied to his wife about how he had come by it.

'I will hold him still, while you irrigate the wound,' he told Holm.

'How foolish of me,' said Holm, backing away. 'I neglected to bring the ointments to . . . do what is necessary when something needs irritating.'

'Irrigating,' corrected Julitta gently. 'You meant to say *irrigating.*'

'I did say irrigating,' snapped the surgeon. 'You will have to do it instead, Bartholomew. Do not worry. I shall not criticise your technique.'

'Thank you,' said Bartholomew drily. He began to work, although he was obliged several times to stop and show the surgeon yet again how to immobilise the limb. Julitta took over the task in the end, leaving Holm to perch on the table and inspect his fingernails in an attitude of boredom.

'How are your various investigations going, Matt?' she asked conversationally.

Bartholomew was not really in a position to concentrate on his answer, with tiny stitches to insert and a woman he loved sitting so close that he could feel the warmth of her breath on his face. He gave a mumbled, disjointed report that had her blinking in confusion.

'The reason I ask is because I saw something odd last

night,' she said, speaking softly so that Ylaria would not hear. 'And I wondered whether Nerli and Lawrence were among your suspects. If they are, I shall tell you something about them.'

'Not Lawrence,' said Bartholomew. 'At least, he is not on *my* list.'

Julitta spoke reluctantly. 'I like him as well, but I could not sleep last night, and looked out of my window at midnight to see him and Nerli sneaking along in the most furtive manner. Nerli was carrying a sword and looked downright dangerous.'

'That hurts, damn you!' said Verius, opening bleary eyes. 'I shall tell the money soldier, and he will slit your throat.'

'It is the ale talking,' said Holm. He flicked his fingers at Ylaria. 'Block his mouth, woman, lest he blurt something that will later embarrass him.'

'No,' countered Bartholomew quickly, when Ylaria stepped forward with a piece of cloth. 'You might cause him to thrash about if you obstruct his breathing.'

'But surely we must respect the privacy of his secret thoughts?' asked Julitta.

'Bartholomew would never do anything so unprofessional as to repeat what a man says in his cups,' said Holm, a little too acidly for the physician's liking.

Verius lapsed into snoring insensibility again, so Bartholomew concentrated on his needlework. Julitta was ready with a clean dressing when he finished, and their fingers touched as she passed it to him. She kept them there rather longer than necessary, and her smile – given so that her husband would not see – tore at his heart. Why had she married a creature like Holm? And why had he not stopped the ceremony and taken her himself, as his friends had urged him to do?

'The money soldier will see me right,' mumbled Verius, settling more comfortably on the floor now the operation was over. 'A fine friend for a poor man.'

'Perhaps he will say something to embarrass *us*,' said Julitta, tearing her eyes away from Bartholomew to look down at the patient. 'Maybe Will should sing, to drown him out.'

'That will not be necessary.' Holm opened the door, allowing a waft of noise to drift in. There was a moment when Bartholomew thought there might be a riot in progress, but then he realised it was the Michaelhouse Choir, turning Tunsted's beautiful *Gloria* into something akin to a battle chant.

'The Fellows of Winwick Hall think they will be the highlight of the ceremony on Tuesday,' Holm sniggered. 'But Brother Michael's rabble will upstage them.'

Verius stirred himself to join in, and Bartholomew was astounded when the ditcher's voice transpired to be a high, clear tenor that was unexpectedly sweet for so hulking a man.

'He has the voice of an angel,' whispered Ylaria, regarding him lovingly.

'If you want to hear the voice of an angel,' declared Holm, 'you should listen to me.'

'A duet, then?' asked Julitta eagerly. 'I should like that very much.'

'Not here,' said Holm loftily. 'I do not perform with drunks.'

As people complained if choir practices went on too long, Michael was obliged to keep them brief, and the bread and ale were being distributed by the time Bartholomew passed St Michael's Church on his way home. There was a lot of angry yelling inside, and he could hear Michael struggling to keep the peace, so he went to help. The latch stuck, reminding him sharply that Hemmysby still lay in the Stanton Chapel.

Once he had wrestled his way inside, he was greeted by pandemonium. Goodwyn and the new medical students had been put in charge of the bread, but their portions were outrageously uneven, and quarrels had broken out. As soon as Michael quelled one disagreement, another began, and Bartholomew could see from the gleeful expression on Goodwyn's face that he was delighted by the trouble he had caused.

Uyten was dispensing ale, but so carelessly that a lot spilled, eliciting roars of outrage from several elderly baritones. The lad eyed them challengingly. His thick ears and missing teeth should have warned the ancients that he was no stranger to brawls, but they persisted in haranguing him, oblivious to or careless of the danger. Richard watched from behind a pillar, safely away from the commotion, with an expression on his face that was difficult to read.

'Help me,' Bartholomew ordered his nephew sharply, 'before someone is hurt.'

There was a moment when he thought Richard would refuse, but then he pushed away from the pier and followed Bartholomew to the bread baskets. Goodwyn blanched when he saw his teacher bearing down on him, and stumbled as he was elbowed unceremoniously out of the way. The furious babble quietened once the pieces were more fairly sized, and it calmed further still when a bass called Isnard the bargeman took over the distribution of ale.

'I need not worry about how to buy refreshments next time,' said Michael sourly, when the bulk of singers had received their victuals and had trooped meekly away. 'The fines I am going to impose on your lads should cover the expense nicely.'

Bartholomew leaned against a wall, tired now the fuss was over. Goodwyn had been sent to rinse jugs at the back of the church, which he was doing with ill grace. Aungel, Uyten and the new medical students were helping, although Richard declined to sully his hands, and came to talk to Bartholomew and Michael instead. So did Isnard, who had developed a very proprietary attitude towards the choir. Like most members, he was Bartholomew's patient; unlike most, he earned a decent living, despite having lost a leg in an accident some years before. He was aware of the importance of free food to his friends, and hated anything that threatened it.

'I do not want that rabble here next time, Brother,' he said, stabbing an angry finger towards the students. 'They lower the tone.'

Richard laughed. 'It was not them who were scolded for spitting during the *Conductus*. Besides, I see nothing wrong with having a few Michaelhouse scholars in the *Michaelhouse* Choir. Without them, the only College member would be the good Brother here.'

'That is because no other scholar has sufficient talent,' explained Isnard earnestly. From anyone else, this might have been interpreted as irony, but the bargeman genuinely believed it. Then he sniffed the air suspiciously. 'What is that reek? Are you wearing perfume, lad?'

'Just a dab,' replied Richard. 'I deemed it necessary to mask the stench of the altos. Can you not ask them to change into clean clothes before coming here, Brother?'

'It would do scant good: those are the only ones they own,' replied Michael. 'And you used more than a dab – you reek like a whore's boudoir. Not that I would know, of course. So apply less in future, if you please. I do not want my singers asphyxiated.'

Before Richard could issue a rejoinder, the monk turned away and began to set the church to rights. Richard was asked to sweep up, but it was not many moments before he took the opportunity to slink away. Goodwyn and his cronies started to follow, but a stern look from Bartholomew made them reconsider. They expressed their resentment by "accidentally" spilling water, and even breaking a brush.

At last they finished, and Isnard invited Bartholomew and Michael for an evening of riotous fun in the Laughing Pig. They declined – it was a particularly rough tavern, and the domain of townsmen, not scholars.

'I am going to pray for Hemmysby,' said Michael, when the thump of Isnard's crutches on the stone floor had faded and the church was quiet again. 'Will you join me?'

Bartholomew knew he should work on his lectures, but his wits were muddy with exhaustion, and he doubted he would achieve much that night. He nodded, thinking it might make him feel less guilty about despoiling his colleague's corpse, and followed Michael into the Stanton Chapel.

'How curious,' said Michael. 'Something has been nailed to Hemmysby's coffin. It was not here earlier. Someone must have done it while my attention was on the music.'

It was a piece of parchment, and he set about removing it while Bartholomew dropped to his knees next to the casket. All was quiet for a moment, then Michael released a gasp of horror.

'We are being blackmailed, Matt! This message says that if Michaelhouse does not pay twenty marks by noon on Monday – three days' time – William's tract will be made public.'

'What tract? The one he and Thelnetham were squabbling about earlier – Linton Hall's heresy transcribed into his own words? Thelnetham will have burned it by now.'

Michael was white-faced with shock. 'He *should* have burned it, and I should have watched to ensure it was done. William must have tricked him somehow . . .'

'William may be a fool, but he is not so stupid as to let that sort of thing fall into the wrong hands,' said Bartholomew comfortingly. 'Do not worry.'

Michael brandished the letter in agitation. 'The author

of this has included two pages of the original, so the wrong hands *do* have it!'

'Then the culprit will be Thelnetham, aiming to give us a fright.'

'This is not his writing,' snapped Michael, rattled. 'And you would not be so glib if you had read Linton's so-called theology. Moreover, William's foreword contains a lot of scandalous remarks about Gilbertines, Dominicans and John Winwick. If those are made public, Michaelhouse will be finished.'

Bartholomew took the missive from him. Its tone was coolly menacing, and it was clear that the anonymous sender meant what was said. The writing was a neat round-hand, and although it was the style used by most literate people, there was something about it that was familiar.

'I think I have seen this hand before,' he mused. 'But I cannot recall where.'

'Well, *try*,' cried Michael. 'It is important!'

Bartholomew did, but was forced to shake his head. 'It is no good. It might have been anywhere. You always have a mass of documents in your office, I marked dozens of essays over the summer, Edith has asked me to read writs regarding Oswald's business . . .'

'Unfortunately, there are no other clues. This is cheap parchment that Weasenham sells by the cartload and the ink is unremarkable. We are doomed, Matt! Damn William and his stupid yen to aggravate Thelnetham!'

Bartholomew was unnerved by the distress with which the Master and other Fellows greeted the news of the anonymous letter, as until then he had been inclined to think Michael was overreacting. The blood drained from Langelee's face, Suttone slumped on a bench, and Clippesby began to cry. William turned accusingly to Thelnetham, but even he could see the Gilbertine's shock was genuine, and that the note had nothing to do with him.

The Franciscan swallowed hard, and his finger shook as he pointed to the pages in Michael's hand. 'Those are from my second draft, the one I wrote in my own words. And they *are* the originals. I recognise the ink blots.'

Michael scowled at Thelnetham. 'You agreed to oversee its destruction—'

'Suttone offered to do it instead,' bleated Thelnetham defensively. 'I thought he could be trusted.'

'I took it to the kitchen,' said Suttone unsteadily, 'to put it on the fire, but we had bread and cheese today, so Agatha had not bothered to light one. She promised to burn it the next time she had a blaze going, so I left it with her. I assumed it would be safe in her domain . . .'

Langelee and Michael hurried downstairs, but it was not long before they returned to report that the laundress had been out for much of the day. The kitchen had been unattended for hours.

'God damn it, William!' cried Langelee. 'I shall go down in history as the Master whose College was suppressed for second-hand heresy.'

'No one will believe that William speaks for us all,' said Bartholomew reasonably. 'I am sure we can distance ourselves from—'

'Two members of Linton Hall tried that defence, and it made no difference,' interrupted Michael savagely. 'They were excommunicated regardless.'

Langelee blew out his cheeks in a sigh. 'Well, we cannot pay this extortionist, so our only options are to catch him or retrieve the text. Does anyone have any ideas?'

No one did, and there were angry recriminations against Thelnetham and Suttone for ineptitude, and William for penning such a thing in the first place. Bartholomew expected the Franciscan to react with his usual blustering defiance, and was alarmed when he muttered a sheepish and very uncharacteristic apology, as it meant that the others' concerns were justified.

'I told you: it was never meant to go outside the College,' he finished miserably. 'It was written purely to annoy this stupid Gilbertine. It is *his* fault that I felt compelled to resort to such measures. And Suttone's for leaving it in a place where it could be stolen.'

'I wish I had never enrolled in this horrid College,' spat Thelnetham. 'It is a disgrace. If William does not see us suppressed, Bartholomew will, for his unseemly fascination with the insides of corpses. No, do not deny it! How else would he know that Hemmysby was poisoned?'

'He did the right thing,' argued Langelee. 'Our colleague was murdered, a foul deed that might have gone undetected if Bartholomew had not had the courage to look beyond the obvious.'

Thelnetham eyed him in distaste. 'Hemmysby was a thief. He did not warrant such a risk taken on his behalf.'

'He was killed before he could answer those charges,' Langelee reminded him. 'Which suggests to me that he was innocent – that someone is using him in the most appalling manner.'

'Yes,' agreed Clippesby unhappily. 'I am sure of it.'

'And now that same villain aims to blackmail us,' Langelee continued.

Bartholomew blinked. 'How do you know the two matters are connected?'

'Because Hemmysby was killed by the person who made off with the Stanton Hutch – the villain who later returned and left "evidence" to make sure he was blamed. Then this same rogue plied his burgling skills a *third* time to steal William's tract.' Langelee turned to Michael. 'Find him, and we will show the bastard what happens to those who threaten our existence.'

He and Michael began a low-voiced discussion about how this was to be achieved, which left Thelnetham and Suttone free to resume their assault on William. The Franciscan sat in dejected silence, and Bartholomew vacated the conclave when he could bear it no longer. When he reached his room, Goodwyn was there, gleefully telling the other students about the near-riot in the church.

'You should not have meddled with the bread,' said Aungel disapprovingly. 'It was cruel.'

'It was fun,' countered Goodwyn, sniggering at the memory. 'There were no injuries, though, which was a pity. I could have bandaged them, and charged for my services.'

'You would not have made much from the choir,' said Aungel. 'They do not have a penny between them. Why do you think they joined? It is not because they love music.'

'It is not because they can sing, either,' chortled Goodwyn. 'My ears still hurt.'

Unwilling to listen to more, Bartholomew grabbed the scroll he needed for his lecture on Galen's *Tegni*, and went to the kitchen to work. He arrived to find Agatha drinking mulled wine with Cynric. She immediately pointed to the table.

'The tract was there. When I returned to find it gone, I assumed Father William had sneaked in and grabbed it, to prevent it from being destroyed.'

Cynric was tight-lipped with anger that thieves had invaded his College yet again. 'The culprit must have watched her leave, then crept in when no one was paying attention.'

'Could it have been one of our new students?' Agatha asked him.

Cynric shook his head. 'Master Langelee set them exercises in the hall, to prevent them from attending that heretical debate. He told me to guard the door to stop anyone from leaving. I did as he ordered, and no one escaped, not even to visit the latrine.'

He and Agatha began a vitriolic analysis of possible

suspects, which was essentially a list of people they did not like. Bartholomew tuned out their acrimonious voices, and began to write his commentary. Not long afterwards, Clippesby appeared with Ethel.

'He has taken to coming here since Hemmysby died,' whispered Agatha, watching him settle in a corner. 'When he is not in the henhouse. He and Hemmysby were friends, and he misses him.'

Bartholomew noted with concern that Clippesby was paler than usual, and his eyes were sunken. He was muttering to the bird, which chuntered back. It did look as though they were holding a conversation, and the physician wondered if he would be regaled with it later, along with some clue to the mysteries he and Michael were trying to solve.

'Agatha boxed Goodwyn's ears today,' announced Cynric with a smile of enormous satisfaction. 'Once he had stopped staggering, he pulled out a knife, but thought better of using it on her when she raised her fist a second time.'

'He did *what?*' Bartholomew surged to his feet. No student of his was going to draw weapons on College staff and expect it to pass unremarked.

'He was scoffing cheese from the pantry,' explained Agatha. 'And when I caught him, he dared me to stop him. He thought himself too old to be belted, but I do not take cheek from students, no matter how grand they consider themselves to be.'

'I am sorry, Agatha,' said Bartholomew. 'It is my fault for not being here to control him.'

She grinned. 'When I told Master Langelee, he offered me a choice of being rid of the boy or having him fined two shillings. I chose the fine, and the Master let me keep it for myself.'

Bartholomew was disgusted that such a serious offence should be so casually handled, and was about to say so when Cynric changed the subject.

'I took this from your storeroom,' the book-bearer said, producing a tiny flask containing a bright blue pigment. 'I hope you do not mind.'

Bartholomew regarded it blankly. 'What is it?'

'The stuff Goodwyn made when he was experimenting the other day. It was clear at first, but had turned blue by the morning. That means he accidentally stumbled across some powerful magic, and I plan to daub some on all the College's walls, to keep us safe in the coming riots.'

'What coming riots?' asked Bartholomew in alarm.

'The ones that will take place when the townsfolk finally despair of all these matriculands,' explained Cynric. 'A few have settled into hostels, but most have declined to put themselves under the University's control and roam in packs, pestering women, picking fights and generally making a nuisance of themselves.'

'There is only so much we can be expected to endure,' added Agatha. 'Folk will snap soon.'

'I will tell Michael.' Bartholomew held out his hand for the phial. 'Meanwhile, you had better give that to me. It is almost certainly toxic, and I should have disposed of it already.'

'If it is toxic, then it means the magic is all the stronger,' said Cynric, pleased. He clutched the little bottle to his chest, and Bartholomew knew he was not going to relinquish it without a fight – which was not something the physician was fool enough to attempt. 'And that is a good thing for us.'

CHAPTER 10

Bartholomew worked in the kitchen until Agatha doused the lamp, obliging him to return to his own quarters. His students were asleep, and unwilling to wake them by lighting a candle, he retreated to the storeroom, where he read until his eyes burned with fatigue. When he closed them for a moment he fell into a deep drowse, and was difficult to wake when Michael came to collect him in the small hours. After several moments of futile shoulder-shaking and increasingly frustrated hisses, the monk solved the problem with a bucket of cold water.

'What?' Bartholomew demanded groggily, wiping the drops from his face. 'Is someone ill?'

'If they were, I would not want you tending them,' whispered the monk waspishly. 'I have never known a man sink so deeply into repose. You were smiling. Was it a pleasant dream?'

It had been. Julitta was in it, and so was Richard, back when he had been a sunny, likeable lad of fifteen. Matilde had made an appearance, too, armed with a heavy purse and announcing her intention to marry Bartholomew that afternoon. Annoyingly, Michael had hurled his water just as Richard was about to divulge a way to wed her and still keep Julitta.

'What do you want, Brother? It is the middle of the night.'

'Yes, and we have work to do. Surely you have not forgotten?'

Bartholomew struggled to rally his sluggish wits. 'What work?'

'Ratclyf. And depending on what you find, perhaps Elvesmere and Knyt, too.'

Bartholomew's mind snapped into focus. 'No, and I have already explained why. Call it superstitious nonsense if you will, but it felt very wrong.'

Michael scrubbed at his face, and Bartholomew noticed again how weary his friend looked. 'You have allowed your imagination to run riot because Hemmysby was a friend. Well, Ratclyf was not, and as I said yesterday, your second victim should be easier than the first. Langelee agrees. Something very sinister is unfolding, and unless we have the full facts we may never catch the villain who has set it in motion.'

'But what if people find out?' asked Bartholomew worriedly.

'No one will,' said Michael impatiently. 'We shall take precautions. Besides, think of your sister and her beloved Oswald. She will certainly want to know if there is a poisoner at large. You must do it for her sake.'

Bartholomew scowled: it was unfair to use Edith as a lever. 'We will never know what happened to Oswald, regardless. Even if you found someone to dissect him – and I can tell you now that it will not be me – he has been in the ground too long.'

'Please, Matt. I understand your reluctance, believe me. I even share it – I would much rather be asleep than helping you defile corpses – but we have no choice. We *need* answers.'

'There must be another way to get them.'

'Langelee and I sat for hours trying to think of one. Nothing came to mind.'

'I shall be decried as a warlock for certain,' grumbled Bartholomew.

'We have until Monday before the blackmailer makes good on his threat,' Michael went on, 'which means we have until Monday to catch him. To do that, we need to know how many victims he has claimed, because Langelee is right – he and the poisoner *are* one and the same. Besides, now you know what to look for, you will use a lighter hand than you did on Hemmysby.'

'Not necessarily. It depends on the—'

'No details, please,' interrupted Michael. 'Now are you coming or not?'

Profoundly unhappy, Bartholomew donned his cloak and followed Michael to the gate. Cynric was waiting there, having sent the porter on some spurious errand so that the three of them could leave the College unseen.

'Follow me and do everything I say,' he ordered. 'I will keep you from prying eyes.'

He did his best, but neither scholar was very good at creeping around in the pitch black. They tripped over unseen obstacles, Michael squawked when his cloak caught on a shoe-scraper, and Bartholomew dropped his medical bag. By the time they reached the church, Cynric was thoroughly exasperated. He led them through the graveyard, shoving them rather roughly into the shadows when a group of matriculands staggered noisily past. Several women were with them, including two of the town's less discerning prostitutes.

'I will not allow this sort of thing once term starts,' vowed Michael. 'I shall recruit more beadles, and we will soon have this riotous behaviour under control.'

'I doubt it, Brother,' said Cynric. 'If they cannot find a College or a hostel, they will fall under de Stannell's jurisdiction. And he is useless.'

'Dick Tulyet will not be gone for ever,' said Michael curtly, disliking the reminder that his authority was not absolute. 'He will support what I am trying to do.'

'Then let us hope he does not return too late,' said Cynric darkly.

He led them to the vestry door, and ordered them to hide behind a buttress while he reconnoitred the church and its environs. He took so long that Michael began to whisper, to stop himself from dwelling on the unpleasant task that awaited them within.

'Did I tell you that twenty-seven new hostels have been founded in the last two months? Most are for clerks, as that is why so many lads came – hoping to study law at Winwick.'

Bartholomew was also glad to be thinking of something else. 'You must be pleased. It means the University is expanding.'

'Yes, but it is happening too fast. Of course, it is Oxford's fault.'

'Oxford's?' Bartholomew was startled by the claim. 'Why?'

'Because if they had kept their ideas on apostolic poverty to themselves, John Winwick would almost certainly have founded his upstart College there. Instead, he foisted it on us.'

'He did not choose us because we are the better school?' joked Bartholomew. 'Besides, I thought you were pleased that he favoured Cambridge over them.'

'I was,' said Michael stiffly. 'But the rising antagonism Winwick Hall is causing has changed my mind. Now I wish he had imposed his patronage on another foundation.'

Bartholomew, sensing a rant in the making, hastily changed the subject. 'Have you found Fulbut yet?'

'No, and as I said earlier, I suspect we never will. Meadowman is the only one still looking for him, as all my other beadles are needed out on patrol. Incidentally, did I tell you about the rumour that the town plans to attack the University at one of three places – this church, King's Hall or Winwick?'

'Why them?'

'Because they are our most conspicuous holdings. I have a bad feeling that the assault will be on Tuesday, at the beginning of term ceremony – which will be grander than usual, as it marks Winwick's official entry into our ranks. Its founder plans to be there, which is a nuisance. I could do without high-ranking courtiers to protect.'

'Perhaps you should cancel it.'

'That would be tantamount to letting the town dictate what we do, and that is a very slippery slope to start down.' Michael sighed tiredly. 'I have lost count of the spats I have quelled of late. There was an especially vicious one today between three new hostels and the bakers' apprentices.'

'What was it about?'

'The burglaries. The culprit – who most people believe to be Potmoor – evades capture with such effortless ease that people are beginning to believe he has help. The students think it is de Stannell, while the town blames the University.'

'Did you speak to Potmoor about the fire in St Clement's?' asked Bartholomew. 'Or his connections to Illesy?'

'Yes, but he refused to comment on either. Did you hear the choir sing my new *Jubilate*, by the way? It was very rousing.'

'That is one way of putting it.'

'It is meant to be loud,' said Michael, offended. 'It is music to celebrate, and you do not do that in a whisper. Here is Cynric at last. Good. If he had kept us waiting much longer, my nerve would have failed me.'

'*Your* nerve,' muttered Bartholomew. 'What about mine?'

St Mary the Great was dark and eerily silent, its thick walls and handsomely glazed windows blocking any outside noise. The only sound inside was the low murmur of prayers, which came from Heyford, who liked earning extra money and was always the first to volunteer when vigils were required. He was in the Lady Chapel with the three coffins.

'He is the only person here,' whispered Cynric. 'You must lure him away, Brother. Then Doctor Bartholomew can do what he likes to these corpses, invisible to all but the spirits.'

Michael pulled a wineskin from under his cloak. 'I shall offer him a little claret to keep out the chill. He claims never to touch strong beverages, but that it is a lie, or he would not have been drunk when his church caught fire. However, he will have to come to my office for it, as I do not approve of imbibing in the presence of the dead.'

Bartholomew snatched the flask and took a hearty swig. He rarely felt the need for a drink, but that night was an exception. He gulped so much that Michael was obliged to tug it away, afraid there would be insufficient left to distract the vicar.

Fortunately, Heyford was more than happy to shirk his duties, and Michael was hard-pressed to keep up with him when he surged to his feet and aimed for the Senior Proctor's elegant office, which was located in the south aisle – a little too close for Bartholomew's liking, but not so far that Heyford would baulk at the distance from where he was paid to be. Bartholomew waited until Cynric nodded to say the coast was clear, and then stepped towards the caskets. He glanced around anxiously.

'Do not worry, boy,' whispered Cynric. 'I bought a charm to protect us. It contains real holy water, so you are quite safe from evil sprites. However, you will not be safe from Heyford if he comes back before you have finished, so you had better get on with . . . whatever you mean to do.'

He retreated into the shadows when Bartholomew unlatched the first lid, unwilling to witness what was being done in the name of justice. The coffin contained Elvesmere, waxy-faced and reaching the point where he had outstayed his welcome above ground. The body had been dressed in a shroud with a lot of fiddly laces, and by the time Bartholomew finally reached bare skin, he was so exasperated that making an incision seemed easy by comparison.

When the examination was complete, he re-dressed Elvesmere, and moved to the next box. His scalpel was just descending towards Ratclyf when there was a great thump on the door, which made him jump so violently that the metal blade slipped from his fingers and clattered ringingly on the flagstones. The muted murmur of Michael's conversation with Heyford faltered.

'Students,' the vicar said disapprovingly, when tipsy giggles followed. 'Relieving themselves in the porch. The scoundrels! I shall tell them what happens to brutes who—'

'Let my beadles do it,' said Michael quickly. 'The troublemakers might be armed, and we do not want you hurt. More wine?'

The argument convinced Heyford, who held out his cup. Bartholomew released the breath he had been holding, and returned to Ratclyf with hands that shook. He finished quickly, then pulled the lid from Knyt's ornate chest.

He stood for a moment, gazing at the kindly features. The Secretary had been a force for good in the town, and he and Oswald had relieved a lot of suffering through the Guild of Saints. It was a pity things were changing now that de Stannell was in charge. Or were they? Julitta and Edith were still members, and they would not condone funds being squandered on less deserving causes.

A burst of laughter from Michael's office pulled him from his reverie – it was hardly the time to ponder such matters. He took a deep breath and began his examination. It took no more than a moment to learn what he needed to know, and he was just straightening Knyt's gown when Cynric came to demand what was taking so long.

'I have finished now,' Bartholomew replied shortly, tempted to point out that dissection was an art, not an excuse for butchery. 'Help me put the lids back on.'

'You have not done it yet?' hissed Cynric in alarm. 'Then hurry! Heyford has finished all the wine and will be out soon.'

At that point Bartholomew discovered that he was less adept at re-attaching clasps than at manipulating dissecting tools, and nervous tension made him more clumsy still. Cynric cursed when he realised they were trying to put Ratclyf's lid on Elvesmere, and gulped audibly when Heyford's returning footsteps sounded in the nave. Michael was at the vicar's heels, gabbling about apostolic poverty in a desperate attempt to distract him a little longer. Then the last clip snapped into place, and there was just enough time to duck behind a pillar. Unfortunately, in his haste to escape, Bartholomew dropped his scalpel a second time. Heyford stopped dead in his tracks.

'Someone is in here, Brother,' he whispered hoarsely. 'A burglar, perhaps, hoping to steal all the ecclesiastical silver that your greedy University has accumulated.'

'It was a bird,' replied Michael. 'One is trapped in here at the moment. But as I was saying, this schism about the relation of grace and merit to dominion is one that will see the whole of Christendom in flames.'

'I hear it has already caused trouble in Oxford.' Heyford dropped to his knees in front of the coffins. 'The King himself has been forced to intervene, and he is said to be furious about it. But we had better discuss this tomorrow, Brother. Now, I must pray.'

'Very well,' said Michael, surreptitiously kicking the scalpel backwards. To his horror, it rattled on the flagstones,

causing Heyford to leap to his feet. 'Lord! What an audacious bird!'

'Perhaps we should look for it,' gulped Heyford. 'It
should be roosting, not flying around making peculiar
noises. Do you think the Devil has possessed it?'

'Of course not,' declared Michael haughtily. 'Satan
would never dare enter St Mary the Great.'

'Then maybe these sinister sounds are not a bird at
all, but three souls crying out from Purgatory. Or rather
one from Purgatory and the other two from Hell.'

'Which two are in Hell?' asked Michael curiously.

'The pair from Winwick. I said from the start that the
place was evil, and when that thieving Illesy was made
Provost, I was sure of it.'

'Are you sure about what happened in Westminster?'
asked Michael doubtfully. 'Illesy does not seem dishonest
to me.'

'Of course I am sure! He is a felon, and his criminal
tendencies are what encouraged Potmoor to hire him as
his legal representative. The pair of them conspired to
burn me alive when I spoke out against their wicked ways.'

'You may be right about Illesy, but that does not mean
the rest of Winwick should be tarred with the same brush.
There is no evidence to suggest that Elvesmere or Ratclyf
were corrupt.'

Heyford pursed his lips. 'Elvesmere was a bigot who
disliked anything not within his narrow remit of virtues,
while Ratclyf was the most deceitful rogue I ever met.
Doubtless that is why they put him in charge of Winwick's
finances.'

'I hardly think—'

'It is common knowledge that if you want a foundation
to prosper, you should appoint a villain to mind its coffers.
Why do you think Potmoor was invited to join the Guild
of Saints?'

'Perhaps that explains why Michaelhouse is poor,' said

245

Michael wryly. 'We have no mendacious felon to manipulate our accounts.'

'Get Thelnetham to do it,' advised the vicar. 'He will see you wealthy in no time at all.'

When Heyford returned to his prayers, Cynric grabbed Bartholomew's arm and bundled him out of the church, taking care to ensure that he did not drop anything else on the way. When they reached the graveyard, both took deep breaths to calm their jangling nerves.

'Well?' asked Michael, making them jump by speaking behind them. He handed the physician the scalpel he had retrieved – the truth would be out for certain if that were found lying around. 'What did you discover? It had better be something worthwhile, because it was not pleasant spending all that time with an opinionated fool like Heyford.'

'It was not pleasant being dragged out to perform anatomies in the middle of the night,' retorted Bartholomew. 'It would not have been so bad if we could have worked openly, with the blessing of all concerned. But what we did felt shabby and sacrilegious.'

'Yes, it did,' agreed Michael. 'But it is over now, so what did you learn?'

'That Elvesmere and Knyt have lesions consistent with *dormirella*, but Ratclyf does not.'

Michael frowned. 'So Elvesmere and Knyt were murdered?'

'I can only tell you that the toxin was inside them. I cannot tell you how it got there.'

Michael pursed his lips. 'Well, Hemmysby, Elvesmere and Knyt are unlikely to have swallowed the same substance by accident on three different days, and the chances of three separate suicides are highly improbable. I think we can safely deduce that they were unlawfully killed.'

'But Ratclyf was not. At least, not with *dormirella*. Perhaps he really did die of a weak heart.'

'So of the six deaths we are investigating, three were poisoned, one was shot, and one died of undetermined causes,' summarised Michael. 'That leaves Oswald . . .'

'I will not dissect him for anyone,' said Bartholomew quietly. 'Not even Edith. You will have to find the killer, and make him give you the names of any other victims.'

'Yes, but how? I was hoping for more than a mere confirmation of what we suspected already. And because we can never tell another living soul what we did tonight, we cannot even reveal that these men were poisoned. People will ask how we know.'

'I have an idea,' said Cynric brightly. Both scholars regarded him warily: his suggestions were not always sensible. From under his cloak, Cynric produced a flask containing more of Goodwyn's blue creation. 'Do you recall how this stuff started off clear, but changed colour during the night? Well, you can claim that the same thing happens with the poison.'

'I do not follow,' said Michael.

Cynric grimaced impatiently. 'You can say that *dormirella* is undetectable at the time of death, but that clues appear on the victim after a period of time. Who will know any different?'

'Lots of people,' replied Bartholomew promptly. He began to list them. 'Langelee, Rougham, Meryfeld, Lawrence—'

'Nonsense,' interrupted Michael disdainfully. 'Lawrence said he had never heard of *dormirella* before we mentioned it, so he is not in a position to argue, while the other *medici* are unlikely to know what the poison can do.'

'And Master Langelee will not contradict us when we explain what we are doing,' added Cynric.

'But what *are* we doing?' asked Michael. 'What kind of clues do you intend to invent, exactly?'

Cynric waved the phial. 'We shall paint their faces blue.'

'I doubt we could make that look convincing,' said Bartholomew, alarmed. 'Moreover, one drip in the wrong place will expose the ruse in an instant.'

'Their lips, then,' said Cynric impatiently. 'Or even one or two judiciously placed spots. Anything that will be obvious to a casual observer.'

'A casual observer who can see through wood?' asked Bartholomew archly. 'They are in sealed caskets, Cynric. And there is no reason to open them.'

'Yes, there is,' countered Michael, visibly warming to the idea. 'We undid Hemmysby's last night, because we forgot to include his pectoral cross. We can say we noticed these marks then. Concerned, I can order the other coffins opened, too. Cynric is right: we can say quite openly that these men were poisoned, and it may panic the killer into making a mistake. At which point we shall have him.'

'But it is a lie,' objected Bartholomew. 'And I am not very good at those.'

'It is not a lie – it is a trap to catch the beast who has taken at least three lives, stolen the Stanton Hutch and arranged for Hemmysby to be accused of it, and aims to destroy Michaelhouse by publishing William's tract. Think of *that* if anyone challenges you.'

'We should paint Ratclyf's lips, too,' said Cynric. 'He was not poisoned, but only one person knows that – the culprit. Our deception will confuse and unsettle him.'

'Excellent!' crowed Michael. 'It is high time we took control of the situation.'

Bartholomew was far from convinced that the plan was sound, especially when it became obvious that he was the one expected to apply the dye. Michael shoved him back inside the church, while Cynric informed Heyford that he had seen a suspicious shadow lurking. The vicar was more than happy to lock himself in the monk's office until told it was safe to emerge.

'Hurry, Matt,' hissed Michael urgently when the physician took an inordinate amount of time to do what was necessary. 'Our scheme will not work if we are caught.'

'It needs to look realistic,' Bartholomew whispered back irritably. 'We will be accused of desecration for certain if we leave obvious brush strokes.'

He finished at last, having applied two or three discreet but noticeable stains on the lips of each corpse. They were as convincing as he could make them, and he left the church with relief. Cynric went to inform Heyford that it was safe to resume his vigil, but the vicar was unconvinced, and ordered the book-bearer to stay with him for the rest of the night. Cynric tried to demur, but Heyford was adamant.

'I was almost incinerated once,' he said. 'I do not intend to give anyone a second chance.'

The escapade left Bartholomew with a deep sense of disquiet, and he knew he would not sleep for what remained of the night, so he sat in his storeroom, a blanket around his shoulders, working on his lectures. The knowledge that he was still far from ready for the start of term ahead forced him to concentrate, so when the bell rang to wake the College for its morning devotions, he was pleased to announce that he had managed to prepare everything that was needed for the second week of teaching. He ignored the fact that another seven and a half still remained, and congratulated himself on his progress.

He went to the lavatorium, where he washed, shaved and donned clean clothes. The lavatorium was a shed-like structure with water piped from the well and drains to channel it away again, built for those who cared about personal hygiene. Bartholomew usually had it to himself, especially after Langelee had declared hot water a frivolous luxury, so that only cold was available. Shivering, the physician trotted across the yard to where his colleagues were gathering.

'Where is Clippesby?' asked Langelee irritably. 'Look in his room, would you, Suttone?'

'He will not be there,' sneered Thelnetham. 'He will be with that chicken. If he were not totally witless, I would say he was communing with the Devil's familiar.'

'Well, he is a Dominican,' said William, who could believe nothing good of that Order. Then it occurred to him that he had just agreed with Thelnetham, and hastened to put matters right. 'But it is the Gilbertines who worship Satan, and if anyone communes with the Devil it is you.'

'As you wrote in your poisonous little tract,' said Thelnetham coldly. 'Well, you had better hope it is never made public, because my Order will sue yours, and mine will win.'

'It will *not* be made public,' vowed Langelee. 'We will outwit this villain, and stop him from harming us. We must.'

'You can try,' said Thelnetham. 'But I suspect he is cleverer than you, so I plan to transfer to another College as soon as one offers me a place. I shall announce my availability at the Saturday Sermon today. It is my turn to preach, and—'

'No!' barked Langelee with such anger that Thelnetham started in surprise. 'You will *not* make self-serving declarations on the day of Hemmysby's burial. And there will be no Saturday Sermon either, out of respect for him. We shall have it on Monday instead.'

Thus admonished, Thelnetham fell silent. Suttone returned to say that Clippesby's room was empty, so Bartholomew went to see whether the Dominican was with the hens in the orchard.

Michaelhouse's poultry led enchanted lives. High walls and secure gates meant they were safe from foxes, thieves and any other predator that might take a fancy to their overfed little bodies, while their coop was a veritable palace, built by a student who had wanted to be a master carpenter. It was not only sturdy, rainproof and airy, but boasted some of the best wood-carvings in Cambridge. Clippesby kept it spotless, and Bartholomew often thought that Ethel and her flock lived in greater comfort than the Fellows.

'Clippesby?' he called as he approached. 'John?'

He was somewhat surprised to see the Dominican emerge through the pop-hole. He had expected him to be talking to the birds, or perhaps letting them out for the day, but he had certainly not anticipated that he might have crawled into the coop with them.

'Is it time for church?' yawned Clippesby. 'I did not hear the bell. I must have been in a very deep slumber.'

'You slept in there?' asked Bartholomew, regarding him uneasily.

'Ethel misses Hemmysby,' explained the Dominican. 'So I decided to keep her company.'

'Please do not tell Thelnetham,' begged Bartholomew. 'We would never hear the end of it.'

'Yes, he has grown opinionated of late. Especially about Hemmysby, who was *not* a thief.'

'No,' agreed Bartholomew, seeing tears fill the gentle Dominican's eyes. 'But Michael will find the villain who wants us to think so.'

Clippesby bent to scoop up Ethel, who was lurking in the hope of treats. 'He said yesterday that it is the same person who aims to blackmail us over William's nasty tract.'

'Yes – the culprit has broken in three times now. Once to steal the Stanton Hutch, once to plant the Cup and the deeds in Hemmysby's room, and once to take William's essay. Our security has never been very tight, so it cannot have been difficult.'

251

'Ethel heard Thelnetham's response when William gave him that tract to read,' said Clippesby, kissing the chicken tenderly on the head. 'As did any number of students. He read a few pages in silence, then began to screech his rage and horror.'

'Well, William did say he wrote it with that specific end in mind.'

'The students must have gossiped about the incident outside the College, where the blackmailer overheard. It explains how he knew what to come here and take. The tract is a horrible piece, Matt – not just the heresy, but the hurtful remarks about other Orders and John Winwick. Our colleagues are right to fear what will happen if it is ever released.'

'Then let us hope that Michael can prevent it.'

Clippesby nodded unhappily, and turned to another depressing subject. 'How is your sister? I cannot imagine Richard is much comfort to her, given the company he keeps – Goodwyn, Uyten, some of the unruliest matriculands. The Bene't hedgehog tells me that there are an unusually high number from London this year, which is why Richard knows so many of them. She wonders whether *he* told them to come and try their luck at Winwick Hall.'

'Then I hope she is wrong,' said Bartholomew fervently.

'The swans predict trouble for Tuesday,' Clippesby went on. 'The town resents lavish displays of grandeur, and they fear an attack on our more ostentatious foundations – King's Hall, Winwick and St Mary the Great.'

'Michael heard that rumour, too. Let us trust that it is groundless.'

'Yes, especially if the Keeper of the Privy Seal is here to witness it. It would be a pity if he told the King that we are as bad as Oxford for quarrels and riots.'

They walked to the yard, Bartholomew brushing telltale wood shavings from Clippesby as they went, lest

Thelnetham guessed what the Dominican had been doing. They arrived to find the other Fellows talking in low, worried voices, while the students waited by the gate.

'I say we charge William the twenty marks,' Thelnetham was hissing. 'It is his scribbling that caused the trouble. And afterwards, he should do the decent thing and resign. Extortionists never stop with one payment, and we do not want any more demands.'

'But I do not have twenty marks,' snapped William. 'And you should accept some of the blame anyway. If you were not such an ignorant pig, I would not have felt obliged to put pen to parchment in the first place.'

'Do not quarrel,' said Clippesby, releasing Ethel so she flapped towards them. Both Gilbertine and Franciscan recoiled in alarm. 'It is unbecoming for men in holy orders.'

'And *you* should resign, too,' snarled Thelnetham. 'Indeed, you *all* should. You are either bigots, lunatics, gluttons, warlocks or heretics. Our founder must be turning in his grave!'

'He will turn even faster if you do not catch this black-mailer,' said Langelee to Michael. 'What did you discover in St Mary the Great last night?'

Michael launched into the tale that he and Cynric had devised, which made Bartholomew look away, lest his more observant colleagues should detect his unease with it. 'So the rogue has claimed at least four victims,' he concluded. 'Hemmysby, Knyt, Elvesmere and Ratclyf. Not to mention trying to extort money from us and stealing our hutch.'

'Then you must do all you can to catch him, Brother,' said William. 'Because I am not giving Hemmysby's killer twenty marks. Even if I did have it to spare.'

The discussion and Clippesby's sojourn in the henhouse meant they were late, so Langelee led his procession up St Michael's Lane at a rapid clip. They were just crossing the High Street when they ran into a group of men who, judging from their bleary eyes and ale-scented breath, had spent the night in a tavern. They were led by Hugo Potmoor, and comprised an odd combination of his father's henchmen and matriculands. Bartholomew was dismayed to see Richard among them. His nephew's was not the only presence to excite comment.

'There is Surgeon Holm,' remarked Michael. 'What is he doing in such unsavoury company?'

'He and Hugo are friends,' explained Clippesby. 'The sparrows tell me they are always together, and are frequent visitors to each other's homes.'

'That does not surprise me,' said Thelnetham. 'Holm is a villain, so of course he gravitates towards men of similar mien.' He shot Bartholomew an unpleasant glance. 'And that includes your nephew, I am sorry to say.'

'Richard is more fool than villain,' said Langelee. 'Tell him to go home before anyone sees him, Bartholomew. He will bring disgrace to your family if he is spotted cavorting with this horde.'

Chagrined that even the hedonistic Master deplored his kinsman's choice of company, Bartholomew went to do as he was told.

'I suppose you have come to recommend that I find myself some more suitable friends,' slurred Richard. 'Well, I am sorry, but I like these. So you can mind your own business.'

Bartholomew stared at him, wondering what had happened to the likeable, ebullient boy he had known and loved. Sensing a quarrel in the making, Richard's companions came to form a semicircle at his back, sniggering and jostling.

'Actually, I came to pass on Langelee's advice,' said

Bartholomew coolly. 'That if you must act like a halfwit, do it somewhere other than the High Street.'

'I am touched by your concern.' Richard waved a careless hand, which caused him to stagger. 'But it is too early for anyone important to be awake, so you and Langelee need not worry.'

Hugo flung a meaty arm around his shoulders. 'On the contrary, your reputation will be enhanced. After all, Holm and I are influential members of the Guild of Saints.'

Richard smiled challengingly at his uncle. 'You will soon get used to me living here again. And I shall be your equal soon – a University Fellow, no less. Now I see what Cambridge has to offer, I wonder why I ever left.'

'The Brazen George awaits!' cried Hugo suddenly. 'And I have a fierce thirst. The last one through the door buys the first drinks.'

There was a concerted lurch towards the tavern, where their braying laughter and drunken hoots drew disapproving glances from scholars and townsmen alike. Richard lost his footing as he tried to join them, and Holm and Hugo made heavy work of pulling him to his feet. Hating to see him make such a spectacle of himself, Bartholomew went to help.

'Perhaps you should just go home, Richard,' he said quietly. 'More ale will—'

'Do not tell him what to do,' interrupted Hugo belligerently. 'It is a good thing you raised my father from the dead or I would trounce you for your audacity.'

'Trounce him anyway,' suggested Holm. 'It might make him less attractive to my wife.'

Hugo laughed. 'It will take a lot more than a battered face to lop *your* cuckold's horns! Just as it will take more than death to lop those of a certain deceased Secretary.'

Holm blinked as he struggled to understand. 'Do you mean Olivia Knyt? She had a lover?'

'Yes – my father. She bought bryony root to cure her husband's fever, but she used it improperly and he died. Which means she is now free to cavort openly, and even remarry if she chooses. Bryony. It sounds so innocent and yet . . . Perhaps you should buy some for Julitta, Will. That would put an end to her brazen wantonness.'

Bartholomew's blood ran cold. 'You would not—'

'Julitta is not wanton,' said Holm, eyes narrowed. 'She loves me, and me alone. Come, Hugo. We have better things to do than bandy words with the man who swoons over my wife.'

They sauntered away arm in arm, leaving Bartholomew staring after them in mute horror, appalled that his affection for Julitta might have put her in danger. Yet Holm had seemed equally averse to poisoning his wife. Did that mean he *did* harbour some feeling for her, and she was safe from harm? But what if—

'You should stay away from them,' advised Richard. Bartholomew had forgotten him, and jumped when his nephew spoke at his side. 'Especially Hugo. I enjoy his company, but he can be . . . disagreeable to people he dislikes.'

'I am sure he can. He takes after his father.'

'You should not have done it.' Richard grabbed Bartholomew's shoulder to steady himself. 'Raised Potmoor from the dead, I mean. It has turned a lot of people against you. You should have kept your smelling salts in your bag. You did not have to use them on him.'

'Of course I did! I took an oath to help those in need.'

'An oath,' mused Richard. 'I am good at finding loopholes in those, and it is obvious that you should renounce that one. I shall want something in return, of course.'

'What?' asked Bartholomew, not bothering to point out

that he had no intention of reneging on a vow, especially one in which he believed with all his heart.

'That you stay out of my affairs. I know what I am doing with . . . I know what I am doing.'

'Doing with whom?' demanded Bartholomew. 'Weasenham's wife? If he catches you, he will destroy you with gossip. He has done it before.'

'If he tries, I will sue him. There is no more effective weapon than the law, and I am an expert at wielding it. And I am serious about what I said – do not meddle in my affairs.'

Richard and his friends were not the only ones worse for wear after a night of drinking. So was Noll Verius, who had collapsed in a heap in St Michael's churchyard. Isnard was with him, but although the bargeman was adept at compensating for the loss of his leg, carrying inebriated ditchers was well past what he could manage.

'Help me, Doctor,' he called. 'His wife will be worried, and I would not have her distressed.'

Bartholomew should have refused and gone to church, but he liked Ylaria, so he obligingly hefted Verius across his shoulder.

'You are stronger than you look,' remarked Isnard, swinging along beside him on his crutches. 'I suppose you are used to lugging your colleagues around after Michaelhouse feasts.'

Bartholomew smiled ruefully, thinking it had been a long time since the College had been able to treat its members to that sort of extravagance. He wondered whether it ever would again.

'Will you tell Brother Michael that me and the other basses had nothing to do with the trouble at the Laughing Pig last night?' Isnard went on. 'I should not like him to think badly of us. Or worse, tell us off in front of the whole choir.'

'Why? What happened?'

'We were sitting quietly, bemoaning the fact that the Guild of Saints will no longer help needy widows, when your nephew and his boisterous friends arrived. We ignored them at first, but then we heard Richard say that *he* had voted against the widows. Well, tempers flared and punches were thrown, although not at him, more is the pity.'

'Agatha told me about Richard's role in that ballot. I will speak to him.'

'Do not bother. He will not listen, and you will be wasting your breath. And do not worry your sister with it either. She is a good lady, and must be heartbroken to see what he has become.'

They arrived at Verius's house, where it took both of them to manoeuvre the ditcher through the door. Ylaria was relieved to have her husband home, and clucked around him like a mother hen.

'He was celebrating,' explained Isnard. 'Brother Michael has given him the solo in the *Recordare*. Michael has a good ear for an angelic voice, which is why he lets me lead the basses, of course. He appreciates my rich tones.'

Bartholomew replaced the filthy bandage on the ditcher's thumb and left, but he had not taken many steps before he was hailed by Rougham, who fell into step at his side. The Gonville *medicus* was in a foul mood, because the Guild of Saints had declined to make its usual yearly donation towards his College chapel. Bartholomew, eager for an excuse to escape the tirade, was glad when he spotted Eyer on the other side of the road.

Rougham followed him to where Eyer was talking to a squat, fierce-faced physician named Nigellus de Thornton, who practised in the nearby village of Barnwell. Nigellus was livid, and the apothecary was trying to calm him.

'Have *you* heard?' Nigellus snarled, making Bartholomew

258

and Rougham flinch at the fury in his voice. 'What Winwick Hall has done to me?'

'No,' replied Rougham. 'But I warrant it will be something nasty. The Keeper of the Privy Seal should have foisted his vile foundation on Oxford instead. We do not want it here.'

'Illesy and his Fellows have rejected my application to teach,' raged Nigellus. 'How *dare* they! I was a physician before most of them were born, and they should have welcomed me with open arms. But they say they have Lawrence, and there is no need for another *medicus*.'

'You should have asked me before submitting yourself to their insults,' said Rougham. 'I could have told you that they are only interested in recruiting lawyers. Lawrence is unusual in that he specialises in both subjects, but—'

'They should have made an exception for me,' blazed Nigellus. 'But I will show them! I have been offered a place in Zachary Hostel, and they will *kick* themselves when they see how many students I attract.'

'He was not rejected because he cannot teach law,' confided Eyer, when the enraged *medicus* had stamped away, 'but because he is not rich enough. Winwick only wants men who can make massive donations to its coffers. I considered applying myself until I realised how much it costs.'

'I imagine you can afford it.' Rougham glanced pointedly towards Eyer's handsome shop. 'You are a member of the Guild of Saints, and they do not admit paupers.'

Eyer winced. 'Yes, but I am thinking of resigning. I would rather my hard-earned shillings went to relieve beggars, orphans and widows, not to buy fancy cutlery for Winwick Hall.'

'I do not see you as an educator anyway,' said Rougham. 'You told me only yesterday that you dislike most of the young men who are applying for places to study here this year.'

'I would make a very good scholar,' objected Eyer indignantly. 'Much better than most of the masters I studied under.'

'You had more than one?' asked Rougham, surprised. 'I thought apprentices in the remedy business tended to stick with the same mentor for the whole of their training.'

'I am different,' retorted Eyer, the shortness of his response making it clear that the discussion was over. Bartholomew was puzzled – most craftsmen were usually only too happy to talk about the painstaking process of learning their trade. Then Eyer forced a smile. 'Are you hungry? I am having crispy fried earthworms and seagull gizzards for breakfast. You are welcome to join me.'

Bartholomew regarded him askance, wondering if he seriously expected such an invitation to be accepted. The earnest expression on Eyer's face made it abundantly clear that he did.

'I am obliged to break my fast in College,' said Rougham, backing away quickly. 'Attendance at meals is obligatory in Gonville, so you must excuse me.'

'It is obligatory in Michaelhouse, too,' said Bartholomew, when Eyer turned hopeful eyes in his direction. He found himself thinking that even Agatha did not serve such unappealing fare, although that might change if the Stanton Hutch was not recovered.

Eyer sighed. 'Pity. Some intelligent company would have been welcome. But I had better return to my shop before my apprentices set it alight. They are lively lads and I love them dearly, but they are inclined to be wild.'

'So are my new students,' said Bartholomew ruefully. 'Aungel told you about their foolish experiments with urine, I believe?'

Eyer nodded. 'Urine *and* your medical supplies, although you have not come to me to replenish your stocks. Have you taken your custom elsewhere?'

Bartholomew smiled. 'Of course not.'

Eyer tapped his chin thoughtfully. 'Your personal finances are none of my concern, but you cannot earn much from your paupers. If you ever find yourself short of the necessaries, I hope you will let me know. I am more than happy to defer payment. I would not extend this sort of credit to the other physicians, but I trust you.'

'Thank you,' said Bartholomew, although he wondered if Eyer would have made the offer if he had known that any bills incurred were unlikely to be paid before Christmas. Before he could say more, Cynric arrived with a summons from a patient who lived in the north of the city.

'Do not forget,' said Eyer, as the physician turned to leave. 'I will not see the poor suffer for want of remedies, and you are always welcome in my shop – if not to dine, then for decent conversation and a chance to relax.'

'You should accept that invitation, boy,' advised Cynric. 'I would never think of looking for you there, and it would do you no harm to escape from patients, students and Brother Michael on occasion. Especially if he wants you to chop up any more dead bodies.'

As Bartholomew walked past St Clement's Church on his way home, he heard Heyford delivering one of his famously feisty sermons. He could see from the road that the church was packed, and, curious to know why the vicar attracted such consistently large crowds, he stepped into the porch to listen. It did not take him long to understand the appeal: the congregation comprised the kind of townsfolk who were delighted to hear that the University had been founded by Satan. They also enjoyed the news that Winwick Hall would soon suffer the wrath of God because it was full of lawyers. It was not only scholars who suffered Heyford's spitting vitriol.

'Potmoor tried to destroy this beautiful church with

261

me inside it,' he bellowed. 'Well, he will burn in Hell for his wickedness.'

'You spout nonsense, priest!' came an equally loud voice, almost in Bartholomew's ear. The physician shot away in alarm when he saw it came from Potmoor – he did not want to be standing next to *him* while he heckled a vicar. The felon strode through the porch to the nave, where others also hastened to give him a wide berth. 'I died and went to Heaven, but God saw fit to send me back to Earth. He loves me, and it is you who will burn.'

'Ever since he died, Master Potmoor has been working on the town's behalf,' added another voice. It was Deputy de Stannell. Illesy was also in the retinue that clustered around Potmoor's heels, but the Winwick Provost took care to stand in the midst of Potmoor's henchmen, either in the hope that he would not be noticed, or because he thought it would be safer in the event of trouble. 'He has donated a fortune to the Guild of Saints, and God applauds his charity.'

'What charity?' demanded Heyford. 'The Guild has been withdrawing alms for weeks now. And why? So the money can go to Winwick Hall! And the reason for this heinous decision? Because the guildsmen want Winwick's Fellows to say masses for their souls when they are dead. It is not generosity that drives them, but self-interest.'

There was a growl of disapproval from the congregation, many of whom had received financial help in the past, and were resentful that more might not be forthcoming in the future.

'And you are a burglar, too,' added Heyford. 'We know who has been stealing from us.'

'Do you indeed?' said Potmoor, speaking over the murmur of agreement that rustled along the nave. 'Then why does de Stannell not arrest me?'

'Because he is your creature,' spat Heyford. 'He does what you tell him.'

'And I do what *God* tells me,' declared Potmoor. He fingered the sword at his side, and two or three of his henchmen drew daggers. The muttering stopped and the church fell silent. 'He blessed me with a glimpse of His sacred face. Can *you* claim as much?'

'You had no holy vision,' sneered Heyford. 'It was a side effect of the *sal ammoniac*. You are a fraud, and the College your Guild supports is an abomination. It should be burned to the ground with all its lawyers inside, just as you attempted to do to me.'

'You try my patience, Heyford,' said Potmoor softly. 'So does anyone who backs you in your vicious claims. Be warned. I shall not turn the other cheek if you continue to preach against me.'

His voice was low, almost caressing, but it carried unmistakable menace. His small, reptilian eyes swept around the building, causing murmurs of consternation as they rested on specific people. By the time he stalked out, the whole congregation had been thoroughly cowed. Heyford began to rant again, but his voice had lost its conviction and his audience soon lost interest.

Bartholomew had not enjoyed witnessing Potmoor's display of power, and he was glad to leave St Clement's for the familiar comforts of home. However, he had not gone far along Bridge Street before he heard someone call his name. Fighting down the urge to keep walking when he recognised Potmoor's voice, he turned slowly and saw the felon hurrying towards him, the henchmen, Illesy and de Stannell at his heels.

'Heyford just made a very unpleasant assertion,' said Potmoor. His face was white, and his small eyes burned with fury. 'You gave me nothing to induce hallucinations, did you?'

'No,' replied Bartholomew. 'But images of unusual clarity are not unknown when—'

'A simple "no" will suffice. Elaboration will vex me,

and I have suffered enough nonsense for one day. No wonder my headaches persist! Fools like Heyford aggravate me at every turn.'

'They do not know what it means to be touched by God,' said de Stannell sycophantically.

'Indeed,' said Potmoor, but the ice in his voice stopped the deputy from adding more. He turned back to the physician. 'I am glad we met, Bartholomew, because I want you to do something for me. Your Benedictine friend has been asking questions about Illesy's past. Specifically, an incident in Westminster.'

'Poor Heyford,' sighed Illesy. 'He is so determined not to be blamed for setting his own church alight that he has resorted to telling some very wild lies about Potmoor and me. He is a man to be pitied, not taken seriously.'

Bartholomew watched him fiddle with the rings that covered his fingers, a restless, nervous gesture that made the physician ask himself if it was Illesy who was lying.

'But people *do* take him seriously,' said Potmoor softly. 'And I dislike him slandering the Provost of the College that my Guild has chosen to fund. If he were not a priest, I would kill him.'

'Now, now.' Illesy laughed, to make light of the remark. 'No talk of murder in front of the Deputy Sheriff, if you please.'

'I thought I was talking in front of the Secretary of the Guild of Saints,' said Potmoor coldly, and Bartholomew glimpsed again the aura of dark power that hung around the man.

'Of course you are,' gushed de Stannell. 'And I—'

'Tell Michael to stop probing this Westminster business,' said Potmoor, his eyes boring into Bartholomew's. 'He will find nothing amiss, and his time would be better spent investigating these burglaries. He claims I have no alibi for them, but I do – I was at prayer.'

'But there have been dozens of thefts,' Bartholomew pointed out. 'Are you saying that you were at your devotions when every single one of them was committed?'

'Yes,' said Potmoor firmly. 'I am.'

'Then you must spend a lot of time on your knees,' remarked Bartholomew, wondering whether the felon seriously expected him to believe such a ludicrous claim.

'Hours,' agreed Potmoor. He whipped around, startling de Stannell so badly that the deputy stumbled as he jerked away. 'Tell Lawrence to tend me in the Brazen George as soon as possible. I need more of his medicine to soothe my pounding head.'

CHAPTER 11

It was almost time for Hemmysby's burial, so Bartholomew hurried to Michaelhouse to don his best cloak and tabard. When the physician was ready, Langelee led his scholars up the lane. There was an unwritten but universally accepted law that funeral processions had right of way, but resentment of the University was currently so high that carts and riders refused to stop, and the scholars were obliged to brave a treacherous gauntlet of vehicles.

They straggled into the churchyard, where Langelee began grappling with the lock. A combination of exasperation, anger and grief caused him to lose patience, and he solved the problem once and for all by stepping back and aiming a powerful kick at the offending mechanism. It flew into pieces and the door swung open.

'It is *its* fault that Hemmysby died out here,' he said sullenly to his astonished colleagues. 'He would have reached the altar if it had not seen fit to be awkward.'

'Yes, but how shall we secure the church when we have finished?' asked Thelnetham.

Langelee did not reply, and only indicated that his scholars should follow him inside. William was just drawing breath to begin the rite when there was a flurry of activity at the back of the church and people began to file in. They included members of the Guild of Saints, scholars from other Colleges and a smattering of townsmen. The Winwick men were neat and dignified in their new livery and Bartholomew felt shabby by comparison, even in his smartest clothes.

'Damn!' muttered Langelee. 'This was meant to be a private affair, but now we shall have to provide wine and cakes for this horde, or we shall be seen as ungracious. Does anyone have any money? The honour of Michaelhouse is at stake here, so do not be miserly, for God's sake.'

There was some discreet rummaging, followed by clinks as coins were handed over. They were pitifully few, and Cynric eyed them doubtfully when Langelee listed all that was needed.

'And tell Agatha to make sure we are respectable,' the Master ordered, before the book-bearer sped away. 'No laundry hanging in the yard, and all our books must be displayed so that people think we have more of them than we do.'

'Winwick has no right to foist itself on us today,' hissed Thelnetham. 'It is not part of the University yet. Not officially.'

'No, but it will have to return the favour when we attend the funerals of Elvesmere and Ratclyf,' said Langelee with grim satisfaction. 'We shall be fed twice for its once.'

'I would not mind a spell inside its lovely hall,' said Suttone plaintively. 'I have not been warm in days, and I dread the thought of winter with no money for more fuel.'

'Winwick's hall is not lovely,' said Thelnetham in disdain. 'It was built too fast, and its mortar was not given time to dry. It sways in the wind, and I should feel sick if I had to teach there.'

'Perhaps *that* is why its Fellows are here,' said William gleefully. 'To stand in a building that does not swing about or reek of wet plaster.'

'They came to pay their respects,' said Clippesby quietly. He was pale, heavy-eyed, and his hair was standing up in all directions. Unusually, he had no animals with him, which made him seem oddly incomplete. 'Do not denigrate them for that.'

Thus chastised, William began the ceremony – a brief

service inside, followed by burial in the churchyard. There would be a more formal requiem later, when it could be properly organised.

'Are you unwell, John?' whispered Bartholomew, as they prepared to carry the coffin out.

'No,' replied Clippesby. 'But I am worried about our sparrows. No one has seen them since Wednesday, and Ethel reminded me today that Hemmysby threw them some crumbs before he went to the debate. Crumbs left from a raisin tart.'

Bartholomew regarded him blankly. 'You think he did something to these crumbs?'

'Of course not. But he died the same day, and Ethel wonders if the poison was in the tart, not the cake from the debate. It would explain why we no longer have any sparrows.'

'Have you been in his room to see whether any of this tart is left?'

'Ethel thought it might be dangerous, so I decided to let you do it. She is terribly unsettled, Matt. She can sense something nasty in the offing, and so can I.'

'What kind of "something nasty"?'

'Bloodshed, as the University goes to war with the town and with itself.'

There was a respectful silence after Hemmysby had been lowered into the ground. Determined to give Agatha and Cynric as long as possible to prepare, Langelee let it stretch on for an inordinate amount of time. Eventually, he raised his head, and was just drawing breath to announce that refreshments would be available in Michaelhouse when Illesy pre-empted him.

'We understand the distress involved in losing a Fellow,' he declared in a ringing voice. 'So to spare Michaelhouse the ordeal of entertaining, we have prepared a small collation at Winwick. Everyone here is invited.'

'What presumption!' spluttered Thelnetham, although his indignation went unheard in the general murmur of thanks from the other mourners. 'It is *our* privilege to offer hospitality, not his.'

'Christ!' breathed Langelee, aghast. 'Now we shall have to do the same for them – for Elvesmere *and* for Ratclyf. The cunning dogs have outmanoeuvred us!'

Resentment in every step, he went to lead the procession to Winwick's repast, bristling with impotent pique when Illesy took the liberty of walking by his side. Bartholomew did not follow. He took a spade and began to fill in Hemmysby's grave, feeling it was the least he could do to atone for his act of desecration. He had not been shovelling long when someone came to help. He assumed it was Clippesby and did not look up, so it was several moments before he realised it was Lawrence. The elderly physician said nothing, and they worked in silence until the task was done.

'Thank you,' said Bartholomew, leaning the spade against a wall. His best habit was streaked with dirt, and his boots were muddy. Somehow, Lawrence had contrived to remain considerably cleaner, although there was a smattering of soil in his white beard.

'He will be in my prayers tonight,' said Lawrence. 'I knew him from Guild meetings, and thought him a fine priest. He even won Potmoor's approbation, and *he* is not an easy man to please.'

'Potmoor,' said Bartholomew, seizing the opportunity to ask a guildsman about the person Edith thought had murdered her husband. 'My brother-in-law did not like him very much . . .'

'Then his antipathy was misplaced,' said Lawrence firmly. 'I became Potmoor's physician after his brush with death, as you know, and I have seen nothing but goodness in him. He is not the evil villain everyone imagines, and is as sweet and munificent as any guildsman.'

Bartholomew regarded him askance, thinking it was either a sad indictment of the other members, or Lawrence was unusually unperceptive. 'Did Oswald and Potmoor quarrel much in Guild meetings?'

'Not that I saw. Indeed, I was under the impression that they did a great deal of business together, so I am surprised to hear that Stanmore did not like him.'

'You mean Oswald sold him cloth?'

'I do not know the nature of their association, Matthew. You will have to ask Potmoor.'

Bartholomew doubted he would be very forthcoming. Then he remembered what Julitta had told him about Lawrence creeping through the town in the dark with Nerli, and supposed he should ask about that, too.

'I am often called out in the middle of the night these days,' he began, intending to steer the discussion to his questions as diplomatically as possible. 'And—'

'I am afraid I cannot accept more of your paupers,' interrupted Lawrence apologetically. 'Not with teaching about to start and Potmoor summoning me every day with headaches.'

'Did he summon you at midnight the other evening?' Bartholomew raised his hands in a placatory shrug when Lawrence regarded him sharply. 'You were seen out with Nerli. He had a sword.'

'You are mistaken. I rarely leave home after dark – I am too old. And while I did tend Potmoor on Friday, it was at dawn, not midnight. Nerli walked part of the way with me, but he was certainly not carrying a weapon. I suppose you spotted me from Julitta Holm's boudoir. It is a bad idea to cuckold the town's only surgeon, Matthew. You may need his help one day, and it would be awkward, to say the least.'

'We meet to practise her reading,' explained Bartholomew.

'Before dawn?' asked Lawrence. He continued before

Bartholomew could correct the misunderstanding. 'Yet I understand the attraction. I might be tempted myself if I were twenty years younger. She is a splendid woman – beautiful *and* a sound financial head on her shoulders. Did you hear about the decision to suspend the beggars' bread and the widows' allowance? That was hers.'

'I did hear, but I cannot believe she would do such a thing.' Bartholomew was bemused by the skill with which Lawrence had taken control of the conversation.

'It sounds heartless, but it is eminently sensible. The money will be lent to Winwick Hall, and will be repaid with interest next year – interest that can then be used to fund other worthy causes. Before she came along, the Guild's finances were in a terrible state, with lots of money one week and none the next. Her plan will ensure a regular and predictable flow of cash.'

'I see. But what happens to the beggars and widows in the interim?'

'I imagine she will look after them herself. She is a generous soul, which is why she was invited to join the Guild. The same is true of all our members. Well, not your nephew, I am afraid to say. *He* was asked out of respect for his father, and because he inherited a vast fortune.'

'I was told that Illesy arranged for him to be elected. And that Illesy will also recommend him for a Fellowship in Winwick Hall.'

'Yes. It is astonishing how wealth opens doors.'

'It is,' agreed Bartholomew sourly. 'But to return to Friday—'

'Poor Potmoor is not responding to my tincture of sage.' Lawrence cut across him. 'I must try something stronger. Valerian, perhaps. However, he is becoming exasperated with my inability to cure him, and may summon you. If he does, stay away from the subject of anatomy.'

'Anatomy?' echoed Bartholomew, startled by the advice. 'I cannot imagine that will crop up.'

'It might – ever since the *sal ammoniac* incident, he has become morbidly fascinated by what happens to a body after death. Personally, I do not consider it healthy. Not in a layman, at least. I have nothing against dissections being conducted by *medici*, as I have told you in the past, although I should not care to do it myself. Not even to an ear.'

Bartholomew blinked. 'An ear?'

'I find them fascinating. Indeed, I have studied one specific condition, which is known in the north as Pig Ear. Shall I enlighten you?'

He began to hold forth, and although Bartholomew usually enjoyed listening to the medical musings of colleagues, the words washed over him virtually unheard that day. Instead, he stared down at the fresh pile of earth at his feet, and bade a final, silent farewell to Hemmysby.

Bartholomew and Lawrence arrived at Winwick Hall to find that the gates had been re-hung, but they did not meet in the middle, so Jekelyn was obliged to stand sentinel in the gap. The porter stepped aside when Lawrence informed him that Bartholomew was a guest, but with such obvious reluctance that he earned himself a sharp rebuke. As the two physicians crossed the yard, the sun came out, bathing the new College in a soft yellow light.

'This really is a pretty place,' said Bartholomew, stopping to admire it. 'But is that a crack running down one wall?'

'The mason assures us that it is quite normal, and to prove it, he dragged us all over Cambridge, pointing out fissures in other buildings. Even Michaelhouse has some.'

'I know,' said Bartholomew wryly. 'Great big ones that let the rain in.'

'Do you like the Winwick coat of arms above the door? The artist finished it today, and the paint is still wet. We are glad – our founder arrives in three days for the beginning of term ceremony, and I imagine it will be the first thing he will look for.'

Bartholomew thought about the Stanton coat of arms at Michaelhouse, which had been so thoroughly battered by thirty-four years of weather that it was virtually invisible. It would not be long before it disappeared altogether, and future scholars would never know it had been there – assuming the College survived the double crisis of blackmail and losing all its money, of course.

'We have sixty students now,' said Lawrence, as he led the way inside. 'It is far too many for a Provost and three Fellows, so we are recruiting reinforcements. It is a pity you know nothing about law, because I should love to have you here. Far more than your nephew.'

They entered the massive chamber that would serve as refectory and schoolroom. Fires blazed at either end, and the benches were unsullied by chips, scratches or stains, although there were not very many of them, and Bartholomew wondered if the Winwick scholars might have to dine in shifts. Light flooded through the windows, all of which were glazed, and plain white walls accentuated the vast airiness. There was a dais in the centre of the room, with a table that had been loaded with food and wine in a casual display of affluence.

The mourners had settled into three distinct groups. The Winwick Fellows were talking to de Stannell, every one of them splendid in his best tabard or robes of office. The Michaelhouse contingent was as far away from them as it was possible to be, huddled with scholars from King's Hall, Bene't and Gonville. Unfriendly glances at their hosts suggested they were disparaging them, although that did not stop anyone from availing himself of the refreshments. And finally there were the guildsmen, a group that included Julitta and Holm, Edith, Potmoor, Hugo, Olivia Knyt and other wealthy burgesses.

Bartholomew edged towards the latter, alarmed by the sight of his sister in company with the man she believed had murdered her husband. He arrived to find Olivia looking distressed.

'I shall escort you home,' said Potmoor solicitously. One hand was raised to his temple, and he looked tired. 'My headache is worse, so I shall not be sorry to return to Chesterton early.'

'It is a reminder of your holy visions, Father,' said Hugo, looking around at the company to ensure they remembered that his sire had been so blessed.

'Michael just told Olivia that her husband was poisoned,' explained Edith to Bartholomew, before turning to look hard at Potmoor. Bartholomew flinched at the brazen accusation in her eyes. 'He spotted telltale blue lesions on Hemmysby's lips, and a hurried inspection revealed the same phenomenon on Knyt, Elvesmere and Ratclyf as well.'

'Lesions that are consistent with death from a poison named *dormirella*, apparently,' added Hugo. His expression was difficult to read. 'It might have gone undetected in all four victims, were it not for the good Brother's vigilance.'

'It is unfortunate that he was not here on Lammas Day,' said Edith, her gaze still fixed on Potmoor. 'He might have seen these marks on Oswald, too.'

There was no discernible reaction from Potmoor, although that was not surprising – the man was alleged to have been involved in countless deaths, and was far too wily to betray himself with careless flickers of guilt. He merely smiled without humour.

'What a pity that no one will ever know. Oswald has been in the ground far too long now.'

'I hope no one thinks *I* had anything to do with John's

demise,' sniffed Olivia. 'Our marriage was not perfect, but he was a good man and I loved him.'

'Oswald had a meeting the night he died,' said Edith before Bartholomew could stop her. 'Was it with you, Master Potmoor?'

'No,' replied the felon, regarding her so coldly that Bartholomew's stomach lurched. 'Once he started opposing all my suggestions in Guild meetings, we had nothing more to say to each other.'

To draw his glittering attention away from her, Bartholomew blurted the first thing that came into his head. 'Did you do business together before that, then?'

'A little,' said Potmoor shortly. 'Come, Olivia. You are pale, and should lie down. These revelations have given you a nasty shock.'

He shoved roughly past Bartholomew, pulling Olivia with him. She went with obvious relief, clearly grateful to be away from the gathering. And as she did not seem to mind being whisked away so precipitously, perhaps she was glad for an opportunity to be alone with her lover, too.

'Go after him, Matt,' hissed Edith. 'It is obvious that he is guilty. Make him confess!'

'Not yet,' replied Bartholomew. 'Later, when we have evidence to—'

'We have it now,' she insisted, her eyes filling with tears. 'Namely, his gloating remark about Oswald's body being too decayed to reveal evidence of poison. *He* killed my husband, just as he dispatched Olivia's, and now he revels in the knowledge that he will not be caught. I cannot sleep at night for thinking about it.'

Bartholomew put his arm around her shoulders. 'I will confront him, I promise, but when the time is right. It would be a shame if he escaped justice because we tackled him too soon.' He changed the subject before she could argue. 'Where is Richard? I thought he would have come today, given that Hemmysby was a fellow guildsman.'

'He went out last night and has not yet returned.' The threatened tears spilled, and she dabbed at them impatiently. 'Oswald would have hated the way he carries on. It dishonours our name, and so does the company he keeps. Will you talk to him again, Matt?'

Bartholomew nodded, although he doubted it would do much good. He felt the familiar surge of anger towards his nephew for putting her through such needless anguish.

'Oh, Lord!' she gulped. 'Here comes de Stannell! I wish he was not Guild Secretary – he keeps pestering me for money to loan to Winwick Hall.'

She ducked away, but de Stannell followed, and Bartholomew was about to rescue her when someone grabbed his hand. It was Julitta, and his skin tingled at her touch. He felt himself blush, and was glad Holm was not watching.

'I have composed a poem,' she confided happily. 'Not a very good one, but the point is that you have taught me enough to manage such a task. I am delighted with myself!'

Bartholomew smiled. 'Perhaps I could visit, so you can recite it to me.'

'I should like that very much, but we shall have to arrange for Will to be out. He does not like poetry, and would be bored.'

Bartholomew refrained from remarking that Holm would be bored with anything that did not revolve around himself, and turned the discussion to the Guild's dubious notion of charity instead. 'Do you really believe it is better to lend money to Winwick than to feed beggars and widows?'

Julitta sat on a bench, and indicated that he should perch next to her. 'The transaction with the College will be like an endowment for the Guild: we set aside a specific sum now, and it will generate a regular income later. It

276

means we shall be limited in the charity we can dispense this year, but our long-term future will be both secure *and* stable. Ultimately, it will help far more beggars and widows.'

'Are you sure?'

'Yes, and your brother-in-law would have supported the scheme unreservedly.' She lowered her voice. 'Poor Knyt spent far more than he raised, and our funds are at an all-time low. We are lucky Winwick agreed to our conditions, or the Guild might have been declared bankrupt.'

'But what will happen to the poor in the meantime?'

Julitta patted his hand. 'I shall not let them starve.'

'I do not understand why Winwick needs so much money when its endowment comprises the tithes from several churches and manors. It is wealthy in its own right.'

'There are details to resolve before the legacy comes into force, apparently. But you should be worrying about more important matters, such as who murdered those poor men. How are your investigations proceeding?'

'Slowly,' replied Bartholomew gloomily.

When Julitta hurried away to liberate Edith from de Stannell, Bartholomew went to talk to his fellow *medici*, who had taken up station near the wine.

'Holm here aims to invent a tonic that will help scholars curb their baser instincts,' said Rougham. He cast a pointed look at Julitta's retreating form. 'Perhaps you should test it for him, Bartholomew. We all know that you have had more lovers than Lucifer.'

'Than Lucifer!' echoed Meryfeld wonderingly, while Bartholomew thought that Rougham was a fine one to preach with his regular visits to prostitutes. 'How do *you* know about Satan's amorous interludes?'

'I have heard reports,' replied Rougham darkly. Then

he turned wistful. 'I wish I had your skill with remedies, Holm. A cure for lust will sell like hot cakes in a University town, and will make its creator very rich.'

'Richer,' corrected Holm, and shot Bartholomew a gloating glance. 'I am already wealthy, thanks to my marriage. I am proud to call Julitta my wife, and no man will ever come between us.'

'Tell us about your other cures, Holm,' said Lawrence, transparently eager to avert a scene.

Holm was all smug confidence. 'I have developed a paste that makes teeth white and strong within a month. No one need suffer from stained or broken fangs ever again.'

'It mends them, too?' asked Bartholomew incredulously.

'Yes, if applied properly. But it is nothing compared to my remedy for gout. I have discovered that a pinch of *dormirella*, along with a few other choice ingredients, will banish it totally.'

'What other choice ingredients?' asked Meryfeld icily. He liked making dangerous medicines for patients himself, and was obviously chagrined that the surgeon should do it, too.

'I decline to say,' replied Holm haughtily. 'It is a secret.'

'*Dormirella* has but one use – as a poison,' said Bartholomew, and because Holm had irked him, he repeated Michael's lie, aiming to see if he could fluster the surgeon into a confession. 'Contrary to popular belief, it is *not* undetectable. Obvious signs appear after a while, as evidenced by Hemmysby, Knyt, Elvesmere and Ratclyf. I do not suppose you treated *them* for gout, did you?'

Holm regarded him with such hatred that Bartholomew was hard-pressed not to recoil and, not for the first time in their acquaintance, he sensed a dangerous core beneath Holm's vanity and casual ineptitude. He remembered the conversation about bryony, and his blood ran cold to think of Julitta living with such a man.

'No,' the surgeon replied shortly. 'None were my patients.'

'Nonsense!' cried Rougham. 'You tended them all at one time or another. However, clients do die, even with the best of care, and no *medicus* can make a pie without breaking eggs.'

'How many eggs do you break a week, Holm?' asked Meryfeld conversationally. 'Roughly.'

'Two or three,' replied Holm. He saw the shock on his colleagues' faces – this was high for a man who only conducted a handful of procedures – and added, 'Although I save far more. Cambridge is lucky to have me, and I shall be missed when I leave.'

'Where are you going?' asked Lawrence, all amiable politeness.

'London, to follow in your footsteps and offer my services to royalty. Julitta will come with me, of course. No man would be complete without a beloved wife at his side.'

Bartholomew tried to mask his dismay, but he knew he had failed when he saw the flash of spiteful triumph in the surgeon's eyes.

'The King has recently hired a Genoese surgeon, one very well versed in dissection,' chatted Lawrence pleasantly. 'Perhaps he will show you some of his techniques.'

'I hope not,' said Holm with a shudder. 'Anatomy is an abomination.'

'Oh fie!' exclaimed Lawrence. 'Studying cadavers will help improve your surgical skills.'

'I am skilled enough already, thank you,' said Holm coolly. 'When you have seen one liver, heart and brain, you have seen them all. They are identical.'

'I doubt the heart of an eighty-year-old woman is the same as that of an eight-year-old boy,' argued Bartholomew. 'All organs will vary with age, sex, health, size and a host of other factors.'

'I agree,' nodded Lawrence. 'And it is my contention that studying these differences will allow us to understand the nature of such diseases as—'

'Dissection will teach us nothing,' interrupted Holm. 'Especially as the specimens available are usually from criminals. They are hardly representative of the rest of us.'

'Would you rather surgeons' cadavers were used, then?' asked Lawrence drolly.

'Certainly not.' Holm glared at Bartholomew. 'And if you lay so much as a finger on mine when I go, I shall return from the dead to haunt you.'

'Please,' said Rougham with a shudder. 'No jokes about necromancy around Bartholomew, if you please. It is rather too close to the truth to be amusing.'

'Who was joking?' asked Holm.

Eyer the apothecary was another guildsman to grace Winwick with his presence. He was standing by the food, his face grave with concentration as he chewed.

'Ginger and cinnamon,' he said, holding up a cake in one hand. Then he raised the other. 'Nutmeg and honey. An apothecary should be able to list the ingredients in anything he eats.'

'It must be a useful skill,' said Bartholomew.

Eyer laughed. 'Yes – for stealing recipes from secretive cooks. Actually, I am here under false pretences – I did not attend Hemmysby's funeral, I came to deliver a poultice for Bon's eyes. But I am glad I stayed, because I want to warn you to be cautious around Lawrence.'

Bartholomew frowned. 'Lawrence? Why?'

'He is not all he seems, and I do not like him.'

'Really? He seems perfectly amiable to me.'

'I knew him before we came here,' explained the apothecary. 'Years ago. I am not sure whether he will recall me, but I certainly remember him. It was in Oxford, where I was learning my trade and he was a master at the University. He made a mistake that caused a man's death . . .'

'It happens, unfortunately. Medicine is not an exact science.'

'Well, this was pure ineptitude,' said Eyer. 'Even I, a mere apprentice, knew that liquorice root can be dangerous to certain patients. God only knows how he won a royal appointment, but perhaps we should not be surprised that the Queen did not last long in his care.'

Bartholomew disliked this sort of discussion, and wondered if Eyer's willingness to disparage colleagues was why he himself always felt slightly reserved in the apothecary's presence.

'She was old,' he said shortly. 'And had been ill for some time.'

'Yes, but ill with what?' pressed Eyer. 'Something that could have been cured by a competent practitioner? And there is something else that worries me, too. All the physicians buy powerful substances from me, and I *always* ask what they intend to do with them – it would not be the first time a patient has died because a *medicus* has failed to appreciate what he has purchased.'

'We are trained to know—' began Bartholomew.

Eyer cut across him. 'Lawrence wanted dwale and hemlock for a specific client a few days ago, but I happened to meet her on my way here, and she had not been in need of them at all. He lied.'

'Perhaps you misunderstood,' said Bartholomew, acutely uncomfortable with the revelations.

'I challenged him just now, but he denied the transaction ever took place, even though it is plainly written in my records and I remember the conversation perfectly. Perhaps the matter slipped his elderly mind, but it has left me very uneasy. Furthermore, since you and I spoke this morning, Nerli came and wanted rather a lot of realgar.'

'Did you sell it to him?' asked Bartholomew anxiously.

'No. He claimed he wanted to set it alight, as he had read that it helps plaster to dry more quickly – a ridiculous assertion, as I am sure you will agree. I told him I had run out, because I was afraid Lawrence had sent him to get it so that he could add it to hemlock and dwale and have the makings of *dormirella*. However, I am not the only person who sells the stuff.'

'You think they have acquired some elsewhere?'

Eyer nodded, then his eyes fell to the cakes he was holding. 'Heavens! Do you think *dormirella* has been sprinkled on these?'

'If so, I think you, of all people, would have noticed – it tastes faintly of garlic.'

Eyer looked relieved. 'Of course! And there was no garlic here. However, one cannot be too careful.' He dropped them on the floor, and wiped his hands on the tablecloth. 'I shall make myself a purge immediately.'

'I seriously doubt the poisoner will strike at quite so many people—'

'Easy for you to say! You came when there was nothing left to eat. *You* are not at risk.'

After Eyer had raced away, Michael approached. The food and wine had run out, so most of the guests had gone home, and it was thus a good time to question the Winwick men about Elvesmere and Ratclyf. The monk wanted Bartholomew with him to gauge their reactions. As they walked to the other side of the hall, Bartholomew summarised his discussion with Eyer. Michael's expression was thoughtful as he advanced on the Winwick men, but before he could speak, Nerli began a diatribe.

'It was a shock to be told that our two colleagues had been poisoned, Brother,' he declared. 'Especially poor Ratclyf. We thought his weak heart had killed him.'

'Which is what the killer intended,' said Michael

smoothly. 'He no doubt believes that *dormirella* is unde-tectable, but he is sadly mistaken.'

'What terrible things you know,' said Bon wonderingly. 'For once I am glad I am blind, because I should not like to see these blue-stained lips.'

'You bought dwale and hemlock recently,' said Michael to Lawrence, then turned to Nerli, 'while *you* purchased realgar. It means the Fellows of Winwick Hall are in possession of three of the ingredients in *dormirella* – the toxin that killed your two friends.'

Nerli's black eyes flashed with anger. 'I did no such thing, and anyone who claims otherwise is a liar. I have no need to murder my colleagues. Or anyone else for that matter. In fact, I am disinclined to believe your tale of blue lips. You made it up.'

'Why would he do that?' asked Bon, bemused. 'It would be a wicked thing to do.'

'To discredit Winwick Hall,' snapped Nerli. 'He is jealous of us, and would love to see us fail. But it is the other Colleges that will flounder. Michaelhouse, King's Hall, Gonville, Bene't – all will fall beneath the steady tread of our advancement.'

'Easy, Nerli,' said Lawrence uncomfortably. 'There is no need for passion.' He smiled at Michael, although the expression was more wary than happy. 'I am afraid you are mistaken about my purchases, Brother. I never use dwale and hemlock, as I feel the risks outweigh the bene-fits. I always have.'

Bartholomew regarded him askance. 'How do you treat severe inflammations, tumours and swellings? Gentle treat-ments are rarely effective on the more serious ailments.'

'I pray,' replied Lawrence shortly, and turned back to Michael. 'And Nerli is right – this tale of blue lips does seem outlandish. Are you sure about it?'

'I am. But if you doubt me, come to St Mary the Great and look.'

Bartholomew was horrified, sure his artwork would never pass muster to sceptical eyes in the cold light of day. And what if the Winwick men wanted to inspect the rest of their colleagues' remains, and the incisions were discovered?

'No!' said Nerli quickly. 'We should leave our dead in peace. Have they not suffered enough? It would be wicked to disturb their rest.'

'I agree,' said Lawrence. 'Indeed, I recommended that they all be buried by now – Michaelhouse did not dally with Hemmysby, and we should have afforded the same consideration to Elvesmere and Ratclyf.'

'You know why we delayed,' snapped Illesy. 'Like Mistress Knyt, we wanted our colleagues buried on a Sunday, which is a holier day than—'

'Superstition,' interrupted Nerli disdainfully. 'Or are you of the belief that our colleagues need all the advantages they can get when their souls are weighed?'

'We all do,' said Illesy shortly. 'Fallible mortals that we are.'

Nerli made an angry gesture with his hand. 'Regardless, I strongly protest against further indignities to their poor corpses. We should leave them alone.'

'They will not object in the interests of truth,' said Illesy, and shot Nerli a look that was difficult to interpret. 'So follow me, and let us see this "evidence" for ourselves.'

Without waiting for a reply, he turned on his heel and marched towards the church, where Michael scowled at the proprietary way he flung open the door. They reached the Lady Chapel, and Illesy indicated with an imperious flick of his hand that his Fellows were to open the caskets.

'You are the *medicus*, Lawrence,' he said, watching Nerli wrestle with the clasps. 'You examine them – not just Ratclyf and Elvesmere, but Knyt, too.'

'I am not qualified to probe the secrets of corpses,' protested the elderly *medicus*. 'And while I have no objection to anatomical studies in principle, I do not want to engage in them myself.'

'I am not asking you to carry out a dissection,' said Illesy impatiently. 'Just to look and see if they have blue lips. Come on, man! It cannot be that difficult.'

With considerable reluctance, Lawrence bent over the coffins, watched intently by Illesy, Nerli and Michael, while Bon cocked his head this way and that as he struggled to determine what was happening from the odd grunt and tut. Bartholomew stood well back, trying to decide whether to take to his heels if the deception was spotted, or stay and attempt to brazen it out.

'Two or three tiny blue blemishes,' said Lawrence eventually, his voice so low as to be almost inaudible. 'On Elvesmere, Ratclyf and Knyt.'

'Are you sure?' asked Nerli in disbelief.

'Yes,' replied Lawrence. 'Come and see for yourself.'

But Nerli shook his head and backed away.

'This is dreadful,' whispered Bon. 'I knew the other Colleges and the town were jealous of our good fortune, but I did not think their bile would extend to murder. Poor Elvesmere! He was my closest friend. And poor Ratclyf, too! He was making great strides towards finalising our College's endowment. How shall we manage now he is gone?'

'I wonder if these "great strides" troubled him,' mused Illesy. 'He spent so much time at prayer that I sometimes wondered whether he was entirely happy about some of the things he was obliged to do as bursar. Money matters are invariably sordid.'

'I had to give him medicine for anxiety,' put in Lawrence. 'And then there was . . .'

'Then there was what?' asked Michael.

Lawrence's expression was bleak. 'I could not reveal this were he still alive, but I came in here on Tuesday, and he was on his knees by Elvesmere's body, begging for forgiveness.'

Michael regarded him sharply. 'Like a killer and his victim?'

Lawrence would not meet his eyes. 'It appeared that way to me. And before you ask, I did not tell anyone, because it was none of my business.'

'You misinterpreted what you saw,' declared Illesy. 'The culprit is someone outside the College. And do not say Potmoor, because poisons are not his style.'

It was hardly a resounding endorsement of his former employer's innocence, and Michael was about to say so when Nerli spoke.

'We shall bury all three today, and to Hell with waiting for Sunday. After all, we do not want anyone else to poke at them for ghoulish curiosity. It would be sacrilege, a crime I abhor with all my heart.'

'Oh,' said Bartholomew guiltily. 'Do you?'

All was bustle and flurry as preparations were made for interring the three dead men. Olivia Knyt was summoned, the gravedigger ordered to ready the holes he had dug, and a vicar hired. The priest was Heyford, ever eager for extra fees. He arrived with one hand to his stomach.

'I was poisoned last night,' he told Michael and Bartholomew. 'I lay deadly sick until dawn, but God saw my suffering and I am now on the mend. Doubtless Potmoor would have preferred to incinerate me, but he dares not try that again. Did I tell you that the villain he engaged for that evil deed was not Fulbut at all, but someone from Winwick Hall?'

'No,' replied Michael, eyeing him warily. 'How have you reached that conclusion?'

'One of my parishioners saw a man racing away from St Clement's shortly before the alarm was raised, and followed him to that Devil's foundation. The scoundrel was in disguise, of course, so my parishioner could not tell which of these rogues is the culprit.'

'Yet you come to bury their dead?'

Heyford sniffed. 'I am prepared to overlook the connection for a shilling a corpse. Besides, I doubt they will attack me in St Mary the Great – not with you looking on.'

The vicar's tale reminded Bartholomew of something he had all but forgotten. Moments before he had seen the smoke issuing from St Clement's, a man in green had almost knocked him over. It had not occurred to him that it might have been the arsonist, especially once Fulbut had been mooted as the culprit.

'What was he wearing?' he asked.

'A grass-coloured cloak,' replied Heyford. 'Why? Did you see him, too, and decide to keep the matter to yourself because it shows your accursed University in a bad light?'

'How could he have seen anyone?' asked Michael sharply. 'He was too busy saving your life. And why have you waited until now to tell us what this witness saw?'

'Because I have only just heard it myself. It came from Verius, who is never very forthcoming with the authorities. However, I shall expect you to investigate Winwick, and bring the villain to justice. I always said there was something diabolical about that College, and I was right!'

'Has Heyford been poisoned, Matt?' asked Michael, when the priest had gone to robe himself for his sombre duties.

'Not with *dormirella*. No one recovers from that once it has been ingested.' Then Bartholomew told him about the collision outside St Clement's.

Michael was thoughtful. 'I wonder which Winwick Fellow owns green clothes. Illesy, who will know all about murder after working for Potmoor? The sweetly smiling Lawrence with his Oxford connections? The sinister Nerli?'

'Well, it was not Bon, as the man I saw was too tall. Of course, it could have been Holm.'

'Holm?' echoed Michael, startled. 'Why would he run to Winwick?'

'Because it is full of guildsmen who would give him sanctuary.' Bartholomew was silent for a moment, thinking. 'It is odd how everything revolves around that College: two of its scholars suffer premature deaths, it is largely responsible for the matriculand trouble, its Fellows possess the necessary ingredients for *dormirella*, and now the St Clement's arsonist flees there.'

'It is not odd, Matt,' averred Michael. 'It is downright suspicious.'

Bartholomew heaved a sigh of relief when Knyt, Elvesmere and Ratclyf were in the ground and the evidence of his handiwork was safely concealed. Langelee was relieved, too, because the hasty burial meant that Michaelhouse could not be expected to provide a reciprocal feast. When the last spadeful of earth was being patted down, Bartholomew went with Michael to talk to Verius. The ditcher was at home, regaling his wife with a romantic ballad. Again, Bartholomew was astounded that such a pure, clear voice should emanate from such a loutish individual.

'Heyford told you?' asked Verius crossly, when he heard why the two scholars had come. 'I knew I should have kept it to myself. Now Potmoor will hear, and come to rail at me.'

'It was Potmoor who set the church alight?' asked Michael.

'No, it was someone from Winwick Hall, but I imagine Potmoor hired him.' Verius played nervously with the bandage on his thumb. 'I was in the church at the time, hiding from a man I owe money to. I saw a rogue in a green cloak lurk in the shadows until Heyford was drunk, then step forward and set the altar cloth alight.'

'And you followed the culprit to Winwick Hall?' asked Michael.

Verius nodded. 'Because I assumed Heyford would smell the smoke, and get up to douse the flames. I did not think *one* jug of ale would send him to sleep. He is a feeble—'

'Winwick,' prompted Bartholomew.

'The man in the cloak walked in there with all the confidence of Satan, so it was clearly his home. The cloak had black edges, and the hood was up, which means I never saw his face. He was of average height and build, though, so it might have been any of that rabble.'

'Not any of them,' countered Ylaria. 'It could not have been that horrible Uyten, because he is tall and brawny. And it could not have been Ratclyf or Bon, because they are small.'

'True,' nodded Verius. 'You can eliminate them from your enquiries, Brother.'

'Good,' said Michael flatly. 'That only leaves the Provost, two Fellows, sixty students and three dozen servants. Solving the riddle will be simplicity itself.'

CHAPTER 12

The following day was Sunday, when there was an extended Mass and a better breakfast. It was egg mash – eggs cooked with smoked pork – and although there was less meat than usual, the food was at least palatable. Afterwards, Bartholomew and Michael set off to Winwick, to ask who had a green cloak with black edging. Needless to say, no one admitted to owning such a garment, and Illesy procrastinated for so long before allowing a search that the guilty party would have had ample time to dispose of it. Michael looked anyway, just to make a nuisance of himself.

'This is a fire hazard,' he declared, when they came to the dormitory above the hall. 'There must be sixty students in here. It was never intended to hold so many.'

'Seventy-three,' corrected Illesy smugly. 'And our lads love it up here. It is new, clean and affords excellent views of the town.'

Bartholomew did not think it was clean – it reeked of sweaty feet – while the views were obscured by the clothes that had been left hanging over the window shutters.

'We shall tidy it up before the founder arrives,' said Lawrence, reading his thoughts. 'Word is that he has already left London, and is on his way. He must be very excited.'

'Are you sure it was wise to invite him?' asked Michael. 'He will learn that his College is unpopular with the rest of the University and the town, and I cannot see that pleasing him.'

'He does not care what people think,' said Illesy. 'If he did, he would not have grown so rich and powerful. Or accepted so many lucrative posts in the Church – a dozen canonries and seven rectories, at the last count.'

'A shameless pluralist,' muttered Michael to Bartholomew, as they walked back down the stairs. 'I shall abolish the practice when I am Archbishop of Canterbury.'

Bartholomew smothered a smile. 'And when will that be, Brother?'

'As soon as the University can manage without me,' replied the monk. 'Which it is unable to do at the moment, so do not fear my departure just yet.'

Bartholomew trailed after him as he looked in the *parlura*, hall and library, but was glad when the invitation to inspect the Fellows' quarters and the Provost's Suite was declined – the point had been made, and anything more would be a waste of their time. Michael did, however, inveigle an invitation to Winwick's mid-morning repast, where he tried every ruse he knew to catch the Fellows out in an indiscretion, but they were lawyers and his efforts to trick them were futile. Eventually, he was forced to concede defeat, and he and Bartholomew took their leave.

'We have two days before term starts,' he said, once they were outside. 'Two days! And we are no closer to the truth now than we were when all this started. Indeed, our position is worse, because we have more victims to investigate. Moreover, we have William's tract hanging over our heads like the Sword of Damocles, and we have done nothing to retrieve our hutch.'

Bartholomew had no words to comfort him. The monk stalked off towards St Mary the Great, where he was needed for decisions about the beginning of term ceremony, after which he would hold another choir practice, while Bartholomew, still plagued with nervous thoughts about dissection, sought comfort in the familiar round of tending patients. There were a lot of them, and they kept him busy well into the afternoon.

All were eager to regale him with rumours about the

agitated state of the town, and he grew increasingly alarmed by the sour atmosphere on the streets. Thus he was uncharacteristically sharp when Warden Shropham stopped him to say that Potmoor had broken into King's Hall on Thursday.

'How do you *know* Potmoor was the culprit?' he demanded. 'Did you see him?'

'I did not need to see him,' replied Shropham, taken aback by the angry response. 'What other criminal would be so audacious?'

'You say a pewter jug was stolen,' Bartholomew went on. 'But I imagine a felon of his eminence would have selected something rather more valuable.'

'He was disturbed before he had the chance to look around,' Shropham flashed back. 'He was obliged to make such a speedy escape that he cut himself on a window, and left splashes of his nasty blood on our nice wood floor. Let us hope it hurts, because it is the only punishment he will ever suffer – de Stannell will not move against a fellow guildsman, and Michael is too busy.'

Bartholomew stared at him. 'The culprit is injured? Why did you not say so? It means that Michael can look for a gash on Potmoor and ask how it happened.'

'Potmoor will lie – say he cut himself shaving or some such nonsense. But something should be done, because he becomes more powerful and dangerous with every passing day. Indeed, I imagine he is behind these murders, too. Felbrigge, Elvesmere, Ratclyf and Knyt.'

'And Hemmysby,' said Bartholomew unhappily.

Shropham softened. 'I am more sorry than I can say about him. He was a good man. Forgive my insensitivity, Bartholomew. I am in a bad mood, because I have just heard that Winwick has almost matched us in numbers. And by the beginning of term, it may even be bigger.'

'Does that matter? There are students enough for both.'

'It is the principle of the thing. We have always been

the largest, and it is not right for this upstart foundation to come along and usurp our place in a matter of days. Moreover, it is *our* prerogative to have first pick of the wealthiest and most influential applicants, but Winwick is poaching them from right under our noses.'

'I hope you will not fight,' said Bartholomew anxiously. King's Hall was jealous of its rights and privileges, and loved nothing more than to defend them with a show of arms.

'I shall try to prevent it, but Winwick tries our patience sorely.'

Bartholomew watched him walk away, then his attention was caught by a group of matriculands, who were throwing stones at a butcher's cart. The town boys reacted with fury, and there was an ugly mêlée until Marjory Starre hurled a bucket of slops over them all. The combatants flew apart with cries of disgust. When two outraged matriculands stalked towards her, Bartholomew hastened to intervene. There was a moment when he thought they would fight him, but several members of the Michaelhouse Choir came to stand next to him, and the matriculands beat a hasty retreat. Marjory began to chortle.

'I have been standing here for ages, waiting for an opportunity to lob. The Devil himself could not have aimed better. Did you see their faces?'

'Yes,' said Bartholomew soberly. 'And you should not do it again. They might hurt you.'

'Nonsense,' she declared. 'They would not dare. And it was good to strike the first blow, for they will be the ones to cause trouble on Tuesday, you mark my words.'

'At the beginning of term ceremony?'

She nodded. 'When the wind will howl for the death of another good man, and we shall have blood flowing in our gutters.'

Her voice had dropped to a whisper, and although Bartholomew knew it was a trick such people often used to make their prophecies sound more convincing, he was unable to suppress a shudder. 'It has already howled for another good man: Hemmysby.'

'It has not finished yet,' she hissed. 'Not by a long way. It blew for Knyt and it blew for Hemmysby – not for Elvesmere and Ratclyf, obviously, as they were not good men – but it will howl a third time before peace reigns again. Perhaps it will be for you. Or for His Majesty's favourite – the man who founded Winwick Hall.'

Bartholomew regarded her in horror. The King would never forgive the University *or* the town if anything happened to his Keeper of the Privy Seal, and a monarch was in a position to wreak bitter and very inconvenient revenge with heavy fines and penalties.

'But better John Winwick than you,' she went on. '*He* does not physick the sick. Would you like a protective charm? I will let you have one for free – payment for all the medicine you give me.'

'It is kind, but—'

'You need one,' she interrupted. 'Some folk wish you harm after what you did for Potmoor. Here, take it. It is the most powerful amulet I own.'

It was a fist-sized stone on a string, etched with runes, and was so obviously heathen that he declined to take it. 'You might need it yourself if your predictions come true,' he said.

'Oh, they will,' Marjory assured him, slipping the stone into his bag. 'I have never been more certain of anything in my life. I have heard about those poisonings, by the way.'

'Oh,' said Bartholomew, startled by the abrupt change of topic. 'Have you?'

'Yes, and in my humble opinion, Potmoor is the most likely culprit.' She did not sound humble at all as she continued to pontificate. 'He is often at Winwick Hall, where Ratclyf and Elvesmere were murdered, and he loves Olivia Knyt, the wife of another victim. You might want to ask what went in the medicine she made to soothe her husband's "colic".'

'Bryony root,' said Bartholomew, recalling what Eyer had said.

'Do *you* cure colic with bryony root? No, you do not. There are other connections to Potmoor as well. Lawrence is his tame physician, and who was the first to arrive when Olivia decided more help was needed? Lawrence!'

'I do not think—'

'You like him because he seems kindly. Well, I have met many a villain with pretty manners, so do not be deceived. Moreover, Surgeon Holm told me that he heard Lawrence arguing with Hemmysby the day before Hemmysby died – on the evening of the first day of the debate.'

'Arguing about what?'

'Hemmysby thought Winwick was being given too loud a voice in the Guild. The row was quite heated, apparently. You watch yourself, Doctor. Trust no one.'

Bartholomew was disturbed by his conversation with Marjory, partly because it was worrying that Lawrence had not seen fit to mention his row with Hemmysby, but also for her prophecies. She had a reputation for being right about such matters, and while he did not believe she had supernatural powers, he certainly believed she was astute – and party to gossip that rarely reached members of the University. He had no doubt that the trouble she foretold would come to pass.

He was disconcerted when he ran into Potmoor almost immediately. The felon nodded amiably enough, although his expression turned suspicious when Bartholomew studied him carefully for any sign of injury. There was none that he could see, so did that mean Potmoor was innocent of stealing the jug from King's Hall?

As he walked away, Bartholomew grew despondent. He

295

and Michael had scant leads to follow for the murders, and the next day was Monday, when the culprit expected to be paid for William's tract. What would happen when Michaelhouse failed to comply? Would the culprit really destroy a foundation by making the thing public? The Fellows would be barred from the University if they were excommunicated, so what would he do? Leave Cambridge and hunt down Matilde? Whisk Julitta away to a place where neither was known, and live together as man and wife? But what about Edith? He could not abandon her when she was so steeped in grief.

Thinking about his sister reminded him that he should visit her. It was a good time to speak to Richard, too, and make him understand how much his dissipation and self-ishness were upsetting his mother. He arrived to find his nephew out, but Edith was pleased to see him, and plied him with cakes while she talked about her continuing trawl through Oswald's box. She had discovered several more unpaid bills, and one transaction that had been brazenly dishonest.

'He must have been ill at the time,' she said defensively. 'Not thinking clearly.'

'These date from two years ago,' said Bartholomew, leafing through the pages she handed him, and noting that the cheated customer was Heyford. The vindictive tone of the accompanying notes suggested that the vicar had been overcharged in revenge for denigrating merchants. 'Oswald was in perfect health then.'

Both jumped when there was a sudden roar of voices.

'Choir practice,' said Edith, rolling her eyes. 'Michael is an intelligent man, so why does he waste his time with those talentless rogues? The only one who can hold a tune is Noll Verius.'

'He does not want to deprive them of free bread and ale. They have come to rely on it.'

'Unfortunately, a lot of matriculands have joined, too,

and while some are in need of a meal, most go just to test his authority. They are certainly wearing him down – I have never seen him look so tired. He has his choir, the beginning of term ceremony, the murders, not to mention preparing his lectures. I hope you are helping him, Matt.'

Bartholomew met the monk at Michaelhouse a little later, listening anxiously to a report that a band of townsmen had been eyeing the College at dusk the previous evening. Walter the porter, pet peacock under his arm, believed they had been reconnoitring in readiness for an attack.

'They probably think we have lots of money,' he said gloomily. 'But they will be in for a shock. We have so little that Master Langelee could not pay me this week.'

Bartholomew wondered how long the College servants would stay once they were not paid the following week either. Would the Fellows be obliged to perform their duties, cramming portering or cooking into a timetable so tight that they did not know how to manage as it was?

'Beadle Meadowman has a lead on Fulbut,' Michael said, when Walter had gone. 'He says he will send me word later this evening. Where are you going?'

'To look in Hemmysby's room for crumbs. I should have done it yesterday, but there was no time.' Briefly, Bartholomew told him what Clippesby had said about the sparrows. Then because it was on his mind, he reported Marjory's tale about the quarrel between Hemmysby and Lawrence.

'But it does not mean Lawrence is the killer,' he finished. 'Holm may have invented it.'

'Possibly,' said Michael. 'But let us hunt for the remains of this tart. Who knows? Perhaps we shall find it in a parcel bearing Lawrence's writing, and we shall solve all our mysteries tonight.'

While Bartholomew searched, Michael flopped wearily on to a chair. It creaked ominously.

'Why do carpenters make furniture so fragile these days?' the monk grumbled. 'I am hardly a heavy man, yet things buckle beneath me as though they were made of straw.'

'Perhaps you are not as slender as you think.'

'My heavy bones require me to eat a certain amount to keep them wholesome. You are the first to stress the importance of a healthy appetite.'

'Yours is rather too healthy, Brother.'

'Rubbish! That is like saying that a library has too many books, or that Aristotle uses too many words. However, there is certainly one instance where "too many" is bad, and that is students. I have more than I can properly teach, and your classes are absurdly large.'

'One will be smaller when I dismiss Goodwyn,' said Bartholomew. 'Edith has offered to lend me the money to repay his fees, so he can start packing the moment it arrives.'

'Wait a day or two before parting with any cash. I saw him talking to Illesy today. They both looked very guilty when they saw me watching, and do you know why?'

'Not really.'

'Because Winwick has been poaching – stealing wealthy students from other foundations. Trinity Hall, Peterhouse, Valence Marie, Bene't *and* Gonville have all complained. However, I am more than happy to turn a blind eye if they relieve us of our malcontents. If they go willingly, we shall not be obliged to refund what they have given us.'

Bartholomew lay flat on the floor to look under the bed. 'I can see a box,' he said, wriggling forward to reach it. 'It must have slipped down here by accident, and ended up pushed right back against the wall. No wonder we did not see it when we searched the last time.'

While he was in this undignified position, Walter poked his head through the window to recite a message from Meadowman: the beadle had located Fulbut's lodgings at last, and had learned that the mercenary was expected to be in them later that night. Michael leapt to his feet.

'He is alive? I was sure he had been executed to prevent him from revealing who paid him to shoot Felbrigge.'

He took two or three steps towards the door, but stopped, startled, when he saw Clippesby standing there with his favourite hen on his shoulder. He had not seen the Dominican arrive, and wondered how long he had been listening. Such unnerving stealth reminded him why Clippesby managed to eavesdrop on so many private conversations.

'Ethel thought you had forgotten her concerns about the sparrows, Matt,' the Dominican said reproachfully. 'She expected you to do something about them yesterday.'

Cobwebs clung to Bartholomew's tabard as he scrambled upright, the box in his hand. He opened it and looked inside. A fruity aroma arose, and a few crumbs adhered to the bottom, still comparatively fresh. Clippesby came to peer at it, head cocked towards the chicken as he did so.

'Ethel says that is definitely the one Hemmysby ate from on Wednesday,' he reported. 'It contained a raisin tart, and he tossed the remains out of the window for the birds. Are there enough fragments left to test for poison, Matt? Preferably without sacrificing some innocent creature?'

Bartholomew nodded and looked at Michael. 'But how will it help us if they do contain *dormirella*? There is nothing on this container to tell us how it came to be here.'

'It was sent – a gift,' supplied Clippesby. 'Ethel saw it arrive. It was not the only one either. You received a parcel at the same time, Brother.'

Michael frowned. 'Did I? Then Walter must have forgotten to give it to me.' His jaw dropped. 'Are you suggesting that it contains tainted food? That someone wants me to die?'

'Ethel thinks so,' replied Clippesby, hugging her. 'She says both parcels came anonymously.'

Michael looked alarmed. 'I am often sent edible treats by those who want to curry favour with the Senior Proctor, and I thought nothing of it.'

Bartholomew hurried to his storeroom and set about assessing Hemmysby's crumbs, while Michael fetched the Lombard slices. It did not take long to set up the necessary experiments.

'How long before we know?' asked Michael in a low voice.

'Several hours,' replied Bartholomew. 'There is plenty of time to catch Fulbut first.'

Dusk was approaching by the time Bartholomew and Michael set out for the mercenary's house. Fulbut lived out past the King's Head, an insalubrious tavern on the Trumpington road, noted for seditious talk and brawls. Cynric accompanied them, unwilling to miss an opportunity to hone his martial skills with a notorious soldier of fortune.

As they passed the inn, Bartholomew was surprised to hear French among the general babble emanating from within. The King's Head was the exclusive domain of townsmen who spoke the vernacular, not the language of the aristocratic elite. He glanced through an open window and saw a large group of matriculands there, all armed to the teeth and making a good deal of self-important noise. The landlord would normally have refused to serve them, but he had been intimidated by sheer force of numbers. His regulars looked on with glowering resentment.

'There will be trouble once the locals get more ale inside them,' predicted Cynric. 'And look by the hearth. Richard is there with your sister's apprentices.'

'Damn!' muttered Bartholomew. 'She will be heartbroken if anything happens to them – she loves them like her own children. And you are right: a fight is all but inevitable.'

'A trouncing might do your nephew good,' said Michael. 'He needs some sense knocked into him. Unfortunately, we cannot intervene. Our priority must be laying hold of Fulbut.'

'You go ahead,' said Bartholomew. 'I will join you there after I have spoken to Richard.'

'He will not listen to you, boy,' predicted Cynric, as the monk hurried away. 'He has grown nasty, and made your sister cry today with a cruel remark. I wanted to punch him, but he was drunk and I was afraid he would fight me. And I should hate to skewer him in front of her.'

Not for the first time, Bartholomew's temper rose against his nephew. Without further ado he marched into the tavern, shaking off Cynric's restraining hand. Fortunately, he was generally regarded as an exception to the no-scholars rule in the King's Head, because many of its patrons were his patients, while others were members of the Michaelhouse Choir. He was not greeted with open arms, but neither was he glared at or threatened. Moreover, Isnard was there, and the bargeman had always been protective of him.

'An ale, landlord,' Isnard called. 'The Doctor is a friend of mine.'

'A friend?' sneered a butcher, one of the few people there who was neither chorister nor the recipient of free medical care. 'I thought you had more taste.'

A dangerous expression suffused Isnard's face, reminding Bartholomew of the many times he had been summoned to patch the bargeman up after fights in this very tavern.

'Mind your tongue, you,' snapped Isnard. He turned to Bartholomew. 'Sit down and drink with us.'

Bartholomew shook his head apologetically. 'I am just here to send Edith's lads home.'

'Please do not,' begged Isnard. 'Because then those would-be students will outnumber us, and we might lose if we challenge them to a battle. Get rid of *them* instead. I will help. Hey, you lot! Get your scabby arses out of here!'

'Now you have torn it, Isnard,' muttered Cynric, as several matriculands came angrily to their feet with knives in their hands. 'There will be a scrap for certain.'

'Stop,' ordered Bartholomew, stepping between the youths and the feisty bargeman. He hoped he sounded more confident than he felt. 'There will be no brawling tonight.'

'And who will stop us?' sneered the leader. It was Uyten from Winwick, cocksure, defiant and very drunk. His tooth-bereft mouth and battered ears were stark reminders that he was no stranger to violence. 'You? I do not think so! Get out of my way.'

'Very well,' said Bartholomew coldly. 'But it will cost you your place at Winwick. There is no room in the University for troublemakers.'

Something in the physician's steady gaze must have penetrated Uyten's ale-inflamed mind, because the lad returned the stare angrily for a moment, but then turned to pick up his cloak.

'This piss is not worth drinking anyway,' he said, pouring the remains of his drink on the floor with calculated disdain. 'We shall go to the Cardinal's Cap instead.'

He waited to see if anyone would react, but when the locals only stared back in stony silence, he indicated with a flick of his head that his friends were to follow him outside. They began to file through the door – until Richard brought them all charging back in again with a mocking jeer.

'My uncle is right, Uyten. Winwick will *not* want doltish louts among its members. And neither shall I, when I am a Fellow there.'

'Doltish, am I?' snarled Uyten. 'What about you, in company with apprentices?'

He injected so much contempt into the last word that Edith's boys leapt up, hauling out daggers, cudgels and a variety of sharpened tools as they did so. The butcher and his friends hurried to stand with them, while the matriculands drew swords. It was not going to be mere fisticuffs this time, Bartholomew saw with mounting horror, but an affray that would result in serious injuries and perhaps even death. And it was Richard's fault. His temper snapped.

'Enough!' he roared, so loudly that it stilled the clamour of taunts from both sides. He stabbed a forefinger at his startled nephew. 'You! Take Edith's boys home at once, and if I see any of them out after dark again, they can look for another apprenticeship.'

'Good,' smirked Uyten. 'They are—'

'And you will return to Winwick.' Bartholomew whipped around to glower at him. Several of the matriculands began to object, but he overrode them. 'Out, all of you! *Now!*'

He stood scowling, first at one faction and then the other, acutely aware that if one individual chose to defy him, there would be a fight, and he was likely to be the first casualty. Then Uyten gave a cool nod and walked away, his cronies at his heels. Richard prepared to follow, but Bartholomew stepped into his path and pointed wordlessly at the back door. With luck, the matriculands would be gone by the time his nephew and the apprentices had navigated their way across a dark and unfamiliar yard.

'Lord!' breathed Isnard, regarding him askance. 'I had no idea you were such a lion, Doctor. Those tales about your valour at the Battle of Poitiers must be true after all.'

'Yes, he is wasted as a physician,' agreed Cynric proudly. 'He should be sheriff.'

Bartholomew stalked into the yard, where Edith's lads were milling about, trying to locate the gate in the gloom. He grabbed Richard's arm, and shoved him against a wall.

'You made Edith cry today,' he said between gritted teeth. 'What were you thinking?'

'Mind your own business. And if you ever speak to me in public like that again, I will . . .' Richard pulled away furiously. 'Just stay away from me.'

Bartholomew stared at him, wrath slowly turning to sadness. 'What has happened to you, Richard? What changed you from my nephew into someone I no longer recognise?'

'I realised that life is for living. It is a lesson my father should have heeded, because then he might still be alive. He tried too hard to be virtuous. He should have let Zachary Steward run his business, and enjoyed a well deserved retirement. Instead, he drove himself into an early grave, just so he could feed a lot of ungrateful beggars and widows.'

Bartholomew almost laughed at the notion that his brother-in-law's dedication to commerce had been motivated by altruism, while the claim that he was 'too virtuous' was patently absurd, as Edith was learning from sorting through his documents.

'He was too good for Cambridge,' Richard went on. 'And too good for her as well. She never really appreciated his worth, and now she delves into his affairs looking for evidence of—'

'Enough,' snapped Bartholomew. 'She loved him deeply.'

'Then she has an odd way of showing it. She should be grieving for him, not probing his finances, looking for inconsistences. She told me today that she plans to ask you for help. However, I can tell you now that if you do, you will be sorry. You will leave my father in peace, or else!'

'What did he say to you?' asked Cynric, as he and Bartholomew resumed their journey to Fulbut's house. Dusk had turned to night, so it was difficult to see where they were going in a part of the town that had few houses and fewer lights.

'Nothing,' replied Bartholomew curtly, unwilling to admit that he had been threatened. Perhaps Richard was drunk, and would apologise the next time they met. Unfortunately, he had the sickening suspicion that their relationship had just crossed a line that would change it for ever, and the thought depressed him profoundly.

'You should have clouted him,' said Cynric. 'And then told him not to squander his inheritance on drink and foolish friends. Did you see Goodwyn lurking in the shadows, by the way? Him *and* the other new lads who want to study medicine with you?'

'No,' said Bartholomew, exasperated. 'They were with Richard?'

'With Uyten. They made themselves scarce when you walked in, but I am sure they would have joined in any skirmish.'

Bartholomew's thoughts were bleak as he followed Cynric down an alley that reeked of urine, and in which the distinctive rustle of rats among rubbish could be heard. It was not long before the book-bearer slowed, indicating with a low hiss that the physician should tread with care. However, it quickly became apparent that stealth was unnecessary, because Fulbut was holding a party, and drunken yells, the laughter of coarse women, and the sound of someone trying to play a bone whistle cut through the silence of the night. Michael and Meadowman emerged from the gloom, two more beadles at their heels.

'I have learned that Fulbut has only been home for a few days,' Meadowman explained in a whisper. 'But this soirée is to let him carouse with old friends before he leaves again. Three barrels of ale have been delivered, along with the best part of a roasted pig. He has invited at least a dozen friends, as well as a goodly number of Frail Sisters . . . I mean prostitutes.'

'Twelve is too many – we are only six,' said Cynric. 'Can you send for reinforcements, Brother?'

Michael shook his head. 'We shall have skirmishes for certain if we pull any more peacekeepers from their patrols. I am afraid we must manage with what we have.'

'Then we shall have to wait until the party is over,' said Bartholomew. 'Nothing will be gained from challenging Fulbut while he is surrounded by friends.'

'We can take them,' said Meadowman confidently. 'You and Cynric fought the French at Poitiers, and are worth ten of the villains in there. We will win with ease.'

'No, we will not,' countered Bartholomew, frowning at Cynric, whose tales of the battle had grown with the telling, so that they had now reached the point where the rest of the English army might as well have stayed at home. In reality, Bartholomew had comported himself adequately, but had been far more useful afterwards, when his ministrations had saved a number of lives.

'Matt is right,' sighed Michael. 'And we cannot leave and come back again, lest Fulbut slips away in the interim. We shall have to lurk out here, which is a wretched waste of time. Go and listen at the window, Cynric. Perhaps the villain will brag about who paid him to shoot my Junior Proctor.'

Cynric went to oblige, but Bartholomew and Michael soon grew tired of crouching motionless in the scrubby bushes that passed as the mercenary's garden, and crept forward to eavesdrop themselves. Unfortunately, Fulbut was more interested in chatting to the women than recounting his misdeeds, and they learned nothing at all. Time passed, and they grew colder and stiffer, their misery intensifying when it began to rain.

'I could be preparing lectures,' grumbled Bartholomew. 'Or checking my experiments on the food that was sent to you and Hemmysby. Or even sleeping.'

'Sleeping?' whispered Cynric. 'But this is fun! Where is your sense of adventure, boy?'

Bartholomew was about to inform him that skulking in the wet outside people's houses was not his idea of good entertainment when the shutter above his head was thrown open. He and Cynric managed to duck out of sight, but Michael's startled face was clearly illuminated by the light that spilled out. Luckily, the revellers were too drunk to notice.

'That is better,' came a voice Bartholomew recognised: Noll Verius. 'It is hot in here.'

'Not him!' groaned Michael. 'Who will sing the solo on Tuesday if he is arrested for hobnobbing with assassins?'

Cynric elbowed him in alarm, warning him to be silent, although the chances of being heard over the raucous yells and hoots within were remote. Bartholomew stood, careful to keep in the shadows, and peered inside. Verius was by the hearth, opposite Fulbut, who transpired to be a wiry, unkempt person with bad teeth. Their companions were rough, soldierly types who wore their hoods up, even indoors. Bartholomew could see one or two faces, but none he recognised.

'My physician tells me that I may lose the feeling in my thumb,' Verius was saying. He scowled. 'King's Hall had no right to put glass in its windows. It is unfair to those who want to climb through them.'

'So that is how he was injured,' muttered Bartholomew, dropping back down to talk to his companions. 'Not in a ditch, as he told his wife. Warden Shropham said the culprit had cut himself when he broke in, and I should have guessed the significance of Verius's wound.'

'Yes, you should,' agreed Cynric. 'Because it means that *Verius* is the rogue who has been robbing the town. Potmoor is innocent.'

'Not necessarily,' said Michael. 'There have been so many crimes that I suspect there is more than one burglar at work. Moreover, King's Hall lost a pewter jug, whereas we lost the Stanton Hutch. Those are hardly in the same class.'

Bartholomew nodded. 'The other Colleges and many townsfolk have been relieved of coins, jewellery and silver plate. King's Hall probably *was* targeted by a different thief.' He thought about the day he had sewed the ditcher's hand back together. 'In his stupor, Verius babbled about the "money soldier". He must have meant Fulbut the mercenary.'

'He said that?' hissed Meadowman irritably. 'You might have mentioned it! Do you have any idea how many hours I have spent tracking this man?'

'What else did Verius say?' asked Michael.

'Nothing,' replied Bartholomew. 'However, Holm was there. It is obvious why, of course.'

'It is?' asked Michael warily.

'I wondered at the time why he came, when there was no question of him being paid, and he rarely performs surgery anyway. He had heard that Verius was drunk and wanted to be on hand to ensure that nothing was blurted to incriminate *him* – and if that failed, be ready to say it was meaningless babble. I have said from the start that Holm is a dangerous man, and this is proof of it.'

'Hardly!' exclaimed Michael. 'And—'

He stopped speaking when there was a chorus of disappointed cries from the house. The second barrel had been broached, but it and the third were sour, unpalatable even to hardened imbibers. Without alcohol, the party soon fizzled out. The prostitutes took their leave and, deprived of their company, the men prepared to follow. Fulbut began to pack a bag, while the others heaved bundles of belongings over their shoulders and made their farewells to Verius.

'They will go to the Fens,' predicted Cynric. 'Where Fulbut will disappear again. We shall have to tackle him with his friends after all.'

A cudgel appeared in Meadowman's hand. 'Well, then. Are we ready?'

'No!' whispered Bartholomew fiercely. 'They still outnumber us two to one.'

'Most will disappear at the first sign of trouble,' declared Meadowman. 'I know their kind. They will drink Fulbut's ale and enjoy his whores, but they will not fight for him. Besides, they are too drunk to be a serious threat. Now, Cynric and I will make sure he does not slip out the back, while you four storm the front.'

'They are not drunk,' argued Bartholomew. 'Not on one barrel of ale. And they look like warriors to me. They are unlikely to run from a skirmish.'

'But we *cannot* let Fulbut escape,' said Michael desperately. 'We need answers. We have no choice but to nab him now.'

'This is madness,' objected Bartholomew, but Meadowman and Cynric had already disappeared, and Michael raised his hand for silence. And then everything happened very fast.

A bloodcurdling yell from the back of the house told them that Cynric and Meadowman had attacked, and there was an immediate clash of arms. The front door flew open with such force that Michael was sent flying, and Verius emerged holding a sword. It was dark, and Bartholomew knew the ditcher would not see that it was his choirmaster he was about to impale. Bartholomew darted forward with his childbirth forceps – a heavy piece of equipment that had served as a weapon far more often than a medical instrument – but Verius swept them from his hands with ease.

'Stop!' shouted Bartholomew. 'Think of your wife. What will she do if you hang for murder?'

But bloodlust burned in Verius's eyes, and he did not hear. He swung his weapon with such force that the blade whistled as it cut through the air. Bartholomew jerked back, then charged at the ditcher before he could regain his balance. Verius swayed for a moment before crashing to the ground, dragging the physician with him. Bartholomew's medical bag burst open, sending pots, packets and bandages scattering in all directions.

He heard Cynric's wild Welsh battle cry, along with the ring of steel against steel, sounds that told him Meadowman's prediction was wrong – Fulbut's friends *had* stayed to fight. Then all his attention was taken by Verius, who was trying to stab him. In an instinctive move that shocked the physician in him, Bartholomew grabbed Verius's injured thumb and twisted. While the ditcher bellowed in pain, Bartholomew scrambled away, feet and hands skidding on the contents of his bag. The twine on Marjory Starre's charm entangled itself around his fingers.

Verius grabbed Bartholomew's leg, and hauled him backwards. The physician ducked the first punch, and to prevent the ham-sized fist from swinging again, he lashed out with the talisman. There was an unpleasant thwack as it hit Verius's nose, and the ditcher crumpled to the ground. Appalled by the sound it had made, Bartholomew knelt next to him and felt for a pulse.

'Verius is dead,' came a shrill shriek from behind. 'And they are defiling his corpse!'

Bartholomew started to say that he was doing nothing of the kind, but the shout had caused panic. Men began to race away, a mad stampede that knocked him head over heels. By the time his wits had stopped reeling, the night was still and silent. He sat up slowly, and was scrabbling for a weapon when someone loomed over him.

'It is only me, boy,' whispered Cynric. 'Are you hurt?'

Bartholomew shook his head. 'You?'

'No, although Meadowman has a slashed arm. You can sew him up in a moment. But first you had better see to Fulbut.'

Dazed, Bartholomew climbed to his feet, noting that Verius's 'corpse' had run off with its cronies. He sincerely hoped he would not be credited with a second resurrection. He followed Cynric into the house, which reeked of spilt ale and the pig that still roasted over the fire.

Meadowman was clutching his wrist, but nodded to say that Bartholomew should tend Fulbut first. The mercenary was near the hearth, a tankard in one hand and a piece of meat in the other – he had been so confident his cronies would win the fracas that he had not bothered to join in himself, and had passed the time eating and drinking. So why was he breathing shallowly, with blood frothing through his lips?

'Save him, Matt,' ordered Michael urgently. 'He cannot die yet.'

'Give him some of that *salt almanac*,' suggested Meadowman.

Bartholomew examined Fulbut quickly. 'A blade has penetrated his lung,' he explained to Michael. 'It is filling with blood, and there is nothing I can do for him.'

'Then ask whether he wants Extreme Unction,' said Michael heavily.

Monks were not priests, but Michael had been granted special dispensation to give last rites during the plague, when men qualified to perform such services had been in desperately short supply, and he had continued the practice since. While he busied himself with chrism and stole, Bartholomew eased the mercenary into a more comfortable position.

'Bastard,' muttered Fulbut between gritted teeth. He spoke with the musical inflection of a man from near the Scottish border. 'I should not . . . have trusted him.'

'Trusted whom?' asked Michael, leaning close to hear. It was not easy: Fulbut had very little breath, and his voice was no more than a rustle.

'The man who . . . hired me. He told me . . . to stay

away after Felbrigge . . . But this is . . . my home now . . . I miss it . . . so I came . . . back.'

'Who gave you these orders?' demanded Michael, seeing the mercenary was fading fast. He put his ear close to the dying man's mouth, then glanced at Bartholomew in despair.

'He is rambling! He just told me that the culprit had a big year. Fulbut, listen to me. You *must* say who hired you.'

'Not everyone here . . . a friend,' whispered Fulbut. 'One . . . stabbed me.'

'Whom did you invite?' pressed Michael urgently. 'Tell me their names. I will catch the killer and ensure he pays for what he has done to you. I promise.'

But Fulbut was dead.

CHAPTER 13

By the time Fulbut had been taken to St Mary the Less, Meadowman had been sewn up, and the rest of the beadles briefed to keep watch for the mercenary's escaped friends, it was very late. Bartholomew trudged wearily back to Michaelhouse, and fell into an uneasy doze in his store-room, where the bubbles and hisses from the experiment brewing on the shelf above his head insinuated themselves disconcertingly into his dreams.

He woke early, aware that it was Monday, and that unless they produced twenty marks at noon, William's intemperate pen might see the College destroyed. Again, he wondered what he would do if he lost his post. Would he be able to track down Matilde? But what about Julitta – could he really abandon her to the villainous Holm? Perhaps he should take her with him instead; they would be happy together, of that he was certain.

He lit a candle and went to check his experiments, but the wavering flame was unsuitable for assessing poten-tially toxic substances so he decided to wait until daybreak. He walked to the lavatorium, still pondering his future. He loved Matilde with an almost desperate passion, but Julitta would probably prove to be the better friend, and would never hurt him as Matilde had done.

'Are you thinking about our mysteries?' came Michael's voice from behind, making him start. The monk had come to wash, retreating prudishly behind a wicker screen with a bucket of water. 'You were in another world. I wished you good day twice without being acknowledged.'

'Yes,' lied Bartholomew, glad his friend could not see the flush of heat in his face. 'What will you do now that

Fulbut cannot tell you who paid him to murder your Junior Proctor?'

'Verius might know. I shall visit his house as soon as Mass is over, and ask his wife where he is hiding. I hope he does not disappear as completely as Fulbut did, or we may never have answers.'

'The culprit is Holm. When I sewed up Verius's thumb, Julitta said that he and Holm were friends, but Holm would never demean himself with such an association. *Ergo*, he foisted himself on us for another reason – namely that he knew Verius and Fulbut were cronies, and was afraid that Fulbut had confided secrets which Verius might blurt out in his drunken stupor.'

'I see,' said Michael flatly. 'And what is Holm's motive for wanting Felbrigge dead, pray?'

'The same as I told you the last time you asked,' said Bartholomew with asperity. 'Felbrigge was a prominent figure in the Guild, and Holm was jealous. Once he saw how easy it was to dispatch rivals, he decided to rid himself of others, too: Elvesmere, Knyt and Hemmysby – all to give himself a louder voice. He went in disguise to Fulbut's house last night, and stabbed him before he could blab any secrets.'

Michael's response was a dismissive snort. 'My money is on Lawrence. He was the first to arrive at Knyt's deathbed, he bought dangerous compounds from the apothecary, he gave Ratclyf a "tonic" to cure his hangover—'

'Ratclyf was not poisoned,' Bartholomew pointed out.

'Ratclyf was not poisoned with a detectable substance,' corrected Michael. 'But he is said to have had a weak heart, yet he had liquorice root in his purse. Lawrence professed to be surprised to see it there, but I imagine it came from him – a man who knew what the effects would be.'

'You have no evidence to make that claim,' argued Bartholomew, although he was sharply reminded of Eyer's tale – that Lawrence had prescribed liquorice root to a

314

patient in Oxford with fatal results. Was it possible that the elderly *medicus* had remembered the lesson, and had used it to eliminate an unwanted colleague? Then Bartholomew pulled himself together. Lawrence would never do such a terrible thing.

Michael continued with his catalogue of reasons. 'He is a physician, yet he claims not to know *dormirella*; Holm overheard him arguing with Hemmysby the night before Hemmysby was murdered—'

'Holm!' spat Bartholomew. 'Of course *he* will want others to come under suspicion.'

Michael ignored him. 'Hemmysby was not the only one who incurred Lawrence's ire: he quarrelled with Elvesmere over whether medico-legal issues are a legitimate field of study. And finally, he is physician to the brutal Potmoor – and Oxford-trained into the bargain.'

'So am I,' Bartholomew reminded him. 'But Lawrence is a good man. He treats the poor.'

'Quite! He is *too* kind and gentle. You must see it is an act. However, there are other suspects, too. I have grave reservations about Illesy, a man desperate to see his new College thrive, and who is also close to Potmoor. Then there is Potmoor himself.'

'And Hugo,' added Bartholomew. 'We tend to overlook him, because he is in his father's shadow, but I imagine he knows all about poisons and killing. I can certainly see *him* inveigling an invitation to Fulbut's party and wielding a sly dagger.'

Michael nodded. 'We also have Nerli. He was seen practising swordplay with Potmoor, and he is Lawrence's armed escort for visits to Chesterton, although he denies any such skill—'

'He studied at Salerno, but I have never heard of that university offering a Masters in Civil Law. Perhaps I should ask him about it.'

'No – there are more important questions he should

answer first. Such as why did he try to buy realgar and later deny it? Why was he so eager to see his colleagues buried? And why did he *really* order the remains of Ratclyf's breakfast pottage thrown away? After all, if anyone knows about poisons, it will be a Florentine. Moreover, he has a dark and angry look that unsettles me.'

'I suppose he is a little sinister.'

'More than a little.' Michael hesitated, but then forged on. 'I am afraid your nephew is also on my list. He is not the man he was, Matt. He—'

'No,' said Bartholomew firmly. 'Richard may have changed, but he is not a killer.'

Michael made no reply, and there was an uncomfortable silence that lasted until the monk asked, 'When will we know whether Hemmysby's tart and my Lombard slices were poisoned?'

'As soon as we can see well enough not to harm ourselves in the process.'

'Good.' There came the sound of a knife scraping across bristles.

'Term starts tomorrow.' Bartholomew slumped on a bench and did not try to keep the dejection from his voice. 'We have six unsolved deaths, Winwick Hall will cause trouble with the other Colleges at the opening ceremony, and Marjory Starre thinks its founder might be assassinated when he visits. And to top it all, we are at the mercy of a blackmailer. I think we may be defeated this time, Brother.'

'No,' said the monk fiercely. 'I am *not* going to lose my College to sly tactics, and a killer will *not* get the better of the Senior Proctor. I will think of something, do not worry.'

He emerged from the screen a new man: his hair was combed, his plump face was scrubbed pink and glowing, and he had donned a fresh habit. He looked fit, strong and he exuded confidence. Perhaps he would do what he promised, thought Bartholomew with a sudden surge of hope.

They walked into the storeroom just as Cynric began to ring the bell to wake the scholars for church. Bartholomew flung open the window shutters, and turned to the shelf on which he had left the crumbs soaking, only to find there was no trace of them. He looked around in consternation. The rank odour of his experiments lingered, although even that was rapidly dispersing in the fresh air.

'You left the door unlocked,' said Michael accusingly. 'And I know exactly what happened.'

He stalked into Bartholomew's bedchamber, where the medical students were donning their tabards and smoothing down their hair. As usual, those with real stubble had not bothered to shave, while those with boyish fluff were making a great show of shearing it off.

'Who has been in the storeroom?' Michael demanded without preamble.

'All of us, sir,' replied Aungel. He shrugged apologetically. 'I know Doctor Bartholomew said not to, but there was a terrible smell, and when we looked inside, there was something brown and squishy on a high shelf. We assumed he had let something rot by mistake . . .'

'What did you do with it?' asked Bartholomew wearily.

'Goodwyn thought it was releasing dangerous miasmas, which he said would make you ill when you sleep in there. So he told us to throw it in the midden.'

'I did,' drawled Goodwyn. 'We cannot have you dead quite so early in the year. Who would teach us how to tend the sick?'

There was a defiant glint in his eye, and Bartholomew had taught enough students to know his authority was being challenged yet again. It could not be allowed to continue.

'Leave,' he ordered.

'Leave what?' asked Goodwyn insolently. 'This room, so

317

you can tell everyone that I am a bad influence on them? I think I shall stay, if it is all the same to you.'

'Michaelhouse. I am not teaching disobedient pupils, and you have had your chance. See whether Winwick will take you. You are more suited to law than medicine anyway.'

'But I do not want to study law,' objected Goodwyn. 'I like it here.'

'You should have thought of that before defying me.' Bartholomew turned to the rest of his silent, stunned class. 'You will be late for Mass if you stand here with your mouths open.'

There was a concerted rush towards the door, and Bartholomew noted wryly that all were careful not to catch his eye.

'You cannot dismiss me,' said Goodwyn when they had gone. 'I paid a term's fees, which gives me the right to stay until Christmas. And Michaelhouse is not so rich that—'

'Your money is forfeit,' interrupted Bartholomew. 'Read the College statutes. We are not obliged to repay anything if a student is dismissed for bad behaviour – and yours has been abominable from the moment you stepped through our gates.'

The blood drained from Goodwyn's face. 'No,' he said, uncertain for the first time. 'If you must insist on ousting me, then I want my money back. It is a colossal sum.'

Cynric was by the door, curious as to what had precipitated the stampede into the yard.

'Goodwyn is leaving,' Bartholomew told the book-bearer briskly. 'Help him pack, and escort him out. I want him gone by the time I return.'

Cynric's grin said he would relish the task. Goodwyn opened his mouth to argue again, but Bartholomew turned on his heel and strode away. Michael followed.

'I liked the lie about the statutes, Matt. You almost convinced me, and I know it is fiction.'

Bartholomew grinned, then went to the back of the

kitchens, where he prodded about in the midden with a stick. 'Here!' he exclaimed triumphantly. 'Yes! The crumbs are still in their dishes. The experiment is not ruined after all.'

'Well?' asked Michael impatiently.

'*Dormirella,*' replied Bartholomew, his exultation draining away as he realised the implications of his discovery. 'The excitement of the debate probably let Hemmysby ward off the symptoms during the day, but they overpowered him when he was walking home in the evening. What he ate in the vestry later was irrelevant.'

'So we wasted our time investigating that?'

Bartholomew nodded apologetically. 'And all because I cannot tell the difference between digested raisin tart and digested fruitcake. Moreover, William said he saw Hemmysby that morning walking "oddly hunched, like Judas in the mystery plays". He offered it up as evidence that Hemmysby had behaved suspiciously on the day that the Stanton Hutch went missing.'

'But he had eaten the poison, and it had started to work,' surmised Michael. 'He might have consulted you at any other time, but he was enjoying his success at the Cambridge Debate too much. He was probably afraid you would order him to stay home and rest.'

'I knew *dormirella* was not instantly incapacitating,' said Bartholomew, scrubbing tiredly at his face. 'I should have taken that into account when we were trying to work out what had happened. It was an unforgivable oversight on my part.'

'And the Lombard slices? Are they poisoned, too?'

'Oh, yes. Enough to kill a horse. Someone does not want you investigating, Brother.'

'Then let us ensure the villain is right to be worried,' said Michael grimly.

As Bartholomew listened to Suttone chanting Mass, the tension within him drained away. St Michael's was a beautiful, peaceful place, and he felt his sagging spirits begin to revive. Unfortunately, his sense of tranquillity did not last long. There was shuffling in the nave, and when it was time for the Magnificat, dozens of bellowing voices joined in. Michael smiled beatifically.

'I thought you might appreciate a little surprise,' he told his shattered colleagues when it was over and he could make himself heard. 'They will perform that piece tomorrow at St Mary the Great. Well? What did you think?'

'Some of the words were recognisable,' replied Langelee, the only one brave enough to venture an opinion. 'And you can certainly be sure of making an impact.'

He indicated that Suttone was to continue the rite, and by the time it was over, the ambiguous remark had been forgotten. The choir lingered, fishing for compliments, and Bartholomew was astounded by the size of it. It comprised not only most of the town's poor, but twice as many students as had been at the practice three days before, when fights had broken out over the bread and ale. The mix remained an uneasy one, and the atmosphere was decidedly edgy.

'Are you sure it is wise to keep them in each other's company?' asked Bartholomew, as he and Michael walked back to the College. 'Some almost came to blows during the Nunc Dimittus.'

'They will not do it again,' vowed Michael. 'The ring-leaders of that unedifying spectacle will be expelled, and the remainder will behave or they will follow, no matter how desperate they are for free food. Hah! There is de Stannell. I want a word with him.'

The deputy was loping along the High Street with a worried, distracted air that did nothing to inspire confidence in his ability to run a large and busy shire.

'What do you want?' he snapped when Michael hailed him. 'I am busy.'

It was no way to address the University's Senior Proctor,

and Michael reined in his temper with difficulty. 'There are rumours that the town will attack our procession tomorrow. How will you prevent it?'

'The tale I have heard is that your clerks will attack each other,' countered de Stannell. 'Those who cannot find a College or a hostel want to vent their spleen on those who have. The predicted trouble has nothing to do with us, so the problem is yours to solve.'

'You know perfectly well that if there is a spat, townsmen will join in,' said Michael irritably. 'You cannot skulk in your castle and pretend that nothing is happening.'

'Declining to risk my troops to protect your scholars is not *skulking*,' flashed de Stannell. 'It is being prudent. If you do not like it, take it up with Tulyet when he returns.'

He stalked off, leaving Michael staring after him in exasperation. 'I never thought to say Tulyet is a fool, but he must have been insane to have appointed that ape as his assistant.'

'Speaking of apes, there is Holm,' said Bartholomew, nodding to where the surgeon was selling one of his new patent medicines to Uyten, assuring the student that his teeth would regrow within four weeks. 'We should ask him about the quarrel he overheard between Hemmysby and Lawrence. Marjory Starre may have misunderstood what he told her.'

'Let me do it,' said Michael. 'You can ask Uyten why he was in the King's Head last night. He is slinking away now he has seen us looking. After him, Matt!'

Bartholomew ignored the order, preferring to question the surgeon than engage in an undignified chase up the High Street. But if he was expecting Holm to incriminate himself with careless slips of the tongue, he was to be disappointed.

'Yes, I heard them,' the surgeon said. 'Lawrence was angry with Hemmysby on two counts. First, for saying that Winwick Hall has too great a say in Guild affairs, and second, for humiliating his colleagues at the debate. Hemmysby told him he would do both again if the opportunity arose.'

'Hemmysby would never have said such a thing,' objected Bartholomew. 'He—'

'Why did you not tell us?' asked Michael, raising a hand to warn Bartholomew into silence. 'You knew he was murdered, and this might have a bearing on the case.'

'Why should I help you? I do not care whether scholars are murdered or not.' Holm looked hard at Bartholomew. 'And stay away from Julitta. She belongs to me, and always will.'

He stalked away, but Michael grabbed Bartholomew's arm before he could follow.

'Leave him, Matt. He is not worth the trouble that would follow if you thumped him.'

'A *confession* might follow if I thumped him,' said Bartholomew sullenly.

'One that would be retracted as soon as the danger was over, and that would make it more difficult to challenge him in the future. If we are going to charge him with anything, we need solid evidence, not suspicions. And especially not the suspicions of the man who hankers after his wife.'

Bartholomew did not answer, because he knew the monk was right. They returned to Michaelhouse, where he was pleased to find Goodwyn gone and Cynric reorganising the room. Then the breakfast bell chimed, and he walked to the hall, noting that no one ran up the stairs any more – the food simply did not warrant the effort.

'Where is Clippesby?' asked Langelee, after intoning one of his eclectic graces and indicating that his scholars could begin eating. A few did, but most looked at what had been provided with a mixture of revulsion and dismay.

'With the chickens again,' replied Thelnetham. 'It is hardly natural, Master, and you should do something about it. Next term promises to be difficult, and his madness will put needless pressure on the rest of us. Dismiss him, and enrol a rational man in his place.'

'He is not mad,' countered William. 'He is eccentric. And he is a better man than you.'

'Defending the Dominicans?' Thelnetham knew exactly how to needle the Franciscan. 'Next you will be saying that you have decided to become one.'

'Never,' declared William hotly. 'They are Satan-lovers, and God will—'

'We should discuss hiring Hemmysby's replacement soon,' said Suttone, cutting into the burgeoning spat. 'Preferably before term starts, as we cannot teach his classes as well as our own.'

'How can we appoint a new Fellow?' hissed Langelee irritably. 'We are destitute, remember? Of course, we may not have to worry about next term if the blackmailer makes good on his threat. He is expecting twenty marks in four hours, and we do not have it.'

'Damn you, William,' muttered Thelnetham. 'As if we did not have enough problems. It—'

'The Saturday Sermon,' interrupted Langelee, changing the subject before the Gilbertine could begin a tirade. 'We postponed it until today because of Hemmysby. I know it is your turn to hold forth, Thelnetham, but I invited the scholars of Winwick Hall to speak instead. You can save whatever you have prepared for next week.'

'Hah!' crowed William. 'He does not want to hear your rubbishy ideas, so he recruited better men.'

'Actually, I did it so that Michael can quiz them about these murders,' countered Langelee. 'He tells me that they are among his suspects for killing Hemmysby, so who knows? Perhaps being in his victim's home will unsettle the culprit and cause him to blurt out something incriminating.'

'Thank you, Master,' said Michael, pleasantly surprised. 'I was wondering how I was going to ask more questions without alienating them with yet another visit.'

'I shall be delighted to hear them preach,' said Suttone. 'I was impressed by Nerli at the debate, although the others were disappointing. Perhaps they will do better in less formal surroundings.'

'Nerli will give the main address,' said Langelee. 'Afterwards, we shall attack his thesis, while his colleagues defend it. It will be disputation in its highest form, so that our new students can appreciate how it should be done.'

'What an excellent idea, Master,' said William. 'It will be much better for them than listening to this boring Gilbertine.'

'However, we *must* emerge victorious,' Langelee went on, ignoring him. 'So do anything you can to score a point, even if it is unethical. As I always tell my teammates at camp-ball games, it is *not* the taking part that is important – it is winning.'

As soon as breakfast was over, Bartholomew and Michael hurried to Verius's house, to ask Ylaria where her husband might be hiding. Michael griped all the way, disgusted that his best singer should become unavailable the day before he was due to give his debut performance.

'And do not suggest Isnard or one of the others,' he grumbled, although Bartholomew knew better than to give advice where the choir was concerned. 'They are hardly solo material.'

Ylaria invited them in, and both scholars were astonished to see Verius huddled by the fire – they had assumed he would vanish into the marshes with the others. Bartholomew felt a stab of shame when the ditcher glanced up to reveal two black eyes and a cut nose.

'I heard you were a skilled fighter, Doctor,' Verius said grudgingly. 'But I never believed it, as you always seem so gentle. I was shocked when you used that stone on me. It was a low trick.'

'So was trying to impale him with a sword,' retorted

Michael sternly. 'You are lucky he was not similarly armed, or you would not be sitting here now, laughing about the situation.'

'I am not laughing, believe me,' muttered Verius ruefully.

Michael wiped the bench with a rag before gracing it with his ample posterior. 'You have two choices: to tell me all you know of Fulbut and his business, or to hang.'

'Fulbut?' Ylaria turned angrily on her husband. 'I thought I told you to send him packing when he came sniffing around the other day. I suppose you defied me and did his bidding anyway. You are a fool, Noll Verius! He has dragged you into dark business, just as I said he would.'

'Very dark,' agreed Michael. 'Fulbut murdered my Junior Proctor, and for all I know, you helped him. So, what will it be, Verius? A full confession, or the noose?'

'Confession,' said Verius quickly. 'Fulbut asked me to break into King's Hall, while he visited the Carmelite Priory. I did it because I needed the money – not that I got much out of it. I filched a pewter jug, but it only fetched a penny at the market.'

'Why attack King's Hall and the Carmelites?'

'Because they had not been raided before, and Fulbut said it meant they were not overly fussy about their security.' Verius looked disgusted. 'It might have been true of the friars, but he was wrong about King's Hall. I was damn nearly caught!'

'You were damn nearly caught in Winwick, too,' said Bartholomew, recalling that here was another crime carried out by an inept culprit who had failed to win much in the way of spoils. 'You only managed to snag a cracked dish before Provost Illesy heard you and drove you off.'

Verius made a curious sideways shuffle, which was not quite quick enough to block the item in question from view. Michael shoved him aside and picked it up.

'You risked the noose for this?' he asked, shaking his head in incomprehension as he turned it over in his hands.

'I do not like that College,' said Verius sullenly. 'So I went there to teach it a lesson for taking all the Guild of Saints' money – funds that should be used for the poor. I hoped to get something better, obviously, but I did not see anything else worth having.'

'What about all the other burglaries?' asked Michael, and began to list them.

'Not me or Fulbut,' declared Verius. 'I swear! Besides, he was in the marshes until recently, hiding out after shooting Felbrigge.'

'Felbrigge,' said Michael. 'Yes, let us discuss him. I know Fulbut shot him, but on whose orders? Potmoor's?'

'No. Work from Potmoor has dried up since his resurrection.' Verius shrugged. 'I cannot prove it, but I thought Fulbut was hired by someone from the Guild of Saints. There are lots of nasty people in it these days – Hugo, the Winwick men, Meryfeld, the Frevill clan, Mistress Mortimer, the Tulyet cousins from the Hadstock Way, the Mayor, Julitta Holm—'

'You mean Surgeon Holm,' interrupted Bartholomew coolly.

'I mean *Julitta* Holm. That surgeon is greedy and selfish, but she is worse.'

'It is true,' said Ylaria, nodding. 'She used to give the Frail Sisters money, but she stopped when they declined to mend their ways. And it was her who told Holm to come here when you sewed up Noll's thumb – she wanted to make sure he let nothing slip when he was drunk, see.'

'Why would she do that?' asked Bartholomew icily, knowing they were trying to divert attention from themselves by attacking the lady he loved.

'Because *she* hired Fulbut,' declared Verius, although the sly cant of his eyes said he was lying. 'She must have heard Ylaria tell you that I cut myself and was getting drunk to deaden the pain. She thought I might blurt out my suspicions, so she and Holm came to stop me.'

'And Noll did blurt,' said Ylaria triumphantly. 'He mentioned Fulbut, who he called the money soldier. Surgeon Holm ordered me to block his mouth, and when you forbade it, Julitta was very quick to say that Noll's remarks were nonsense. See? It all makes sense!'

'Enough fantasy,' said Michael sharply. 'Tell us about Fulbut.'

'In the past, I helped him collect money,' obliged Verius. 'Money owed to Potmoor, usually. Sometimes we had to be a bit . . . forceful, but the pay was good. I did not want to work for a felon, obviously, but only a fool says no to Potmoor. I had no choice, Brother.'

'Neither did Olivia Knyt, I imagine,' said Ylaria, aiming again to distract them from her husband's misdeeds. 'And now she is carrying his child.'

'She is pregnant?' asked Michael, startled. 'How do you know? Did she tell you?'

'She did not have to,' replied Ylaria loftily. 'I am a woman.'

Bartholomew pulled Michael to one side. 'Actually, Ylaria may be right. Olivia bought bryony root, and we know that she and Potmoor are close . . .'

'I have no idea what you are talking about,' snapped Michael impatiently.

'Bryony does not ease colic, which is what Olivia told Eyer she wanted it for. However, it can be used to end unwanted pregnancies, although not always effectively.'

Michael turned back to Verius. 'What else can you tell me about Fulbut? And think very carefully, because the paltry information you have provided so far is not enough to save you.'

'But that is all there is!' cried Verius, dismayed. 'He was close-mouthed about his business, which is why Potmoor hired him.' He flailed about for someone else to incriminate. 'I know! Richard Stanmore. He is as nasty a fellow as I have ever . . . Oh, Christ!' He put his hands over his face. 'I forgot! He is the Doctor's nephew!'

'But that does not make him decent,' put in Ylaria quickly. Bartholomew was sorry when he heard the desperation in her voice, unable to imagine the terror she must feel at the prospect of losing the man she loved to the scaffold. 'He inherited none of his mother's goodness, but all his sire's avarice and cunning.'

'Yes!' Verius nodded eagerly. 'Oswald Stanmore might have been nice to his family, but he was ruthless and deadly in business. He founded the Guild of Saints to make up for the bad things he did to others. And Richard is exactly the same, but with less charm.'

'Is there no one you will not malign in the scramble to exonerate yourself?' asked Michael in distaste. 'I want facts, not unfounded accusations.'

Verius frowned as he racked his brains for something else. 'I can tell you that Fulbut was ordered to disappear after he shot Felbrigge. It was a clean kill and no one saw him, but it was part of the agreement that he should leave and never return, lest he be caught and forced to talk.'

'But he did return, and someone stabbed him,' said Michael. 'So who was at his house last night?'

'His soldier friends, but they will have melted into the Fens by now, so do not waste your time looking for them. That surly porter Jekelyn from Winwick Hall was there, too.' Abruptly, Verius stopped speaking and stared at Michael. 'I have just remembered something, Brother. Something true this time! Jekelyn was wearing a green cloak with black edging.'

'Like the one on the man you followed after the St Clement's fire?' asked Bartholomew.

Verius nodded eagerly. 'I cannot say for certain that Jekelyn set the fire, but the cloak was the same. It is either his, or he borrowed it.'

'And you just happen to remember this now?' asked Michael sceptically.

'I really have,' said Verius fervently. Then he looked sly. 'My wits are awry from the blow the Doctor gave me. It is *his* fault that I forgot this important detail. Will this be enough to save me, Brother? I do not want to hang.'

'We shall see,' said Michael, and sailed out of the house.

'Here is the connection we have been looking for,' said the monk, once he and Bartholomew were hurrying back down Bridge Street. 'If Jekelyn killed Fulbut, then the chances are that a Winwick scholar ordered him to do it.'

'Can we trust Verius's testimony?' asked Bartholomew doubtfully. 'I did not see anyone in a green cloak last night.'

'It did not occur to me to look, to be honest. I only had eyes for the villain who murdered my deputy. But yes, I think we can believe Verius about this. And it means that someone from Winwick hired Fulbut to shoot Felbrigge, then sent Jekelyn to kill him when he reneged on the pact to leave Cambridge.'

Bartholomew remained uncertain. 'Verius was so desperate to exonerate himself that he would have said anything. So would Ylaria.'

'Not everything they bleated was fiction – Oswald *was* ruthless and *did* indulge in dubious business practices. And I am afraid there may even be truth to their claims about Julitta. Several people have told me that she gives less money to worthy causes than she once did.'

'Holm,' said Bartholomew in disgust. 'Her property is legally his now, and she is not at liberty to dispose of it as she likes. It is his fault that she can no longer be open-handed. Yet she remains loyal, and will never hear a bad word about him.'

'I am inclined to share their views about Richard, too,' Michael went on. 'I have not wanted to worry you, but he

329

has been at nearly every spat my beadles have had to quell of late. He does not fight himself, but stands in the shadows and goads them on.'

'No,' said Bartholomew stubbornly. 'I do not believe it.'

'Well, there he is,' said Michael, nodding across the street. 'And to prove my point, he is in company with a lot of matriculands. And the reprehensible Goodwyn, who I imagine has wasted no time in blackening your name with him.'

'I doubt Goodwyn's opinion will make much difference to the way Richard sees me,' said Bartholomew unhappily. 'We are not as close as we once were.'

Michael shot him a sympathetic glance. 'It is difficult to believe he is Edith's son. She is so honest and kind, while he is . . .' He waved a hand to express words he did not like to speak. 'Indeed, he makes me glad I do not have children. I should be mortified if they turned out like him.'

Many of the young men who formed the noisy, whooping pack had been in the King's Head the previous night, and it was clear that they had not gone home as ordered, but had continued to carouse. The odour of ale was detectable from some distance, and most were unsteady on their feet. One lurched away suddenly and was sick against a wall. His cronies cheered.

Richard looked worse than most: his long hair was lank and greasy, his fine clothes were stained, and there were bags under his bloodshot eyes.

'The Devil must be proud to see so many of his minions enrolling in your University,' came a snide voice. It was Heyford. 'I shall preach a sermon about it this afternoon.'

'Please do not,' begged Bartholomew. 'There is trouble enough already.'

'Trouble that is none of the town's making,' retorted Heyford. 'It is the University's fault for inviting all these Satan-spawn to join it.'

330

'They were not invited,' objected Michael. 'They just came.'

Heyford sniffed. 'Regardless, I must warn people about tomorrow. There will be violence, bloodshed and chaos, and decent folk should stay indoors. Personally, I think you should delay the beginning of term ceremony until you have more control over your scholars.'

'The dates are determined by statute,' said Michael irritably. 'We cannot change them to suit ourselves. But are you feeling better? You claimed you were poisoned yesterday.'

'I *was* poisoned,' declared Heyford. 'By someone who hopes to still my tongue. But God protects me from evil-doers, as you saw for yourself, Bartholomew, when He sent you to carry me from my burning church. Look at those villainous matriculands now! One has turned his bile on the Franciscans. I shall certainly include *that* in my sermon.'

He scurried away, and the two scholars turned to see Goodwyn taunting three novices. The Grey Friars recruited their members very young, and these were mere boys, frightened and uncomfortable in their new habits.

'Enough,' Michael ordered. The friars scurried away in relief. 'You should know better.'

'And so should you,' sneered Goodwyn. 'I am ousted from Michaelhouse, so you have no authority over me now. It was only a bit of fun anyway. Can no one take a joke?'

'There is nothing amusing about bullying,' said Michael.

'No,' agreed Goodwyn acidly. 'Yet you do it with your levying of fines for whatever takes your fancy, while Bartholomew is a despot who terrifies his students.'

He made an obscene gesture, which caused his cronies to cheer. While Michael reasserted control with some scathing remarks that wiped the grins from their faces, Richard sidled towards Bartholomew.

'I am sorry about last night,' he whispered. 'It was the ale speaking. Can we be friends again?'

'We will always be friends,' said Bartholomew, wishing the apology had sounded more sincere. 'But you are breaking your mother's heart with your riotous behaviour. Either stay and keep out of mischief, or leave so she cannot see how you spend your life.'

Something unpleasant flared in Richard's eyes, although he inclined his head amiably enough. 'You are right. I shall give your advice serious consideration.'

He sounded so disingenuous that a terrible thought insinuated itself into Bartholomew's mind: perhaps Richard *was* involved in the mischief that was unfolding. He had changed so much that his family no longer recognised him, so who knew what he was capable of now?

'Have you ever met a mercenary named Fulbut?' he asked, dreading the answer.

Richard blinked. 'Credit me with some taste! A mercenary indeed!'

'Then what about Jekelyn, the porter from Winwick Hall?'

Richard indicated his companions. 'These are the sons of knights, merchants and diplomats, and some have even been presented at Court. They are not porters, mercenaries or any other low-born scum. They are respectable.'

'Yes,' said Bartholomew flatly. 'So I see.'

Richard scowled. 'How can you criticise them when your patients include some of the worst rogues in the town? And do not preach virtue at me either, not when you are brazenly wooing Julitta Holm – a married woman.'

'I hardly think—'

'At least I offered to marry the Earl of Suffolk's daughter,' Richard forged on. 'But you make Julitta a whore. It would be easy to get an annulment, given that I doubt her union with Holm has been consummated, but you prefer to sully her good name by visiting while he is out.'

Bartholomew was taken aback by his nephew's assault. 'I have not—'

Richard cut across him again. '*Does* she care for you, or is she just using you to punish her husband for taking Hugo as his lover? Personally, I hope she is acting to avenge herself on Holm, because I do not want her as an aunt.'

'And why is that?' asked Bartholomew coolly.

'Because she inherited her father's business acumen *and* his powerful persona. Such parents leave their mark, and shape us into what we become.'

And with that enigmatic remark, Richard turned on his heel and marched after his friends.

Bartholomew's thoughts were in turmoil as he and Michael resumed their walk to Winwick, and he barely heard the monk's diatribe on unruly matriculands. It had never occurred to him that Julitta could apply for an annulment. Would she do it? He thought she might – her marriage was a sham, after all. He was suddenly filled with hope for the future – until he remembered something else Richard had said, at which point he burned with shame. His love for her *was* damaging her reputation, given that half the town seemed to know about their trysts. It was hardly gallant, and Richard was right to condemn him for it.

He was sufficiently unsettled that when Michael was diverted from their mission by University business at St Mary the Great, he went to Milne Street to see Edith. It was partly to ensure that Richard's night of debauchery had not upset her, but mostly because he was in need of a sympathetic ear. Unfortunately for him, she had uncovered another instance of Oswald's dubious dealings, one that had deprived St John's Hospital of a significant amount of money, and she was too distraught to think about anything else.

'At first, I thought he had made a mistake,' she whispered, ashen-faced. 'But subsequent documents show that he knew exactly what he was doing. Perhaps I should have listened to Richard and burned everything, as then I would not have learned these horrible secrets. Have you made any progress with identifying his killer?'

'No,' replied Bartholomew, hating to see the disappointment in her eyes. 'Not yet.'

'Then be careful. The deeper I delve, the more I realise that he dealt with some very unsavoury individuals. Potmoor was the worst, but he also worked with that loathsome Frevill clan, the Bishop, Mistress Mortimer, members of King's Hall and Winwick, Mayor Heslarton . . .'

The list went on for some time, and Bartholomew listened with growing dismay. Some were convicted felons, most were of dubious probity, and the rest were powerful men who would resent being questioned. And while he had known that Oswald's business practices were sometimes unethical, he had not appreciated quite how many were downright criminal.

Edith was so unsettled by her discoveries that it took a while to soothe her, and by the time he had succeeded, it did not seem appropriate to burden her with his own problems. He left her in a more quiescent state, although his own mind churned with uncertainty and torment. He collected Michael from the church, and they walked towards Winwick in silence. Bartholomew was so distracted by his concerns that he did not see Eyer until he had collided with him.

'Ouch!' The apothecary hopped about on one foot, his pink face twisted in pain. 'Watch where you are going, Matt! Did you not hear me calling?'

'Sorry.' Here was one man Bartholomew could not afford to annoy: the health of the town's poor would depend on his largesse until Michaelhouse was able to pay its Fellows' stipends. Assuming the College was not dissolved in the interim, of course. 'Did you want me for something?'

'Only to invite you to try some of my mushroom wine. I added a dead squirrel to enhance fermentation, and I should like your opinion on the result.'

'Gracious,' said Bartholomew, wondering how to refuse without causing offence.

'I appreciate that you will be busy with term starting tomorrow,' Eyer went on, 'so come next week, when things are quieter. I invited Bon, too. Many folk consider him peevish and unfriendly, but he is charm itself when you come to know him. Unlike his Winwick colleagues.'

'Oh?' probed Michael keenly. 'You do not like Illesy, Lawrence and Nerli?'

'Not really. Especially Lawrence. And there are rumours about all three – that they are closer than they should be to Potmoor, and that they aid him in his depredations.'

'I cannot see Lawrence climbing through windows to rob wealthy homes,' said Bartholomew, disliking the apothecary's penchant for gossip and unfounded speculation.

Eyer regarded him soberly. 'Perhaps not, but he is often out at night. *Not* visiting patients as he would have us believe, but on other business, about which he lies whenever I raise the subject. Nerli is often with him, and I do not believe it is for company as they claim. Meanwhile, Potmoor would be behind bars were it not for Illesy's cunning legal advice.'

'He is right, Matt,' said Michael, when the apothecary had hurried away on an errand of mercy to Olivia Knyt, who was suffering from stomach cramps. 'Potmoor would be in my cells if Illesy had not been there to supply fictitious alibis.'

'He is not right about Lawrence, though.' Bartholomew's stomach lurched suddenly when the bells of St Mary the

Great rang for sext. 'It is noon, Brother! The extortionist will be waiting for his twenty marks.'

'Forget about him. Langelee dealt with several matters of this nature when he worked for the Archbishop, and he says he has a plan. We must trust him to carry it out while we attack the villain on another front – by laying hold of his helpmeet Jekelyn.'

Winwick's gates were off their hinges again when they arrived. There was no sign of the porter, so Bartholomew and Michael walked into the College unchallenged. Inside, they were greeted by uproar, and soon learned why. Illesy and his Fellows had gone to St Mary the Great to prepare for Michaelhouse's 'Saturday' Sermon; unsupervised, the students had run riot.

There were at least sixty of them in the yard, watching a boxing match between servants. Wine was being swigged from flasks, bets were being placed, and there was a lot of yelling and cheering. Others were hanging out of the dormitory windows or lounging in corners to mutter in low voices. At least a dozen Frail Sisters were there, surrounded by pawing admirers.

'It is more like a brothel than a College,' said Michael in distaste. 'The other foundations are right to voice their reservations about it. Illesy will have to make adjustments to discipline after tomorrow, or I shall petition for the place to be closed down.'

There was a sudden clatter on the far side of the yard. A tile had slipped from the roof, and the muddle of shards already on the ground indicated it was not the first time this had happened.

'The builders cut corners in the race to finish Winwick by the beginning of term,' said Bartholomew, squinting up at it. 'Which means much of the work is shoddy. The roof should not be falling to pieces so soon, and nor should the plaster be flaking off the walls.'

'A substandard hall is not Winwick's only problem,' said

Michael. 'Tynkell told me that *ninety* new students have been accepted, more than all the other Colleges put together. They have been picked for their wealth, not for academic merit, so they will be all but impossible to teach.'

'I cannot see the founder being impressed when he arrives tomorrow. Perhaps he will have second thoughts and withdraw his patronage.' Bartholomew gestured at the noisy throng. 'After all, he will not want this sort of lout braying that he was educated at Winwick Hall.'

'What do you want?' came a belligerent voice from behind them. They turned to see one of the matriculands who had been with Uyten in the King's Head the previous night. He was older than most new students, and looked more like a soldier than a budding lawyer.

Michael regarded him coolly, disliking the lack of deference. 'And who are you, pray?'

'Sir Joshua Hardwell, not that it is any of your affair.'

'Who is in charge while the Fellows are out?' Michael kept his temper with difficulty.

'I am,' replied Hardwell. 'But do not think you can fine us for drinking and gambling, because we will not be bound by your rules until tomorrow. And perhaps not even then. We all hail from important families, and we are not men to be restrained by silly strictures.'

'We shall see,' said Michael, his confident tone suggesting that Winwick would lose that particular battle. 'But we came to speak to Jekelyn, not you. Where is he?'

'There,' said Bartholomew, stabbing a finger towards the porter, who was sneaking towards the gates, resplendent in a green cloak with black edging. When he saw he had been spotted, an expression of alarm suffused Jekelyn's face. He whipped around and aimed for the hall instead.

'After him, Matt!' cried Michael. 'I shall be right behind you.'

Bartholomew darted towards the hall, swearing under his breath when he tripped over a carpenter. He had only

337

just regained his balance when he heard a door slam at the back of the building. He hared towards it, and flung it open to see that it led to an orchard. Jekelyn was jigging through the trees, making for a gate at the far end, at which point he would disappear into the tangle of lanes that emptied on to the Market Square.

Bartholomew tore after him, but arrived to find the gate still closed – the porter had not yet gone through it. He stood still, listening intently. All he could hear was the students' cheering. There was a snap behind him as a twig broke underfoot. He spun around quickly, but not quite fast enough. A cudgel swung towards him, and although he managed to throw up an arm to protect his head, the blow sent him flying. He landed with a thud that drove the breath from his body.

CHAPTER 14

Bartholomew was not sure how long it was before his wits stopped spinning, but when they did, he was lying on the ground with Michael leaning anxiously over him.

'Thank God!' breathed the monk, crossing himself. 'For one dreadful moment I thought I was going to have to solve all these mysteries by myself.'

'Thank you for your concern.' Bartholomew winced as he sat up. 'Where is Jekelyn?'

'Gone. I could have followed, but I did not like to leave you here unattended.' Michael hauled him to his feet. 'We had better return to Michaelhouse, or the Saturday Sermon will have started and Langelee will have invited Illesy and his Fellows into our home for nothing.'

They left Winwick through the back gate, and hurried through streets that pulsed with tension, eventually reaching Michaelhouse to find it transformed. The yard had been swept, the gates washed, and the hall given a thorough scour, so it smelled clean and fresh. What little silver the College still possessed had been polished and placed on display, and the woodwork gleamed. William and Suttone had begged platters of delicacies from their friaries, while Thelnetham had borrowed money for wine. Deynman the Librarian had removed all the books from their chests and set them on shelves, and Agatha had broken out the ceremonial linen.

'Oh, dear,' she said, deliberately spilling a cup of claret, just as the Winwick men were shown in, 'but never mind. If the stain does not come out, we shall throw this table-cloth away and buy another. Money is no object to us. Is it, Master?'

'Not at all,' declared Langelee. His eyes were puffy, as though he had been crying. Bartholomew was alarmed. What had happened to drive the manly Master to tears? 'We older Colleges are rolling in it, and it is only the new ones that must rely on loans from town charities.'

'We are proud of our association with the Guild of Saints,' said Illesy icily. 'Indeed, we have invited them here today. It is the first time we have been asked to take part in a disputation with another College, and it is only right that they should witness our victory.'

Langelee gaped at him. 'I think you will find that it is *my* privilege to issue invitations to events in my own home.'

Bon smiled in his approximate direction. 'Yes, but we knew you would not object. You must have great respect for our talents or you would not have solicited our presence here today.'

'But the Guild has females in it!' cried Thelnetham, appalled. 'You know – *women*! And we do not allow those on the premises.'

'I am sure you can make an exception just this once,' said Illesy. 'Ah! Here they come now.'

There was a commotion on the stairs, and Edith and Julitta walked in. Thelnetham crossed himself in abject horror, although the other Fellows were more concerned with who was on their heels. It was Potmoor, with Walter scurrying behind him. The porter was wringing his hands, and his lugubrious face was full of dismay and agitation.

'I tried to keep him out,' he wailed to Langelee. 'But he *looked* at me, and the next thing I knew, he was across the threshold.'

Hugo and Holm were next, their heads inappropriately close as they sniggered at some private joke; Bartholomew bristled at the open insult to Julitta. De Stannell followed them, wearing the ceremonial robes of Deputy Sheriff, although had had evidently taken a tumble from his horse en route, as they were stained with muck from the road.

Behind him was Meryfeld, grinning his amusement at the sight, with Eyer chatting amiably at his side.

'Winwick did this on purpose,' Langelee hissed furiously, as other guests entered in their wake and began to avail themselves of the refreshments. 'They knew we would not expect to cater for so many, and want to humiliate us in front of all these dignitaries.'

'Then they will not succeed,' vowed Thelnetham. 'I shall send to the Gilbertine Priory for more wine, even if it means I spend the rest of the year paying off the debt. I may not intend to stay here much longer, but I will not see our noses rubbed in the dirt.'

'The Carmelites will help, too,' declared Suttone, while the other Fellows made similar promises. Bartholomew had no Order to raid, but help came in the form of Edith, who whispered that she had apprentices waiting with edible offerings in the yard below.

'Julitta warned me,' she confided. 'She does not want Michaelhouse embarrassed.'

'No,' agreed Julitta. 'I do not like most of the Winwick men. Illesy is oily, Nerli is sinister, and Lawrence makes me sick with his false sweetness. Bon may be bad-tempered and acid-tongued, but I admire his honesty. He has been given the task of recruiting more masters, so I hope he picks some who are more pleasant than the current horde.'

Bartholomew wondered whether Richard would be among their number. Thoughts of his nephew reminded him of their last conversation, but before he could mention the prospect of Julitta annulling her unsatisfactory union with Holm, Edith spoke.

'Richard told me a few moments ago that he has invited Goodwyn to stay. I would not mind, but Goodwyn promptly spouted a lot of lies about you – how you cheated him of his fees, how you stole a valuable hutch to buy medicine, how you itch to raise more felons from the dead . . .'

'Perhaps the tale about William seeing the Dominican

Prior riding across the sky with the Devil on his back originated with him, too,' added Julitta. 'It sounds like the kind of spiteful nonsense Goodwyn would invent.'

Bartholomew regarded her in horror. 'What?'

'Weasenham the stationer told me,' replied Julitta. 'But do not worry. I know it is a malicious fiction, and so will anyone else who matters. William would never have written such vile nonsense and given it to the scribes to copy. Where is he, by the way?'

'Unwell,' replied Bartholomew, looking away so he would not have to meet her eyes. The truth was that Langelee did not trust William to behave, so the Franciscan had been ordered to stay in his room until the debate was over.

'Perhaps it is the shock of hearing what has been penned in his name,' suggested Edith. 'And there is more to come, apparently. Weasenham's scribes were only given the first two pages, but have been informed that the finished tract comprises at least thirty more. Poor William! He must be mortified – terrified of what will be attributed to him next.'

'Did these two pages mention apostolic poverty?' asked Bartholomew nervously.

'No, just the tale about Prior Morden,' replied Edith. 'The scribes are delighted by the prospect of copying more. They say theology has become boringly conventional since Linton Hall in Oxford got into trouble for its radical opinions.'

So the blackmailer had issued a warning, thought Bartholomew numbly: pay up or else. Clearly, whatever plan Langelee had devised to deal with the situation had been unsuccessful.

'How are your investigations?' asked Julitta, breaking into his tumbling thoughts. 'Are you close to catching whoever murdered Hemmysby, Knyt and the others?'

'Not really,' replied Bartholomew, although he was barely aware of speaking. What would happen to Michaelhouse now? Would the Dominicans sue for defamation? Morden was a reasonable man, but he could not be expected to ignore that sort of insult. If he did, credulous people might assume the tale was true.

'I wish *he* was not here,' said Edith, indicating Potmoor with a nod of her head. 'I find it difficult to be in the same room as him. Indeed, I declined the invitation to come today, which is why I did not mention it when you visited, Matt. But Julitta persuaded me to change my mind.'

'I thought it would do her good,' explained Julitta. 'She spends far too much time poring over documents and fretting over her son these days. It is hardly healthy.'

'No,' agreed Bartholomew, grateful to her for enticing his sister out, even if it was only to a dull debate and some mediocre refreshments.

'Yet she is right about Potmoor,' Julitta went on. 'It would not surprise me if *he* poisoned all those men, perhaps to ensure that they do not stand witness against him for robbing half the town. And look at how he smirks and simpers with Nerli and Lawrence.'

'Nerli is exactly the kind of person I would expect Potmoor to befriend,' said Edith sourly. 'He is sinister and vicious, like the henchmen Potmoor employs. Lawrence is nice, though.'

Julitta's expression was troubled. 'Then why do I always feel that is what he *wants* me to think – that I am being manipulated with benign smiles and grandfatherly goodness?'

Eventually they moved away to talk to Clippesby, leaving Bartholomew to fret about the blackmailer's mischief, Edith's pallor and how to obtain a declaration of nullity. He was not left alone for long. Langelee approached, rubbing his swollen eyes.

'Have you heard that the extortionist has struck?' he spat angrily. 'The bastard! After I gave him ten marks, too.'

Bartholomew gaped at him. 'You *paid* him? What with?'

'A loan from your sister. Do not glare at me! I did not tell her why I needed the money.'

Bartholomew was appalled. 'You should not have done it! And certainly not without Michael and me there to help you lay hold of him when he came to collect.'

Langelee scowled. 'I thought *I* could lay hold of him. After all, I outwitted several demands of this nature when I worked for the Archbishop. I took Walter and William with me, but he threw sand in my face, and was off before the other two could grab him.'

Bartholomew turned the Master's head to the light, to examine his eyes. 'So he avenged himself with the tale about Morden, and now we owe Edith ten marks into the bargain.'

'Worse,' said Langelee through gritted teeth. 'Another note arrived a few moments ago. The rogue has issued a second demand.'

He held it out. Again, the clerkly writing was familiar, but Bartholomew still could not place it. His heart sank when he read that if fifty marks were not left at a particular tomb near the Round Church by midnight, more of William's tract would be made public.

'You have made the situation worse by attempting trickery,' he said accusingly. 'He will be on his guard now, and we may never catch him. Has Michael seen this?'

'No – he has gone to question Weasenham's scribes. Ah! Here he comes now.'

When he read the blackmailer's latest communiqué, the monk's expression turned more grim than ever. 'William's pages were left at the shop anonymously, along with payment for ten copies to be made,' he reported tersely. 'Weasenham showed me the originals. They are so obviously William's that we will never deny it convincingly.'

'It was just the bit about Prior Morden?' asked Langelee anxiously.

Michael nodded. 'Nothing about apostolic poverty yet,

thank God.' He indicated the new message. 'Although that might change tomorrow. The culprit must hate us very deeply, to murder Hemmysby, steal the Stanton Hutch, and set the Dominicans at our throat.'

'Or perhaps we are just the instrument with which he aims to damage the whole University,' suggested Langelee soberly. 'The King will be livid that the example of Linton Hall went unheeded, and might arrange for the whole *studium generale* to be put under interdict.'

'Lord!' breathed Michael, appalled. 'You may be right.'

Langelee glanced behind him, where the hall teemed with people. 'And the culprit might be here right now, so for God's sake go and catch him before he succeeds.'

The thought that such a person – Hemmysby's poisoner – might be settling himself comfortably on a bench in Michaelhouse's hall made Bartholomew feel physically sick. He leaned against the wall at the back and watched the guests avail themselves of the refreshments, which were distributed in dribs and drabs as they arrived from the various priories. There was, however, no contribution from the Dominicans, despite repeated appeals from Clippesby.

Potmoor stood near the door, so as to be first at the platters when they appeared. Hugo and Holm were giggling together on his right, and de Stannell was on his left, nodding sycophantically at everything he said. Julitta sat by Edith, and Bartholomew was not sure who was comforting whom as they clutched each other's hands. Holm's fondness for Hugo was hurtful to Julitta, while Edith kept staring at the man she believed had murdered her husband.

The Fellows of Winwick stood near the dais, the brooding Nerli, Illesy with his fingers thick with rings, and Bon gripping Lawrence's arm. Bartholomew watched the elderly *medicus* direct his charge to a chair. Were Julitta and Michael right to question Lawrence's character? When the old man abandoned his Winwick colleagues to chat to Meryfeld and Eyer, Bartholomew joined the three of them, supposing he should try to find out.

'If Holm really *has* discovered a cure for gout,' Meryfeld was saying sulkily, 'he should tell us what is in it, so we can help our own patients. It is unethical to keep the secret to himself.'

'He does not want the competition,' said Eyer, tactfully not mentioning that Meryfeld never shared his own remedies. 'Still, he told me that his potion comprises mostly angelica and powdered chalk, so if it does not work, at least we can be assured that it will do no harm.'

He glanced at Lawrence, making it clear that he thought the same could not be said of *his* treatments. Lawrence only beamed back, and Bartholomew gazed at him in wonderment. Was he really such an innocent that he could not see the obvious challenge in the apothecary's glare?

'I thought you might like to read this,' Lawrence said, tearing his eyes away from Eyer to hand Bartholomew a scroll. He smiled genially. 'It is a little treatise I composed on ailments of the ears, which may be of interest to you.'

'I dislike reading,' declared Meryfeld, watching the parchment change hands with marked distaste. 'I always say that if something needs to be written down, then it is not worth remembering.'

'That is a crass remark to make in a hall of learning.' They all turned to see Holm standing behind them. 'What a fool you are, Meryfeld! No wonder Lawrence has poached all your best patients.'

'I have done no such thing,' objected Lawrence, blushing uncomfortably.

'What about Potmoor, then?' demanded Holm. 'He was Meryfeld's, but now he is yours.'

'That was Potmoor's decision, not mine.' Lawrence flailed about for a way to change the subject. 'What a delight it is to be here! I have never been inside before. It is very . . . cosy.'

'He means poky,' translated Holm, looking around disparagingly. 'I cannot imagine it is pleasant in winter. None of the windows are glazed, and there is only one fireplace.'

'We manage well enough,' said Bartholomew, disliking criticism from such a quarter. Before he could add more, Holm was off on another contentious subject.

'I fed some *dormirella* to a rat yesterday, and *its* lips have not turned blue, which is curious, given what Brother Michael claimed about the stuff.'

'Why did you do such a thing?' asked Bartholomew, immediately suspicious.

'I have an enquiring mind, and I do not believe everything I am told.'

Holm looked so hard at Bartholomew that the physician wondered whether he knew the truth. If so, did it mean *he* was the killer, and had conducted the experiment in a panic? It certainly made sense that he was the blackmailer – by attacking Michaelhouse, he struck a blow at his rival for Julitta's affections.

'I had never heard of *dormirella* before Michael mentioned it the other day,' said Lawrence amiably. 'But Nerli tells me that burning it is an excellent way to dry wet plaster.'

'Actually, it is not,' countered Eyer. 'I can suggest much better remedies. Cheaper ones, too. Using *dormirella* to air out rooms is like using wine to clean latrines.'

'I see,' said Lawrence, and hastened to change the subject again, presumably to conceal his ignorance. 'Come with me to talk to Nerli, Matthew. He studied in Salerno, where you attended all those dissections. Perhaps you and he have mutual acquaintances.'

Holm immediately embarked on a vicious denunciation of anatomical studies, and Bartholomew was glad when Lawrence tugged him away, as he had no desire to listen to such an unintelligent tirade. He happened to glance back as he went, and was stunned by the look of black hatred on the surgeon's face. It was quickly masked, but told him yet again that Holm was a dangerous adversary who meant him serious harm.

'Ignore him,' said Lawrence in a low voice. 'He is a snake. Meanwhile, Meryfeld is an ass, and Eyer is a pompous bore with shameful secrets.'

The apothecary had said much the same about Lawrence, Bartholomew recalled. Had Lawrence heard that his past had been gossiped about, and decided to retaliate in kind? Bartholomew was no more comfortable listening to him than he had been listening to Eyer, but before he could change the subject, the elderly *medicus* began muttering in his ear.

'It concerns an incident in Oxford many years ago, and—'

'Be careful, Lawrence.' Both physicians turned to see that Eyer had followed them. 'Slander is a criminal offence, you know.'

Lawrence's expression was coolly aloof. 'It is only slander if the tale is untrue. But you seem to have done well for yourself in your current occupation, so let us say no more about it. Unless you want to confide in Matthew, of course. But that is your decision, not mine.'

Eyer scowled at him. 'I think we both know that I have no choice after *that* cunning little speech.' He addressed Bartholomew stiffly. 'The truth is that I have not always been an apothecary. I was training to be a physician in Oxford, but was . . . asked to leave.'

'Sent down,' elaborated Lawrence. 'For experimenting on patients before he was qualified – with herbs and potions of his own devising.'

'Herbs and potions that worked,' flashed Eyer. 'My punishment was a gross miscarriage of justice, and all because the local apothecaries were jealous of my success. They hounded the Master of Balliol until he was forced to dismiss me. But I always was more interested in cures than diseases, so perhaps it was a blessing in disguise.'

'Perhaps,' said Lawrence archly. 'But the episode means that you are unlikely to be endorsed by a professional body, so your practice here is almost certainly illegal. Charitably, I have turned a blind eye, but perhaps I should not have done.'

As trade associations tended to be fussy about who they sanctioned, and would certainly not overlook the kind of confrontation Lawrence had described, Bartholomew imagined Eyer probably *was* operating without the necessary licence. And Lawrence's tale explained a great deal – the inconsistencies in Eyer's stories about his past, his occasionally puzzling manner, and his trespassing on the physicians' domain by making diagnoses. It also explained why Eyer had tried to blacken Lawrence's name: it had been a preemptive strike against a man who could destroy him.

But for all his flaws, Eyer was a reliable practitioner, and Bartholomew had not forgotten his willingness to provide free medicines for the poor. Such generosity deserved its reward, and he felt it was incumbent on him to repair the rift if he could.

'If you expose him, he will be forced to leave,' he told Lawrence. 'And we shall be deprived of a decent apothecary. That would be a pity – for us and our patients. Moreover, I have no complaints about the service he has provided, and neither have Rougham and Meryfeld.'

'True,' sighed Lawrence, and favoured Eyer with one of his kindly smiles. 'Shall we be friends, then? Perhaps you will dine with me in Winwick one evening next week.'

Eyer muttered his acceptance and hurried to an open window, where he began to gulp down deep breaths of fresh air. Lawrence watched him thoughtfully, then resumed his walk towards Nerli without another word. Was that a flash of spiteful satisfaction in his eyes, Bartholomew wondered – glee that he had exposed the apothecary's dubious past while deftly deflecting attention from his own? Bartholomew was tempted to pursue Eyer's allegations, but pragmatism prevailed. He had more important questions to ask.

'Did you argue with Hemmysby about him savaging your colleagues in St Mary the Great, and the fact that Winwick has too great a say in Guild politics?'

'No,' replied Lawrence, rather more sharply than was his wont. 'As I have told you before. We had a mild exchange of opinion. William and Thelnetham were there in the vestry with us, so ask them about it if you do not believe me. They will confirm what I say.'

'I meant after the first day,' said Bartholomew. 'Were any threats exchanged then?'

Lawrence laughed, although there was a brittle quality to the guffaws. 'Of course not! He was not the kind of fellow to issue threats, and I am sure you cannot imagine *me* doing it.'

He had hailed his Winwick colleagues before Bartholomew could question him further. Illesy scowled, Nerli grimaced, and Bon wore a moue of distaste, as if being in Michaelhouse was beneath him. None were expressions that encouraged Bartholomew to make them welcome, and he felt his hackles begin to rise. He struggled to mask his objection at having such people in his home.

'Are we ready?' Lawrence asked jovially. 'The honour of Winwick rests in our hands today.'

'We shall prevail,' said Bon. 'Michaelhouse's reputation in the University is poor, while our minds are honed sharp.'

Bartholomew would not normally have challenged a guest, but there was something about the Winwick men that made him unwilling to stand meekly by while his colleagues were insulted.

'I seem to recall that we destroyed you the last time we met in the debating chamber,' he said coolly.

'How kind of you to remind us just before we re-enter

the fray,' said Illesy. 'However, your sly attempt to disconcert will not succeed, because this time the subject is law,
not theology. Bon is right: we will prevail.'

'Bartholomew has visited Salerno, Nerli,' said Lawrence
quickly, before a quarrel could erupt. 'He witnessed a
number of dissections there that—'

'*I* never saw any dissections,' interrupted Nerli indignantly. 'How dare you suggest I might! I am a lawyer, not
an anatomist.'

'Of course,' said Lawrence. 'But I imagine you will find
common acquaintances if you—'

'No,' said Nerli curtly. 'I would never demean myself
by associating with anyone who condoned such diabolical
matters. We will share no mutual friends.'

'I am sorry, Matthew,' said Lawrence, as the Florentine
stalked away. 'I was not aware that he felt so negatively
about dissection. It just goes to show that even those you
think you know can surprise you sometimes. As you
learned with Eyer just now.'

At last, Michael indicated to Bartholomew that he was
ready to put more questions to the men from Winwick
Hall. Dutifully, the physician stood at his side to watch
for telling reactions.

'Matt and I were in your domain earlier,' Michael began
pleasantly. 'To speak to your porter. Unfortunately, he
bolted when he saw us. Why would that be, do you think?'

'Why did you want Jekelyn?' asked Illesy suspiciously.
'Has he done something wrong?'

'Oh, yes,' replied Michael. 'He was at the home of a
notorious mercenary last night – the one who murdered
my Junior Proctor.'

'Perhaps he was drunk, and did not know what he was
doing,' suggested Bon, turning his milky eyes towards the
monk's voice. 'He is a terrible sot, and we should never
have hired him.'

'No, you should not,' agreed Michael. 'And you will notify me the moment he reappears.'

Illesy bristled. 'You have no right to order us to—'

'Your porter is implicated in the murder of a University proctor,' interrupted Michael sharply. 'So either you accede to my terms or I shall fine you for refusing to cooperate with an official investigation.'

'Very well.' Illesy capitulated with bad grace. 'But I am sure he had nothing to do with Felbrigge's death. His only crime will be a poor choice of friends.'

'On the contrary,' said Michael coldly. 'He is a killer himself. He stabbed Fulbut.'

'Nonsense!' cried Illesy. 'However, even if you are right, all it means is that he has rid you of a dangerous assassin. Surely you will not punish him for that?'

'Of course I will! We do not take justice into our own hands in Cambridge.' Michael smiled without humour. 'Incidentally, Fulbut took a while to die, and talked a great deal before breathing his last.'

There was silence, and Bartholomew read unease in all four Winwick men. Illesy began to fiddle with his rings, Lawrence gulped, Bon paled, and Nerli hissed between his teeth.

'It seems murder is not Jekelyn's only crime,' Michael went on. 'We also have reason to believe that he set fire to St Clement's Church – a blaze in which its vicar might have died.'

'No!' breathed Lawrence, shocked. 'Jekelyn would never do such a wicked thing.'

Nerli and Illesy exchanged a brief glance that suggested they were not so sure.

'I agree,' said Bon. 'Jekelyn is . . .' He trailed off when someone approached their group, and tilted his head in an effort to identify the footsteps. It was Potmoor with de Stannell at his heels.

'Are you discussing Goodwyn's transfer to Winwick

Hall?' asked the felon. 'He tells me there is a misunderstanding with his fees, so I hope it can be resolved.'

'It is not a misunderstanding,' countered de Stannell. 'Michaelhouse took the lad's money, but now refuses to give it back. It is brazen theft.'

'Goodwyn,' sighed Michael. 'What a sad case! The lad has a pox that eats the brain, and one cannot believe a word he says. Have you accepted him yet, Provost Illesy? If so, you might want to give him his own room, as Matt thinks his condition might be contagious.'

'Heavens!' gulped Illesy. 'Are you sure?'

'Oh, yes.' Michael regarded de Stannell kindly. 'You are *probably* safe, but you might want to take a few precautions. Eat a pound of raisins every day, and abstain from meat for a month.'

'*I* need not worry,' declared Potmoor smugly, although the deputy's eyes widened in alarm. 'I have God's protection, which is much better than raisins.'

He began to hold forth about his resurrection, and the Winwick men took the opportunity to drift away. Frustrated, Michael signalled to Langelee that the debate might as well start, muttering to Bartholomew that they were wasting their breath by trying to wring clues from the likes of Illesy, Bon, Nerli and Lawrence. They were lawyers, and it would be easier to lay hold of an eel.

'Nerli is the main speaker today,' announced the Master, once he had welcomed everyone and issued the unusual edict that the occasion would be in the vernacular, out of courtesy to those guests who had no Latin. 'He will outline his thesis, Michaelhouse will rebut it, and Winwick will try to respond. Whichever side offers the best arguments will be deemed the victor.'

'And what *is* your thesis today, Signor Nerli?' asked Suttone pleasantly.

'That the Bible lays out clear guidelines for the levying

of taxes,' replied the Florentine, in English that was a good deal less thickly accented than his Latin.

'For Heaven's sake!' muttered Michael. 'Could he not have chosen a more lively topic? I know nothing about the theology of taxation. How am I supposed to defeat him?'

'Cheat,' Langelee murmured back. 'And that is an order.'

As there were not enough benches, the Michaelhouse Fellows were obliged to stand at the back of the hall. Bartholomew did not mind, as it gave him an opportunity to observe his suspects without them realising what he was doing. As far as he was concerned, there were only five: Nerli, Illesy, Holm, Potmoor and Hugo. He ignored the nagging voice which told him that perhaps Richard should also be included.

He watched Nerli first, noting the man's arrogant confidence. If the Florentine had poisoned Hemmysby, then he suffered no remorse about being in his victim's home. Meanwhile, Holm and Hugo sat indecently close together, whispering and giggling like teenagers. Potmoor was in the front row, looking around him with so much interest that Bartholomew wondered whether he was assessing it for a future break-in. Illesy was staring at Nerli, but creases of concern in his smooth face suggested that his mind was not on his colleague's monologue.

'He spoke well,' murmured Langelee, when Nerli eventually sat and Suttone rose to refute some of his points.

Michael nodded. 'His slight hesitation of manner says that he has not taken part in many of these occasions, but once he gains some experience, he will be formidable.'

'He told me that he has been a scholar all his life,' said Bartholomew. 'How much more experience does he need?'

Michael shrugged. 'Perhaps debates do not take this form in Salerno.'

Bartholomew was about to inform him that they did when Suttone began his analysis. The Carmelite was followed by Illesy, who spoke for some time without saying anything of substance.

'He has a slippery tongue,' murmured Michael. 'I am not surprised he kept Potmoor out of trouble for so long.'

Bartholomew was startled when Langelee called on him to take the floor. He was not a lawyer or a theologian, and had expected to be spared. Then he saw that Clippesby had Ethel on his head, and understood the Master's reluctance to rely on the Dominican to make a good impression. He stepped on to the dais, and managed to acquit himself adequately. Edith and Julitta clapped when he had finished, which put Holm in a jealous sulk.

Bon made some stumbling, uncertain points that Michael refuted with his usual incisive logic, and then it was Lawrence's turn – a good-natured but rambling discourse that was difficult to follow. Langelee had saved the best for last. Thelnetham was an eloquent and witty orator, and some of his remarks had everyone roaring with laughter, no mean feat given the dry subject matter. The Gilbertine dismissed Lawrence with a few well-chosen words, destroyed Illesy in a sentence, picked Bon up on a few points that Michael had missed, then neatly demolished Nerli.

There was no need for Langelee to announce a winner, because it was obvious. The Winwick Fellows nodded curt acknowledgement of the applause that followed the Master's concluding remarks, and prepared to leave.

'I am sorry you felt the need to embarrass us a second time,' said Bon coldly, when the Michaelhouse men went to thank them for coming. 'We are still novices, and you might have made allowances accordingly.'

'Moreover, I am not sure that all Thelnetham's points were legitimate,' added Nerli. 'I shall check his references

355

when I get home, and will be disappointed if he fabricated them.'

'Of course he did not fabricate them,' declared Langelee, conveniently forgetting that he had charged his Fellows to cheat. 'We are simply more masterly than you in the debating chamber.'

'For now,' said Bon sulkily. 'But that will change – unlike your status as inferior College. I may not be able to see your hall, but I warrant it is not as fine as ours. *And* we have more students.'

'Come,' said Lawrence, tugging on his arm before he could add more. 'Our lads are meant to be reading Gratian's *Decretum,* but they are a lively horde, and I have a feeling we shall find them doing something else. Thank you for your hospitality, Langelee. We enjoyed ourselves very much.'

With a stiff bow, Illesy swept from the hall, his Fellows at his heels. Most guildsmen followed with relief, having been extremely bored. Bartholomew went to speak to Edith, who confessed miserably that she did not want to go home in case Richard was there. She held a book, and twisted it agitatedly in her hands as she spoke. It had a gold-leaf cover, and was clearly valuable. Puzzled, Bartholomew took it from her. Inside were drawings of exotic beasts.

'Clippesby asked me to look after it,' she explained. 'Ethel wants to read it, apparently, but he is afraid her beak will damage the binding. I assume he refers to the chicken and not a person? It is sometimes difficult to be sure with him.'

'When did he give it to you?' demanded Bartholomew.

'Just now.' Edith frowned at the urgency in his voice. 'Why? Is something wrong?'

'Yes! I suspect this is the tome that Thelnetham left as a pledge in the Stanton Hutch.'

Like many people, the Gilbertine's ears were attuned

to hearing his name, even across a large room. Keen to know what was being said about him, he sailed over.

'My bestiary!' he cried, snatching it to clutch against his breast. His delighted shriek brought the other Fellows clustering around. 'Thank God! I shall not ask how you came by it, Matthew – I am just glad to have it back. Now I can leave this accursed place with all that is mine.'

'You will have to wait for another College to accept you first,' said Langelee. 'And—'

'One has,' interrupted Thelnetham. 'Bon has just offered me a Fellowship at Winwick Hall. He was impressed by my performance today, and says I am exactly the kind of man he needs. So I resign from this house of thieves, fools and lunatics, and good riddance to you all!'

'You cannot go to Winwick!' cried Langelee, dismayed at the notion of losing his best disputant. He flailed around for a reason that would convince. 'You told us that its hall has been raised too quickly, and sways in the wind. You said it would make you sick if—'

'I have changed my mind. And now, if you will excuse me, I am going to pack.'

With mixed emotions, the other Fellows watched him flounce away. His acerbic tongue and haughty manners were a trial, but he was a gifted teacher, and he certainly raised Michaelhouse's academic standing. They would miss him, no matter what William might claim to the contrary.

Bartholomew tore his eyes away from the Gilbertine's retreating form. The return of the bestiary answered a lot of questions, and he now knew exactly where the Stanton Hutch was, and who had put it there. 'Where is Clippesby?' he asked.

'In the henhouse, I expect,' replied Langelee, after a quick glance around established that the Dominican was no longer in the hall. 'He spends all his time there these days, except when I roust him out to attend his duties. However, I wish I had left him alone today. He should not have attended the debate with a chicken on his head.'

'The Stanton Hutch is in there,' explained Bartholomew. 'We thought from the start that the culprit was someone in College, and he – citing Ethel as his source – has been oddly insistent that our money will be returned. *He* took it, then left the cup and the deeds in Hemmysby's room, probably to ease our minds.'

'He might be a lunatic, but he is not a thief,' said Michael, shocked. 'He would never steal from us or anyone else. And never put us through such torment, either.'

'Well, there is only one way to find out,' said Langelee. 'Suttone, stay here and ensure that our remaining guests do not run off with the tablecloths. Bartholomew and Michael, come with me.'

He led the way to the orchard at a rapid clip, and began to bawl for the Dominican as he neared the coop. Clippesby's muted reply could be heard within. As he declined to come out, Bartholomew was obliged to crawl in after him.

'Oh, John,' he said sadly, when he saw the missing chest against the back wall, partly covered in straw and with Ethel preening on top of it. 'What have you done?'

Clippesby did not answer, and only watched as Bartholomew pulled the hutch outside, where Langelee flung open the lid and pawed through it. When the Dominican finally emerged, Bartholomew was appalled by the change in him. He was thin, and his face was grey with strain.

'It is all here,' said Langelee in relief. 'Every penny. We are saved.' He rounded on Clippesby. 'But you owe us an explanation.'

'I brought it here, as it was the safest place I could think of,' replied Clippesby. 'And I have stayed with it as often as I can. So has Ethel. But the damp was beginning to damage Thelnetham's bestiary, so I took it out and gave it to Edith to mind.'

'But why?' asked Langelee, stunned. 'You are not a thief. And please do not say Ethel did it.'

'Do not be silly, Master,' said Clippesby irritably. 'She could not possibly lift something this heavy. I took it from the cellar because a thief *did* intend to make off with it. He has been burgling other Colleges with great success. You must have heard about him.'

'Yes,' said Langelee, struggling for patience. 'But how did you know he wanted our hutch?'

'Because Hemmysby told me. It was his idea to "steal" it and put it somewhere else. He made me promise not to tell anyone, and the hens said—'

'*Hemmysby* told you?' interrupted Bartholomew.

'Yes,' replied Clippesby. 'He overheard some rats talking at a meeting of the Guild of Saints. They were discussing a plan to filch the Stanton Hutch from our cellar.'

'I imagine he did hear rats,' said Langelee wryly. 'But human ones, not rodents.'

Clippesby frowned. 'He was using the word as a term of abuse? He did not mean animals?'

'Wait,' said Michael, holding up his hand. 'Are you saying that the people responsible for all these burglaries are guildsmen?'

'Well, Hemmysby referred to the ones who aimed to go after us as "the rats in the Guild". He was determined that they would not have our property, and asked me to help him thwart them. And we did: Ethel saw them invade our College on Friday, and leave empty-handed and furious. Poor Hemmysby was dead by then, of course, so never knew that his precautions had paid off.'

'What did these villains look like?' demanded Michael.

'Ethel could not tell, because they kept their faces hidden. All she can say is that one was bigger than the other, and both were well dressed.'

Langelee shook his head in bewilderment at the revelations. 'So why were the deeds and the Stanton Cup in Hemmysby's quarters? Bartholomew thinks you put them there.'

Clippesby hung his head. 'I could not bear your distress, so I took them from the chest, and was going to ask Hemmysby to return them to you while we kept the coins hidden until the danger was past. But he died and you ransacked his room . . .'

'Do you think that is why he was killed?' asked Bartholomew uneasily. 'Because he heard the thieves plotting and so was in a position to expose them?'

'He could not expose them because he did not see their faces,' said Clippesby unhappily. 'That was the problem.'

'Then was he poisoned because they knew he had listened in on one of their discussions?' pressed Bartholomew.

'I do not know,' said Clippesby wretchedly. 'I have thought of little else for days.'

'Why did he not tell *me* his suspicions?' demanded Langelee. 'I am not exactly a novice in thwarting criminals.'

'Because you always discuss such matters with the Fellows,' explained Clippesby. 'And he was afraid that William or Thelnetham would blurt out the secret in one of their stupid rows. He also thought that I could find a more secure hiding place than anyone else.'

'You have,' conceded Langelee grudgingly. 'I cannot imagine any thief searching a hencoop.'

'Yet I do not think they left Michaelhouse empty-handed,' said Bartholomew. 'They would have had to go through the kitchen to reach the cellar, and what was lying on the kitchen table on Friday? William's tract, left there by Suttone for Agatha to burn on the fire. They must have snagged it on their way out, in revenge for being foiled over the hutch.'

'Which means that the thieves and the blackmailers *are* one and the same, just as we thought,' surmised Michael. 'And almost certainly the poisoners, too.'

Langelee hefted the hutch on to his shoulder. 'I shall look after this now. However, I want all the Fellows – except Thelnetham, of course – available at midnight tonight.'

'Why?' asked Clippesby.

'Because instead of fifty marks behind this tomb, these damned rogues are going to find some very angry Michaelhouse men.'

While Michael disappeared to follow some leads he claimed to have gleaned from interviewing the College's guests that day, Bartholomew escorted Edith home to Milne Street, where both were relieved to find that Richard and Goodwyn were out. With a weary sigh, she summoned Zachary Steward, and opened the box containing her husband's documents.

'She is finding more evidence of Master Stanmore's trickery now we are nearing the bottom,' Zachary confided, watching her. 'Obviously, he did not have time to dig this deep when he set about destroying what he did not want his family to see.'

Bartholomew blinked. 'How do you know—'

'I was his right-hand man for fifteen years. He did very little without my knowledge, and I am amazed that he managed to wipe so much clean before he passed away. I noticed the tang of burning around him several times during his last few days, but it never occurred to me that he was destroying evidence until this week.'

Bartholomew gazed at him. 'If you are right, then it means he knew he was going to die, and took steps to put his affairs in order first. To protect his reputation.'

Zachary nodded towards Edith. 'To protect her. You already knew he was not always ethical, and he did not care about anyone else, except perhaps Richard. But you are right: I think he did know his end was near, although I have no idea how.'

The revelation troubled Bartholomew, as did the notion that the discoveries Edith had made were probably slight compared to what Oswald had managed to conceal. He watched the pair work for a moment, then took his leave, loath to be a witness when she found something else that would upset her.

He hesitated once he was outside, not sure where to go. He did not want to return to College, where all the talk in the conclave would be about Thelnetham's defection, Clippesby's antics and the blackmailers, and he had no patients needing attention. He found himself walking towards the High Street, feeling a sudden need for the haven of Eyer's shop. He arrived to find the apothecary preparing a salve for Bon, steeping ragwort and rose petals in a bowl of water. Eyer's welcoming smile was strained; clearly, he had not forgotten what had transpired earlier.

'May I have some of that for Langelee?' Bartholomew asked, nodding towards the dish. 'Someone threw sand in his eyes.'

'At a camp-ball practice? I do not know why that game is legal. It nearly always ends with someone being hurt.'

'I think that is why Langelee likes it.' Bartholomew sat down and helped himself to a stick of liquorice root. He could not remember the last time he had eaten a decent meal, and its earthy flavour reminded him that he was hungry. 'It caters to the innate soldier in him.'

'Did you mean what you said in Michaelhouse?' blurted Eyer. 'You will still use my services, even though you now know me as a disgraced physician?'

'I know you as a good apothecary – which is all that matters, as far as I am concerned. And I shall say so to Rougham and Meryfeld if they ask.'

Eyer grasped Bartholomew's shoulder in gratitude. Neither spoke for a while, and they sat in companionable silence, Bartholomew relaxing after his fraught day and Eyer concentrating on his salve. Eventually, the apothecary began to confide details of the Oxford debacle, and Bartholomew felt the reserve that had existed between them begin to lift. He was sorry the matter had not come to light sooner, as it would have eliminated weeks of unnecessary wariness.

'Yet perhaps it is as well I did not become a scholar,' Eyer concluded ruefully. 'I barely understood a word of that debate, and the whole affair was unconscionably dull. But you look tired and sad, my friend. Would you care for a bowl of frog and bean soup? It is very nutritious.'

Bartholomew accepted, and was surprised to find it reasonably palatable, although he declined to gnaw on the bones at the bottom, as the apothecary encouraged him to do.

Alone in his storeroom later, he tried to work on his lectures for the third week of term, but his thoughts kept returning to his worries. He tried to push them to the back of his mind, but he knew Galen's *De elementis* too well for it to hold his attention, and he was eventually forced to concede that he was wasting his time.

Idly, he picked up the scroll that Lawrence had lent him. He did not think he would be able to concentrate on it any more than he had his work, but Lawrence had an easy style, and he soon became engrossed. He had almost finished, when something made him frown. Lawrence described a condition known in the North Country as Pig Ear, defined as a thickening of the visible part of the ear following a blow or other trauma. Langelee was beginning to show signs of it from his love of campball, but it was far more pronounced in Uyten, who had earned it from his fondness for brawling.

Something was scratching at the back of Bartholomew's

mind, and he knew it was important. It was to do with Fulbut's dying words, when the mercenary had talked in his distinctive brogue about the man who had hired him to shoot Felbrigge – someone who had had a 'big year'. Understanding came in a flash. Fulbut had not been saying 'big year' but 'pig ear'. He had been referring to Uyten!

Flushed with triumph, Bartholomew raced up the stairs to Michael's room, only to be told that the monk was out on patrol with Meadowman. He left the College at a run. On the dark streets, beadles were out in force, along with noisy bands of matriculands and apprentices, although troops from the castle were conspicuous by their absence.

'De Stannell has recalled them all,' said Michael, tight-lipped with fury when the physician finally caught up with him. 'He says the trouble is of our making, so we must resolve it ourselves.'

'The apprentices are not ours. Nor is that horde from the King's Head. But never mind them, Brother. I think I know the identity of the killer.' Excitedly, Bartholomew told the monk what he had read in Lawrence's scroll.

Michael was thoughtful. 'Do you think Lawrence lent you that text with the specific intention of leading you astray – to shift blame away from himself?'

'Of course not!' Bartholomew was disappointed by the monk's response. 'He could not know I would read it today. Or at all, for that matter. It would be an extraordinarily elaborate ruse.'

'But why would Uyten poison all these people?'

'You know why! Felbrigge was telling you just before he was shot that he had put measures in place to control Winwick Hall. Obviously, Uyten does not want his College regulated by guildsmen. He killed Felbrigge first, then dispatched Hemmysby, Elvesmere, Ratclyf and Knyt to ensure that they could not put these safeguards into force either.'

'But Elvesmere and Ratclyf were Winwick men. They

were unlikely to support their College being manipulated by an external authority, and would have been in Uyten's side.'

Bartholomew shrugged, unwilling to admit that Michael had a point. 'Perhaps he felt they could not be trusted.'

'And what about Oswald?' pressed Michael. 'I sincerely doubt *he* was interested in managing Winwick. He always kept out of University affairs, in deference to you.'

'He founded the Guild to help the poor,' argued Bartholomew. 'He would not have wanted its funds diverted to a wealthy College. And if Uyten did kill him, I want him brought to justice. For Edith's sake.'

'Very well,' sighed Michael. 'We shall tackle Uyten in the morning.'

'Why not now?'

'Because Illesy has sent him to Ely for parchment, and he is not expected back until tomorrow. Bon told me when I asked why there was no student-guide to accompany him to the debate earlier. Do not worry, Matt. Uyten has no idea we suspect him, so he has no reason to flee.'

'I imagine we will see him at midnight,' said Bartholomew dourly. 'At the Round Church, waiting for his fifty marks.'

'Perhaps. But go home now, and try to sleep. One of us should be alert if we are to thwart blackmailers and killers later.'

Bartholomew started to walk to Michaelhouse, but happened to glance into the Cardinal's Cap as he passed, and saw Rougham sitting inside with Meryfeld and two women. He entered the tavern, and joined their table uninvited.

'Keep taking the tonic, mistress,' said Rougham, blushing furiously because his companion was Yolande de Blaston, the town's most popular prostitute. 'Goodbye.'

'And the same goes for you,' said Meryfeld, shoving

Yolande's friend off his lap with such vigour that she stumbled. 'And if you feel faint again, sniff the *sal ammoniac* I prescribed.'

She frowned her confusion. 'But you gave us that for patrons who fall asleep in our beds after they have finished with us. We do not need it for ourselves.'

'Come, sister,' said Yolande, quicker on the uptake. 'Let us leave these medical men to discuss dissection and anatomy. We have other fish to fry.'

'Do not fry them too long,' said Meryfeld, trying to wink meaningfully without Bartholomew seeing. 'You may need to consult us again.'

'It is all right,' said Bartholomew wearily. He had known for years that Rougham enjoyed a lively relationship with Yolande, and it came as no surprise that Meryfeld did likewise. 'Your personal lives are none of my concern. I just wanted some company.'

'Those were patients,' said Rougham sternly. 'You do not have a monopoly on paupers, you know. However, I am disturbed that they think we discuss dissection and anatomy when we are together. I have never talked about those in my life, except to condemn them.'

'Nor have I,' agreed Meryfeld in distaste. 'They strike me as most unhygienic activities, as I cannot imagine that the inside of corpses are very clean.'

Bartholomew glanced at Meryfeld's grimy paws, and thought a dissector could slice up a hundred corpses without his fingers being half as filthy.

'Much can be learned from the art,' he said, then wished he had held his tongue. He remained troubled by his examination of Hemmysby, and did not want to defend such procedures when he was not entirely sure they were ethical.

'It would not result in anything *I* should want to know,' declared Rougham. He leaned a little closer, and his voice turned gossipy. 'Did Father William really pen those poisonous words about the Dominican Prior and Satan?'

'William did not make them public,' hedged Bartholomew. 'And it is a foolish distraction when we should be concentrating on the murders of our friends and colleagues – Hemmysby, Knyt, Elvesmere, Ratclyf, Felbrigge, Oswald Stanmore—'

'Stanmore was not murdered,' declared Meryfeld, startled.

'Of course not,' agreed Rougham. 'Although you are not in a position to say so, Meryfeld. I was the one who tended him on his deathbed.'

'Yes,' acknowledged Meryfeld. 'Edith sent for you. However, she was not to know that he was actually *my* patient. I had been treating him while Bartholomew was in Peterborough.'

Bartholomew frowned. 'Treating him for what? And why did you not tell me?'

'Because I did not want to distress you.' Meryfeld glanced at Rougham. 'Or embarrass *you* by revealing that you had made a mistake. You see, Stanmore did not die of marsh fever.'

'Yes, he did,' countered Rougham crossly. 'I suffer from it myself, and I know the signs.'

'Signs that are also consistent with a failing heart,' said Meryfeld. 'Which is what killed him. He came to me three weeks before he died, and every day after that. He was worse each time.'

He then gave a detailed account of Stanmore's case. The symptoms were unequivocal, and when he had finished, both Bartholomew and Rougham were forced to concede that his diagnosis was correct.

'I have no cure for sicknesses of that magnitude,' he concluded, uncharacteristically humble. 'So I did not attempt one. I prescribed a little peppermint and valerian to calm him, but that was all.'

'So why did Edith not tell me all this?' demanded Rougham irritably. 'I might have treated him differently had I been in full possession of the facts.'

'She did not know,' explained Meryfeld. 'He did not want to spoil the little time they had left together, so I was sworn to secrecy. He would not even let me visit their home. He always came to my house instead. Indeed, I summoned him there the evening he died.'

'Why?' demanded Bartholomew, 'when there was nothing you could do to help him?'

'Because Lawrence happened to mention that some chest pains can be eased by a hot compress. I knew Stanmore would struggle to sit through a long Guild meeting comfortably, so I made him one, and sent a note inviting him to visit.'

'In French?' asked Bartholomew, recalling the message that Edith had found.

'Of course. I do not debase myself with the vernacular when dealing with wealthy clients. I cannot have them thinking me coarse. I used my best parchment and expensive purple ink. He said he felt a little better after I applied the compress, although the effects wore off all too quickly.'

'He went straight to the guildhall when you had finished?' asked Bartholomew.

Meryfeld nodded. 'We walked there together. No one killed him, Bartholomew. He left Milne Street to come directly to me, and we were in each other's company until I left him by the door of his house when the meeting was over. I would have stayed the night, as I could see the end was near and I wanted to be on hand to help, but he would not let me.'

'Did he eat or drink anything in all that time?'

'Nothing. He had no appetite.'

Relief surged through Bartholomew, and he gripped Meryfeld's hand. 'Thank you! Edith will be hurt that he did not confide in her, but it is better than thinking someone poisoned him.'

'He might have lived longer had he not worked so hard when he should have been resting,' said Meryfeld. 'There were things he did not want her to discover, you see.'

'What things?' asked Rougham curiously.

'He did not say, but I suspect they pertained to the way he ran his business. One night when he came to see me, there was a reek of burnt parchment on him, and I had the strong sense that he had been destroying records.'

Bartholomew left the Cardinal's Cap and hurried to Milne Street. It was late, but he knew Edith would not mind. He told her everything he had learned, and then sat with her while she wept for the man she had loved, and the knowledge that he had tried so hard to spare her pain.

CHAPTER 15

Bartholomew returned to Michaelhouse to find the other Fellows waiting for him, their expressions grim. It was almost eleven o'clock, and late for them to be awake. The elation he had felt on discovering the truth about Oswald evaporated when he recalled what they had to do that night.

'We *must* catch them this time,' said Langelee. 'If they escape, it will not matter that we have retrieved the Stanton Hutch – they will make good on their threat and we shall be destroyed.'

'Perhaps we should go to Ely and arrest Uyten,' suggested Bartholomew. 'Then we will be spared this reckless escapade.'

'I do not believe Uyten is the culprit,' said Michael, after Bartholomew had explained his theory to the others. 'He is not sufficiently clever.'

'Then perhaps he is following orders,' suggested Langelee.

'It is possible,' acknowledged Michael. 'But I doubt he will be entrusted with tonight's delicate business. He is too brutal and clumsy. This is a task the rogues will tackle themselves.'

Everyone except Bartholomew agreed, and turned their attention to Langelee's plan.

'We had better take *some* money with us,' said William worriedly. 'They will not approach if they think we have come empty-handed.'

'I have prepared this.' Langelee produced a parcel that clinked metallically. 'It is roughly the weight of fifty marks in shillings, but comprises a lot of nails. It should be enough to draw them in. And then we shall pounce.'

'Heavens!' gulped Suttone. 'Are you sure there is no other way? They will almost certainly be armed, and one of us may be hurt.'

'You only have yourselves to blame,' said Thelnetham, who had been listening to the discussion with aloof disdain. 'I told you that William's disagreeable opinions would cause trouble, but you would not listen. You should have dismissed him years ago.'

'And you should never have been appointed,' flared William. 'You are a spiteful old—'

'Thank God I am leaving at the end of the week,' interrupted Thelnetham, crossing himself piously. 'I cannot tell you what a relief it is to be going to a respectable foundation.'

William drew breath to retort, but the Gilbertine put his head in the air and minced away. Under the sober habit of his Order he was wearing bright red shoes.

'We are better off without him,' said Langelee, watching him go. 'He might rise above the rest of us in a debate, but he is of an unpleasantly quarrelsome disposition.'

'He is,' agreed William. 'And his manner of dress sets a bad example to our students.'

'We should go,' said Michael, after a brief moment during which everyone contemplated the fact that the Franciscan's unkempt mien was hardly something to which young men should aspire either. 'Or the culprits might arrive first and see us slipping into our hiding places.'

'Is that the plan?' asked Bartholomew uneasily. 'But it is what they will expect us to do!'

'Credit me with some sense,' said Langelee irritably. 'I have chosen positions where they will not think to look. No, Clippesby, you cannot bring the chicken. Put it down.'

'Perhaps he should stay here,' suggested Bartholomew, suspecting the traumatic revelations earlier had taken their toll and it would be safer for everyone if the

Dominican was left behind. 'We should not strip the College of all its Fellows when the town is so uneasy.'

'And Thelnetham no longer counts,' growled William. 'He does not care what happens to us now. The selfish, ungrateful pig! After all our kindness towards him, too.'

'I had better stay behind as well,' said Suttone. 'You are right: we cannot trust Thelnetham to act in our best interests, while John has been odd since Hemmysby died. I am worried for him.'

'Worried for himself more like,' muttered William, as the Carmelite led Clippesby away before anyone could object. 'You had better recruit a few beadles to help instead, Brother.'

'No,' said Langelee. 'We cannot involve outsiders. We do this alone or not at all. But do not worry. Cynric will help, and I will not be defeated a second time. We *will* prevail.'

Bartholomew's heart pounded with tension as they walked to the north of the town, where the Round Church was a barrel-shaped mass in the darkness. The streets were unusually busy with bands of townsfolk, students and matriculands, all armed and obviously looking for trouble. Fortunately, Langelee and Cynric were formidable in their half-armour and broadswords, so no one bothered the Michaelhouse contingent.

When they arrived, Bartholomew was allocated a spot at the back of the graveyard, a dismal location near the reeking, fetid canal known as the King's Ditch. William was not far away, while Langelee and Michael were on Bridge Street, and Cynric had been given the Barnwell Causeway. Langelee's parcel had already been deposited behind the stipulated tomb.

The night was dark and cold, and a strengthening wind made it difficult to listen for stealthy footsteps. Time passed slowly, and Bartholomew grew increasingly chilled, but dared not move lest the culprits were watching. He heard the bells in the nearby Franciscan Priory chime for nocturns, which meant it was after two o'clock – the blackmailers were obviously in no hurry for their money – but still nothing happened. The friars' chanting wafted towards them, melodious and serene.

Then he saw a shadow near the tomb. It could not have come from either of the roads, so he could only suppose there was another way into the cemetery of which Langelee had been unaware when he had deployed his troops. At the same time, he heard crooning above the buffeting wind: William was joining his brethren's night office, probably on his knees with his eyes closed, which meant he was unaware that their quarry had arrived.

Bartholomew picked up a pebble and lobbed it in the friar's direction, but the singing continued. He peered into the darkness, hoping to see Langelee, Michael or Cynric stealing forward, but they were watching the streets, not anticipating that the culprits might approach from another direction. The wind tore the clouds from the moon, and he saw the shadow clearly – a figure wearing a hooded cloak, his movements brisk and confident as he weighed the parcel in his hand.

Bartholomew exploded from his hiding place with a furious yell. He heard Langelee's answering shout, and lumbering footsteps told him that William was also on his feet and running. Then the clouds obscured the moon, and the figure vanished in the sudden blackness. By the time Bartholomew reached the tomb, the shape had gone.

However, while the moon's silvery light had still glowed he had spotted a path, and knew the blackmailer had taken it. It was narrow and nearly impossible to follow in the dark; brambles tore at his clothes as he blundered along it. He stopped and listened intently, but all he could hear was Langelee cursing somewhere behind him.

Then there was a gleam of light – Cynric had had the wit to bring a lamp. The book-bearer shoved past

Bartholomew and began to race along a thin, all-but-invisible track that snaked through the tangle of brush towards Bridge Street. Bartholomew followed, but was knocked flying when Langelee barrelled into the back of him.

'Move!' bellowed the Master, pounding past.

As Bartholomew scrambled upright the clouds parted for an instant and illuminated a fork in the track. Cynric and Langelee had chosen the broader more obvious route to the left, so he took the other, shouting for William and Michael to do the same. It made a sharp right turn, then ended at the King's Ditch so abruptly that he was obliged to flail with his arms to avoid pitching in.

Not far away was a boat, one person rowing and another sitting in the stern. Bartholomew put one foot in the water, the chase so hot in him that he was willing to leap in and swim after it, but the ditch was icy cold and reeked of sewage. It brought him to his senses. The chances of catching a moving boat were slim, but he might well catch something else, and he could not afford to be ill at the beginning of term.

'No,' he shouted, when William made as if to stage a running dive. 'It is too late.'

The figure in the stern leaned back nonchalantly as the little craft gained speed, and raised a hand in a taunting gesture of farewell. William released a string of oaths no friar should have known, and Bartholomew thought he heard mocking laughter float across the water.

'Damn!' hissed Langelee, coming to stand next to them. 'I searched this place thoroughly and saw no sign of these paths. The bastards must have concealed them. Did you see anything that will allow you to identify them?'

'No,' replied Bartholomew despondently. 'It was too dark.'

Later, the Fellows sat in the conclave, analysing what had gone wrong. Langelee was pale and sullen, hating being bested a second time, while Cynric was furious with himself for not guessing that the culprits might travel by water. William was indignant that the crime should have taken place during a holy office, and Michael was worried about what would happen when the blackmailers arrived home to discover that they had been given a parcel of nails.

'The figure I saw was too small to be Uyten,' said Bartholomew. 'Perhaps he was the one rowing the boat.'

'Not if he is in Ely,' said Michael. 'Besides, I was sceptical when you first outlined your theory, and nothing has changed my mind. But we shall certainly speak to him in the morning.'

'You mean in an hour or two,' put in William. 'The night is almost over now.'

'Do not waste your time on Uyten,' ordered Langelee. 'We have too much else to do. The villains will make good on their threat when they discover that we have deceived them, and we must be ready for the resulting trouble. We shall start preparing our defences at first light.'

'I hardly think the tract will result in an assault on our College, Master,' said Suttone. 'Most people do not care two hoots about heresy. And the Pope and the King are unlikely to invade.'

Langelee shot him a withering look. 'Excommunication and dissolution are what we face in the long term, but before we reach that stage, we must weather the reactions of those William insulted in his foreword. The Dominicans will seek reparation through the courts, but the Gilbertine novices are an unruly horde, and will come at us with weapons.'

'So will John Winwick's scholars,' added Michael.

'Then we had better start preparing now,' gulped William, and the fact that he did not try to argue told an alarmed Bartholomew that Langelee's concerns for the College's safety were justified. 'I shall rouse the students at once.'

The wind had picked up further since they had been at the Round Church, and was gusting hard. Bartholomew recalled Marjory Starre's prediction that the next blow would presage another death, perhaps his own. He slipped his hand in his bag and felt the comforting smoothness of the charm she had given him, but then chided himself for a superstitious fool.

He followed his colleagues out of the hall, and it was not long before Michaelhouse was in the grip of frenzied activity. Buckets were filled with water, ready to combat fires; any objects that could be used as weapons were stacked in readily accessible piles; and baskets of stones were collected to lob from the tops of walls and the gatehouse.

'Term starts today,' gasped Michael, struggling to help Bartholomew and Langelee block the back gate with a stack of logs. 'And I have never known a less scholarly atmosphere. I predict that far more students will immerse themselves in trouble than in a book.'

Langelee agreed. 'Tynkell said that licences were issued for eighteen hostels last week alone, and the University has never seen such a massive influx of new members. Nearly all are louts.'

'It is Winwick Hall's fault,' said Michael bitterly. 'It has attracted entirely the wrong kind of applicant, and Thelnetham will soon learn that he has made a mistake.'

'He has been seduced by its grand position on the High Street and handsome uniforms,' said Langelee. 'Perhaps you should refuse to let its people matriculate, Brother. That would show it what the University thinks of its upstart ways.'

'If I did, ninety Winwick men would be mortally offended, and we should have a riot for certain. However, I might postpone the opening ceremony. I hate to cave in, but I have received notice from King's Hall, Bene't, Gonville, Peterhouse *and* Valence Marie saying that they will react with anger if Winwick does anything boastful or glory-seeking.'

'And it will,' predicted Langelee. 'Illesy bragged yesterday that he will be first in the procession out. But I shall not yield precedence, and neither will the other Colleges.'

They turned as William hurried up, holding a letter bearing the familiar clerkly scrawl. His face was as white as snow, and he was closer to tears than Bartholomew had ever seen him.

'This was left at the porter's lodge,' he said in a small voice. 'No one saw it arrive.'

Langelee read the missive, then tore it into tiny pieces in impotent fury. 'We are to expect retribution for our deceit,' he reported tightly, once he was able to speak. 'But we are to be given one last chance before the full tract is released. A hundred marks is to be left behind St Radegund's Priory by noon tomorrow.'

'They must know we cannot pay by now,' said William wretchedly. 'Why do they persist?'

'They know nothing of the kind, thanks to our pride,' said Michael grimly. 'We put on a fine display yesterday, and they were almost certainly here. They think we are loaded with money.'

'Here is Meadowman,' groaned Langelee, as the beadle dashed towards them. 'Now what?'

'I have just been told that Jekelyn the porter has gone to St Clement's Church,' gasped the beadle. 'Do you think he is going to set it alight again?'

It was still dark as Bartholomew and Michael, with Meadowman at their heels, ran towards Bridge Street, although dawn was not far off. The physician could not recall when he had last seen so many people out at such an hour, and it was clear that none had work in mind. He pulled up his hood to cover his face when he heard several cursing Potmoor's penchant for other people's property.

'This wind does not help,' muttered Michael, when one particularly violent blast made even his solid person stagger. 'It is getting stronger by the moment.'

'It means someone good will die,' said Bartholomew. 'Or so Marjory Starre says.'

'You should know better than to listen to that sort of nonsense,' said Michael sternly.

They made the rest of the journey in silence, and arrived to find St Clement's full of townsfolk, all listening to a pre-dawn rant by Heyford. There was a resentful murmur when three University men joined them, so Bartholomew huddled further inside his hood and retreated to the shadows with Meadowman. Michael was too large for hiding in dark corners, and was too princely a figure to try. He strode to the front, glaring up at the pulpit with his hands on his ample hips. Intimidated, Heyford finished his diatribe very lamely.

'So the University *will* suffer hellfire and death,' he said in a much meeker voice than he had been using moments before, 'but they are for the Lord to inflict. Now, I have kept you all quite long enough. God be with you, and do not forget to leave your donations in the box on the way out.'

The congregation looked startled by the feeble conclusion: evidently they had expected something rather more rousing. Some began to murmur that it was time to oust an establishment they had never wanted in the first place, but the muttering stopped when Michael took up station at the door and greeted people by name as they shuffled past. Some were members of his choir, while others relied on the University for custom. Most left the church deflated and uncertain, a far cry from the braying mob that Heyford would have set loose.

Watching, Bartholomew saw what a charismatic figure

his friend had become. Authority and age had imbued him with a power he had not possessed a decade before, and it occurred to him that the monk might be right when he claimed he was indispensable to the University. If the mere fact of his presence could silence a feisty orator and compel a would-be mob to exchange pleasantries with him, then perhaps the *studium generale* would founder without his guidance.

'What do you want?' asked Heyford when his flock had gone. 'You should not be here.'

'A Benedictine is unwelcome in your church?' asked Michael archly. 'I must tell the Bishop, so he can appoint a vicar who *does* embrace my Order.'

'A Benedictine is welcome,' said Heyford shortly. 'The Senior Proctor is not, and nor is any member of your wicked University.'

Michael sighed irritably. 'I do not have time for your histrionics today, Heyford, so we shall resume this discussion tomorrow. In the meantime, you can tell me where Jekelyn is.'

'The Winwick porter? How should I know? He is hardly likely to come here. His nasty College is the foundation I most deplore.'

'He is under the altar,' explained Meadowman, happy to leave the safety of the shadows now that the congregation had dispersed. 'He crept in when no one was looking, apparently.'

'What?' cried Heyford, outraged. 'A holy place? How dare he!'

He stormed into the chancel and hauled up the altar cloth before the others could stop him. Meadowman's hand dropped to his cudgel, ready to defend the priest, but Jekelyn sat in a dejected huddle and made no effort to emerge.

'Come out,' ordered Heyford angrily. 'You cannot lounge there. It is sacred.'

'I know,' said Jekelyn, not moving. 'That is why I came. For sanctuary.'

'Sanctuary from what?' asked Michael coldly. 'From me, because I intend to charge you with the murder of Fulbut? We know you attended his party, where you stabbed him before he could be arrested and forced to reveal who hired him to shoot my Junior Proctor.'

Jekelyn licked dry lips. 'I suppose my knife might have slipped into his vitals, but he was an evil man, and Heaven will not mourn him.'

'Very possibly,' said Michael. 'But that is not for you to decide. Now come out before I lean in and drag you out by the ears.'

Jekelyn cowered away from him. 'No! You cannot touch me here.'

Bartholomew was studying him thoughtfully. 'You admit to killing Fulbut, so that is not the crime which troubles you. Is it the fire that plagues your conscience?'

Jekelyn swallowed hard, and would not look at Heyford. 'It was not my idea. I should not go to Hell just because I carried out orders.'

'Whose orders?' asked Bartholomew. 'Uyten's? I know he told you to murder Fulbut.'

'He gave me up?' gulped Jekelyn. 'The bastard!'

'Fulbut was told to disappear permanently,' Bartholomew continued, while Michael blinked his astonishment that the physician should have been right. 'But he was homesick and came back, so Uyten arranged to have him killed.'

Jekelyn looked away. 'Fulbut's only loyalty was to his purse, and his presence here put Uyten in danger. He had to die. But I was never happy with burning this church, so I only lit a small fire in the hope that it would be spotted and doused. And it was, so God *has* to take that into account!'

'You consider burning a church a worse sin than murder?' asked Michael, startled.

'Of course.' Jekelyn's face was earnest. 'No one will care about me dispatching a mercenary, but damaging a House of God . . . I heard Father Heyford preach about it and . . . well, I came here in the hope that St Clement would forgive me.'

'He will not, and you will go to Hell,' declared Heyford angrily. 'Nothing can save you.'

'But I could grant you absolution,' said Michael quickly. 'In exchange for information and surrender. You will be tried for the murder of Fulbut, but you will not be judged on the arson.'

'Now just a moment,' began Heyford as relief flooded into Jekelyn's face. 'He committed a terrible crime against me, and—'

'Yes, he did,' interrupted Michael. 'But you have been whipping up fervour against the University, which is just as bad. And the Bishop will agree when I send him my report.'

Heyford glowered, but said no more, and Jekelyn began to speak.

'I am amazed,' said Michael as they hurried out of the church a short while later, leaving Meadowman to take Jekelyn to the proctors' gaol. Day was breaking, filling the streets with a dull, leaden light. 'I was sure you were mistaken about Uyten. We had better confront him at once.'

'We cannot.' Bartholomew was struggling against the weariness that threatened to overwhelm him after yet another virtually sleepless night. 'He has gone to Ely, remember? I doubt he is back yet.'

'He has ordered murder and arson for the sake of his beloved Winwick,' said Michael, 'so I doubt he will abandon it when it might need him most. I suspect he never went.'

Bartholomew skidded to a standstill. 'Then he will be

furious when he learns his crimes are revealed – the resulting scandal will certainly damage his College's reputation. He has already killed at least four men to protect it, and might decide that two more are neither here nor there. And we are unlikely to stand much chance against him if he enlists the help of ninety loyal students.'

'They would not dare harm the Senior Proctor.'

'Were it any other College, I might agree, but it is Winwick – a new foundation with members who do not know the University and its ways. It would be reckless to march into the place alone.'

'Perhaps you are right,' conceded Michael. 'I shall take some beadles then, although I hate to pull them away from their stations when we are a hair's breadth from a serious riot. God only knows what it will be like when people start to assemble for the beginning of term ceremony.'

'I thought you were going to cancel it.'

'I shall, but scholars will still congregate, and so will many townsfolk.'

They ducked as a shower of pebbles sailed towards them, lobbed by a group of matriculands. Catcalls followed, centred around the claims that Bartholomew was a necromancer and Michael had murdered his deputy. Then the leader muttered an order, and the accusing jeers faded into a silence that was far more unnerving. The matriculands began to advance, slowly and with unmistakable menace.

'Stop!' roared Michael in his most commanding voice. 'And go home before—'

'He thinks he can tell you what to do,' interrupted the leader mockingly, and Bartholomew was not surprised to recognise Goodwyn. 'What do you say to that?'

There was a howl of outrage and weapons were drawn. Bartholomew fumbled for his childbirth forceps, knowing there was little he could do against so many but determined to put up a fight; Michael produced a stout stick from somewhere about his person. Just when they thought it could get no worse, Goodwyn and his cronies were joined by men from one of the new hostels. The ex-student's face was bright with vengeful triumph when he saw his little army double in size, and Bartholomew knew that he and Michael would not be allowed to escape alive.

Then a score of warrior-nobles from King's Hall happened past. Goodwyn's mob outnumbered them two to one, but forty cudgels were no match for twenty swords, and King's Hall knew it. They surged forward with blood-curdling whoops, scattering Goodwyn and his men in terror. The King's Hall party was too dignified to give chase, and war cries turned to laughter as their charge petered out. They went on their way without so much as a backward glance at the men they had saved. Bartholomew shot Michael a feeble grin.

'There is nothing like the threat of death to sharpen one's wits. I do not feel at all tired now.'

'Then use them.' Michael's voice was urgent. 'Did you see what happened just now? Hostel men racing to support Goodwyn's louts?'

'Yes. What of it?'

'They *mingled*, Matt! They did not form discrete groups, as they would normally have done, but stood shoulder to shoulder with people who should have been strangers. However, I strongly suspect they were not.'

'I have no idea what you are talking about.'

'They *knew* each other,' snapped Michael impatiently. 'Not a superficial acquaintance from a night in a tavern, but something of longer duration. They are all recent arrivals, which means they must have been friends already. So why did they all suddenly decide to come here?'

'Because Winwick is recruiting, and they are eager for a lucrative career in law.'

'No,' said Michael. 'We have never been overwhelmed with new students in such numbers before. I think *some* came in the hope of winning a place at the University, but many have no intention of studying. They roam in packs, doing nothing but drink and carouse. So if they did not come for scholarship, they came for some other purpose, and the way they have behaved from the start suggests to me that the whole thing is orchestrated.'

'You mean someone told them to descend on us?'

'Yes. And as most hail from London, I suggest we discuss this with your nephew.'

Bartholomew gaped at him. 'You think *Richard* brought them? But that is ludicrous!'

'Is it? Then why does he stay here when our little town must be dull after the wild delights of the city? Why do so many of these matriculands come from the place where *he* lived until recently? Why does he know so many of them? And why is he always on hand when trouble arises?'

'He would never do such a thing. And he has stayed for two reasons. First because he, thinks his father was murdered—'

'A recent suspicion. Not one that explains his presence here since August.'

Bartholomew ignored him. 'And second, because he wants a Fellowship at Winwick Hall.'

Michael pointed. 'Well, there he is now with some of the worst offenders. And look at them – men in their mid-twenties, too old to be aspiring students. They are not here to study. There is mischief afoot, and we need to find out what it is before our poor town explodes into violence.'

Richard and his cronies numbered roughly a dozen men, all dressed in the latest Court fashion: long hair, shoes with pointed toes, and elaborately embroidered gipons. Bartholomew recognised at least three who had led packs of matriculands at different times, while others had been in the King's Head two nights before. Michael was right, he thought: these were not men who wanted to study.

Moreover, something Clippesby had said was niggling at the back of his mind: that the Bene't hedgehog thought Richard had encouraged the matriculands to try their luck at Winwick Hall. In other words, the Dominican had detected something odd in Richard's behaviour, even if his saner colleagues had missed it. Then Bartholomew shook himself impatiently. No! This was his nephew – the lad he had known since birth. Richard would never orchestrate such dark mischief.

Michael strode up to Richard and pulled him to one side. The others immediately stepped forward to intervene, but Richard made a sharp gesture telling them to stay back. They obeyed at once, and Bartholomew felt a cold dread settle in his stomach. The fact that his nephew could so effortlessly control a lot of arrogant hotheads told him more than words ever could.

'There are an unprecedented number of matriculands this year,' began Michael, ice in his voice. 'Can you tell us what brings them here?'

'Perhaps they have heard of you, Brother,' said Richard with an insolent smirk. The grin did not quite touch his eyes, though, which were wary. 'And they came to see you in action.'

'They came because of you,' said Michael harshly. 'Goodwyn told us that he knew you from a London tavern, and you are friends with a lot of other louts as well.'

Richard laughed harshly. 'I know I am popular, but I do not have *hundreds* of acquaintances who would follow me into the Fens. And you have it the wrong way around, anyway: I choose to stay *because* so many of my London companions have elected to study here.'

Bartholomew felt sick: he could tell Richard was lying. 'You met Uyten in London – the man whose Provost has sponsored your election to the Guild of Saints, and has promised you a Fellowship at Winwick.'

'What of it?' shrugged Richard. 'It is not a crime to know people.'

'*Please* tell us the truth! Edith will suffer if there is trouble. Cambridge is her home.'

'Yes, and it should not be,' flared Richard. 'She should be living in respectable widowhood at Trumpington, not prodding around in Father's affairs to expose his . . . oversights.'

Bartholomew's first reaction was indignation that Richard should presume to judge Edith, but then he saw the angry confusion in his nephew's eyes, and irritation gave way to understanding. 'You tried to burn those documents, then ordered her to stay away from them because you guessed what she might find.'

'I guessed nothing!' snarled Richard, although the truth was in his eyes. 'Father was a good man. He founded the Guild of Saints and was generous with alms.'

'Yes, he was,' said Bartholomew gently. 'But that does not mean he always stayed on the right side of the law. What happened? Did someone in London tell you that Oswald's affairs were not always honest?'

Richard glared and him, and when he spoke, it was through gritted teeth. 'I was made aware of certain rumours, so I hurried here to put an end to them. Unfortunately, a brief glance through that box told me that there might be some justification to the tales.'

'So why did you not destroy its contents – prevent Edith from learning things that have hurt her?'

'I thought I had,' replied Richard shortly. 'I put it on a fire at the bottom of the garden, but the flames must have gone out, and she found it – unscathed – when she went for a walk last week.'

'I see.' Bartholomew was unimpressed to learn that Richard could not even be trusted to incinerate a box properly. Doubtless, he had been too keen to return to his drunken friends.

'I tried to take it from her,' Richard went on. 'But all that did was give her the idea that there was something in it of interest.'

Bartholomew was thoughtful. 'In Weasenham's shop the other day, you said you knew what you were doing. I thought you meant with the stationer's wife, but you meant something else entirely. But you *don't* know, Richard. You have everything wrong.'

'Yes and no,' said Richard tightly. 'I might have been unaware of the way my father conducted his affairs – I am not interested in cloth, so we never discussed it. But I *do* know it was not his choice to break the law. Evil people corrupted him, and when he tried to extricate himself from their vile clutches, they poisoned him. A friend in London told me all about it.'

'Oswald was not poisoned,' said Bartholomew, and outlined everything that Meryfeld had told him, concluding with, 'So your friend was lying.'

'In other words, your vengeance on the town you think led Oswald astray is woefully misplaced,' said Michael. 'I cannot imagine how you, an experienced lawyer, can have been so scandalously credulous.'

Richard gazed at them. 'So he was not murdered?' he asked in a voice that had lost its arrogance. 'And he was more likely to have defrauded others than been cheated himself?'

Michael gave a sharp bark of laughter. 'The person has not been born who could deceive Oswald Stanmore. He was the most astute businessman the town has ever seen, and it is common knowledge that he was ruthless, calculating and devious.'

'Not all the time, of course,' added Bartholomew kindly. 'And he never preyed on the weak, the poor or the vulnerable.'

'Who was the friend who spun you this yarn?' asked Michael. 'Uyten?'

Richard nodded and looked away. 'So he took advantage of my grief? That was a low trick.'

'If you want him brought to justice, you had better tell us exactly what he told you to do,' said Michael briskly. 'Come on, man. Time is passing, and we cannot afford to waste it.'

Richard's face was white. 'To recruit as many men as possible, and bring them here to create a rumpus. It was easy: London is full of lads who are game for fun. I brought about twenty, but they invited their own companions, so there are probably in excess of fifty of us here now, plus a lot more who heard about Winwick through us, and came of their own volition to try their luck in winning a place.'

'Who funded all this mischief?' demanded Michael.

'I did.' Richard's voice was little more than a whisper. 'That is to say I paid for a lot of them to get here. I was told that they would be given places at Winwick when they arrived, but Illesy will only accept wealthy applicants, so there are a lot of disappointed paupers wandering around . . .'

'Where did you find all this money?'

'My inheritance – avenging Father seemed a good way to use it.' Richard's shock slowly turned to anger. 'Damn Uyten! I will make him pay for this.'

'No, you will not,' said Michael firmly. 'You have done enough harm. Leave him to me.'

'You?' Richard had regained his composure and the hubris was back. 'He has outwitted you at every turn, and there is no reason to assume that anything will change. But I am a patient man, Brother. Cambridge will not hold Uyten for ever, and when he slithers back to London I shall be waiting for him.'

'London?' pounced Michael. 'You are leaving?'

'There is nothing for me here now. I shall go today.'

'What about your Fellowship at Winwick Hall?' asked Bartholomew.

'One has been offered, but for more money than I am willing to pay. It proves what I have suspected from the start – that the Provost and his Fellows do not want me, they want my fortune. But they will not have it. I can think of a hundred better ways to spend it.'

'Then let us hope that they do not all involve drink and fickle friends,' muttered Michael, watching him stalk away.

CHAPTER 16

The streets were more uneasy than ever as Bartholomew and Michael resumed their journey to Winwick Hall. The groups of students, matriculands and townsmen were larger and more heavily armed, and Michael's beadles had given up ordering scholars home: instead they were concentrating on trying to keep the factions apart. The wind did not help. It gusted fiercely, sending leaves, twigs and rubbish cartwheeling along the road, and people were obliged to shout to make themselves heard. Yells were misinterpreted as threats or insults, and offence was quickly taken.

'It is like trying to control the sea,' muttered Michael in despair. 'Too many folk want mischief, and my beadles are too few to stop it. Perhaps Marjory Starre's prediction about wind and death was right, Matt, and *I* shall be the great man for whom it blows.'

He pointed to where another surly band was preparing to advance. Head pounding with tension, Bartholomew tugged out his childbirth forceps again, although it was the appearance of members of the Michaelhouse Choir that encouraged their would-be assailants to retreat, not the sight of his weapon.

'What will happen to Richard?' he asked in a low voice, as they began walking again.

'We shall let him disappear to London,' replied Michael, 'but if he ever shows his face here again, the University will hold him to account for what he has done.'

'I will warn him to stay away,' said Bartholomew. 'Poor Edith.'

'She will—' Michael stopped speaking as the Chancellor hurried up.

'I have just had a message from John Winwick,' Tynkell gasped. 'He will arrive at noon.'

'Then ride out and intercept him!' cried Michael, horrified. 'He cannot be here. If he sees us in such turmoil . . . well, suffice to say it will do us no good.'

'I will try,' gulped Tynkell. 'But he is a determined man, and I am not sure I shall manage.'

'Nor am I,' muttered Michael, as Tynkell hurried away. 'And for once I wish we had a Chancellor with more backbone.' He narrowed his eyes against the wind as he squinted up the High Street. 'Is that de Stannell? I thought he planned to spend the day cowering inside his castle. I wonder what has drawn him out.'

'The gale has damaged the guildhall's new roof,' explained the deputy. 'And I am needed to hire a ladder. Potmoor is terribly upset, as he paid for those tiles himself.'

'Hire a ladder?' echoed Michael in disbelief. 'Surely you have more important matters to attend – like preventing riots in your town?'

'The guildhall is important,' snapped de Stannell, annoyed by the censure. 'And the Sheriff of Cambridgeshire and Huntingdonshire knows his duty.'

'You are not Sheriff! Dick Tulyet still holds that post, thank God.'

'No, he does not.' De Stannell's smile was gloating. 'If you had wanted him to remain in office, Brother, you should have exerted more control over your colleagues. *I* am Sheriff now, and I shall *never* let the University rule my town like he did.'

'What are you talking about?' demanded Michael irritably.

'He was beheaded last night in the Tower of London.'

De Stannell's monkey-face blazed with gleeful spite. 'As a punishment for allowing Michaelhouse to write treasonous words about the Keeper of the Privy Seal. I heard it in Weasenham's shop not an hour ago.'

'And you believe it?' Bartholomew regarded him wonderingly, amazed that a royal official should have been taken in by so far-fetched a rumour.

'Why should I not? I warned Tulyet that his fondness for scholars would end in trouble, and I was right. He should have crushed your University, not allowed it to flourish. I shall not make the same mistake.'

'Who told you this ridiculous story?' asked Michael crossly. 'Weasenham?'

'No, Uyten from Winwick Hall,' replied the deputy smugly. 'And the tale is true, because the tract containing these seditious remarks is being copied by Weasenham's scribes as I speak.'

'You are a fool, de Stannell!' said Michael in disgust. 'First, how can Tulyet have been executed for something that is not yet fully in the public domain? Second, it takes a full day for news to travel between London and Cambridge, even with the fastest messengers. And third, being Sheriff of a place where such statements originate is not a capital offence. Can you not see that this is a scheme to cause trouble between us?'

'I see nothing other than that Tulyet's association with the University has brought about his downfall.' De Stannell was clearly delighted by the prospect of being rid of his superior. 'You should watch yourself, Brother. He was popular, and I imagine folk will hold *any* Michaelhouse scholar responsible for his fate, regardless of who actually wrote the words that lost him his head.'

Michael strode away, unwilling to waste time listening to such rubbish, and Bartholomew followed. The wind chose that moment to hurl a mat of wet leaves into de

Stannell's face, and his indignant diatribe about unmannerly scholars dissolved into splutters.

'So Uyten strikes again,' said Bartholomew, torn between concern and disdain. 'We will not survive to be excommunicated at this rate – we will be attacked and destroyed long before the King and the Pope read William's stupid ramblings.'

'It is an outrageous story,' said Michael dismissively. 'No one with wits will believe it.'

'Unfortunately, the people who itch for a riot will not care whether it is true or not. Townsmen will feel justified in rising against the University, while scholars will feel justified in taking exception to such an outlandish claim.'

'You are right,' gulped Michael, breaking into a trot. 'It may well provide the spark that sets us alight. Clever Uyten! Who would have thought he had it in him?'

Bartholomew was glad when Michael dragged half a dozen beadles from their peace-keeping duties to accompany them to Winwick, anticipating an ambush at every step. They arrived to find the gates still off their hinges, and as Jekelyn had not been replaced, there was no one guarding the entrance. They entered unopposed and were astonished to find the yard deserted. In confusion they looked around, and Bartholomew noted that a buttress had collapsed. It lay in a heap, and the wind was now so strong that it sent some of the smaller pieces tumbling across the yard.

'Uyten!' he exclaimed, spotting a pale hand poking from under the debris, so ham-like it could belong to no one else. He raced towards it.

'Oh, no!' groaned Michael. 'Yet again, we are to be deprived of answers.'

They began hauling away debris. Fortunately for Uyten, the buttress was constructed of cheap rubble masonry – nothing heavier than lumps of damp mortar and small

393

pieces of rock. If he had not suffocated, there was a chance that he was still alive. They grazed knuckles and tore fingernails in the frantic race to dig him out. The hand began to flap as they exposed an arm and then a shoulder, and ignoring Bartholomew's pleas for care, Michael grabbed it and hauled with all his might. Uyten came free in an explosion of dust and gravel.

'Help me,' the student groaned, as Bartholomew knelt to examine him. 'Illesy . . . *he* did this.'

'Why would he mean you harm?' asked Michael, watching Bartholomew take a bucket of water from one of the beadles and begin to rinse the filth from Uyten's face.

'Because I did not go to Ely as he ordered – I could not leave Winwick when the town felt so uneasy. You had better arrest him, Brother, before he kills anyone else.'

'How did he cause you to be buried?' Michael's voice was thick with doubt. 'Did he push the buttress over?'

'Not that I saw.' Uyten coughed when water went in his mouth. 'But he is Provost. There is nothing he cannot organise.'

'So where is he?' Michael gestured at the deserted yard. 'In fact, where is everyone?'

'The students have gone?' croaked Uyten, struggling to sit up. 'The bastards! They could have dug me out first. They have been itching to join the fun outside for hours, but I have kept them in. I want them here to greet the founder when he arrives, you see.'

'Where is Illesy?' demanded Michael again.

'Gone to the guildhall with his Fellows.' Uyten began to pat himself all over to test for injuries. 'Probably to consort with Potmoor and put some villainous plan into action.'

'And what about *your* villainous plan? Let us start with the tale that Tulyet is beheaded.'

'Oh,' said Uyten sheepishly. 'That was fast. Weasenham wastes no time.'

'How could you have done such a thing?' asked Bartholomew reproachfully. 'Tulyet has a wife and child. How do you imagine they will feel when they hear this story?'

Uyten waved a dismissive paw. 'Dickon will not care. The boy is a monster.'

There was a cut on one of his fingers, and as he peered worriedly at it, Bartholomew saw blisters on the palms of his hands, of the type that often appeared when some unaccustomed activity was undertaken. An activity like rowing.

'It was you who paddled the boat up the King's Ditch last night,' he surmised. 'You were not the one who collected the parcel from the tomb – that person was smaller.'

With detached fascination, he watched Uyten's ponderous mind sort through its options: deny the charge, bluster or own up. In the end, the lad settled for a scowl.

'You should not have left us a packet of nails. It was stupid. You have cost yourselves extra money, and another uncomfortable rumour into the bargain.'

Michael regarded him with dislike. 'You had better cleanse your soul with a full confession, because you are bound for a very dark place indeed. That head wound looks nasty. Does it hurt?'

Alarm flashed in Uyten's eyes as he raised a hand to his temple and it came away stained with blood. He gulped audibly. 'Confession? You mean I am dying?'

'It is time to make amends,' said Michael. 'But quickly. Time is short.'

The colour drained from Uyten's face, leaving him so white that Bartholomew was almost moved to pity. 'I did not mean to embark on such wicked business. I swear it!'

'Start with Fulbut,' ordered Michael. 'And do not think of lying, because we already know the truth. Jekelyn told us everything.'

'Oh, Lord, did he? I knew he could not be trusted. He is a slippery—'

'You hired Fulbut to shoot my Junior Proctor,' interrupted Michael. 'But when he reneged on the agreement to leave Cambridge, you sent Jekelyn to murder him, lest he broke his silence.'

'Yes, but the orders came from Illesy. He does not have the courage to deal with me face to face, so he writes notes and gets poor blind Bon to deliver them. Bon thinks they are reading lists and lecture notes. Illesy does not work alone, though. He has help from the Guild.'

'Who?' asked Bartholomew. 'Holm?'

'Oh, certainly,' gabbled Uyten, desperate to ingratiate. 'Along with others. Richard Stanmore is easy to manipulate – a few careful words and he leapt at the chance to cause trouble. He thinks the town corrupted his father, although from what I understand, it was the other way around.'

'How will having the town in flames benefit anyone?' asked Michael, shooting Bartholomew a warning glance to prevent him from diverting the discussion by responding.

'Simple – if the other Colleges are destroyed or weakened, Winwick can expand unfettered.'

'I hardly think—' began Bartholomew, seeing serious flaws in the plan.

'Our founder wants it to be the biggest and best College in the country – a school of law founded by a lawyer, training men to rise to great power and influence. Illesy has a remit to do whatever is necessary to achieve it. He has been recruiting wealthy students as fast as he can, and he hates the fact that the Guild holds the purse strings. Please believe none of this is my fault.'

Bartholomew regarded him sceptically. 'And what do you gain from all this?'

'The founder promised to make me a prefect next year, and possibly even a Fellow.' Uyten's expression was bitter. 'Then my family would *have* to acknowledge that I am no dunce.'

'Oh, but I am afraid you are.' Michael stood abruptly, and beckoned to his beadles. 'He has told us all he knows. Take him away.'

Uyten gaped at him. 'Take me away? But you cannot cart a dying man around!'

'You are not dying,' said Bartholomew. 'In fact, you are barely hurt at all. It will take more than a bit of rubble to make an end of a brawny lad like you.'

'You mean you tricked me?' cried Uyten, as the beadles pulled him to his feet. 'I am not destined for Hell after all?'

'I imagine you are – just not yet,' replied Michael. 'When I said you were bound for a dark place, I was referring to the proctors' gaol. Did you misunderstand? How unfortunate.'

'Nothing I said will stand in a court of law,' shouted Uyten desperately. 'My "confession" was obtained by deception. You made me think I was dying, and promised absolution!'

'I promised nothing,' said Michael coldly. 'You were complicit in killing my Junior Proctor, and I could never pardon you for that.' He looked around him. 'But Illesy and his Fellows are reckless to have gone out today. What will happen to their College while you are in gaol and all the other students have disappeared to cause mischief?'

'You cannot let any harm befall Winwick just because Illesy is an incompetent villain!' cried Uyten, distressed. 'Let me go, Brother. I will stay here and protect it. Please! Our founder will be broken-hearted if his College is damaged.'

'You should have thought of that before embarking on this wild plan,' said Michael, indicating that his beadles were to haul the lad away. Uyten howled and writhed furiously, and they were hard-pressed to subdue him. Michael turned to Bartholomew. 'We need to find Illesy – fast.'

'We do, but Uyten is right: his testimony and Jekelyn's will not convict someone who has made his living by outmanoeuvring the legal system. Unless you want Illesy to walk free, we need a more credible witness to stand against him. Such as one of his accomplices from the Guild.'

'Do you have anyone particular in mind?'

'Holm. He will turn King's evidence to save his own neck.'

'Why am I not surprised that you should choose him?' muttered Michael.

The two scholars aimed for the surgeon's house. It was difficult to keep their hoods up in the gusting wind, and whenever they blew back to reveal their faces, people glared. Bartholomew was grateful for the two beadles at their side, although he wished there were more. It had required three of them to drag a frantically struggling Uyten to the gaol, while another had been needed to inform Meadowman and his patrols of what was afoot.

'We are going to be lynched,' he muttered. 'People are angry about Dick Tulyet.'

'Not everyone.' Michael was puffing hard at the rapid pace the physician was setting. 'Isnard is waving a friendly greeting, and so is Ylaria Verius.'

It was a small ray of hope in an otherwise bleak situation.

'Illesy,' said Bartholomew, flinching when the wind ripped a tile from a roof and it smashed on the ground nearby. 'I suppose we should have guessed.'

'Yes,' panted Michael. 'Founding a new College is expensive, and he will need all the funds he can get. John Winwick and the Guild have been generous, but more will always be required. He blackmailed us for money, and I cannot help but wonder whether he persuaded his friend Potmoor to use his talent for theft – that the proceeds from all these burglaries are in Winwick's coffers.'

'Not all, Brother. Verius and Fulbut were responsible for some. And Illesy certainly would not have ordered Fulbut to commit crimes in the town – he wanted him dead or vanished, lest he was caught and decided to talk.'

'True,' acknowledged Michael. He sighed bitterly. 'If we had not gone to Peterborough, none of this would have happened. I could have slowed everything down, thus allowing time for Winwick Hall's money to be raised legitimately.'

'You might have tried, but Felbrigge was shot when *he* attempted to introduce measures to curb its progress, and—'

He stopped when he saw Julitta, serene and beautiful in a pale blue dress and cream cloak. Knowing he would be unable to lie convincingly if she asked where he was going, he attempted to sidle past her, but she grabbed his hand and brought him to a standstill. Michael, wheezing and grateful for the respite, staggered to a halt beside them.

'You two should not be out today,' she chided, her lovely face creased with concern. 'Not with all these silly tales about Sheriff Tulyet. I ordered Weasenham to desist, but it was too late. Go back to Michaelhouse and stay there until the town has something else to gossip about.'

'Is your husband home?' asked Michael, to prevent time being lost on a wasted journey.

'Yes, with Hugo,' replied Julitta. 'They are discussing—'

'Please excuse us,' said the monk, beginning to trot again. 'We are in a hurry.'

But he was still winded, so it was easy for Julitta to keep pace. At first he refused to say what was afoot, but she was a determined lady, and soon had the whole sorry story out of him.

'Will has his failings, but he would never condone poisoning,' she stated firmly. 'Or setting churches alight. You are mistaken.'

'Illesy is the mastermind behind all this trouble,' said Bartholomew. 'A man with sinister connections to Potmoor. And your husband spends a lot of time with Potmoor's son . . .'

Julitta glared angrily at him. 'And you think Will's friendship with Hugo means he is part of this nasty affair? Well, you are wrong. He is not a brave man, no matter what impression he tries to give, and would never have the nerve to throw in his lot with poisoners and arsonists.'

'Uyten said otherwise,' rasped Michael, while Bartholomew thought Julitta's defence was a poor indictment of Holm's character – that she thought him innocent only because she considered him too cowardly for anything so daring as breaking the law.

'Uyten is a ruffian,' said Julitta tightly. 'How can you believe anything he says? Will would never harm the town *or* the University.'

'Yes, he would,' countered Michael. 'He hates scholars, because Matt and you . . .'

'Are friends,' finished Julitta. 'Yes, he does not like the situation, but he is not so low as to wreak revenge by embroiling himself in a plot to murder people. However, I have never liked his association with Hugo, and I rue the day that Lawrence introduced them to each other.'

'*Lawrence* did?'

'He is not only Potmoor's personal physician, but his

400

confidant and adviser. Potmoor and Illesy do nothing without *his* blessing.'

'No,' said Bartholomew impatiently. 'Lawrence is not involved.'

Julitta shot him an irritable, exasperated glance. 'I know this is difficult, Matt, but look at the evidence. Lawrence says he wants to dedicate his evening years to teaching, but it is rumoured that his incompetence killed Queen Isabella—'

'So what? Even if the tale is true, it does not make him a criminal.'

'No, but it makes him a liar. And while he pretends to be kindly and amiable to his fellow *medici*, he steals their best patients behind their backs – just ask Meryfeld and Rougham. He has probably taken yours, too, but you are too busy to notice. Moreover, I have not forgotten that he quarrelled with Hemmysby. Did you ask him about that?'

'Yes,' replied Bartholomew. 'He denied it.'

'Well, there you are, then! More proof that he is not a truthful man. He is almost certainly Illesy's helpmeet in whatever is unfolding.'

'He probably just enjoys teaching,' persisted Bartholomew stubbornly. 'Like me.'

But Michael agreed with Julitta. 'Men do not give up lucrative posts for no reason, and I have always been suspicious of Lawrence. I strongly suspect that he *did* fail the old Queen, and aims to worm his way back into royal favour by making a success of Winwick.'

Bartholomew looked from one to the other, unwilling to concede they might be right. 'We still need to talk to Holm,' was all he said, then broke into a run that had them both scrambling to keep up.

It did not take long to reach the surgeon's elegant house on Bridge Street, and Julitta led the way into the cosy parlour where she and Bartholomew had spent so many enjoyable evenings while her husband was out. Holm and Hugo were standing on either side of the hearth, and it was clear that a disagreement was in progress.

'We have very little time and a lot of questions,' began Michael, too breathless from the rapid dash to provide explanations. 'If you cooperate, I shall see what can be done to save you.'

'Save us from what?' Holm glanced uneasily at the two beadles who stood in the doorway. 'We have done nothing wrong.'

'Except peddle false cures,' growled Hugo. He wore a sword, and Bartholomew was suddenly seized with the conviction that the situation was going to turn ugly.

'Leave, Julitta,' he said in a low, urgent voice. 'Find somewhere safe to wait while—'

'They are not false,' snapped Holm. 'You just did not follow the instructions properly.'

'Lawrence says my gums might never recover from your stupid tooth-whitener,' snarled Hugo. 'And your remedy for gout made my grandmother worse. You are a fraud!'

'Now just a moment,' said Julitta indignantly, pulling away from Bartholomew, who was trying to manoeuvre her towards the door. 'No one *forced* you to take Will's medicines, Hugo.'

'See?' sneered Holm. 'You only have yourself to blame. It—'

The end of his sentence dissolved into a squeal of alarm when Hugo whipped out his blade. The beadles surged forward to prevent a skewering, and there followed a vicious exchange of blows. Michael snatched up a poker and waded into the affray, while Bartholomew hauled out his trusty forceps, shouting again for Julitta to leave. He had taken no more than a step forward when Holm moved. The surgeon had a dagger, and Bartholomew only just managed to avoid the swipe intended to disembowel him. Holm prepared to strike again, but the physician was quicker. He lunged with his forceps and knocked Holm to his knees.

Julitta released a horrified cry and darted forward to place herself between them, and it was sheer bad luck that the punch Bartholomew aimed at Holm struck her instead. She slumped to the floor, and while he gaped in stunned disbelief, Holm attacked again. Bartholomew raised the forceps so the killing blow was deflected, but he was off balance, and a well-aimed kick drove him headfirst into a pile of cushions.

By the time he had fought his way free of their pillowy softness, Hugo had been defeated by the beadles, Michael had Holm pinned against a wall with the poker, and Julitta lay where she had fallen. Stomach churning, he scrambled to her side. There was a cut on her nose, and she would have a black eye. He burned with shame: he had not only struck a woman, but one he loved. And at that moment he knew he would marry her as soon as her union with Holm was dissolved. Matilde was a distant dream, but Julitta was real, and he had learned to his cost the price of dallying. He hovered over her anxiously, willing her to open her eyes.

'Will she live?' asked Holm. When Bartholomew nodded, the surgeon smiled; it was not a nice expression. 'Good. I am fond of her, although she should not have forced me to befriend Hugo so we could learn his father's plans. It worked, of course. Hugo told me everything.'

'What are you saying, you bastard?' snarled Hugo, struggling furiously in his captors' grip.

He might have broken loose, but rescue came in the form of Cynric, who appeared suddenly in the doorway. The book-bearer dealt Hugo a sharp tap on the head, which was enough to daze him without knocking him completely insensible. Michael indicated that the beadles were to drag him away before he regained his senses. Bartholomew saw none of it: all his attention was on Julitta. Cynric started to speak, but Holm cut across him.

'You think Potmoor is the culprit,' he crowed, 'which is exactly what we intended. You are fools to have fallen for it.'

'We fell for nothing,' lied Michael. 'We have known all along that the real villain is Illesy.'

'Illesy?' blurted Holm in unfeigned surprise. '*He* gave Julitta orders?'

'I want the truth about this unsavoury affair,' said Michael sternly. 'Not malicious lies *or* a shameful attempt to place the blame on your unconscious spouse.'

'It *is* the truth. Julitta was told what to do – by Illesy, if you can be believed – and she told me. I had to obey, or she would have made life unbearable for me. She found a loophole in her father's will, you see, which means she controls our finances. Bartholomew should not have taught her how to read.'

'You never loved her,' snapped Bartholomew, goaded into responding. 'You married her for money and now you are trying to implicate her in a crime, just to be rid of her. You are despicable!'

Holm sneered. 'You think you know her, but you do not. She is more devious than any man alive – she takes after her sire in that respect. And do not think to have me hanged so that you can marry her instead. She would never allow it. You do not have a glittering future like I do.'

'Enough!' Bartholomew spoke so sharply that Julitta stirred. Cynric tried again to intervene, but Holm over-rode him a second time.

'She is not the generous soul you think. It was *she* who arranged for the beggars' alms to go to Winwick Hall. And when I treat patients who fail to pay, she hires louts like Hugo, Fulbut and Verius to take my fees by force.'

'We are more interested in *your* role in this affair,' said

404

Michael quickly, when Bartholomew came to his feet with a dangerous expression on his face. 'The murders of Felbrigge, Elvesmere, Ratclyf, Knyt and Hemmysby; the burglaries; the attempt to blackmail—'

'I know nothing of murder.' Holm giggled in a manner calculated to aggravate. 'However, it was a delight to watch Michaelhouse squirm over William's tract. Langelee thought he could end it with ten marks. What an ass! Now the price is a hundred. However will you pay?'

'You are involved in that, too?' Bartholomew's voice dripped disgust. 'I might have known!'

'You will be excommunicated when the essay appears in full, and will have to leave Cambridge. Your sister will miss you, especially as her loathsome son is in the process of slinking back to London. Would you like me to look after her for you?'

Bartholomew was gripped by a rage so intense that he barely heard Michael's sharp words of caution about not letting himself be provoked. He took three or four steps towards the surgeon, but Cynric blocked his path.

'Pummel him later, boy.' The book-bearer turned to Michael, his voice urgent. 'I came to tell you that there are two separate mobs on the rampage, Brother. The first is a mixture of matriculands and scholars from Winwick—'

'No surprise there,' interrupted Michael. 'They are men brought here for that very purpose.'

'They claim they are appalled by the University's corruption and arrogance, and want to make an end of its evil ways.'

'So that is how Illesy plans to be rid of his rivals,' surmised Michael, ignoring Holm's shrill giggle of triumph. 'And the second mob? Who has joined that?'

'A lot of troublemakers from the other Colleges, along with a smattering of fractious townsmen. They say Winwick is an upstart foundation and intend to teach it a lesson. I do not think I have ever seen an angrier horde.'

'It sounds too deadly to stop,' gloated Holm. 'The University will be destroyed. What a pity!'

'Lock this creature in the cellar,' ordered Michael, but Cynric had hurried away the moment he had finished delivering his message, so the monk bundled Holm into the basement himself. Outraged howls drifted out.

Meanwhile, Bartholomew's feelings were in turmoil. Julitta was not seriously hurt, but he was appalled by what he had done. Part of him blamed Holm, and he was sorry that Cynric had prevented him from battering the smug face to a pulp. He glanced up as the book-bearer reappeared, ushering Edith in front of him.

'I saw her go past, so I fetched her back,' Cynric explained. 'She can look after Julitta, while we disband these two rabbles before they do serious damage.'

'I will stay with Julitta, Matt,' promised Edith. 'You must help Michael before it is too late.'

'I am not going anywhere as long as she is insensible,' said Bartholomew unsteadily. 'She may need me when she wakes.'

But at that moment, Julitta's eyes fluttered open and she started to sit up.

'Did you hit me?' she asked, wincing as he eased her back down. 'Where is Will?'

'You see?' said Edith. 'She needs a kindly nurse, not a physician. Now go.'

Bartholomew was not happy about abandoning two people he loved when the town was on the verge of a serious disturbance, but Michael insisted that he could not manage alone, and when Julitta assured him that she did not need his protection, he was forced to relent. He glanced back at her before he left, hating leaving her.

Outside, the air rang with angry voices, and he could hear the clash of arms from at least two directions. All the shops were closed, their doors and windows barred against invaders. Anxious faces peered from the upper floors, and the acrid reek of smoke told of some building that was aflame. The wind was now a gale, ripping twigs and small branches from flailing trees. It blew so hard that it set the bells in St Clement's swinging, sounding an eerily discordant alarm for the brewing turmoil.

'I hope Tynkell manages to stop John Winwick from coming,' gasped Michael as they ran. 'He must not see us like this – especially as the last time he was here, my Junior Proctor was shot. He will think we spend all our time in a state of constant turmoil!'

'But this turmoil is *his* fault,' hissed Cynric. 'Him and his upstart foundation.'

He shoved the two scholars off the road and into an alley, and moments later a vast body of men thundered past. They were the matriculands and Winwick students. Michael blurted an oath, appalled by the size of the multitude that had been mustered.

'And that is not all of them,' cautioned Cynric when they had gone. 'They have another group laying siege to Bene't College.'

They continued on their way, buffeted by the wind and the occasional rock lobbed by those who recognised the Senior Proctor's distinctive bulk – it was not easy to disguise so princely a figure in its flowing Benedictine habit, even with the cowl drawn up to hide his face.

'What will happen, Brother?' called Warden Shropham from the top of the King's Hall gatehouse. 'There is talk of a mob coming to attack us.'

Michael skidded to a standstill. 'One might, so keep your lads inside until further notice.'

'I am afraid most are already out,' said Shropham apologetically. 'Aiming to teach Winwick a lesson. Do you want the rest of us go and look for them?'

'No!' Michael was alarmed at the notion of yet more

angry scholars on the streets, sure the ineffectual Shropham would be unequal to keeping them in order. 'Stay where you are.'

Bartholomew began sprinting again. He was so tense that his head throbbed, and he felt cloudy-witted. Or perhaps it was fear for Julitta and Edith that prevented him from concentrating on the mass of facts he had accumulated. He knew he had learned enough to answer some of the questions that had plagued him that week, but he was wholly unable to apply his mind to the task.

A sudden roar from outside Gonville Hall made him stop to look. An enormous crowd had gathered, and he recognised several Winwick students. They were hurling stones and howling abuse. Rougham appeared in the gatehouse window and the clamour slowly died away.

'Go away,' the *medicus* ordered imperiously, his voice shrill above the wind. 'Because if so much as a single tile of ours is damaged, Winwick Hall will pay the bill.'

There was a furious bellow at this, and another barrage of missiles was loosed. Fortunately for the defenders, Gonville, like all Colleges, had been built to withstand such onslaughts. Some of the besiegers had swords, and most had cudgels and knives, but as long as the gates held, there was little such weapons could do. If one gave way, however, the slaughter would be terrible.

'Come away, Matt,' hissed Michael. 'I would intervene if I had my beadles, but I am not such a lunatic as to try it alone.'

It was not far to Winwick Hall, and they arrived to find it much as it had been left. A solitary beadle – a squat, dim-witted fellow named Giles – was on guard outside, while the doors still leaned uselessly against the wall. He almost wept with relief when he saw Michael.

'I think a mob is about to descend on us, Brother! A lot of College men and townsfolk are in the Market

Square, listening to rousing speeches. The College men are fools! They should be securing their own foundations, not attacking this place.'

'Yes,' agreed Michael. 'They—'

'I told Provost Illesy about the danger,' Giles gabbled on. 'But he does not believe me. He says no one will dare assault Winwick, and—'

'Where is he?' interrupted Michael. 'Inside?'

Giles nodded. 'With Potmoor.' He said no more, but the expression on his face made it clear that he disapproved of anyone in the University associating with such a man.

'Who else is in?' demanded Michael. 'Or are they alone?'

'He is with his three Fellows and half a dozen students. The rest are off assaulting Gonville, and they plan to march on King's Hall afterwards. Michaelhouse is safe, though, because the choir is guarding it. They know where their free bread and ale comes from.'

'At least they are good for something then,' muttered Cynric.

'Come inside and shut the gates,' instructed Michael. 'With luck, the mob will lose interest when they see they cannot get in.'

'I wish I could, Brother, but the doors are off their hinges.'

'Then we shall lift them into place.' Michael indicated that Bartholomew and Cynric were to help. 'It may be enough of a deterrent, although obviously a good shove would see them topple.'

'Then let us hope no one shoves,' grunted Giles, as he lent his strength to the task. It was quickly done, although the wind was strong enough to make them sway precariously.

'If we can squeeze a confession from Illesy, we may yet avert a crisis,' said Michael. 'I shall order him to make a public apology, which might take the wind out of the College men's sails.'

'But what if they meet the other horde?' asked Cynric worriedly. 'The Winwick lads?'

'One thing at a time,' said Michael.

When six indignant students raced from the hall, demanding to know why the Senior Proctor was meddling with their property, Michael ordered them to build a barricade to shore up the gates. He started to stride to the *parlura* to confront Illesy, but the Provost saved him the trouble.

'What are you doing here, Brother?' he demanded. 'How dare you—'

'I am trying to save your College,' snarled Michael. 'Although God knows it does not deserve it. And you have a lot of explaining to do. Where is Potmoor?'

'Potmoor? How should I know where he—'

'Enough!' snapped Michael, as a vengeful cheer from the Market Square indicated that the speakers had almost inflamed their listeners to the point where they would be ready to march. 'This is no time for lies. Where is he? In the Provost's Suite?'

He stalked towards the rooms in question without waiting for a reply, leaving Illesy too startled to stop him. Bartholomew followed, his nerves jangling with tension. He entered the building full of disquiet, then gaped in astonishment as he looked around.

Illesy's quarters belied their grand name, and were poor and mean, their furnishings shabbier than anything at Michaelhouse. There were no books on the shelves, and the floor was bereft of rugs. The bed was old, and there did not seem to be enough blankets. No fire was lit in the hearth, and the only personal items were a bronze statue and a ceramic bowl.

'Now you know why we always entertain in the *parlura*,'

410

said Illesy sourly. His habitual oiliness had been replaced by a dark, sullen resentment. 'We do not want outsiders to know that we are not yet as wealthy as we would have everyone believe. It was a scramble to deceive you when you came to help Ratclyf.'

Michael gestured to the ornaments. 'These were in his room . . .'

'Potmoor lent them to us. We deploy them when they are needed to impress, although we keep people away from our private rooms if we can.'

'But you have plenty of money,' objected Michael, although Bartholomew chafed at the discussion. 'A beautiful new hall, the promise of churches and manors in your endowment—'

'Precisely,' snapped Illesy. 'The *promise* of churches and manors. We do not have them yet, and we need money now. The student fees we have collected do not cover all our bills – builders, carpenters, tilers, bakers, brewers, the stationer. Then there is the staff needed to run the place. Why do you think I have not replaced Jekelyn?'

'But your fine new livery.' Michael looked pointedly at Illesy's hands. 'Your rings.'

'Potmoor's. He also bought the Fellows' clothes; the students are rich, so they purchase their own. We know how these things work, Brother. One whiff of weakness and the other Colleges will home in on us like jackals. They will use our fleeting moment of poverty as a stick with which to beat us, and we might never recover our rightful status as premier foundation.'

Michael blinked his surprise. 'So Winwick Hall is destitute?'

'No, we have a temporary problem with our cash flow,' corrected Illesy stiffly. He grimaced. 'It is because we came so rapidly into being. John Winwick should have ensured that our endowment was in force before raising buildings and opening our doors to pupils.'

411

'But you provided lavish refreshments after the debate and Hemmysby's funeral—'

'The Guild of Saints helped with the debate, while Potmoor paid for Hemmysby. It was all a ruse, to maintain the illusion of affluence.' Illesy's voice was bitter. 'You will not understand the necessity, of course.'

'No,' lied Michael. He blew out his cheeks in a sigh, stunned. Then he caught Bartholomew's agitated expression. 'But fascinating though this is, it is not why I am here. I ask again: where is Potmoor?'

For a moment, it seemed that Illesy would deny entertaining the felon, but then he shrugged, and led the way to the hall. As they walked, Bartholomew glanced across the blustery yard and saw with alarm that the students' barricade was perilously top-heavy. Cynric thought so, too: he made a frustrated gesture to say that he had said as much, but had been overruled.

'Potmoor has been good to us,' Illesy was saying. 'He not only made donations from his own purse, but he has encouraged the Guild to be generous as well. He and Julitta Holm. I do not know what we would have done without them.'

'Yet some of your Fellows object to their College's association with a criminal,' remarked Michael.

'Because none of them knew how heavily we rely on his largesse. Until today, that is, when I felt compelled to tell them.' Illesy gave a rueful grimace. 'Even in an enlightened establishment like a university, there are those who refuse to believe that malefactors can reform. My Fellows were among them, although I hope we have rectified that misapprehension now.'

'Why today?' demanded Michael.

'A few disparaging remarks against Potmoor are not a problem – it reduces the chances of anyone guessing that he is a major benefactor. However, Bon in particular is a little *too* censorious, and Potmoor finally had enough. He understands that we cannot risk an open association, but he does not like being continuously insulted by those he is trying to help. But my Fellows know the truth now, so I hope we can strike some sort of balance.'

He opened the *parlura* door to reveal the felon sitting at the table with Lawrence. The account books were open and the elderly physician had been reading them aloud – for the benefit of Bon, who was by the window, head cocked as he tried to gauge what was happening outside; and for Potmoor who, like most townsfolk whose occupations were manual, was illiterate. Deputy de Stannell was there, too, hovering at Potmoor's side as usual, while Eyer was by the hearth, mixing another poultice for Bon's eyes. Nerli was reading in a corner, brooding and baleful.

'What is happening?' demanded Bon, when he heard his Provost's voice. 'All is not well. I can hear horrible sounds.'

'We are about to be besieged,' replied Illesy shortly. 'Our lads are raising a barrier to repel the villains who dare set angry eyes on our property.'

Before he had finished speaking, there was a furious clamour of voices from the Market Square, followed by the sound of marching feet. The attackers were on their way.

CHAPTER 17

There was a stunned silence in the *parlura*, then de Stannell raced to the window and peered out. Eyer's hands flew to his mouth in horror, Lawrence looked frightened, Nerli seemed surprised, and Bon's face flushed with indignation. Only Potmoor remained unmoved, giving the impression that he rather relished the prospect of violence.

'Who?' shouted Bon furiously. 'Who dares assault us? Do they not know that our founder will be here at any moment? Order them to disperse, Brother. You are Senior Proctor, are you not? Use the authority vested in you.'

'It is too late.' Michael rounded on Illesy and Potmoor. 'Your ostentatious College has done great harm, but not nearly as much as the crimes you have committed – murder and theft.'

'Not me,' declared Potmoor, his small eyes glittering. 'God would not approve of his beloved breaking the law, so I have abstained from wrongdoing since my resurrection.'

'You have done nothing of the kind,' said Michael accusingly. 'You have been out a-burgling virtually every night, as your lack of alibis attests.' He glared at Illesy. 'And I mean *reliable* alibis, not ones brazenly fabricated by your lawyer or the ludicrous claim that you were praying.'

'I have alibis,' flashed Potmoor, nettled. 'Just not ones I am prepared to use.'

'Olivia Knyt,' blurted Bartholomew in sudden understanding. 'Of course!'

'Leave her out of it,' snapped Potmoor angrily. 'I will not have her name sullied. Or Knyt's. He was a good man, although as dull as ditchwater. Lord! My head pounds! Sometimes I wonder whether my glimpse of Heaven was worth this agony. Give me more tonic, Lawrence.'

'And you need not pretend to be bewildered either,' snarled Michael, rounding on the elderly physician. 'I know your close friend Potmoor does nothing without your blessing.'

Both men regarded him askance, and when Potmoor spoke he sounded amused. 'I have every respect for my *medicus*, but why would I need his blessing when I have the Almighty's?'

'And I neither sanction nor condemn what my patients do in their spare time,' added Lawrence. 'Whatever gave you the notion that I might?'

'Because you have lied,' Michael forged on. 'You deny that you argued with Hemmysby the night before he died, but witnesses say you did.'

'Then they are mistaken,' objected Lawrence. 'I have never—'

'And I do not believe that you came here because you love teaching,' interrupted Michael.

Lawrence groaned. 'Do not tell me that you credit the tale about me killing the old Queen! You should know better, especially if you have heard the one about Sheriff Tulyet's execution. They are malicious falsehoods, Brother, designed to damage the innocent and cause trouble.'

'That barricade is not going to hold!' shouted Nerli urgently. 'Everyone, come with me to shore it up! No, not you, Bon. You will be in the way.'

'Stop,' snapped Michael, as Lawrence hastened to oblige. 'I have not finished with you.'

'Later, Brother,' ordered Nerli. 'When we are not under siege.'

'He means when outsiders are not here to hear Winwick's crimes unveiled,' muttered Michael, as Lawrence, de Stannell and Eyer raced away on Nerli's heels, Lawrence with obvious relief. Bon fluttered uncertainly, but Potmoor and Illesy stayed put, clearly of the opinion that they were too grand to sully their hands with menial tasks. The monk rounded on the Provost again. 'Why did you send Uyten to Ely last night?'

'To buy parchment. It is cheaper there, and every penny counts, as you have just forced me to confess. Unfortunately, he disobeyed me, and did not go.'

'I tackled him about that,' added Potmoor. 'He said he wanted to be on hand to monitor Lawrence, whom he believes is a poisoner. I could not tell if he was lying.'

'*Is* Lawrence the villain, Brother?' asked Illesy, his voice suddenly tired and plaintive. 'If so, you cannot imagine the damage it will do us. Wealthy and powerful men will not send their sons to a foundation where they think they might be murdered by its Fellows.'

'There is no evidence to accuse him,' said Bartholomew stubbornly.

'Actually, there is a great deal,' countered Michael. His voice became urgent as a crash from the High Street indicated that time was running out. 'If you two have any love for this place, you will confess to your misdeeds before this mob destroys it. An apology *might* avert a disaster, although it will have to be a remarkably abject one, or—'

'What misdeeds?' interrupted Potmoor indignantly. 'I have just told you that I have not committed any since God showed me His face.'

'You and Illesy ordered my Junior Proctor shot—'

'What?' cried Illesy, shocked. 'Why would we do such a thing?'

'Because he aimed to control you, and instigated measures to do it. You disapproved.'

'Well, yes, I did,' conceded Illesy. 'But I am lawyer enough to circumvent whatever he had put in place. I kept a violent crim— Potmoor free for twenty years. I am good at legal loopholes.'

'Then there was Elvesmere.' Michael spoke more quickly when the mob reached the gates and began to pound on them. The frail barrier wobbled. 'Who died here the evening Potmoor visited, although Potmoor lied about it until we produced witnesses.'

Potmoor shrugged. 'It was none of your business, and I was only here briefly anyway – Illesy took my donation of ten marks, and saw me out. However, I did not kill Elvesmere. Why would I? I barely knew the man.'

'And I did not do it, either,' said Illesy. 'Do you hear me, Bon? I can see you shooting me nasty glances. I did not like Elvesmere, but he was a gifted teacher, and like any responsible Head of House, I am able to set the good of my College above personal preferences.'

'And Ratclyf?' asked Michael.

'He was nervous and uneasy after Elvesmere died,' replied Illesy. 'And it stressed his weak heart, no matter what you say about blue lips and poison.'

'I miss Elvesmere.' Bon's voice was accusing, and it was clear that he was not convinced by the explanations. Bartholomew was beginning to be, though, and a quick glance told him that so was Michael. 'He was my closest friend.'

'Do not say we conspired to poison Hemmysby and Knyt either,' Illesy went on. 'Hemmysby was a nobody, not worth the bother, and we liked the way Knyt ran the Guild.'

'Moreover, Olivia wanted her baby to carry *his* name, not mine.' Potmoor shrugged and looked away. 'She is right. Hugo suffers cruelly from his kinship with me, and my unborn child deserves better, much as it pains me to say it.'

'But you mentioned professional killers and spillages of blood,' pressed Michael, looking from one to the other sceptically. 'You were overheard in All Saints churchyard.'

Potmoor and Illesy exchanged a mystified glance, then Potmoor released a bark of laughter. 'We were talking about the pig we slaughtered for today's feast – John Winwick likes pork. It was nothing to do with dispatching people. We met secretly, so that no one would guess the depth of my involvement with Winwick Hall.'

'We should have hired a butcher to deal with the pig,' added Illesy, 'but I wanted to save money, so Nerli did it. Unfortunately, his inexperience resulted in a terrible mess . . .'

'Then what about the St Clement's fire?' pressed Michael, but the conviction had gone from his voice and he sounded defeated. 'Heyford was vocal against your College . . .'

'Terribly,' agreed Illesy. 'And it was gratifying to see his domain in flames. But arson is not in our interests. Donations were given for its repair that might have come to us.'

'But you were angry with him for his slanderous sermons. And after the fire, he annoyed you with his tale about stealing from the royal coffers.'

'Of course I was annoyed,' said Illesy irritably. 'It was low to gossip about another man's youthful indiscretions. However, he will not do it again. He will be "offered" a new parish today – in the Fens, where his poisonous sermons can do no harm. Effective immediately.'

'Offered by whom?' asked Bartholomew, thinking it was hardly fair that Heyford should be banished, as the tale about Illesy's dishonesty was apparently true.

'John Winwick, who is friends with the Bishop. But it proves my innocence – I would not have bothered to find Heyford a new home if I intended to solve the problem with murder.'

'Is this your writing?' Michael picked up the accounts book from the table. Illesy nodded, and the monk sighed as he turned to Bartholomew. 'It is a different hand from the blackmail notes, and Potmoor is illiterate. They are not the extortionists. Uyten misled us, and so did Richard.'

'Richard Stanmore?' asked Illesy, looking from one to the other. 'I would love to snag him as a benefactor. He wants to be a Fellow, so we shall charge him handsomely for the privilege.'

'Damn!' murmured Michael, when Illesy and Potmoor went to look out of the window. 'They are not our culprits and we have wasted valuable time proving it. Now it is too late to avert trouble.'

A thundering crash as the barricade toppled suggested that he was right.

Bartholomew watched helplessly as baying College men and townsfolk began to swarm across the fallen barrier. De Stannell, who should have been leading the effort to drive them back, promptly turned and bolted for the sanctuary of the hall, so it was Cynric and Nerli who bore the brunt of the invaders' charge. Lawrence and Eyer tried to help by jabbing with sticks, but it was a battle they could not win, given the attackers' superiority of numbers. Bartholomew leaned out of the window, unwilling to watch them die for a lost cause.

'Fall back!' he yelled, struggling to make himself heard over the wind. 'To the hall.'

Nerli and Cynric stood shoulder to shoulder, repelling the attackers with their swords until the others had staggered to safety, then turned and fled themselves. They reached the hall, and there came the sound of the door being slammed shut and a bar being slotted into place across it.

'Such rough treatment!' cried Illesy in alarm. 'I am not sure the building can take it. A buttress fell today . . .'

'Uyten claims you arranged for it to collapse on him,' said Michael, although he spoke distantly, as the answer no longer mattered.

'On the contrary, I warned everyone against going too close,' objected Illesy indignantly.

'It sounds to me as if Uyten and Richard have made some very unpleasant accusations,' mused Potmoor, his small eyes hard and cold. 'But we shall discuss them later, when we do not have a fight on our hands. Everyone upstairs to the main hall. It will be easier to defend.'

They followed him up the steps, and by the time they arrived, the yard had filled with rioters. Michael flung open a window and yelled an order for them to disperse. The wind tore away his words, but the mob would not have obeyed anyway. Most were inveterate troublemakers, who liked nothing more than an opportunity to go on the rampage, and where better than a foundation they all hated? They surged towards the door with the clear intention of forcing their way in.

'It will not hold for long,' predicted Nerli grimly. He turned to Cynric, instinctively recognising a fellow warrior, thus telling Bartholomew that the Florentine had lied about being a scholar all his life. 'Cynric, go to the dormitory, and start organising something that will make them think twice about using a battering ram. I will try to brace it with another bench.'

Bartholomew followed the book-bearer to the top floor, where the wind was shaking the tiles on the roof, making a tremendous clatter. The students, Eyer, Lawrence and Beadle Giles were peering out of the windows in horror at the scene below. Cynric quickly set them to filling basins, buckets and jugs with water from the washing butt. Bartholomew raced back down to the hall and, not caring that he was overstepping his authority, ordered everyone upstairs to help. De Stannell opened his mouth to object, but Potmoor muttered something about it being wise to obey a veteran of Poitiers, and led the way. Only Bon remained, on his knees at the far end of the room, praying fervently that any damage would be repaired before the founder arrived.

'We are not deprived of all our suspects,' said Michael, speaking in a low voice so as not to disturb him. 'We still have the falsely smiling Lawrence and the sinister Nerli, who is rather too competent a military strategist for my liking. *And* he was the one who insisted on a hasty burial for our murder victims.'

Below, the mob clustered around the door as they debated how best to break it down. They scattered angrily when water was hurled down on them, and several prepared to lob missiles of their own. Then someone jabbed an indignant finger to where some of their number were disappearing inside the Fellows' quarters.

'They are going to loot without us!'

There was a furious howl, and everyone piled after them. The respite would not last long – they would return with renewed vigour when they found there was nothing to steal.

'The culprit is de Stannell,' said Bartholomew in the eerie silence that followed. 'It explains why he is always with Potmoor, grovellingly determined to win his favour.'

'But Potmoor is irrelevant,' said Michael, most of his attention on the yard as he waited tautly for the assault to resume.

'Not so. He has just told us that all the burglaries were committed when he was with Olivia Knyt – times when he had no usable alibis. And who knew where he planned to be? His dogged shadow de Stannell.'

Michael regarded him askance. 'And why would de Stannell want Potmoor accused?'

There was a sound behind them, and both scholars whipped around to see the deputy standing in the doorway, a crossbow trained on them.

'You should have kept your mouths shut. Now I am going to have to kill you.'

De Stannell kicked the door closed behind him, and although Bon turned slightly at the sound, he immediately resumed his prayers. Bartholomew considered yelling a warning, but what would be the point? A man with hypochyma could do little to help.

'Yes, it has suited me to have Potmoor blamed for the burglaries,' whispered de Stannell. He glanced at Bon, but the murmured prayers did not falter. 'Why do you think I have kept him such close company recently? It is so I shall know his whereabouts and plans. It has not been pleasant, but it has certainly worked.'

'It has,' agreed Michael. 'People do think Potmoor is guilty. Unfortunately for you, they also think you are his accomplice, and that is not the sort of man they want running their shire. You will not retain your post for long after Tulyet returns.'

'He will not return,' said de Stannell confidently. 'And if he does, I shall arrange for him to have an accident. Do not think of calling for help, by the way. I shall shoot whoever tries, and cut down the other with my sword. Bon will not see, and everyone else will assume the mob did it.'

'So are we to believe that you are the burglar?' asked Michael, eyeing him in distaste. 'Slipping out to raid your town while Potmoor frolics with Olivia Knyt?'

De Stannell shot him an unpleasant look. 'Of course not. Potmoor's religious conversion left a number of his henchmen unemployed, and as Sheriff, I knew their names. They now work for me.'

'But why involve yourself in such a vile scheme? You are already wealthy.'

De Stannell gestured to the hall. 'This place is costly, and some guildsmen are beginning to object to the amount of money we plough into it, so I have been obliged to devise other ways of raising funds. None of the proceeds have been for me.'

'So what *do* you gain from the arrangement?'

'Immortality! The College will soon be renamed Winwick and *de Stannell* Hall.'

'I think the founder will have something to say about that.' Michael regarded him with rank disdain. 'And Matt is wrong, because you are *not* the clever mastermind behind this scheme. To be frank you are not sufficiently intelligent.'

De Stannell scowled as he aimed the weapon, but the monk only gazed back defiantly, and the crossbow wavered. Young Dickon had been right to question the deputy's abilities as a soldier, thought Bartholomew. Clearly, de Stannell did not have the courage to shoot.

'Your master is Lawrence,' Michael went on. 'The man whose incompetence killed the Queen, who lied about his interactions with Hemmysby, who has poached his medical colleagues' best patients, and who ensured that Hugo and Holm became friends so that he would have a second spy among Potmoor's intimates.'

Bartholomew was suddenly assailed with an uncomfortable thought. All Michael's 'evidence' had come from one source: Julitta, who had always been quick to disparage the elderly physician. Irritably, he pushed such treacherous suspicions away. This was the woman he intended to marry!

'You should have asserted your authority as Senior Proctor more rigorously,' said de Stannell, and the sly grin he flung at Bartholomew told the physician exactly what was coming next. 'If you had put an end to your friend's unseemly lust for the wife of—'

'Stop,' snapped Bartholomew through clenched teeth. 'Leave Julitta out of it.'

'She is a cunning woman,' de Stannell went on gleefully. 'The clever daughter of a powerful and extremely ruthless man, from whom she learned her business acumen and her ability to deceive. It has not once occurred to you that she has been *using* your infatuation for her own ends.'

'No,' said Bartholomew fiercely. 'She would never—'

'She has been monitoring Michael through you ever since we feared he might interfere with our plans – long before you went to Peterborough. But you will never have her. She loves Holm and he loves her, as far as he is able. They are more similar in temperament than you know.'

'And why would Julitta conspire with the likes of you?' asked Michael scornfully.

'Why do you think? The rewards for supporting Winwick Hall will be vast. Powerful men will appreciate clerks trained to their specifications, and the clerks themselves will be grateful for the opportunity to further their ambitions.'

'So you ordered Felbrigge shot to ensure that the College could expand unfettered,' surmised Michael, while Bartholomew shook his head, unwilling to believe de Stannell's gloating words. 'But why kill Elvesmere? Surely he was happy to have won such determined supporters?'

'I thought the same, and was astonished when he announced his conviction that Winwick should remain a modest foundation. I was obliged to stab him, to shut him up.'

Illesy had mentioned Elvesmere's preference for moderation, so that was likely to be true, thought Bartholomew, but de Stannell was no killer. Again, it was something Dickon had said that provided the proof that the deputy was no threat.

'You were taking a riding lesson at the castle when Elvesmere died. You are not the culprit, so do not try to claim credit in the hope of making us think you are dangerous. You are a pitiful excuse for a villain.'

'Then who did dispatch him?' asked Michael, while de Stannell blustered and huffed in indignation. Both scholars ignored him.

Bartholomew had been aware for some time that the devotions muttered by the window were gibberish. Bon

424

was not praying, but listening to every word. And he knew why.

'Bon,' he said softly. 'De Stannell is just his monkey.'

The wind was gusting so hard that it made the timbers in the hall creak and its steady roar was almost louder than the racket made by the invaders, who were pouring back into the yard after their fruitless foray to the Fellows' quarters. Bartholomew jumped in alarm when a violent blast cracked one of the windowpanes, and there was a series of crashes as tiles were torn from the roof. There were screams, too, either because they had landed on the men milling outside, or as a result of Cynric's resumed barrage from the dormitory.

'Me?' asked Bon, turning his milky eyes towards Bartholomew as he climbed to his feet. 'How? I am blind, in case you had not noticed.'

'You cannot deceive me about hypochyma,' said Bartholomew. 'I know what it entails. You cannot read, perhaps, but you have sufficient vision to let you carry out your wicked plans. And you had Uyten. Through him, you hired Jekelyn and Fulbut to commit murder, and tricked Richard into bringing his friends here.'

Bon spread his hands. 'Uyten told you that Illesy did all that.'

'A claim you cannot have known unless it originated with you,' pounced Bartholomew. 'We have told no one else, and he is in prison.'

'In prison?' echoed Bon uneasily.

'You used and misled him, just as you have used and misled everyone else. He will not stand by you when he learns what you have done. He will tell us everything in an effort to save himself.'

'But I cannot see,' pressed Bon, all wounded reason. 'How can I have written letters to Uyten purporting to be from Illesy?'

'And there is another slip! How could you know that the orders came in the form of letters unless you had sent them? And you do not need to have written them yourself. You can dictate.'

For the first time, Bon looked directly at him, and the smile he gave was cold. 'But no one can prove it. Uyten thinks he was following *Illesy's* instructions, and you will not be in a position to put him right. I shall not bear the blame for any scandal that comes to light. *Illesy* will.'

There was a sudden cheering roar from the invaders below. Someone had found a robust piece of scaffolding that would serve as a battering ram.

'What is going on, de Stannell?' demanded Bon, going to the window. 'I cannot make out who is doing what. Tell me!'

'It is the sound of your machinations about to destroy you,' said Michael. 'The burglaries, the murders, the blackmail of another foundation – all these have made you enemies.'

'I did what was necessary to ensure our survival. This is a noble venture, and I look to the day when the whole country is run by Winwick-trained lawyers. Nothing can stand in the way of such a dream. Our founder is a true visionary.'

'Then I imagine he will be appalled when he learns what you have done.'

'He will never find out. Everyone who knows the truth is either an ally or will be dead.'

Bon turned to de Stannell, to give the order to shoot, but both Bartholomew and Michael knew that by far the greater danger was the mob below. Desperately, the physician racked his brain for ways to restore calm, but nothing came to mind.

'Elvesmere was your friend,' said Michael, his voice full of distaste. 'But you killed him without a second

426

thought. *You* stabbed him, not this silly deputy here, but your poor eyesight prevented you from making a clean job of it.'

Bon grimaced. 'It was fortunate a more loyal friend was on hand with poison – and to carry the corpse out of my room, where its discovery would have been awkward. I wanted to take it to another College, but there were too many beadles about, so we were forced to settle for the latrine.'

Bartholomew took over the discussion, to give the monk a chance to think of a way to quell the turmoil that boiled in the yard below, for his own mind was blank. He realised that they had been unforgivably careless when they had interrogated Uyten: they had not asked who had been with him in the boat, and Uyten had not volunteered the information.

'Your hypochyma is no obstacle to collecting blackmail money in the dark,' he said to Bon. 'You have skills the rest of us lack, as you spend your whole life moving through shadows. Afterwards, Uyten rowed you away.'

'Did you really think I would not guess that you were waiting? Or that I would march openly along a main road to collect my spoils? You should have paid and been done with it. The other Colleges did.'

'You have blackmailed them, too?' Bartholomew supposed he should not be surprised.

'They all have secrets – and money to spare. Why did Michaelhouse refuse?'

Another violent gust shook the building, and an agonised yowl caused Bartholomew to glance through the window. Nerli's sword, hurled like a spear, had impaled someone. Unfortunately, far from deterring the invaders, it drew a chorus of outraged yells, and the assault intensified.

'Enough,' snapped Michael. 'We must bring an end to this before we are all torn to—'

'No one will touch de Stannell and me,' averred Bon

confidently. 'We are members of the Guild of Saints, which is loved for its charity.'

'Not since you have taken the food from the mouths of widows and beggars,' said Bartholomew warningly. 'Which is why you killed Knyt, of course – a man who was beginning to baulk at the amount of money Winwick wanted. And you tried to kill Michael with poisoned cakes, while you succeeded in dispatching Hemmysby with a gift – no doubt sent after he overheard you making plans to burgle Michaelhouse.'

Bon's milky eyes narrowed. 'I killed Hemmysby for humiliating me at the debate. He should have eaten the raisin tart on the evening of the first day, and I was livid when he appeared to belittle me again the following morning. I shall kill Thelnetham when he arrives to take up his Fellowship, too, but only after he changes his will in Winwick's favour, of course.'

'Ratclyf was not poisoned with *dormirella*, though,' said de Stannell. 'Regardless of the tale you put about.'

'He died of remorse,' declared Michael. 'Lawrence saw him next to Elvesmere's coffin, weeping and begging for forgiveness. *He* felt guilty about a colleague's murder, even if you do not.'

'You were afraid he would break and expose you,' said Bartholomew. 'And he *was* poisoned, but not with *dormirella*. He had a sore throat, so you gave him liquorice root, knowing exactly what it would do to his weak heart.'

Bon shrugged. 'It was for the greater good – the future of Winwick Hall. He was a vile man.'

'What is wrong with letting Winwick grow naturally, like the other Colleges?'

'That will take years, and I want my rewards now,' replied de Stannell. He smirked. 'So the decision was made to speed it along.'

Bon ignored him, and Bartholomew saw he had scant regard for his helpmeet. 'Our founder took a chance with me – no one else wanted a blind scholar – so I have taken one for him.' He turned to de Stannell. 'He will be here soon, so oust those louts from our yard before—'

'What about Heyford?' interrupted Michael. 'Did you poison him, too, after Jekelyn failed to incinerate him for you?'

'Yes, with dwale. It did not work.' There was another chorus of howls from below, and Bon made an impatient gesture to de Stannell. 'Shoot this pair, and then get rid of that mob before they do us any damage. We cannot have the founder—'

'It is the burglaries that have done the greatest harm,' interrupted Michael, ignoring the deputy's show of taking a firmer grip on the weapon. 'By stealing for Winwick Hall, you have destroyed the fragile truce between University and town, and set us at each other's throats.'

'Which is exactly what Bon intended,' explained de Stannell, clearly glad of a few more moments to summon up his courage. 'The other Colleges will be destroyed or weakened by it, thus eliminating the competition. Moreover, it was clever to have Potmoor blamed.'

'Hardly!' exclaimed Michael. 'He is Winwick Hall's biggest benefactor.'

'Something Illesy should have told me sooner,' said Bon sourly, while de Stannell blinked his astonishment at the revelation. 'I thought Potmoor was just a felon whose fondness for our College was an affront. I would have used another scapegoat had Illesy been open with us.'

'Do you really think the University will survive with just Winwick and a handful of hostels?' asked Michael scornfully. 'The Colleges give it stability: without them it will founder. So unless you want Winwick to fail before it is properly established, help me put an end to this mischief.'

'Winwick will not fail.' Bon glanced irritably towards de Stannell. 'Hurry *up*, man! Or do you want me to come and do it?'

Bartholomew winced as the battering ram dealt the door such a blow that he felt the vibrations through the floor. 'Winwick *will* fail if they break in. They mean you serious harm.'

'De Stannell!' barked Bon. 'For God's sake, kill this pair and oust that rabble before—'

'Oust them?' echoed Michael. 'And how do you propose he does that?'

'They will disperse on my orders,' bragged de Stannell. 'I have soldiers waiting. All I have to do is yell, and they will race to save us. Bon? Shall I?'

The battering ram struck home so violently that the whole edifice trembled, and a clump of plaster dropped from the wall. Bon started in alarm.

'Yes, call them. Quickly!'

The deputy went to the window and bellowed at the top of his voice. The wind snatched his words away, although there were answering jeers from the yard. He tried again.

Suddenly, there was a crack that was far louder than anything they had heard so far. Everyone looked around in alarm, and Michael stabbed his finger at a large fissure that had appeared in the wall. Moments later, Illesy thundered down the stairs and flung open the door.

'The fallen buttress, the wind and the battering ram have rendered the building unstable,' he yelled. 'We cannot stay here a moment longer. It is set to collapse!'

'Collapse?' echoed Bon. 'No! It is the best hall in the—'

'Fool!' shrieked the Provost. 'It was raised so fast that the foundations are too shallow, the mortar was not given time to set, and the workmanship is shoddy. If you were able to see, you would not be making asinine claims about its quality.'

Furious at the insult, Bon tore forward with a knife in his hand. The Provost was too startled to defend himself, and went down in a flurry of blows. He was dead before Bartholomew or Michael could move to help him.

'There,' said Bon in satisfaction, keeping a grip on the weapon and obviously ready to use it again. 'Now I shall be Provost.'

When Bon and de Stannell began an urgent discussion in hissing undertones, Bartholomew decided it was time to make a move before anyone else died. De Stannell posed no threat, so he hurtled towards Bon, but the lawyer's reactions were faster than he had anticipated, and he was sent sprawling by a well-timed punch. Moments later, Lawrence entered. He faltered at the sight of Bartholomew on the floor and de Stannell with a crossbow. When he saw Illesy, his face drained of colour and he hurried to kneel next to him. Then Nerli arrived.

'What is going on?' demanded the Florentine. 'Did that rabble kill Illesy? By God and all that is holy I will track down the villain and make him pay.'

'I think we have found our culprits at last, Nerli,' said Lawrence in a small voice, looking first at de Stannell and then at Bon. 'You crossed Bon off our list of suspects, but . . .'

'*You* have been investigating?' asked Bon dangerously.

Nerli reached for his sword, only to find it was not at his side. He grimaced, but his voice was steady as he replied. 'Two of our Fellows vilely poisoned, along with Knyt and Hemmysby, who were the best of men? Of course we were looking into the matter.'

'You are part of it, Lawrence,' said Michael accusingly. 'Do not try to deceive us.'

Bartholomew glanced at Nerli, and saw the Florentine's muscles bunch as he prepared to leap at Bon. But there was a sudden movement behind him, and he pitched forward with a cry of pain. Eyer stood there, his pink face cold and hard. The apothecary held a crossbow in one hand and a bloodstained dagger in the other.

431

'No,' whispered Bartholomew in stunned disbelief. 'Not you as well.'

'I should have known,' said Lawrence contemptuously. 'You were a rogue at Oxford, and you are a rogue now. I should have spoken out the moment I recognised you, but I thought you deserved a second chance. I suppose you did it for money? You always were a greedy fellow.'

Eyer shrugged. 'Establishing a new business is expensive, so I was delighted to start earning profits sooner than I expected.'

'But you are wealthy,' objected Bartholomew, bewildered. 'A member of the Guild of—'

'I joined for appearances' sake, as I told you,' snapped Eyer. 'People are more likely to trust a rich apothecary than one who can barely make ends meet.'

'Then why have you been giving me free remedies for the poor?'

'To put you in my debt, so you will feel obliged to buy medicines from me in the future. I did the same with the other physicians, careful to make each think that he is the only one so favoured.'

Answers tumbled into Bartholomew's head. 'You tried to make me suspect Lawrence and Nerli by telling me that they were Potmoor's minions. You also said they engaged in questionable business after dark, and bought realgar, dwale and hemlock—'

'Lies,' interrupted Lawrence contemptuously. 'I am too old to venture out at night, and I rarely use potent herbs – I have seen too many accidents to be comfortable with them. Such as at Oxford, when a certain patient was killed with liquorice root.'

Eyer smiled coldly. 'A lesson that has been of considerable use to me in eliminating rivals, as Ratclyf learned to his cost. I imagine your heart is not what it was when you were young, so perhaps I shall give you a dose, too.'

'Enough!' snapped Bon, as another crash on the door

caused a sconce to drop off the wall. He gestured to Bartholomew. 'Pick up Nerli, and put him in the corner. I can hear him breathing, and we do not want him sneaking off while we are not looking.'

The Florentine had been saved from serious injury by the thick leather of his sword belt, and feigned unconsciousness as he was dragged across the room. Unfortunately, Eyer was alert for tricks, and Bartholomew hoped Nerli understood the warning pinch he managed to deliver before he was ordered to stand with Michael and Lawrence against the far wall. Eyer kept the crossbow trained on his captives while he held a muttered conference with his associates.

'We should have rushed de Stannell while we could,' whispered Michael, disgusted with himself. 'Now we are in trouble, because Eyer will not scruple to shoot unarmed men. We were stupid, too greedy for answers.'

Upstairs, and oblivious to the drama unfolding in the hall below, the defenders continued to lob anything they could find out of the windows, while the wind screamed through the broken panes and made the timbers groan. Bon broke away from his accomplices, and began to strip the rings – Potmoor's rings – from Illesy's fingers.

'I am the stupid one,' mumbled Lawrence. 'Eyer is often here with potions for Bon's eyes, but we all know there is no cure for hypochyma. He came to plot with his paymaster, and I should have guessed it, especially knowing what he was capable of from Oxford.'

'The writing on the blackmail letters,' said Bartholomew in a low voice. 'Now I know why it was familiar: it is on the medicines I buy. Doubtless, Eyer also penned the notes to Uyten, the ones purporting to be from Illesy.'

Eyer overheard and shrugged. 'Your Michaelhouse colleagues are unlikely to make the connection, and you will not be alive to tell them. I defeated them with ease when I collected the five marks they tried to fob us off with on Monday.'

'You mean ten marks,' said Michael.

'He is trying to make trouble,' said Eyer to Bon. 'For spite, because I flung sand in his Master's eyes. It was only five marks, I assure you.'

'Never mind this now,' said de Stannell urgently. 'Illesy was right when he said the building is ripe for collapse. That crack is getting bigger.'

Everyone looked at it: the dust that trickled out in a continuous stream did not bode well. Another thud from the battering ram shook loose a more vigorous fall. When a mighty gust of wind buffeted the building, it opened even wider.

Bartholomew turned back to Eyer. 'You are the "friend" who helped Bon poison Elvesmere when the stabbing went awry. And you supplied him with *dormirella*, confident in the belief that it is undetectable.'

'I thought it *was* undetectable. I have never read anything about blue lips.'

'Did you invade Michaelhouse, too?' asked Michael. 'And steal William's tract when the Stanton Hutch was unavailable?'

'The tract,' grinned Bon. 'As soon as it was read to me, I knew we could put it to good use. We shall make it public later, and when you and Bartholomew fail to return home today, everyone will assume you fled to avoid the consequences.'

'Potmoor has suffered from headaches ever since I used your *sal ammoniac*,' said Bartholomew, fearful now that he knew the apothecary was so coldly ruthless. 'What was in it?'

'A toxin of my own creation,' replied Eyer. 'I shall sell it to wealthy clerks in time, men who will pay handsomely for an easy way to be rid of inconvenient enemies.'

'We hoped you would kill a few paupers with it,' added

Bon, 'which would have turned the town against Michaelhouse *and* reduced the number of beggars demanding alms – money that could then come here. It seems our plan misfired, given that Potmoor has been generous to us.'

Bartholomew continued to stare at Eyer. 'But you are not a bad man. You helped me rescue Heyford from the fire.'

'You misread my intentions.' When Nerli stirred slightly on the floor, Eyer tensed, fingers poised ready to shoot. 'I was going to *stop* you from saving him, but then I remembered that you had fought at Poitiers.'

The whole building released an ominous creak, and the wind ripped another four panes of glass from their lead frames with sharp pops.

'No!' cried Bon, gazing at the ruined windows in dismay. Then he became businesslike. 'De Stannell, go and delay the founder for the time it will take us to disguise the damage. Potmoor will lend us a tapestry to hide the crack, and a glazier can be hired to—'

'It will take more than a tapestry and a few new panes to convince John Winwick that all is well,' interrupted Michael. 'It is over, Bon! You have lost.'

'The barrage from upstairs has stopped.' De Stannell's voice was suddenly shrill with alarm. It grew more so when he glanced out of the window to assess what was happening in the yard. 'And the mob is now swollen with matriculands who seem to have forgotten which side they are on. Perhaps the Michaelhouse men are right – we *are* in danger!'

'There is only one way to survive,' declared Michael. 'By putting aside our differences and joining forces. The invaders want blood, and if we fight among ourselves, they will have it.'

'Shoot him, Eyer,' snapped Bon. 'Then kill the physicians. De Stannell, shout to your troops again. The rabble will disperse when they see armed soldiers coming.'

There was another almighty crash from downstairs, followed by a deep, penetrating groan that suggested some vital support was in the process of disintegrating. Then the floor tipped violently to one side. Bon staggered and Eyer grabbed a windowsill for support. De Stannell dropped his crossbow.

It was the chance Bartholomew had been waiting for. He hurled himself at Eyer, and was aware of Nerli leaping up to tackle de Stannell, leaving Bon for Michael. Physician and apothecary crashed to the floor, where they began a frantic tussle for the weapon. Upstairs, the students screamed in terror, and part of the ceiling fell, narrowly missing Lawrence. The building torqued enough to pop out all its remaining panes, and there was a wild cheer from the yard below.

'The stairs!' shouted Lawrence. 'Quickly! It is—'

But his words were lost in another deafening groan and the building began to topple.

For a moment, Bartholomew heard nothing but the tortured squeals of flexing timbers. He staggered upright, which was not easy when the floor was tilting at such a crazy angle. Eyer snatched at his legs, then disappeared in a cloud of dust.

Coughing hard, Bartholomew scrambled towards the door, stopping only to haul Nerli to his feet. He saw Michael's bulky form ahead, but there was no sign of the others. They had been closer to the exit, so he could only assume they had already left.

'Follow me!' cried Lawrence, arriving from the dormitory with the surviving defenders at his heels. Bartholomew was relieved to see Cynric among them. 'The back door – hurry!'

It was a terrifying journey down the stairs. Lumps of masonry plummeted all around them, and the student in front of Bartholomew was killed instantly when a piece landed on his head. Lawrence stopped to tend him, but Bartholomew shoved him on, not wanting those behind them to be delayed for a lost cause. Grit and dust swirled so thickly that they could not see their own feet. Then Lawrence fell, tumbling down several steps in a flurry of flailing limbs.

'I cannot see,' he rasped. 'I am disorientated . . .'

Bartholomew staggered as someone tried to shove past him. It was Bon, for whom blinding dust was less of a problem. Bartholomew grabbed his tabard, and although the Winwick Fellow tried to punch him away, he refused to let go. Bon screeched when a stone struck his shoulder, and broke into a stumbling trot, unwillingly towing Bartholomew after him. The physician kept hold of Nerli with his other arm, yelling for the others to follow his voice. They struggled down more stairs and along a hallway.

He felt wind on his face, and although he still could not see, he was aware of daylight ahead. Lawrence surged past, and began to wrestle with the clasp on a window. It flew open with a metallic screech, ripped from his hand by the gale. De Stannell batted him out of the way, desperate to escape first, but the mob was at the back of the hall as well as the front, and the deputy disappeared in a sea of clawing, punching hands.

'A cruel choice,' gasped Michael. 'Being crushed or torn to pieces.'

Another beam fell, and dust belched thickly out of the window. It drove the invaders back, so Bartholomew used it as a shield to conceal him as he scrambled out – it was more instinct than a rational decision about the way he wanted to die. Michael followed, murmuring prayers of contrition under his breath.

Then Potmoor emerged with a sword, and the diabolical shriek he gave as he plunged among the attackers was enough to scatter them in alarm. He laid about him wildly until someone lobbed a knife that took him in the back. Bartholomew hurried towards him, but was knocked to the ground with a cudgel. Dazed, all he could think was that he had to reach Potmoor and help him. More of the building fell, and no one took any notice as he crawled towards the fallen felon through a sea of milling legs.

'You will have to resurrect me again,' whispered Potmoor. 'Where are your smelling salts?'

Bartholomew had lost his medical bag in the hall, but Potmoor's eyes closed in death, so it did not matter. He sensed, rather than saw, someone come up behind him, and whipped around just in time to avoid a jab from a makeshift spear. He recognised his assailant as one of the soldiers from Fulbut's party, and supposed the fellow had joined the riot to avenge his friend. The soldier raised the weapon to strike again, but Bartholomew managed to grab a piece of scaffolding from the ground and sent the fellow flying with a wild swing that hit its target more from luck than skill.

There was a low rumble as more of the hall fell, sending a blast of debris into the desperate mêlée. Several attackers dropped as if poleaxed. Then someone came at Bartholomew with a sword. He raised the strut, but it flew to pieces in his hands, leaving him defenceless. The swordsman prepared to strike the killing blow, but the swipe was blocked by another weapon. Bartholomew could not see his rescuer in the billowing dust, but there was a waft of familiar perfume.

'Richard?'

His nephew was howling at the top of his voice, but Bartholomew could not make out the words at first. Then he caught 'Michaelhouse Choir', and was suddenly aware that a number of those around him were singers. Verius was fighting like a lion, valiantly repelling a group of townsmen determined to make an end of an enticingly prostrate Senior Proctor.

The fracas ended when the hall finally gave up the ghost, and combatants on both sides were forced to run for cover or risk being buried alive. Bartholomew, Verius and Richard dragged Michael to his feet, and took refuge behind a stable as the wind swept a treacherous barrage of splinters and plaster fragments over them, forcing them to hunker down with their arms over their heads. It seemed an age before they were finally able to stand up.

'Well,' breathed Michael, staring at the heap of rubble that was unrecognisable as Cambridge's newest College. 'I wonder what John Winwick will say about *that* when he arrives.'

'He is not coming, Brother,' said Richard. 'At least, not today – Tynkell just told me. He sends his apologies, and hopes you will enjoy the start of term without him.'

Michael sagged. 'I do not know whether to laugh or cry.'

He emerged unsteadily from behind the shed, then flinched when someone lobbed a rock at him. The culprit was Sir Joshua Hardwell, the soldierly matriculand who had been left in charge when Winwick's Fellows had gone to practise for the debate with Michaelhouse.

'The next person who does that is a dead man,' came the angry and distinctive voice of Isnard the bargeman. 'Brother Michael is under *my* protection.'

Hardwell gave a jeering bray of laughter. 'You imagine you are a match for me?'

He stepped forward threateningly, but stopped when Isnard bellowed a summons and choir members appeared from all directions to stand at his side.

'Fight him, and you fight us all,' growled Verius. 'Right, lads?'

There was a chorus of rumbled agreement, deep from the basses and higher from the tenors.

'Oh, Christ!' blurted Hardwell, looking along the serried ranks in alarm. 'I think they are going to *sing*.'

He hurtled towards the back gate, and his sudden, agitated flight caused others to follow.

'Sing,' mused Isnard. 'Now there is an idea.'

'Especially as the University's opening ceremony has been cancelled,' added Verius. 'It would be a shame not to warble *something* today, after all our rehearsals.'

There was a lot of preparatory throat-clearing, and they launched into something that might or might not have been Michael's newly composed *Conductus*. The trickle of men hurrying to the gate became a flood, particularly when it became clear that Winwick would not be providing much in the way of pillage. Meanwhile, the singing grew steadily louder, until it drowned out both the wind and the settling remains of the ruined hall.

'I thought you were leaving,' shouted Bartholomew to his nephew.

Richard smiled. 'I was, but it occurred to me that you might need help, so I fetched these fellows, along with a lot of your patients. You have some very ruffianly clients, you know. It is hardly respectable.'

'Perhaps not,' said Bartholomew. 'But I would not change them for the world.'

EPILOGUE

It was a subdued, sombre congregation that trooped into St Mary the Great for a belated beginning of term ceremony two days later. Most matriculands had slipped away the day before, evidently of the opinion that life would be dull if they were obliged to spend their time studying.

The occasion began with a mighty explosion of sound as the choir sang the opening anthem. Michael waved his arms frantically to remind them that it was meant to be *pianissimo*, but to no avail. Through the open door, Bartholomew saw a horse rear and a dog run away with its tail between its legs. Pleased with their performance, the singers went for an unsolicited encore.

Before they could do it again, Chancellor Tynkell embarked on a short speech that made no mention of Winwick Hall, and instructed each foundation to bring forward any student who wanted to matriculate. This they did in strict order of foundation, with Peterhouse, King's Hall and Michaelhouse first, followed by the other Colleges. The hostels were next, with some jostling among those that had only come into being in the last month. There were more than there had ever been before, and the principals of some looked little older than their charges.

As the matriculands gave their names to Tynkell's clerks, Verius sang – saving the Senior Proctor's life had earned him a pardon for his role in the troubles. The sweet beauty of his voice did much to ease the lingering antagonism caused by the disagreements over precedence, and Michael's expression grew smug when he saw the startled pleasure on his colleagues' faces.

A number of townsfolk were in the congregation, including Sheriff Tulyet, who had returned home the previous evening. Cambridge already felt safer with him in residence. The two surviving Fellows of Winwick Hall stood together – Lawrence with a bandaged head, and Nerli with his arm in a sling. The few Winwick students with a genuine desire to study had been offered places in other foundations, but most had left the town without a backward glance.

'Did you hear that the Guild of Saints will be dissolved today, Matt?' whispered Michael. 'Its name is tainted now, and it has no money anyway. Eyer left it all his worldly goods, but these only just covered its outstanding debts. Its whole fortune was either gobbled up by Winwick Hall or was stolen by Holm and Julitta when they made their escape.'

Bartholomew gaped at him. '*What?*'

'The moment we left, Julitta told Edith that she was no longer needed, released Holm from the cellar, grabbed everything she could carry – including the Guild's remaining funds – and fled. You did not believe Holm's taunting claims in their house, but he was actually telling the truth.'

'I know.' Bartholomew was unable to keep the hurt from his voice. He had doggedly maintained Julitta's innocence for as long as he could, but as the evidence against her had mounted, even he had been forced to admit that she had played him for a fool, probably from the first time he had set eyes on her.

'I should have seen it weeks ago,' Michael went on. 'Someone clever ordered Holm to befriend Hugo – watching Potmoor through his son is not something our silly surgeon would have thought of doing himself. Moreover, Julitta also asked about my investigations every time we met. I thought it was polite interest, but she was actually fishing for information.'

'She questioned me, too,' said Bartholomew

442

wretchedly. 'I probably did all manner of harm by confiding in her.'

'Unlikely,' said Michael kindly. 'We spent most of the time floundering around in the dark, so you had very little of value to pass on. And she deceived everyone, even me, so do not feel too badly about it. Incidentally, she left you a letter.'

He held out a folded piece of parchment with Julitta's neat roundhand on the front – letters Bartholomew himself had taught her to make. Then he noticed that the seal had been broken.

'It tries to justify what she did,' said Michael. 'And promises you a warm welcome if you ever visit Paris. I should avoid the place if I were you.'

'How does she justify it?' Bartholomew felt no compunction to read the missive himself, and did not care that Michael had opened something that was very clearly marked 'private'.

'By saying that she and Holm aimed to *help* the University by spying for Bon and urging the Guild to divert its charity to our newest College. She denies making more than ten marks from the arrangement, although Bon's records suggest otherwise. He paid a fortune for her help.'

'She was not always a bad person,' said Bartholomew unhappily. 'Earlier this year, she was generous, good and gentle with the wounded soldiers at the castle.'

'That was to impress Holm, to ensure he married her. Once she had him, she reverted to her true self – ruthless, scheming and greedy, just like her father.'

Bartholomew recalled her sweet face, and the intimate evenings they had spent together when Holm had been out. It was difficult to accept that it had all been part of a grubby plan to draw him into her confidence and allow her to monitor the Senior Proctor.

'She told some shocking lies,' the monk went on. 'Holm

was never burgled; Lawrence never had a serious row with Hemmysby – a tale spread by her puppet husband; Nerli never practised swordplay with Potmoor; Lawrence's incompetence did not kill the Queen and nor did he poach patients, introduce Holm to Hugo, or exert influence over Potmoor. Moreover, she *encouraged* Weasenham to gossip about Tulyet's "execution", rather than ordering him to desist as she claimed . . .'

'Yes, Clippesby told me. He also says it was her and Holm who came to steal the Stanton Hutch from Michaelhouse. He recognised the cloaks they wore, which were left behind in the race to escape. Which means that they also stole William's tract . . .'

'Of course! It had to be someone who knew where Langelee kept the key to the cellar. Did she worm the information out of you?'

Bartholomew nodded miserably. 'Ylaria and Verius knew what sort of person she was. They guessed exactly why she had appeared to "help" with his thumb, and we should have listened.'

'And her motive was money and power, as promised by Bon. Yet I doubt Hemmysby knew that she and Holm were the ones charged to invade us, although his suggestion to look in Winwick Hall for the culprit tells me that he might have suspected Bon.'

'I cannot believe she gave him William's tract,' said Bartholomew bitterly. 'She must have known what he would do with it. I thought she harboured *some* affection for Michaelhouse – and for me. Yet she was willing to see us excommunicated for her ambition.'

'Well, she is foiled on that front. Langelee found the work in Bon's room and we burned it.'

'But the damage has been done – relations between us and the Dominicans are damaged—'

'Not so.' Michael smirked. 'I used Weasenham's penchant for gossip to say that the essay was not by William

444

at all, but by Bon. The Dominicans have apologised for thinking badly of us, and we are friends again. The matter is closed.'

'Thank God! I like the Dominicans, and do not want them to be enemies.'

Michael nodded at the letter. 'This contains a lot of claptrap about love, and how Julitta thinks Michaelhouse's disgrace would have been good for you. In her eyes, the University is holding you back from reaching your full potential as a physician.'

Bartholomew grimaced. 'She would not think that if she knew what I did to Hemmysby and the others in the name of justice – with the Senior Proctor's connivance.'

'Yes, – thank heavens you did not confide that little secret! Of course, the business with the tract was your fault. If you had not taught her to read, she would never have known that it was something worth stealing.'

'Holm probably wishes she had stayed illiterate, too,' said Bartholomew wryly. 'It was because of her skill with letters that she found the loophole in her father's will – the one that allows her to control the marital finances. I doubt he would stay with her if the money was his.'

'No,' agreed Michael, not mentioning that a letter informing the surgeon that Julitta had made a mistake in her interpretation was already on its way to Paris. It was revenge of sorts, as Holm would certainly act on it. 'You do know she was only pretending to be stunned when you hit her? She sat up very quickly when you announced an intention to stay. She wanted you gone, so she could escape. She knew Bon's plans were falling apart, and that flight was the only option.'

'Founding a College should be a noble feat, yet so much evil has come from it – Felbrigge shot; Elvesmere, Knyt and Hemmysby poisoned with *dormirella*; Ratclyf given medicine that stopped his weak heart; relations damaged between University and town, perhaps irreparably; Illesy, de Stannell, Eyer and Potmoor killed at Winwick Hall . . .'

'Along with Goodwyn, who was looting when it collapsed. He was paid to insinuate himself into Michaelhouse, you know. Or rather, he was told that if he enrolled, he would be rewarded ten times what he forked out in fees. The same happened in other Colleges, where young men had a remit to cause trouble, learn our secrets and spread discontent.'

'Who told you that, Brother?'

'Documents in Bon's room. Richard was not the only one recruited to bring friends here – at least another dozen men did likewise. Losing his sight has turned Bon bitter and vengeful, because he thinks it encourages people to undervalue his intellect – which caused him to be overly devoted to the one College that was willing to accept him.'

'He is wrong to blame our low opinion on his hypochyma. The truth is that he is just not a very good scholar, as evidenced by his dismal performance in two debates.'

'Yes,' sighed Michael. 'And it is a pity he escaped.'

'You still have not found him?'

'Not yet. I shall send his description to all four corners of the kingdom and he will not stay free for long. He cannot – until he is caught, I dare not eat gifts of cakes, lest they are poisoned.'

'A fine reason for wanting to snare a killer,' said Bartholomew, although the remark made him smile. Then he became sombre again. 'Marjory Starre said there would be a fierce gale, and that a good man would die. She was right.'

'She was not,' countered Michael. 'No one who died on Tuesday was *good*, and there are often strong winds in October. There was nothing magical about her prediction.'

'What about Potmoor? He was innocent of the

burglaries, and after his resurr— after his bout of cata-lepsia, he did try to make amends for his past.'

'It was too little, too late. Moreover, we might have solved the case a lot sooner if he had confessed to his affair with Olivia Knyt. Is she better, by the way? I heard you were called out to tend her last night.'

Bartholomew nodded, but said no more. Olivia's first reaction on discovering that she was carrying her lover's child had been to dose herself with bryony root and get rid of it, but then she had changed her mind. Unfortunately, the herb was still going about its business, and it had taken the combined skill of two midwives, Marjory Starre and Bartholomew himself, to reverse the process.

'Then we could have stopped assuming that Potmoor was guilty of the burglaries,' Michael went on when there was no reply. 'And looked for the real culprit.'

'Who was the real culprit? The minions Potmoor no longer needed after his brush with death, as de Stannell claimed?'

Michael nodded. 'They stole a veritable fortune, although Bon's records reveal that de Stannell kept a lot for himself. Doubtless Bon would have poisoned him in time. And Uyten, whom I interviewed at length last night. He is stunned to learn that his master was Bon, not Illesy. He really is a fool. As if the likes of him would ever be made a University Fellow!'

'What will happen to him?'

'He will face trial, but will claim benefit of clergy, so will probably be exiled.'

Bartholomew sighed. 'No wonder this case was so diffi-cult to solve. Bon had a grand plan, but all his helpmeets were in it for themselves.'

'For money,' nodded Michael. 'Like Eyer. Or for pres-tige, like Uyten. Or for both, like Holm, Julitta and de Stannell – who rashly expected the College to be renamed after him.'

Bartholomew nodded to where John Winwick was talking to the Sheriff. 'He is unwilling to concede defeat, and wants to try again.'

'Yes. I have suggested he does it in Oxford.'

Bartholomew laughed.

'I am serious. They pride themselves on their adaptability, so they can accommodate his impatience. However, we at Cambridge are unsuited to hurried decisions.'

'Yet some good came out of all this. I learned that no one murdered Oswald, and Richard proved himself to be decent in the end.'

'There is hope for him, I suppose. He goes home older and wiser, especially about his sire.' Michael sniggered suddenly. 'Did you know that Thelnetham wants to be reinstated at Michaelhouse? Langelee has refused, so our conclave will be a haven of peace once more.'

'William will be pleased.'

'There is something else that is good, too. We have discovered a new weapon in our battle against killers – dissection.'

'Oh, no! My conscience will not let me do that again.'

'Yes, it will,' countered Michael. 'Several bodies have been recovered from Winwick's ruins, and we need to be sure that they are crushed looters, not hapless souls poisoned by Bon. There is a great deal of work for you once this ceremony is over.'

Bartholomew's reply was drowned out by the choir, beginning the jubilant anthem that marked the end of the ceremony, but this time Michael made no effort to quieten them. He shrugged and pointed to his ears when the physician tried to make himself heard, then turned towards his singers with a complacent smile. He could not have timed their interruption better himself.

Bon had not fled when Winwick Hall and all his dreams had collapsed. He had hidden in the rubble, feeling anger burn within him. He would repay those who had thwarted his plans, and when they were dead he would rebuild his College better, bigger and stronger than ever. He was there now, listening to the choir bellow the closing anthem. He pushed the din from his mind, and thought about the task that lay ahead.

He did not need good eyesight to tell him that the hall was past saving, and that the tottering remains would have to be demolished in order to start afresh. He would not make the same mistakes again, though. His new College would be raised slowly and painstakingly, and it would stand for centuries, outlasting Peterhouse, Gonville, Clare, Trinity Hall and all the other foundations that had called it an upstart.

He groped his way to the cellar, the cool vaulted chamber below the hall that should have been full of ale, wine and food for the coming term. When he thought about all he had lost, his temper boiled again, and he thumped a wooden post with all the force he could muster, wishing it were Michael, Illesy, Lawrence, Nerli or Bartholomew instead.

But for once his poor vision worked against him, and he did not know that the strut was one that had been inserted to shore up the roof until it could be dismantled safely. Bon's blow knocked it from its moorings, and it crashed to the floor. For a second nothing happened, then the ceiling caved in. It happened so quickly that Bon was barely aware of it. One moment he was standing in silent fury, and the next he was buried under tons of masonry.

There was only one witness to his death. Clippesby had been appalled by the loss of life at Winwick Hall, and had gone there to pray for the souls of the dead. Unnoticed, he watched Bon slouch to the cellar, and his keen ears caught the bitter curses hissed into the darkness. Then he heard Bon strike the post, and knew from the sound of the resulting collapse that the man would not be coming out again. He bowed his head, and added another name to his prayers.

Winwick Hall's desirable location on the High Street meant it was not long before the site was sold. One parcel of land was purchased by Nerli, who decided to settle in Cambridge once Bartholomew had made it clear that he would not try to discuss mutual acquaintances at Salerno. Nerli had been appalled when the well-intentioned Lawrence had tried to initiate the conversation, sure he was going to be exposed as an imposter, as not only had he never been to the place from which he claimed his impressive string of degrees, but he had no qualifications whatsoever. He had read widely, though, and knew he was more than a match for more formally trained minds.

His land contained the collapsed cellar, but the rubble was nicely packed, so he used it as the foundation for his new home, a pretty cottage that he named Knyt Hostel, in honour of the murdered Secretary of the Guild of Saints. He only ever took three students at a time, but he trained them with such meticulous diligence that kings and bishops clamoured to hire them when they graduated. He ran Knyt Hostel for the next six decades, and was much mourned when he died just short of his hundredth birthday.

Beneath him, Bon's bones gradually turned to dust, and although Michael continued to hunt, no trace of the blind lawyer was ever found. It was generally believed that he had fled to the Fens and had drowned in one of its treacherous marshes. Only Clippesby knew different, but he saw no reason to disturb the dead.

HISTORICAL NOTE

The position of anatomy in university curricula was a delicate one. The great medical schools at Salerno, Bologna, Montpellier and Padua had long since recognised it as a good way for surgeons to learn about the human body; dissections were also conducted for legal reasons, to assess whether someone had been the victim of foul play – the first autopsies. The Church did not ban the practice, but it was frowned upon in England, and there is no evidence that it formed part of a medical education. Physicians, considered at this time to be superior to barber-surgeons, would certainly not have sullied their hands with anything so base.

One reason for the lack of enthusiasm was that contemporary books and authorities thought they had a pretty good idea of the way things worked, so inclined to the opinion that not much could be learned from dissection anyway. The intricacies of comparative anatomy were a long way in the future, and the feeling was that once you had seen one liver, heart or stomach, you had seen them all.

Another hot topic in medieval universities was apostolic poverty. The debate had continued for centuries, but had another airing in the 1300s, when Pope John XXII went head to head with the Franciscans about it. His bull *Ad conditorem* was vigorously contested by the Grey Friars, including William of Ockham, who wrote *Opus nonaginta dierum* (the Work of Ninety Days). The debate grew so heated in Oxford, that the King was obliged to issue an edict in 1358, forbidding its scholars from discussing the matter, and several bishops banned men from their dioceses from enrolling there, lest they picked up nasty heretical ideas. No doubt Cambridge made the most of the situation by opening its doors a little wider.

Most of the people in *Death of a Scholar* were real. Michaelhouse, founded in 1324 by Hervey de Stanton, had a Master in 1358 named Ralph de Langelee, and his Fellows included Michael (de Causton), William (de Gotham), John Clippesby, Thomas Suttone, William Thelnetham and Simon Hemmysby. John Aungel and John Goodwyn were later members.

William Rougham was an influential member of Gonville Hall and became its Master in 1360. William Heyford was vicar of St Clement's in the 1350s; John Felbrigge was a University proctor, although not until the 1370s; John Weasenham was the University Stationer; and there were a number of scholars named Ratclyf. Geoffrey de Elvesmere, a University clerk, was stabbed in the back in 1371. Albizzo di Nerli hailed from the Carmelite convent in Florence, and came to study in Cambridge in the 1370s. He had a reputation for great sanctity, and died in 1428.

Outside the University, Nicholas Fulbut was a burglar, Roger Verius was convicted of robbery and John Jekelyn was a thief, all active in Cambridge in the 1330s. Nicholas de Stannell was Sheriff of Cambridgeshire and Huntingdonshire in 1358, and the Tulyets were a powerful local family throughout the fourteenth century. In the early 1300s, John Bon murdered John le Knyt, aided and abetted by Hugo, son of John Potmoor. William Illesy was also involved. None were ever convicted of the crime, with Hugo and Bon dying in prison before the case could be heard. There is no record of what happened to Illesy.

John Meryfeld was a famous physician at about this time, while William Holm held a royal appointment as surgeon. So did Master Lawrence, one of the medics who tended Queen Isabella on her deathbed in August 1358. She died shortly after swallowing a purge made up by Thomas Eyer the apothecary, although there is nothing to suggest that this was anything more than coincidence.

Colleges were different from hostels, because they were endowed – they had a pot of money at their fingertips that made them more stable than those that relied solely on fluctuating student fees. As such they tended to have a greater say in University affairs, although some hostels were exceptions to the rule. There was a little flurry of new Colleges in Cambridge in the mid-fourteenth century, with Pembroke (Valence Marie), Gonville Hall, Trinity Hall and Corpus Christi (Bene't) founded between 1347 and 1352. Then there was a significant hiatus, and no more appeared until Magdalene in 1428.

There was never a Winwick Hall in Cambridge, although there was an influential clerk named John Winwick who founded a College, named after himself, in Oxford. It was one of two pre-1400 Colleges in that University which failed to survive, although it might have done had John Winwick not died before matters were fully settled.

John Winwick was an extremely able public servant and a noted pluralist, both of which served to make him very rich. He began as a lowly clerk from Huyten (Uyten), now in Merseyside, but quickly climbed the slippery pole until he became one of Edward III's most trusted administrators. He was appointed Keeper of the Privy Seal in 1355, a post he held until his death in 1360. He was a canon in nine different cathedrals, not to mention accruing lucrative posts in York, Clitheroe, Shrewsbury and Ripon.

Winwick College was for lawyers, and the founder's will stipulated that the funding was to come from the church at Ratcliffe on Soar, the title of which the College was to hold. The Pope failed to ratify the arrangement, and Winwick's executors did not press the matter, perhaps because they wanted the tithes for themselves. Had it survived, Winwick College might have been as much a household name as any of the medieval foundations in Oxford and Cambridge, but it faded into oblivion from lack of funds, and is now no more than a footnote in the history books.